Frank Barnard trained as a journalist before moving into public relations. He worked as managing director for major international consultancies before quitting at fifty to write full-time and race cars. He is married with two children and four grandchildren with whom he enjoys sailing and sea-fishing near his home in Rye, Sussex.

BLUE MAN FALLING

FRANK BARNARD

headline

Sur les Quais de vieux Paris, written and composed by Poterat/Erwin
© 1939 by Les Editions Musicales VOG
© 1951 Les Editions Leon Agel
Used by kind permission of Les Nouvelles Editions Meridian, France

First published in 2005
by HEADLINE BOOK PUBLISHING

7

Cataloguing in Publication Data is available from the British Library

ISBN 978 0 7553 2555 9 (B format)
ISBN 978 0 7553 3154 3 (A format)

Typeset in Galliard by Palimpsest Book Production Limited,
Polmont, Stirlingshire

Printed and bound in Great Britain by CPI Antony Rowe, Wilts

Headline's policy is to use papers that are natural, renewable and recyclable
products and made from wood grown in sustainable forests. The logging and
manufacturing processes are expected to conform to the environmental
regulations of the country of origin.

HEADLINE BOOK PUBLISHING
A division of Hodder Headline
338 Euston Road
London NW1 3BH

www.headline.co.uk
www.hodderheadline.com

To Jan

AUTHOR'S NOTE

Blue Man Falling is a work of fiction. The squadron depicted did not exist and neither did its personnel, whether in the air or on the ground. Similarly, many of the place names in France, England and the United States will not be found on any map. *Blue Man Falling* describes the kind of events that occurred during the Phoney War of 1939–40 and subsequently during the German invasion of 10 May 1940 onwards, but does not deal with real incidents or experiences. The narrative is, however, placed in the overall context of historical verisimilitude and the achievements and sacrifices of the pilots, other air-crew and ground-crews of the Royal Air Force in the Battle of France, men of many nationalities, remain an inviolable reality. *Blue Man Falling* is dedicated to those men who, together, fought the first desperate battles in the skies of France and laid the foundation for still greater battles to come . . .

Overture to war

On 15 May 1940, at about half past seven in the morning, the British prime minister Winston Churchill received a telephone call. He was still in bed. The prime minister of France, Paul Reynaud, said, in English: 'We have been defeated.' Churchill did not immediately respond. Reynaud repeated: 'We are beaten. We have lost the battle.'

Churchill said: 'Surely it can't have happened so soon?'

Reynaud replied: 'The front is broken near Sedan.'

The agony of France would take weeks to reach its conclusion but in that brief exchange Reynaud and Churchill acknowledged that all hope, for France at least, was gone.

Defeat had come swiftly, too, for the Royal Air Force in the Battle of France: they were vastly outnumbered, employing outdated tactics in the air and without the benefit of radar. Yet the few Hurricane fighter squadrons that met the German onslaught accounted for at least three hundred enemy fighters and bombers at the cost of fifty-six of their own pilots killed. For Hitler's Luftwaffe it was to prove a Pyrrhic victory, thanks to the air-combat lessons learnt in the skies of France, the fighting spirit of the RAF pilots; and, perhaps most of all, to the stubborn resistance of the iron-willed chief of Fighter Command, Air Chief Marshal Sir Hugh Dowding, to committing reinforcements to the conflict being waged in Europe. By preserving his scarce resource of Hurricanes and Spitfires he

1

was able, three months later, to lead his pilots to victory in the Battle of Britain . . .

The so-called Phoney War or, to the French, the Drôle de Guerre had ended brutally on 10 May 1940 when Germany invaded Belgium, Holland and France by land and air: Blitzkrieg.

Within two days Holland had fallen and Belgian forces were forced to retreat. The German advance was swift and inexorable. Allied resistance – the British, French and Belgians – was dogged and courageous, but the German combination of fast-moving armoured and infantry divisions, supported by squadrons of Luftwaffe bombers and fighters in overwhelming numbers, prevailed. By 20 May they had reached the Channel coast and were heading for the key ports to the west. By 26 May the remnants of the British Expeditionary Force were gathered at Dunkirk for a desperate evacuation. On 14 June the Germans entered Paris and eight days later, on 22 June, France surrendered. It was little more than nine months since Britain and France had declared war on Germany following the invasion of Poland.

When France surrendered on 22 June 1940 the RAF had lost 959 aircraft. Only sixty-six of the 452 fighters dispatched to France returned. But Dowding's unshakeable belief in preserving what he could of the home defence resources had been vindicated: fewer than eight hundred Hurricanes and Spitfires, with second-line support, fought the Battle of Britain outnumbered by at least three-to-one but, helped by inspired leadership and the unblinking eye of radar, they proved sufficient to beat the Luftwaffe in the air.

Many of the hard lessons learnt by the RAF pilots and their commanders in the Battle of France proved vitally important in that crucial victory . . .

Part one

'Looks as though they mean it this time, sir.'

One

At three in the morning it was already light – everything conspired to cheat the pilots of sleep: the low sun filtering through the windows of their billets in Fonteville; the spasms of anxiety about what the day might bring; and the growing tumult of sound to the east, where an almost continuous barrage of anti-aircraft fire blended with the drone of aero-engines and the thud of bombs. Maybe they'd been right at Wing in calling for readiness at dawn. Perhaps this wasn't just another false alarm . . .

Kit Curtis was already dressed when Madame Bergeret tapped on his door. Her eyes were filled with tears and she brushed them away with her apron – every day a clean one for the proud old woman who had cared for him now for more than half a year.

'So,' was all she said.

They knew instinctively that, with the dawn, everything had changed. Really, it came as no surprise. For weeks the Hun had been growing more aggressive, no longer content to probe Allied defences with Junkers, Heinkel and Dornier bombers on reconnaissance flights but dispatching sizeable formations of fighters to test the resolve of the Royal Air Force and l'Armée de l'Air. Days before, Kit, at the head of B Flight, had encountered three squadrons of Messerschmitt 109s on a high-altitude sweep between Metz and Nancy. But without the advantage of height

– and fearing Brewster's wrath more than the Luftwaffe – he had turned away.

When Madame Bergeret saw that he had packed his gear, her hand went to her mouth. Everything had gone: his blue service shirts, from the hangers suspended on the curtain rail; his civilian clothes – the good tweed jacket, cords, woollen ties, brogues; his few well-thumbed books, Froissart, Gibbon, Conan Doyle; the Box Brownie snap of his parents, posed rather awkwardly on the York-stone terrace of an English country house. The small damp-smelling refuge, of which he had grown fond, was now as bare and cheerless as if he had never been there.

He tried to think of something to say that might comfort her but nothing came. She reached out and touched his cheek, her work-worn fingers rough to his skin, then smiled hopelessly at him, just as she had smiled at the husband who had marched away so jauntily to his fate at Verdun, and the son who was facing the Good Lord knew what odds with his armoured division near Namur.

Down the lane from the farmhouse, facing the church of Saint-Saulve, with its tombs of warriors who had fought the English, the pilots were gathering in front of the sandstone *mairie* that had served as their mess since September. The thunder of warfare was almost comical now in its frenzy, and by contrast there was a stillness about Kit's farewell to Madame Bergeret. They said little but their silence meant much.

'This is probably a fuss about nothing. What's for supper?'

'Rabbit.'

'I will try not to be late.'

'I will not start to cook until you return.'

'Madame . . .'

'My name is Delphine.'

'I know.'

'Always so correct.' She patted his arm. 'When you are old no one is left to call you by your name.'

6

'Yes, I suppose so. It must be odd.' A pause. 'Someone may collect my gear . . .'

'Until tonight, my son.'

'Until tonight.'

'Goodbye.'

'Goodbye Delphine.'

'Readiness at dawn' was not an unusual command but this time there had been something chilling about it, coming amid a welter of wild rumour and speculation: tales of German paratroops behind Allied lines, of fifth-column saboteurs, of panzers massing on the borders, of the abundant resources available to the Luftwaffe and the prodigious performance of their fighters, particularly the Me-109s. 'Readiness at dawn': the pilots were aware that with the simple words came a reluctance to acknowledge that a crisis might be approaching – embarrassment, almost, that struck to the heart and tested their resolve. The order gave them plenty of time to brood, to remember narrow squeaks, brolly-hops, and nursing damaged aircraft back to base; airmen, Hun or British, falling to their deaths in the roaring oven of a stricken fuselage; bodies plummeting to the ground, parachutes destroyed; burned comrades pulled from charred cockpits and loaded into blood-wagons; and Dinghy Davis dying before their eyes on the runway at Revigncourt six months ago.

The eruption of gunfire and detonating bombs, overlaid by the growl of aircraft that built in volume, had not disturbed them. They had been awake already, would have said they had never slept, although they had, fitfully. Like Kit they had tugged on their uniforms, washed and shaved, staring at their faces in small cracked mirrors and, carefully avoiding speculation about mortality, dragged combs through their hair, lit the first fag of the day and stowed their gear in case they were ordered suddenly to move. Since the previous summer most had settled into easy, affable relationships with their hosts. A dozen Madame Bergerets clung at doors waving goodbye. Small boys and girls watched mute, wide-eyed, or shouted shrill reminders about promised gifts.

There was no need, then, for Corporal Evans from the aerodrome to knock them up, leaving the engine of the three-ton Bedford running while he raced from billet to billet ignoring curses and threatening Brewster's wrath. They were waiting for him, and watched as the lorry slewed to a standstill in front of the *mairie*.

Evans thumped the gear-lever into neutral, jumped down from the cab and ran towards the pilots, only to lose his footing and sprawl in the gravel. With his pale face and red cheeks, he resembled a clown at the end of an unfunny turn. 'We've been attacked. A Dornier. Machine-gunned some of the French kites. We thought it was an exercise.'

'Christ,' said Buster Brown. 'So it really has started.'

The last few pilots, marginally better sleepers than the rest, were straggling in from their billets: the new boy, Kenny Rains, and Goofy Gates.

'What's up?' shouted Gates, as they piled into the back of the lorry.

'Can't you hear, you cloth-eared sod?' said Buster.

'Oh, that,' said the sergeant pilot, apparently noticing the din to the east for the first time. 'I suppose that means the balloon's gone up.'

In the few minutes it took to reach the aerodrome, bouncing across the ancient bridge spanning the Meuse and grinding up the incline to the flat plain of Revigncourt, Kit surrendered to the usual funk. There was nothing he or any of the others could do about it – a few denied it, but they all felt the same. And with the wave of apprehension came an insidious inner voice with the unanswerable question, 'What am I doing here?'

The sun was a little higher now but a thick haze clung to the ground. The Hurricanes stood ready, props angled skywards, facing the direction of take-off. They looked elegant and deadly.

On the southern side of the perimeter a pillar of blue-black smoke puffed and billowed from the remains of the two l'Armée de l'Air Moranes, destroyed by a single Dornier 17 that had sped in low and undetected. The stench of burning fuel hung in the air. A good show, really, one had to admit – daring, dammit . . .

Over by his Hurricane Kit said: 'All set, chief?'

Flight Sergeant Jessop nodded, and with Taggart, his fitter, and Gray, his rigger, Kit ran up the engine and completed a full pre-flight check. It came so easily to him now. Little more than six months ago he had been consumed with fear that he might forget a critical element of the routine. Today, hardened by combat, with two Heinkels and a share in an Me-110 to his credit, he faced different dangers: familiarity and complacency. He forced himself to check and check again. Then, satisfied, he gave the crew a thumbs-up and eased himself out of the cockpit as the LACs wheeled away the trolley accumulator.

'Looks as though they mean it this time, sir,' said Jessop, as Kit hopped down from the port wing.

'Looks that way,' said Kit, aware that Jessop expected a more pugnacious response and that Buster would have come up with something apt and pithy. Over at Readiness he went through his usual ritual: resting his parachute on the tip of the port wing, one strap already clicked into the lock so that he could loop himself in on the run and snap in the second strap; his flying helmet on the cockpit gunsight, plugged in ready, beside his gauntlets. He was superstitious about following the same procedure. Silly, really, but you never knew. He was wearing standard-issue overalls that had once been white, and steel-tipped lace-up shoes. He had dispensed with the heavy flying boots, so valuable during the vicious winter: shoes gave him more feel on the rudder pedals, another little edge . . .

The six Hurricanes of A Flight were already up, clearing the perimeter in twin vic-formations, neat but not tucked in too tight, eager and aggressive; the flight commander Ossie Wolf was waggling his wings.

'That bloody Yank always was a line-shooter,' Buster grunted.

Kit noted grins break out on faces around him. 'Give him a break, for Christ's sake.' He was aware of his own mettle rising with the roar of the Merlins. The airmen on the buckboard were handing out mugs of sugared tea with slices of bread and jam. Somehow word had got round that the Hun were bombing airfields. But, apart from the saucy Dornier, Revigncourt had escaped attack. Nobody knew why – not even the CO, who came out now from his office in the nearby Nissen hut, the wooden door slamming behind him. He was still walking with some difficulty, although the doc had dug out most of the pellets.

Brewster was embarrassed by his wound – its location, in his left buttock and upper thigh, and the manner in which he had suffered it, peppered by a peasant with a shotgun as he floated to earth on his 'chute after his machine had brewed up while he was mixing it with Me-110s to the west of Nancy. The peasant had been aghast when Brewster ripped off his overalls and jabbed at his RAF wings, roaring and purple. The man had started forward, his hands in a supplicating gesture, but was swiftly felled by a meaty fist and his weapon hurled into a nearby pond. Now Brewster was impatient to be back in the air, but the doc was firm. He had been compelled to yield leadership of A Flight to Wolf. It was a touchy subject – 'sensitive as his arse', as Buster Brown put it.

Brewster had never been a patient man but now, grounded, he badgered and bellowed more than ever at his brood of young pilots. They loved him for the way he sliced through red tape to get them the supplies and equipment they needed, the way he would forget in moments an entirely justified bollocking and administer a thump on the back with a blue joke about a Bar-le-Duc hot-spot; the way he would spot a faltering spirit and prescribe a three-day pass to Paris. He sought constantly to make their lives safer and longer, not comfortable or easy, perhaps, but safer and longer . . .

B Flight gathered round the stocky squadron leader, a head shorter than most of them. For the moment his big fat-fingered paws had to do his flying for him. First they swooped and dived to show the relative positions of Hun bomber formations and, a few thousand feet above and slightly behind, the fighters. Then one of the Brewster mitts became B Flight ignoring the bombers and engaging the fighters. 'This is the sermon for today,' said Brewster. 'You are after the fighters. Repeat, you are after the fighters. We have every reason to think this is the big one. I do not want to lose one bloody aircraft. If anyone comes wandering back with his stick in his hand he'll have me to contend with, never mind the bloody Hun. It is imperative that you gain height advantage and keep it. When you attack don't dive your height away. Get back up as fast as possible. Don't be tempted to follow somebody down, even if you reckon one more burst will do it. Your job is to draw off the fighters and leave the bombers unprotected. Someone else can deal with them. You're after the escort. All clear? Understood?'

There was a general murmur of assent, a few displays of bravado here and there; an insouciant grin, a murmured joke – black, of course – but most of the faces were pale and reflective, thoughts full of battle at 20,000 feet, with hefty formations of the nimble, lethal Me-109s and formidably armed 110s. 'Good,' said Brewster. 'End of lesson.'

As the group dispersed to await orders, Brewster took Kit aside. 'For Christ's sake, make sure they've got the message. I'm relying on you to curb the wilder spirits in your charge Kit. Some of the chaps up at Dampierre copped it yesterday. Spotted a juicy formation of Dorniers and sailed in for the kill. Got bounced by 109s lurking above them. Two Hurricanes lost, one pilot killed, another lucky to walk back through the lines.'

Kit found Taggart and Gray and fussed over his machine, checking what had been checked three times already. He wanted to be off, to know the wave of relief as the demands of the sweep consumed his concentration. He knew it would be all right then. It always was: that sense of control over an aircraft primed and ready for action, wings bristling with Brownings, the thrill of emerging from haze into rolling landscapes of sun-drenched clouds, immense vistas on every side, his comrades around him, their Hurricanes jinking this way and that, the constant scanning for the tell-tale black specks that could be on you in an instant, their tracer zipping past you – never through, no, not you – and the surge of cold fury as you turned aggressor, throwing your machine around the sky in crazy manoeuvres that no air show had ever seen, intent on getting off a quick burst, a nice double-deflection shot, and nailing the bastard.

For the second time in half an hour Kit visited the latrines, the heavy dew soaking his shoes, and wondered if he had been spotted – nipping to the bogs was a clear sign to all that you had the wind up.

Kenny Rains was having a pee and Kit lined up alongside. 'Have the chaps christened you yet?'

'I'm not with you, sir,' said the pilot officer. He had a shock of reddish hair, fine features, a vestigial fair moustache. He looked about fifteen.

'You know, a nickname.'

'Oh. Some of them call me Claude. Haven't a clue why.' He made it sound as though it wasn't worth knowing.

'Bad King John,' Kit said. 'Actor. You know, Robin Hood, the film.'

'Oh,' said Rains. 'I must have missed it.'

'Bit tenuous, I admit. They'll probably come up with something better.' Rains had been with the squadron for less than a week. Kit wondered if they'd have time.

Rains shook himself off in matey fashion. He seemed quite assured.

'Talking of christenings, Rains, it looks as though you're going to have something of a baptism.'

'Got here just in time, then, sir.'

Cocky little tick, thought Kit, parroting what he thinks Teacher wants to hear, just as they all had at the beginning. They were outside now, not the slightest breeze to disperse the haze. It was a scene at any flying club on an English summer weekend. 'How many hours did you say you've got on Hurricanes?'

'Thirty, sir. Any tips?' Rains's manner was easy, almost condescending. He had been judged a natural, the best pilot of his intake, and wore the accolade like a medal.

'Don't waste ammo. You might have eight Brownings but you've only got sixteen seconds of firepower. Single squirts, not more than a second a burst.'

'Yes, I know about that.'

'No doubt, but you haven't been in a scrap so far, have you?'

'No – I don't imagine I'll forget, though. Thanks anyway.'

Christ Almighty, thought Kit. 'You know about deflection, of course?' He felt a sudden urgent need to make sure the arrogant little fellow had every chance to survive.

'In theory,' said Rains, airily, unconsciously making things worse.

Over by the machines there was a flurry of activity. They broke into a trot.

'You clocked the blackboard in Dispersal?' shouted Kit. 'You're flying Blue Two. If we find some trade stick to my tailwheel. Don't let it out of your sight.'

'Righty-ho,' said Rains.

At six a.m their orders came through. 'B Flight patrol Metz, 15,000 feet.' Taggart pulled Kit's harness so tight he winced. No give in the straps – like there had been last October when he nearly brained himself on the hoops of the canopy, lunging this way and that as his stricken Hurricane decided to fly itself. Now the aeroplane came alive, vibrating to the thunder of a thousand horsepower, the wing-tips flexing, the fat tyres thrusting at the chocks. Its power permeated his body. He imagined his blood frothing. A glance to right and left, just to make sure Buster Brown and Kenny Rains were set, a final thumbs-up to Jessop and the crew, and he taxied away, craning his neck to see either side of the steeply raked snout. Behind him thundered Pip Fuller, the gruff New Zealander Eddie Knox and the weaver, arse-end Charlie, Goofy Gates.

As the flight soared over the perimeter fence, Kit glanced sixty feet to starboard and caught Buster Brown's eye. On impulse he waggled his wings and gave him a V-sign. Buster thrust out his lower lip and nodded. He'd got the point. To port Rains leaned forward at the controls, tongue at the corner of his mouth – as though he was struggling with a taxing prep.

B Flight pierced the haze at five hundred feet half expecting the sky to be black with Hun. Not a sign, but visibility was perfect as they continued to climb. The low sun was in league with the Luftwaffe, refracting on every scratch, mark and fleck of engine-oil on the Perspex canopies. Did the bumptious Master Rains know he should clean the canopy with only the softest cloth? 'In theory,' Kit could hear him say.

Almost unconsciously he flicked on his gunsights, checked the range and wing-span indicators, set the gun-button to fire, scanned the engine instruments and altimeters, then resumed his systematic search of the sky, his eyes moving in a methodical zigzag, high and low, left to right, and then again . . .

They were maintaining a model vic formation. Kit negotiated a gentle turn to port. Rains throttled back instantly to keep position. The boy was good, no doubt of that. Beyond the accelerating Buster Brown, Kit saw the second vic of B Flight following his lead, Goofy Gates weaving back and forth slightly above Knox and Pip Fuller, the flight's insurance against being bounced.

He snapped on his R/T. 'Good stuff, chaps.'

'Thanks awfully, Blue Leader,' said Buster.

There was a faint crackle in Kit's headphones, a voice with a distinctive twang that sounded a long way off. At first he couldn't make it out. Then: 'Enemy aircraft going west, enemy aircraft going west, direction Joinville. Get the lead out and hit the sods.'

'That's the infernal Yank. Surprised he's still up. He must be running low on juice by now.'

'Put a cork in it, Buster,' said Kit. 'R/T silence.'

Over Joinville fifteen Dorniers were bombing the railway yards from 5,000 feet, an efficient squadron in no particular hurry to flatten the target. They levelled the station for good measure. Cars and taxis parked outside were pitched into the air or obliterated. Many SNCF sheds were ablaze, and locomotives pierced with bullets belched steam. Rolling stock trundled down the warped tracks, propelled by the force of countless bullets.

'This is Blue Leader, Blue Leader, do not attack, do not attack. Where are the fighters?' Kit held his flight in the sun at 15,000 feet.

'Don't see 'em.' That was Goofy.

'There is no bloody escort,' said Buster.

'Okay,' said Kit, 'let's give it a whirl. Line astern, line astern, go.' The five Hurricanes formated smoothly on his machine, still unseen by the Dorniers below. The Hun was enjoying his work. 'Number one attacking, number one attacking. Go!' Kit fought to keep his voice calm and unruffled as he nosed into a dive and opened the throttle, black smoke streaming from the Merlin's exhaust.

The grey-green pencil-shaped fuselage of a Do-17, white-edged black crosses on its wings, swastikas on its twin rudders, loomed huge in his windscreen. For a moment the image froze. He could see the crew clearly, intent on the damage they were inflicting on the ground. The pilot was grinning and shouting over his shoulder to the navigator. Kit's bullets tore through the plexiglass canopy, raking towards the nose.

Abruptly the Dornier's wings folded at the roots. One broke away with its engine in flames. The other screened the last moments of the crew as they fell towards the carnage they had created below.

The Dorniers, underpowered and without armour, scattered like geese alarmed by a fox. Kit was down on the deck now, scarcely five hundred feet above the ground. Even in the tumult of the raid, people were in the streets, running from houses, waving. Barrelling into a steep climb, he came up beneath the pale belly of another Hun. The front gunner was cranking his machine-gun down and to the right towards the Hurricane but the bullets flew wide. The Brownings chewed along the fuse-lage, whipping through the floor-pan and into the cockpit. The Dornier sagged away, turning east. The starboard nine-cylinder Bramo was blazing.

Kit gained height, poised for the kill. Blue Two, Kenny Rains, sailed across his bow and let loose a perfectly judged one-second burst, just as teacher had told him. Then another. The Dornier dropped a wing, rolled on to its back and spiralled down. A single parachute opened and sailed clear. The German was going to land close to the town. Kit speculated on the reception he would receive.

The surviving Dorniers were heading for home, helped by the still dense haze. Kit could not imagine they had not called up fighter support. He called off the attack. He had no idea how many they downed but he was pleased with his own performance: one definite and a share of another, though he'd let Rains revel in the glory. Cheeky little sod, nipping in front of him like that. He realised his hands were wet with sweat and trembling on the controls, his mouth and throat dry. He began to laugh, without knowing why.

As though nothing had happened, B Flight resumed its neat vics. They had suffered no losses, no damage to the machines. Rains's grin stretched from ear to ear. Perhaps, Kit thought, the Hun was not as formidable as they'd feared. Not smart, after all, to embark on the Joinville raid without an escort. If this was the big push, might they be betrayed by arrogance and compla-cency? Perhaps it was possible to halt the sods . . .

Low on fuel Kit peeled off and turned for Rouvres, home to the Hurricanes of 73 Squadron. Buster Brown assumed the role of Blue leader and guided the flock back to Revigncourt.

Shimmers of heat rose from Kit's machine as the Albion three-point bowser moved in to top up the wing-mounted fuel tank and check the reserve in front of the cockpit; the reserve Kit had switched to for safety's sake five minutes before landing. Odd: he'd get the fuel lines checked at Revigncourt. Usually it was the wing men who consumed more fuel, constantly on the throttles to keep pace and position with the flight leader. Piss-poor, not dropping back to Revigncourt like that, to be part of the post-sortie jollifications. He felt he was missing out.

Meanwhile, as a fresh stock of .303 bullets was fed into the ammunition boxes, Kit nabbed a willing LAC to clear the windscreen and canopy of muck and oil, then run the canopy back and forth in its grooves to make sure it moved easily in case he needed to exit in a hurry. It had been a cakewalk so far. But on the ground, with time to think, he had no reason to believe that that would last.

Cradling a mug of tea and a bacon sandwich, adrenaline dissipating and overcome by fatigue, he became aware of a familiar figure sprawled under an ash tree by Dispersal. It was Johnny Balbec, a bulky yellow Mae West over his flawlessly tailored dark blue l'Armée de l'Air uniform. His facial burns were stark in the vivid morning light. He beckoned Kit with raw red fingers. Nearby, a gaggle of French pilots chattered excitedly. They appeared to be waiting for something.

'Ah,' said Balbec. 'What news of my good friend Buster?'

'Alive,' said Kit, shortly. 'What's going on?'

'We are falling back,' said Balbec, 'to Berry-au-Bac.' He seemed content about it.

'Reims?' Kit was confounded. 'Christ, the show's hardly started yet.'

'For you, perhaps. For us it appears to be over. We are awaiting transport.'

'Transport? But where are your Moranes?'

Again a gesture with the burnt hands. 'Regrettably the Boches have rendered them unserviceable.' Balbec indicated a conflagration on the far side of the aerodrome. 'We were awaiting orders but unfortunately they arrived too late. Instead we received a visit from a very proficient squadron of Heinkel 111s.' He smiled wearily. 'No doubt you will be appalled to hear that I am less than desolated. Perhaps it is better to be destroyed on the ground than in the air. At least the pilots survive to fight another day.' He noted Kit's expression. 'Even you, my friend, must acknowledge that the Morane is no Hurricane. Personally I was reluctant to provide the Boches with what you call the sitting ducks but, of course, if the orders had come through in time . . .' He shrugged.

The French squadron was piling into the back of three l'Armée de l'Air Renault trucks. Balbec waved them off. Then, with Kit, he strolled across to his powder blue 135 Delahaye, parked between two Nissen huts, climbed behind the wheel and fired up the V-12. The rorty boom caught the attention of the LAC working on Kit's machine. He shouted something.

'What is he saying?' cried Balbec, over the bellow of the engine.

'I think he is suggesting that your parents were not married,' said Kit.

'Again?' said Balbec, cupping his ear.

Kit shook his head and stepped back. The Frenchman accelerated smartly away, shifting through the gears with a racing driver's skill. He would be on the outskirts of Reims within the hour.

'Sorry about that, sir,' said the LAC, levering himself off the wing of the Hurricane and on to the grass.

'He may be a fucking bastard,' said Kit, 'but the fact that he's French has nothing to do with it.'

'I'll remember that, sir.'

'Do so. They are our allies, after all.'

The airman grunted. 'They were quick enough to obey instructions to bugger off.'

'Meaning?'

'They got their bloody orders same time as us. Our blokes were in the air in about four minutes. By the time the Froggies got through gassing about it the Jerries had bombed their kites to buggery. You should have seen their faces, sir. Like kids at Christmas.' He paused. 'Are we for it, sir?'

'Don't be ridiculous,' said Kit.

'I was just wondering how we're expected to get out.'

'It won't come to that. The Hun aren't as hot as they're cracked up to be. My chaps have just given them a proper pasting.' He saw relief in the airman's eyes and felt a pang of guilt. It was so easy to trot out glib comfort when doubts and fears were creeping into your own soul.

Taxiing in at Revigncourt, his canopy thrust open, his body soaked from the heat of the engine and the rapidly rising temperature of a perfect early-summer day, Kit discovered he had already missed a second sweep. He doubted that Buster Brown was still enjoying leading B Flight. The Luftwaffe appeared to have learned its lesson. Fighter escorts, Messerschmitt 109s and 110s, were coming over in strength now, supporting the bombers. Railways, troop concentrations and more airfields were being hit. The squadron had received unconfirmed reports of Allied forces pulling back in disarray, of whole communities taking to the roads, of civilians strafed by Heinkels. Sickened by the speed of it all, he realised he hadn't given the Maierscheldts in Nancy, eighty miles further east, a second thought. Hannah, he knew, was in Paris. But what of her parents?

In the CO's office Kit found Brewster bent over a map of the Marne-et-Meuse, spread on the green baize card table he had brought with him from Tangmere. It gave the scene a domestic air: a doting father, perhaps, planning a diverting trip to amuse his children. His stubby forefinger with its blackened nail appeared to be tracing a route west, in the direction of Reims. Beside him Spy Turner, the intelligence officer, was nodding, making notes, face drawn. Seeing Kit, they fell silent. Brewster made a stab at nonchalance, strolling over to his desk to receive Kit's report. But the implications were obvious. The voice of the LAC at Rouvres came to Kit like an echo: 'I was just wondering how we're expected to get out.' Again, he experienced a wave of guilt. By now the man might have realised the emptiness of his easy reassurances . . .

Two

Friday, 10 May 1940 (morning)

The Readiness 'phone was as startling as a scream. Momentarily the pilots appeared frozen by the shock of it. Then the voice of the duty corporal bawling the orders was drowned by the crash of thrown-down chairs and the pounding of booted feet. Moments later came the breaking song of the Merlins. It was A Flight's third sortie of the day. The tally was good: two Dorniers, a Heinkel, a Henschel Hs-126 and two probables, with only one pilot down, Beaky Parker, hit by shards of the fragile Henschel army co-operation plane he had blown apart like a clay-pigeon. To be downed by a Henschel – he'd suffer for that. But his 'chute had opened safely and he had been seen to land close to French lines. Word had got round – nobody knew how – that he had liberated a motorbike and was speeding cross-country back to Revigncourt.

Another bomber-cover job, Ossie Wolf learned, this time over Luxembourg: a swift climb to 15,000 feet, a link-up with Blenheims and Battles over the target, then stick around for twenty minutes as they hit their objectives. It was simple enough. But Luxembourg? 'Jesus Christ, sir,' Ossie Wolf shouted to Brewster from his cockpit, 'surely the Hun can't be there already?'

The CO had scrambled on to the wing beside him and nodded, hair flattened by the force of the air thrown back by the three-blade propeller. 'For your ears only,' he roared, 'we may be relocating. The ground party's standing by. Orders in the air. But if you get confirmation, choose your moment when you pass it on. I want no doom and despondency.'

'Poor old Beaky,' said Ossie. 'He's going to find himself roaring back to the arms of the Wehrmacht.'

'He didn't make it,' Brewster said. 'He took a load of shrapnel in the gut. The French say he was dead when they got to him.'

'The motorcycle?'

'Wishful thinking, I'm afraid.'

'Shit.'

'Indeed,' said Brewster. He patted the top of the American's leather helmet. 'Get some back for Parker. That's an order. And don't lose any more. That's an order too.'

'My kind of orders, sir.'

'Glad to hear we've stumbled on some you approve of.'

The previous evening, in the mess at Fonteville, the tall windows open to admit the cool air and sweet fragrance of the countryside, Ossie had given Beaky Parker a game of darts. Parker was good. 'Hand-eye co-ordination, old chum,' he'd grinned, 'that's the name of the game.' Then he thumped in another winning double. 'It's the same in the air.'

'No,' said Ossie. 'In the air there's a guy about to throw a dart in your back.'

'Point taken, Red Leader. Middle for diddle?'

Later, as they nursed beers on the gravel terrace of the *mairie*, with the black bulk of the church sharp against the purplish sky, Parker said: 'I saw England today.'

'In your dreams.'

'No, not in my dreams. You know my kite's been guzzling fuel? The blokes fixed it this morning so I took her up to make sure all was well. Amazing visibility so, just for a lark, I nipped up north and stooged along the coast for a bit. Blighty's still there, all right, white cliffs and all. Quite brought a lump to the old throat.'

'So you celebrated by beating up the airfield at two hundred feet and topping it off with that goddammed climbing roll,' said Ossie, suddenly Flight Commander. 'Do it again, you bloody idiot, and I'll have you court-martialled.' But now, sighting the Blenheims and Battles wheeling over Luxembourg, he was cheered by the thought of Beaky relishing a final glimpse of his homeland.

Sluggishly the British bombers struggled to regain height, rising out of the haze now mingling with the smoke belching from their targets. For A Flight it was impossible to glimpse what had been attacked: bridges, troops, tanks? Ossie counted the machines – nearly forty had gone in. Ten, fifteen, twenty . . . twenty-one . . . twenty-three . . . Christ . . .

As the survivors turned for home Ossie gathered A Flight 3,000 feet above and behind them. Even at that distance he could see the damage the bombers had sustained: the long, vulnerable canopy of a Fairey Battle smashed, the pilot half collapsed over the controls; another, its port elevator secured to the tailplane only by a single hinge, swooping and whirling like a child's kite about to hit the ground; a Blenheim trailing smoke from its starboard Bristol Mercury, changing from white to black now until the propeller stopped and flames streamed back across the wing. Then, very slowly, the starboard wing tip of the Blenheim tilted down and it began a graceful curving turn to the east. Perhaps he was going to put it down. But no, the bank became a savage spin and the machine was quickly swallowed in the haze. No 'chutes . . .

Over the R/T a sudden shout from Al Miller: 'Hello, Leader, weaver calling. Enemy aircraft, enemy aircraft, two o'clock below, going west, going west.'

'Red Leader, Red Leader, I see 'em Al, I see 'em.' There they were, a formation of fifteen Dornier Do-17s. Jesus, it was tempting. 'Where are the fighters? Where are the fighters?'

In an instant Ossie had his answer. A flight of Me-109s zipped through them line astern, straight out of the sun at 360 m.p.h.

A Battle detonated like a grenade. Simultaneously Al cried out, 'I'm hit, I'm—' Then nothing.

Ossie caught a yellow-nosed 109 at the top of a loop, just as it hung there for a moment, perfect. A one-second stab on the gun-button and it fell away, its tailplane severed. The pilot had flung back his side-hinged canopy ready to jump but the flailing mass scythed into one of the Dorniers he had been sent to protect and together the locked machines tumbled earthwards. Another Dornier faded across Ossie's windscreen, right to left and slightly above. He snapped to port, was astonished to see, on the bomber's fuselage alongside the usual Luftwaffe insignia, the white Andreas cross of the Condor Legion. His thoughts flicked back to the skies of Spain three years before. The Dornier dived away and Ossie went with it but only briefly, snapping off a couple of hopeful bursts at lengthening range. To his surprise, there was a heavy detonation somewhere amidships and the machine lurched upwards as though the control cables had been damaged. Ossie re-engaged but the German was an old hand and turned somehow to face his attacker. Bullets from the twin-fixed MG-15s in the cowling keened round and through the Hurricane. Miraculously unscathed, Ossie fired again but as he saw his .303s strike home there was a searing explosion in the fuselage behind his seat, an odd racket like a thousand ball-bearings dropping on to a corrugated roof, and a triumphant Me-109 pulled away into the safety of the sun.

The Hurricane shuddered and Ossie felt the stick go loose in his hand. The plane dipped into a dive, then pulled itself up into a loop so tight that the G-force blacked him out. His sight returned as the fighter dived out on the other side but still the controls would not respond. The goddammed elevators were jammed . . .

The Hurricane built up speed and threw itself into a second loop. Flames were lashing back from the engine, licking the outside of the canopy. Fuel spilled into the cockpit, soaking Ossie's overalls, and he blacked out again. He was preparing to fry. A spark was all it needed. For a moment his vision was restored, and again the machine charged down to embark on another loop. Ossie wrenched at the pin of his Sutton harness. It resisted, then suddenly fell away. The belts came loose. At the top of the loop he threw back the canopy and fell out, clear of the flames. Still giddy from the effects of G-force he yanked his D-ring – aware immediately of his mistake. As the 'chute deployed, the rigging lines streamed between his legs, tangling chaotically, suspending him upside down beneath the canopy. He stared at the fields and woodland below, exhausted, incapable. Then, with a lunge, he seized the rigging lines and pulled himself upright. His legs came free and he dropped down, upright and secure in his harness. He was a thousand feet up, sweeping towards a knot of woodland. To his left, his Hurricane completed a final neat loop and buried itself in a patch of marshland. Five hundred feet now. He sailed over some high-tension cables and instinctively lifted his legs though the cables were far below. The ground was coming up fast. It was almost exhilarating. He could make out green sprigs of a crop showing through the dun earth of the fields encircling the copse. The trees were rising to meet him. Seconds before he struck them he glimpsed a Dornier on a rise half a mile away. Figures were moving nearby and they stopped to watch his descent . . .

The noise was startling as he plunged through birches, oaks and beeches, branches and twigs cracking and snapping, tearing at his clothes as he tumbled down between the trunks. He tried to shield his face with his arms but they were pulled back and agonisingly upwards by the force of his passage. Ten feet from the woodland floor he bounced in his harness like a puppet. Blood flowed from his nose. A pheasant gave a belated screech of alarm and flapped away into the undergrowth. He pulled off his leather glove and wiped away the blood, which was dribbling on to his ripped Mae West. His nose felt odd, flat and malleable but numb, and a knife-like pain was apparent in the joint of his left shoulder. He moved it and heard a shrill scream

25

echo round the woodland: his own. Below, on the flat carpet of dry leaves, he could see his flying boots, standing upright and together as though placed there by a conscientious batman.

He still seemed a long way from the ground, too far to risk popping his harness and trusting to luck: two busted legs and he'd be stuck in this goddammed wood for a good long time – Jesus, maybe they'd never find him. Anyway, he'd already pushed good fortune to its limits. Then, as he swung gently back and forth, he heard distant voices and feet crashing through the undergrowth. He opened his mouth to shout out but stopped as the discussion became more distinct. They were speaking German.

Two men emerged into the clearing and stared up at him. They wore the buff overalls of a Luftwaffe bomber crew. The taller was thin, almost gaunt, his hair sparse on a domed crown; round spectacles gave him a professorial air. The other was younger, no more than twenty, stocky, snub-nosed, his blond thatch close-cropped. They began to laugh but a *Hauptmann* thrust his way into the clearing, gripping a small pistol. This was a solution that Ossie had not considered: to be shot like a possum in a trap. 'This is probably the shit who shot us down,' said the officer, in German. His finger tightened on the trigger of the 7.63-calibre Mauser. His face was scowling, filthy with dirt and oil, but Ossie recognised him: Claus Diechmann.

The moment passed. Diechmann thrust the pistol into his overalls and stood with his feet apart, left arm folded over right, the hand cradling his right elbow in the manner of the Führer, nodding his head with satisfaction. His forage cap was tipped over his left eyebrow but the rakish effect was spoiled by the newly blackened eye below. 'Put the swine out of his misery.'

Snubnose moved forward, pulling a clasp-knife from his pocket. So, they were going to save a bullet. Probably wise, thought Ossie, given the fluid nature of the front. Why give away their position? He wondered whether Snubnose would choose chest or throat. He considered telling Diechmann who he was, in fluent German naturally. To hell with him, he decided. Why give the bastard the satisfaction? He'd probably finish him off anyway. Snubnose was scrabbling on the tree-trunk behind him and Ossie waited for the blow. Instead the knife rasped at the taut rigging lines. They began to give and he felt his weight supported from below.

Snubnose was back on the ground and together he and the studious-looking *Feldwebel* released him from his tangled harness and lowered him to the woodland floor. Ossie crouched on his haunches, wavering and off-balance, his hand on his shoulder. Diechmann gave it a sharp jab with his flying boot and Ossie rolled over on to all fours, clenching his teeth against the pain. The bespectacled *Feldwebel*, sweat staining the front of his overalls, glanced at his officer apprehensively. Diechmann pulled out the Mauser once more and studied it, as though weighing his options. Then, with a slight smile, he returned it to his pocket and gave Ossie another shove with his foot. He fell on to his side, and Diechmann said, in English, 'You understand you are our prisoner. Play games with us and my little toy comes out again. Now, however, we must be patient. Our comrades will be here soon. For you the end. For us, as you say, business as usual.'

He was crouching, evidently puzzled by Ossie's lack of response, his head tilted sideways. Ossie was amazed that he hadn't recognised him. His face must be in a worse state than he'd thought. Fresh blood dripped from his battered nose and an egg-like swelling was developing on his right temple. Lucky, otherwise the million-to-one shot might have singled him out for special treatment . . .

Ossie rose shakily to his feet and surreptitiously smeared the blood over his features. Diechmann had changed little in the three years since they had come across each other during the war in Spain. His skin was pale, though, no longer tanned by the Spanish sun. The man was staring hard at him now. Was there at last a hint of recognition? The German's hand went once more to his pocket. Ossie braced himself for the bullet.

Instead Diechmann held out a crisp white linen handkerchief and jerked it irritably at him. Ossie shook his head and dragged his sleeve across his bloody nose.

Diechmann let the handkerchief drop. 'It is no matter to me, one way or the other.' He stepped on it and twisted it into the mud with his heel, snapping in German: 'March the swine to the machine.' He turned away and strode back down the animal track leading from the wood.

Ossie took a pace or two but stumbled on the tangle of parachute harness at the base of the tree. Automatically the *Feldwebel* extended a hand to steady him, jarring his damaged shoulder. Ossie gave an involuntary yelp of agony. The man said automatically, 'Excuse me, please.'

From the edge of the wood Diechmann shouted, 'My God, you apologise to this bastard who tried to kill us? Stand away. Get your hands off the pig.'

His fury came and went like the wind, just as it had in Spain. Ossie remembered how, his sweating fingers clasping and unclasping the controls of the Junkers Ju-52 over Guernica, Diechmann had at one moment screamed obscenities at the Reds and the Jews he claimed were concealing themselves within the populace of the city below, and at the next whooped with glee as his aircraft lifted to the release of its bombs and he heard the whistle of their descent.

Slowly Ossie climbed the crest of the rising ground where the wreck of the Dornier sprawled. Oil and fuel seeped from the smashed engines, and the propellers had been bent back against the nacelles by the force of the landing. Thin shafts of light shone through the bullet holes in the metal skin. The cockpit was a ruin – Diechmann had done well to get it down.

The *Hauptmann* had regained his composure. 'A strong old cow,' he said, in decent English, thumping the fuselage approvingly. 'She will fly again. Built to last, like the Reich.' Then he shaded his eyes, peering to the east. 'Very soon our fellows will be here. We have not long to wait.' But Ossie detected a trace of concern in his tone.

Overhead large formations of bombers were growling westwards. Somewhere, not too far away, anti-aircraft guns were loosing off; then he heard the thinner crackle of machine-guns, the thud of mortars, the clank and grind of tank tracks. 'No longer a rehearsal,' said Diechmann. He tapped the Andreas cross on the bomber's flank. 'You know this?' Ossie shook his head. 'I had the honour to serve with Kampfgruppe 88 in the Spanish war. For the Luftwaffe the great rehearsal, but, of course, for my comrades and me simply a holiday, just tourists. Fliers on vacation.' He laughed at the deceit. 'Wonderful. And the world looked on.' He paused. 'Perhaps you knew little of these matters living out your narrow existence on your tiny island. You should not have been so blinkered, my friend. Now you will find out how well we learnt our lessons.' He tapped the Condor insignia again. 'One must guard against sentimentality, but why not celebrate the old times, the good days? They made us what we are today.'

Still Ossie said nothing.

Diechmann lost patience and turned away, which suited Ossie just fine. 'Arno, rouse yourself,' Diechmann shouted. 'Interrogate this insolent pig.'

The *Feldwebel* ambled over, suppressing a yawn, and said to Ossie in English: 'It is less painful now, the shoulder?'

'You astound me, Arno,' said Diechmann. 'How can you indulge in petty courtesies with the swine who brought us down? One day I will have you shot. You are not the stuff of which the Reich must be composed. You still yearn for your fat wife, your cosy fireside, your schoolroom, those little heads bent over arithmetic books. You fail to see the broader canvas, the opportunity to play your part in the great scheme of things. In Spain—'

'You have told me of Spain,' said the *Feldwebel* wearily.

Diechmann ignored him. 'In Spain every man was a volunteer.

We were proud to invest our lives in the greater future. We had vision. We believed. In what do you believe, Arno?'

'I believe I am an excellent navigator,' said the *Feldwebel*, stolidly. 'I can tell you exactly where you have crashed our machine.'

'You oaf,' said Diechmann, with a quiet menace. 'One day, yes, I will have you shot. Perhaps I will do it myself, with great pleasure. Tell me what you get out of this idiot. Use the arm to encourage him.'

The *Feldwebel* leant back against the nose-cone close to Ossie and began to clean his spectacles with a rag. He replaced them carefully, adjusted them on the bridge of his nose, and said quietly, 'Do you speak German perhaps?' Ossie shook his head. 'I thought maybe you did. It seemed to me you were following our conversation.' Again Ossie shook his head, wondering where this was leading. Perhaps the *Feldwebel* wasn't as guileless as he appeared. Now he took Ossie's left arm in both hands and looked him straight in the eye.

Oh, Christ, thought Ossie, can I stand this?

'You permit?' said the German, moving the arm.

'Fuck you,' said Ossie. He was surprised by the sound of his voice: he had not spoken since his brolly-hop.

The *Feldwebel* laughed gently. 'No, you do not understand. I believe you have a dislocation, nothing more. I can restore it for you but it will be painful.' His fingers probed the shoulder. Then he grunted, satisfied. 'Yes, it is as I thought. You wish?'

'Yeah, I wish,' said Ossie. What the hell? There was something about the *Feldwebel* that suggested maybe he was okay and, anyway, he felt almost too bushed to care. He let his head fall back, staring at the sky. Its expanse was scored with condensation trails, like patterns left by skaters on an ice-rink. He felt the German grasp his arm, firmly but without force, and extend it sideways. 'Do not attempt to be courageous. The *Hauptmann* will enjoy hearing you scream.'

There was a brief, experimental lateral tension, then a swift jerk. Ossie felt the joint snap back into place. The pain was extreme but less than he had feared. He hollered anyway, to help things along for the *Feldwebel*. Immediately the shoulder felt easier. 'Where in hell did you learn to do that?'

'Many misfortunes occur in the playground, my friend.' Then: '*Sind Sie unverletzt?*'

'Yeah, I'm fine.'

'So,' grinned the *Feldwebel*, with obvious satisfaction.

'Okay, so I have a little of your lingo,' said Ossie, cursing himself inwardly. Had this been a subtle ploy after all?

'Don't be concerned. But it is perhaps as well that you keep this to yourself. You understand, of course, that the *Hauptmann* demands certain other information.'

'That's easy. Name, Beery, Christian name, Wallace. Rank, flight lieutenant. Number, 5066609.'

'You are not English,' said the *Feldwebel*.

Ossie was shaken. This was one shrewd fellow, not to be under-estimated. He cursed himself again – he should have put on a Limey accent. His shoulder was throbbing now. 'Canadian,' he said.

'Your squadron?' Ossie shook his head. 'Location? Aircraft?'

'Tiger Moth.'

The German laughed. 'The latest model, yes. A great improvement.' Then, with a touch of pride despite himself: 'But no match for a Messerschmitt, *hein?*' With his hands he mimicked the Me-109 bouncing Ossie's Hurricane. 'You forget, I had a grandstand seat. A Tiger Moth built by Hawker maybe?'

Diechmann was back, walking round the tip of the drooping wing. Snubnose, the little bomb-aimer, scuffed the heels of his flying boots behind him. Diechmann had heard Ossie yell. He said, with ponderous irony: 'I am surprised, Arno, that you should resort to such vulgar tactics to ensure co-operation. Shame on you. Your information, please.'

Now his face clouded. What few facts the *Feldwebel* passed

on he greeted with derision and no mention was made of Ossie having German . . .

Diechmann ordered Ossie to stand. 'So, Canadian then. Tell me, why does the British Empire pretend to respect the rights of countries under its sway when it expects them to sacrifice themselves in hopeless and stupid resistance?'

'Go chase yourself,' said Ossie.

Diechmann pumped his fist into Ossie's battered nose. He went down, hard, striking his head against the Dornier's nose-cone. Diechmann dragged him to his feet. 'Have you searched the shit?' The *Feldwebel* looked hopelessly at Ossie. Ossie said: 'Yeah, he did.'

'You lie! All lies!' said Diechmann. He seized Ossie's right ear and twisted it round and upwards. Ossie rose on to his toes. Diechmann let go and snatched the standard-issue Elgin watch from his wrist. Then he fumbled through the American's pockets: a pen that concealed a silk map of the Franco-German border country, a scrap of paper, a tiny compass, a creased sepia photograph.

Diechmann thrust the watch and pen into his overalls, inspected the paper, tossed it away, and stamped on the compass. 'No need for a compass, Mr Lumberjack. You are going in one direction only. East.' Then he glanced at the photograph . . .

Ossie remembered it being taken, that time Kit Curtis had shot a roll of Kodak in the Jardin du Carousel in the Tuileries when they'd had that good time with Hannah and Bébé – at least, it had been a good time until he had known for certain that Hannah wasn't Kit's girl, noticed how she had studied Bébé, like she was some kind of reworking of herself, so much the same yet stunningly not. Before they had begun to suspect . . .

'She looks like a dirty French Jewess,' Diechmann was saying, 'only good for shagging. They will quickly learn what real men are when we enter Paris.'

'She's my sister,' said Ossie. 'She died of cancer a year ago. She was going to be a nun in Toronto.'

Diechmann's mouth fell open. He flushed crimson. Ossie

caught the *Feldwebel*'s eye. He was shaking. He'd got it, all right. Ossie also felt an urgent desire to laugh. Diechmann thrust the photograph back into Ossie's pocket, roughly, to show he didn't care.

Less than half a kilometre away across the open fields thin poplars marked the course of a road traversing the plain. Where the road came into view, skirting a straggle of farm buildings, a dustcloud rose. Gradually, lumbering black shapes could be seen groaning and rattling along the *pavé*: tanks, and behind them figures, many of them freakishly tall, could be dimly made out, moving with purpose in two columns.

Diechmann was exultant. As the troops came nearer he waved joyously, perched on top of the Dornier fuselage. To make sure he had been seen he pulled out his pistol and fired several times in the air. Then he set off across the fields. The columns had halted, faced right then advanced through the ankle-high crop towards him in a wide, unhurried line.

'It does not occur to the fool,' said the *Feldwebel*, bleakly, 'that these troops have come from the west.' Back on the road the tanks had halted, the chugging of their engines beating out a primitive rhythm. Ossie recognised them as Renault R-35 ten-tonners.

Diechmann's lone figure was swallowed up in a swirl of soldiery that milled about him, then swept him back towards the wreckage of the bomber. Their faces impassive, the Senegalese *tirailleurs* booted him before them. Some still carried their packs on their heads; a custom that at a distance had given them the appearance of giants. Diechmann's cheeks and forehead had been slashed with a sharp blade. His overalls were scarlet with blood. His arms were pinned behind him. He was sobbing with fear and impotent fury at the ignominy of black hands thrusting him forward.

A single French officer presented himself. At a glance he took in the situation, noting Ossie's RAF wings. He gestured him aside curtly, issuing orders in rapid French. The *Feldwebel* and the bomb-aimer were seized, their hands strapped behind their backs with webbing strips and forced on to their knees beside Diechmann. They seemed struck dumb by the speed of it all. A Senegalese corporal, taller than the rest, had turned his back on the three Germans. With professional zeal he was testing the blade of a machete, watched by his grinning comrades.

'Jesus Christ,' said Ossie. 'What do you think you're doing?'

The French officer pushed him aside impatiently. 'Three kilometres from here are many dead people, old, young, mothers, children, babies. Machine-gunned on the road as they fled. Murdered by the Boches.' He tried to appear reasonable. 'We are in no position, my friend, to take prisoners. Do you really suggest that we leave them here to return another day and butcher once more?'

'But this?' Ossie's voice was dry with horror.

The Frenchman shrugged. 'It is their way.'

There was a dull thump followed by an odd gasp from the Senegalese, a mixture of gratification and revulsion. Diechmann's severed head lay on the rich reddish earth with its green summer shoots. The mouth was gaping, working; the eyes flickering, opening, shutting, amazed. Another thudding impact. The trunk of the little bomb-aimer fell forward, the head rolling down the gentle slope, its blond hair picking up mud and tiny stones as it went, blood spurting from the severed neck. A Senegalese booted it on its way to pitiless laughter . . .

The *Feldwebel* had only moments to ready himself. His face was expressionless, resigned. His chin was high. He was looking towards the east – remembering what? The fat wife, the children he had guided and tended? Perhaps he also mourned the dead piled high on the road beyond the poplars . . .

The French officer casually lit a Gitane, watching impassively as the Senegalese threw the three corpses into the fuselage of the bomber, retrieved the heads and jammed them on to stakes swiftly fashioned from fallen branches in the wood. These they positioned, with some care, in front of the shattered Dornier before piercing its fuel tanks with bullets and setting it ablaze. The Frenchman offered Ossie a cigarette, the smell of crude tobacco blending with the stench of burning flesh. He pushed the pack away.

Unmoved, the officer glanced at his watch. 'As you wish. Keep the sun to your left, my friend, and you should regain our lines. But pay close attention. The Boches are everywhere, most particularly where our command tells us it is impossible for them to be.' He flicked his half-consumed cigarette towards the blazing Dornier.

Ossie noticed that Diechmann's hair was alight, the face frozen in anguish.

On a snapped command the Senegalese *tirailleurs* formed up and swept back across the field towards the waiting tanks. The French officer followed them for a pace or two, halted, then strolled back to Ossie, who stood motionless, unable to grasp the enormity of what had unfolded in front of him. 'Ah yes, my *sergent-chef* retrieved this souvenir from the overalls of the Boche pilot. From the make, I imagine it's yours. I prevailed upon Diouf to acknowledge that you have a greater need for it. Besides, where we are going I do not want him counting the hours that may be left to him.' He pressed the Elgin wristwatch into Ossie's palm. It was half past three.

By the time Ossie had strapped on the watch the French officer had regained the road and gave a jaunty wave. He did not respond. The gesture was too dismissive of the horror that had taken place just minutes before. Once, he had taken a tumble from a bronc during a vacation on a dude ranch in Wyoming. He felt that way now; every joint and muscle protesting at the least movement. His neck felt weak, unable to support his head. It would be so easy to rest awhile, stretch out on the warm earth, wait to be found, maybe. But found by who? And what of the grisly spectacle only yards away and the loathsome odour? Ossie forced himself to take a step, then another, heading slowly towards the distant road and the poplars.

Moving away from the burning Dornier, not looking back, Ossie, sensed his first few steps towards freedom and safety being reflected in those dead unseeing eyes, glazed now, in the sockets of the impaled skulls behind him . . .

Three

Floating in impeccable formation at 20,000 feet over Sedan, shepherding a dozen Blenheims on their way to knock out pontoon bridges which spanned the Meuse and were vulnerable to the advancing Panzers, Kit became aware that he was cupping the knob of his Hurricane's throttle lever, easing it almost imperceptibly back and forth. He took pleasure in hearing the engine revs rise and fall, a sing-song, monotonous refrain that was more heartening than any of the *marche militaire* that crackled incessantly from French stations on the wireless.

It hadn't been like that on the first sweep. Even at the time he had sensed the slightest hesitation in the engine's response, a fractional labouring when he opened the throttle. It was the kind of gremlin that would guzzle fuel. But his desire to prove worthy of leading B Flight in what promised to be the first big engagement of the campaign, the responsibility he felt for the men around him, the need to do everything right and not balls things up had compelled him to ignore his sixth sense about things mechanical, the subtle indicators that something was playing up. Fired-up, he had taken not the slightest notice of something so relatively minor. And he'd got away with it: simply a brief diversion to Rouvres before he dropped back to Revigncourt where Sergeant Jessop and the lads had found some offending gunge in the fuel lines, just a fleck or two but enough to account for the Merlin's sudden thirst.

His momentary sense of well-being was quickly dismissed: even a touch of euphoria was dangerous when the skies were filled with Hun trying to kill you. Inevitably his thoughts turned to Ossie Wolf, that time six months earlier when he had raged at what he saw as Kit's naivety about the approaching conflict. 'You don't really hate the Hun. To you and your sort they're just guys on the other side. Guys much like us, perfectly decent, really. I got news for you. They're not. They're murdering thugs. I've seen what they did in Spain. And while you're flying round the fucking clouds like Sir Lancelot looking for the Holy Grail, down below the Krauts will be destroying civilisation. Wise up buster. There's only one rule you need to remember. Do it to him before the sonofabitch does it to you. Period.'

The bitter confrontation had been compounded by the American's rank. No sergeant, however gifted in the air, should be permitted to harangue a senior officer in this way. But despite this Kit had been forced to wonder whether there was truth in what he had said so he suppressed his mounting anger: 'Believe me, I'm under no illusions.' Today he knew otherwise.

And now it seemed that Ossie had bought it. It was shortly before take-off that B Flight learned the A Flight leader was officially posted missing. The CO was reluctant to confirm the news, clearly hoping that even now Ossie would find his way home, perhaps at the controls of a barely airworthy and badly mauled machine or at the wheel of a venerable Citroën or Renault commandeered from a handy farmer. It was his style, to reappear suddenly, refusing to be quizzed about his adventures and demanding another Hurricane. They knew he had been hit, that was all, bounced by an expertly flown Me-109. No one had seen him go down. But surely he'd make it. After all Al Miller, A Flight's weaver, had got back okay, his R/T controls smashed, his engine streaming glycol, uncertain whether his damaged undercarriage would survive the landing. If he could do it, surely Wolf would. But as the hours passed and the shreds of information filtering through the grapevine proved as baseless as those that surrounded the fate of Beaky Parker, the pilots were forced to confront an uncomfortable truth: that if it could happen to Ossie Wolf it could happen to anyone.

The loss of their most colourful character shook the squadron. He had seemed invulnerable, their best, most canny flier, a little older than the rest with a raw, ruthless edge, five victories already and the promise of more to come. He was a model in some ways – his professionalism in the air, his qualities of leadership that had pitched him, reluctantly, from sergeant pilot to acting flight lieutenant and A Flight Commander within six months – in others, a mystery: his prickly views on the English class system, his resistance to authority, his tight-lipped response to questions about his background in the Midwest and, most of all, about his time in Spain where he seemed to have fought for the Republicans and witnessed events that had scarred him somehow. Few of the pilots could get close to him. He'd counted his fellow sergeant Dinghy Davis a buddy, but Dinghy was dead, burned in his kite back in November. To the squadron, then, it was a puzzle that only Kit Curtis had built with him some kind of trust, odd because Kit seemed the epitome of everything the American detested; assured, well-educated, privileged, popular, 'a goddammed golden boy', as Wolf had once observed to his fellow NCOs. Everyone knew that in the early days the pair had had their run-ins, but around the turn of the year there had been a change in the way they regarded each other, a subtle bond, almost as though a secret was shared, an understanding established. Suggestions that it had to do with women were dismissed by both men with red ears and a swift change of subject. Yes, definitely odd . . .

The twelve stub-nosed Blenheims prepared for their bombing and strafing run. They would dive out of sight of the waiting Hurricanes, be lost in the persistent low haze, find themselves horribly exposed to flak and fighters as they climbed away from their targets. A few years before their speed had been judged remarkable. Now they gave away 100 m.p.h. to a Messerschmitt

109. Already the losses were catastrophic and not one of the Blenheim crews dipping away from their protective escort could have been under any illusion about their chances. But still the voice of the flight commander came through on the R/T without a tremor: 'Thanks a lot Watchdog. Back in a jiffy.'

Eyes red from ceaseless scrutiny of the cloudless, brilliant sky above and around them, the pilots of B Flight watched for the merest hint of something, somewhere, at 30,000 feet, swooping for the kill or climbing foxily from 10,000, hiding in their blind-spot and ready to pounce. Only a multitude of contrails, streaming west, was visible at high altitude. Then—

'Blue Leader, Blue Leader, our flock is back.'

'Okay, Goofy. Watch for fighters, watch for fighters.'

A single Blenheim laboured towards them, clawing for precious height on full throttle. On its camouflaged wings and fuselage the yellow, blue, white and red roundels stood out in startling clarity. The dorsal turret, housing the single Vickers machine-gun, swung vigorously back and forth. The bomber appeared undamaged.

'Thank you Watchdog. Time to go home.' It was a different voice.

'Say again,' said Kit, incredulous but striving to sound casual. This was it. No more to come. More than thirty men lost in as many minutes.

The Blenheim pilot did not respond. Instead he dropped on to his course and powered for his base at Plivot, shadowed by Buster Brown, Kenny Rains and Pip Fuller. Kit banked away with the Kiwi, Eddie Knox, and Goofy Gates. He was consumed with sick fury. The tears starting in his eyes were not merely from the strain of remaining vigilant.

The three Hurricanes curved away north of Verdun, sweeping eastwards over the Forêt de Spincourt. The haze was thinner here. Thousands of hectares of deep-green wooded heights passed below, a few tortuous white roads, rust-hued dwellings, cream, black and brown beasts in the fields, crops tinged emerald and small lakes sapphire blue in reflected light, haphazard touches of colour like oil-paint on an artist's pallet, serene, timeless, normal. But 25,000 feet above, pinned into their tiny cockpits, sucking oxygen, eyes raw behind their goggles, Kit Curtis, Knox and Goofy Gates knew life was anything but normal, as they flicked on their gun-sights, set gun-buttons to 'fire', checked instruments and altimeters. They were hunters now, no longer shepherds guarding a threatened flock but wolves scenting a kill.

Near Mars-le-Tour, just west of Metz, Gates sang out, 'Enemy aircraft, enemy aircraft, eleven o'clock and below. Twelve of the sods.'

'Stukas, by Christ,' said Knox.

The angular silhouettes of a *Staffel* of Ju-87s were wheeling over a road junction that, as the Hurricanes side-slipped their height away for a clearer view, they saw was jammed with an extraordinary multitude of humanity and conveyances: cars, smart and dilapidated, a country autobus or two, lorries, ancient farm wagons, tiny hand-carts, anything on wheels that could move and carry. Many of these contrivances were piled high with possessions: tables, chairs, wardrobes, cupboards, pictures, clothing, and children. Except nothing was moving, just the Stukas hanging over the scene, their dangling wheel-pods like the talons of birds of prey.

In a steep vertical bank Kit made out military transport, mostly trucks, whether British or French it was impossible to tell, immersed in and immobilised by the chaos. Closer still he saw bodies, whole or in parts, strewn across the ground and sprawled in ditches, the burning skeletons of bombed vehicles. The fear and panic were almost tangible.

'Oh, my God,' Knox was shouting over the R/T, 'the shits, the absolute shits.'

'For Pete's sake, shut up, Eddie,' rapped Kit. 'Prepare to attack. And, Goofy, keep a bloody good look-out. Where the hell's their ruddy escort?'

The bombs had done their work. Now the Stukas were calmly proceeding with the second phase of their routine: the business of strafing those who might have survived. This was Poland all over again: the methodical pummelling of targets frozen with dread by the howl of sirens and the earth-shaking impact of bombs. No need for fighter cover, particularly this far east: the word 'Stuka' struck terror into the boldest heart. But this was not Poland . . .

The Hurricanes were down to 8,000 feet now. Still they had not been spotted. What a gift. Then Gates bawled: 'Hurricanes above us and coming down. To the right, to the right.' Not Hurricanes, though. Stubby, blunt-nosed, almost toy-like, half a dozen fighters thundered past to starboard, throttles wide open at 300 m.p.h., trailing black exhaust smoke. The wings and fuse-lage bore roundels, the rudders tricolour flashes, but French not English.

'Where did those ugly buggers come from?' The New Zealander's voice was almost squeaky with surprise.

'It's Rupert Bear and his pals,' said Goofy Gates.

'Curtis Hawks,' said Kit. 'Wrap up and enjoy the show.' He pulled the Hurricanes away to gain precious height and watch for Me-109s who might choose to spoil the duck-shoot.

Like the Blenheims, the point of utmost danger for the cumbersome Stukas was the moment they attempted to climb away from their target. To the fast-closing l'Armée de l'Air fighters sweeping in from behind with a 100 m.p.h. advantage their only defence was the single flexibly mounted 7.92mm machine-gun in the rear cockpit. In less than eight minutes all twelve Ju-87s and their crews were burning on the ground. No survivors. And no losses among the Curtis Hawk 75s who passed the Hurricanes at 15,000 feet rocking their wings. Some of the pilots were bouncing in their seats with exultation, giving jubi-lant thumbs-ups as they soared past. Kit seemed to hear again the savage voice of the LAC at Rouvres as Johnny Balbec and his boys motored smartly down the road to Reims: 'Fucking

French bastards.' He wanted the man to hear about this. Maybe he'd have a chance to tell him. You never knew. War had a habit of throwing people together . . .

To the tiny figure making painful progress alongside the *grande route* from Metz to Verdun, the three Hurricanes were mere dots turning away and crawling west. But they were high enough to catch the sunlight under their wings and Ossie Wolf knew them for what they were. He felt abandoned. The guys would have written him off by now, no question. He caught himself – Jesus, he was acting like a soft kid. He'd made it this far. No reason why he shouldn't make it all the way. It was down to him, nobody else, and that was fine, the way he liked it – had always liked it. But keep away from that goddammed road with its blinding white dust and its treacherous heat-haze. Anything could emerge from those shimmering mirages. And there was plenty of stuff in the air: it would be all too easy to get knocked off by some trigger-happy Kraut air-gunner presented with a cute little running target. He'd already heard the ruckus of some low-level show going on, ten or fifteen miles away. He thought he'd seen Stukas too and maybe Spits or more Hurrys. It was hard to tell as they'd been obscured by the pillars of smoke soiling the sky. Yeah, he reckoned he'd be some mug to take to the road, relatively smooth and tempting though it was, so he stumbled along ditches and across reedy, stinking streams, keeping close to whatever shelter there was, throwing himself flat at the first hint of danger.

Only minutes earlier a Panzer motorcycle combination, on reconnaissance and moving fast between the lines of poplars, had almost caught him in the open. He'd clawed the ground behind some tussocks of grass waiting for the shot but the growl of the BMW motor had receded. He raised his head, tasting mud, and watched them go; three helmeted and goggled soldiers, two on the bike with automatic rifles slung across their shoulders, the other in the sidecar, swivelling the machine-gun mounted in front of him. They were joking together, confident, apparently heedless of what might await them a few miles down the road. In about five minutes, Ossie reckoned, they would reach the French tanks, holed up in the beech woodland.

He'd come across them an hour ago, forcing his way between dense foliage and emerging into a clearing, horrified to be confronted by a trio of tanks – but French, thank Christ, 32-ton Char B1 heavies, their motors silent, stinking of fuel and oil, their guns black-muzzled, still hot from recent action, the steel clicking and creaking as it cooled. The crews, perched on the armour plating, were incurious at first, seeing him as no kind of threat, hardly caring whether he was friend or foe. He was unarmed, alone and thus irrelevant. They stared down at him, gnawing stale baguettes and passing round unlabelled bottles of coarse red wine. Then they took in the RAF wings on his tunic, the mud-clogged flying boots, the battered state of his face. '*Merde, vous êtes pilote anglais?*'

An officer jumped to the ground, handed him a few hard crusts and watched curiously as he swigged the wine to soften them. He felt the alcohol flow through him, inducing fatigue. He passed the bottle back quickly. '*Vous avez de l'eau?*'

'*Non.*'

'*Où sont les allemands?*'

The officer spread his hands and raised his eyebrows. They were lost themselves, scattered after an encounter with Panzer 1 six-tonners. He held up three fingers and mimed an explosion. '*Les Boches, poom, poom, poom.*' He drew a finger across his throat. '*Quels salauds.*' He rattled off a torrent of French describing their battle.

Much of it was lost on the dazed American, but not enough. He wanted it to stop.

The tank crews, flushed with wine and the thrill of action, spurred the officer on, cutting in with details of their own, shouting that no, the Panzer with the red and gold turret flash was ours not yours, cursing the Germans in intricate, colourful ways, throwing back their heads and slapping the sides of the tanks as they elaborated on the death-throes of the Panzer commander who had emerged from his turret, well alight, and set the undergrowth ablaze. They fell against each other at that with morbid glee.

Ossie tried shaking his head. '*Je regrette mais je n'parle pas bien français.*' It was a phrase Bébé had taught him. He had it off so well that people thought he was fluent. Now the French officer laughed, thought he was being modest, and forged on with his account of the engagement.

'Okay,' said Ossie finally, 'okay. Yeah, good show. *Félicitations. À bas les Boches.*'

But now they wanted to hear from him. '*Combien de victoires? Cinq? Vraiment? Pas mal, mon copain.*' They demanded more, so with his hands he demonstrated how it was done – a lesson in killing – and, reluctantly, how he'd been bounced by that sonofabitch Me-109. He was dismissive of his brolly-hop, made no mention of Diechmann, the scholarly *Feldwebel* and the little blond bomb-aimer, pushing away the image of those three slack-jawed heads on stakes ten miles back. He felt crowded by death.

He made to move. 'Yeah, well . . .' The French tank crews gathered round him, slapped him on the back. He winced, and the garrulous officer gave a cry of sympathy. He pushed the others away roughly, gathered him to his chest and kissed him on both cheeks. They pressed more bread on him. '*Les rosbif, ils sont là.*' A wave down the road. '*Bonne chance, mon copain.*'

Now, with the rattle of the German motorcycle combination receding, he slid down the bank of a ditch and found himself ankle-deep in a meagre, sluggish streamlet. He thrust both hands through the mantle of green weed and cupped noxious water in his palms then gulped it so rapidly that he choked. His stomach, full of bread, became swollen and taut. He loosened the top buttons of his fly. Then he sank to his knees in the marshy channel and thrust his head through the weed, holding his breath and allowing what current there was to soothe his wounds.

A prolonged burst of machine-gun fire rang out some way off, followed after an interval by three deliberate single shots: the thin reports of a pistol. The Panzer recon guys had come across the French tank crews.

On the road the traffic, all of it German, was growing: more motorcycles, trucks, half-tracks, the occasional staff car swerving between the slower vehicles, raising dust. Cover was sparse. Ossie knew he had to find shelter until dark. Cooler now, he stumbled on to a stony track that left the road beside a stump of a shrine containing a weather-beaten effigy of the Virgin and Child. It curved away to the right and led to a group of farm buildings, huddled beside a patch of woodland that formed a natural windbreak where the ground fell away to a densely forested valley. Close to the buildings three Panzer tanks were burning. It was from this valley, Ossie realised, that they must have emerged, unwittingly presenting their bellies to the waiting French B1s. Two had been destroyed on the spot, a third had advanced a few hundred yards, then slewed to a halt and brewed up. Ossie approached the scene cautiously.

He passed the first Panzer 1 six-tonner with his hand over his mouth, his thumb and forefinger clamping his nostrils. The trapped crew had been broiled: a pool of iridescent fat had spread under the tank and glimmered dully in the sunlight. On its fringe regiments of ants were exploring its possibilities.

At the farmhouse it was clear that they had been watching his approach. A yellowing lace curtain moved in an upper room. A skeletal hound tied with string to the wheel of a farm-cart yelped without pause, its front paws leaving the ground with the effort. Wavering on the worn sandstone step he seized the rusting iron knocker, moulded like a clenched fist, and rapped urgently on the brown-painted door. He could hear people moving inside but no one came. He slammed the knocker hard and long. Finally the door was unlocked and an unshaven face peered out. A gust of wood-smoke escaped from the unlit interior, the smell mingling with the odours of long-eaten meals, stale cigarettes and animals. Ossie tried out his bad French. '*Je suis votre ami*—' The door closed and was bolted.

He stepped back and stared up at the window with the lace curtain. A woman met his gaze, gaunt, agitated, her hands clenched beneath her chin, trembling. She jerked her head. She wanted him to go. Or did she mean the barn? He turned back, questioningly, but she'd vanished, the curtains drawn. Then he realised she hadn't meant either.

A platoon of four Panzergrenadier half-tracks had pulled off the road. Now two launched themselves across the open fields towards the carcasses of the nearby tanks. Behind each driver half a dozen infantrymen sat neat as toy soldiers, the barrels of their rifles pointing skywards, wavering with the motion of the vehicle. Caught in the yard, Ossie knew he'd been seen.

The darkness of the barn was startling after the glare outside and, for a moment, he could see nothing. Startled chickens burst past him in a flurry of feathers. He closed the sagging door behind him. Gradually he made out farm implements stacked against the walls, caked with mud and rusting. Horse-collars and harnesses hung from hooks and dung was thick on the cobbled floor. A rough wooden trough stood against the wall, empty. No loft, no stalls, not even a pile of hay. Nowhere to hide or even burrow. At the far end of the building a second door stood open, creaking in the breeze. A shadow passed across it. No dice there. Ossie looked again at the array of tools: some useful scythes and pitch-forks. Who was he kidding? He heard a commotion over by the house, that goddammed knocker being worked good, then the crash of a door being kicked in. Some kind of scuffle and a man being dragged into the open, pleading. A woman screamed, shrill, terrified. The man was whining, '*Mais, Monsieur, Monsieur . . .*'

There was a heavy blow and a cry of pain. An officer shouted in German: 'Leave him alone, you damned fool. Who do you think we are? The bloody SS?' Things quietened down. These were ordinary soldiers, Ossie told himself, professionals. He was in the bag, sure enough, but maybe he'd be okay.

The voices were perceptibly softer now. The officer had dropped into fluent French, talking to the peasant in a reasonable, even tone, almost friendly. The man was reassured, relieved that he was being listened to. And he was eager to please, hoarse with desperation, explaining that a British airman had arrived only moments ago, that they had naturally refused to even speak to him, that they wanted only peace and to be left alone, that they believed the fugitive was now sheltering, absolutely without their permission, in the *étable à vache*.

'Right place for him, the animal,' someone said in a Bavarian accent and there was a burst of laughter, instantly silenced by a snapped order. Then the soldiers sprang to their task with a clatter of boots. The barn was being encircled.

Ossie walked out slowly into the sunlight, his arms spread in a gesture of resignation. He was careful to appear calm and composed but he was darned if he'd raise his hands in meek surrender. The soldiers facing him, weapons aimed and cocked, were curious and impassive, but those who had inspected the ruined tanks were rejoining their comrades now, shaken, sickened, enraged. Their mood was dangerous and unpredictable but at a curt command they gathered themselves, still sullen but once more yielding to the will of their young *Hauptmann*. They regarded him with respect, eyes full of trust. He had led them half across Europe. Why doubt him now?

The *Hauptmann* gave Ossie a casual salute and a slight smile. 'So,' he said in flawless English, 'bad luck. We come to investigate our comrades and we collar you. Wrong time, wrong place.' He was thin and tall, six-two, six-three, olive-skinned with straight black hair, almost Latin. Next to the stocky American the contrast was droll: the one elegant and assured, the other pugnacious and defiant.

'You understand I need to know certain information,' said the German. He signalled to an *Unterfeldwebel*, who bustled over, pulling a notebook and pencil from his tunic.

48

'Beery,' said Ossie. 'B-E-E-R-Y.' He spelled it out slowly watching the man write it down. 'First name Wallace.'

'Ah,' said the officer, taking the notebook from the surprised NCO and ripping out the page. 'I much admired your portrayal of Long John Silver. You must tell me about your most interesting interpretation before we unite you with the many thousands of your comrades we have already taken prisoner.' He returned the notebook to the bemused *Unterfeldwebel* and nodded at the smouldering tanks. 'Advise Command that those poor devils are beyond help. And make a point of saying the peasants had nothing to do with anything. No, add that they helped us capture a terror-flier. That should preserve their wretched skins a little longer.'

The peasant had been frantically scanning the *Hauptmann*'s face for signs of hope, understanding nothing that had been said. Now, something in the German's demeanour told him that perhaps, after all, he and his wife would not be put up against a wall and shot. The man was under no illusions: he was old enough to have lived through the last invasion by the Boches. He seized the *Hauptmann*'s hand and pumped it up and down with tears in his eyes. The young officer pulled away and wiped his hand on his jacket.

Alarmed again, the peasant scuttled back to the farmhouse. At the weatherbeaten brown door the woman appeared. The man attempted to restrain her but she thrust him away and advanced a few steps into the yard. She stood there, her mouth open, shivering violently, whether with fear, despair or disgust it was impossible to tell. She wore the usual garb: shapeless cotton dress, bilious floral apron, ankle socks, clogs. She had once been comely. Ossie could make out the vestiges of beauty in her face: fine eyes, a broad, intelligent forehead. She was staring at him with something close to anguish. He nodded deliberately, trying to show he understood. Her brow cleared. Then she turned and went back into the gloom of the farmhouse.

The *Hauptmann* gestured Ossie to follow him to his grey Hanomag 251 command vehicle. The mighty Maybach engine burst into life. As they climbed up into the front seat of the half-track, Ossie pinned between the *Hauptmann* and the driver, the officer said, with a crooked grin: 'And now, my friend, I really do implore you to be a little more co-operative, in your own best interests. I have no idea who we will hand you over to and, from the look of you, I would say you have suffered enough.' They were bouncing at some speed across the fields to the road. Ossie reached for the top of the windscreen with both hands. A click sounded behind him as the *Unterfeldwebel* slipped the safety lever of his 7.65 Luger. Ossie pulled himself upright and spat over the *Hauptmann*'s head. Most of the spittle flew backwards and streaked the flanks of the half-track but a few flecks soiled the officer's uniform. The NCO gave a bellow of outrage and thrust the barrel of the Luger into Ossie's ear. But the *Hauptmann* waved him back into his seat, shaking his head and studying the passing countryside with what appeared to be genuine interest, only his eyes betraying the faintest sign of amusement.

Ossie wriggled back into his seat. 'Something left a nasty taste,' he said, then added: 'I'm glad you enjoyed *Treasure Island*.'

Four

After a tense, laborious climb to 25,000 feet Kit gathered B Flight into two neat vics, careful to maintain height and, alert to the position of the lowering sun, led the six Hurricanes in gentle, curving turns to port and starboard. They were looking for trouble and growing impatient. They reckoned they'd been flaunting themselves long enough. No Blenheims and Battles to shadow this time but an offensive sweep over Bar-le-Duc with a brief from Brewster to seek and destroy enemy fighters. 'The news we're getting from HQ at Reims is that when we draw off the escorts and leave the bombers exposed whole raids are turning back, the windy sods. So get cracking and hit the fighters hard. Remember, this is our sky not theirs.' Now they had a chance to avenge the bomber crews they had witnessed going so stoically to their death.

All the boys were jumpy. Despite the loss of Beaky Parker and Ossie Wolf they knew that good fortune had been with them, none more so than Al Miller, laughing one moment, close to tears the next, hair still clogged with oil, eyes scarlet from glycol. Nursing his shattered machine back to Revigncourt after the ill-fated sortie on which Wolf had gone down, Miller climbed from his cockpit, stained with traces of the excreta that had seeped through his trousers. Nothing was said.

Even phlegmatic Goofy Gates was twitchy. Just before take-off Kit had caught him by the buckboard, slurping a mug of tea with a face like a stricken bloodhound. Never had his nickname suited him so well. 'You're looking browned off, Sergeant. What's up?'

'This arse-end Charlie business, sir. Why does it always have to be me?'

'Because you're good at it, Sergeant. You've saved our skins often enough. Anything else?'

'No, sir. Yes, sir. I still think someone else could have a bash. Pilot Officer Rains for a start.'

'When I need your advice on how to run the flight, Sergeant, I'll ask for it. Finish your char and go and check your aeroplane.'

'I've done that, sir.'

'I gave you an order Sergeant. Go and check your aeroplane. You're being wet, and I'm not about to trust my life to some clot who's moping about feeling sorry for himself. You've probably forgotten something vital. Now, get your bloody finger out.'

'Yes, sir. Sorry, sir.'

'For Christ's sake, Gates, it's the same for all of us. We're all feeling the pressure. What did you expect? All I know is you're the best bloody weaver in the business. If I didn't believe that I wouldn't ask you to do it. Now, get a grip and make sure we don't get bounced. I'm relying on you.' He expected a rueful grin, some sign that his words had struck home, but Gates said nothing. Avoiding Kit's eye, he replaced the china mug on the tailgate of the buckboard and walked away, head down, hands thrust deep in his pockets.

Kit cursed himself for failing. Just a stupid bloody pep-talk, automatic, superficial, ill-judged. He felt a deep unease: it had been no way to talk to a man he respected. Worst of all, it hadn't helped.

Now he sang out over the R/T: 'Keep 'em peeled, weaver.'

'I am doing.' Gates's voice still held a testy strain.

'Good show.' Kit left it at that. Nothing he said seemed right. Cloudlets had started to form in the late afternoon from the water vapour swept aloft by the air rising from the baked earth. As the hours passed they mingled and became huge, billowing masses stretching to the horizon, flat at the base, lively and full of movement above, transforming themselves into fantastic shapes: gargantuan beasts, grotesque parodies of vegetation or massifs that dwarfed any terrestrial mountain range.

Against this grandeur the sturdy Hurricanes made a brave sight: Kenny Rains fifty feet to Kit's left, Buster Brown to the right. Behind them and a little above, the second vic; the squadron favourite Pip Fuller and the two sergeant pilots, Eddie Knox and arse-end Charlie, Goofy Gates. Fuller was drifting out to port, eighty feet, ninety, a hundred. 'Keep it tight, Pip, keep it tight,' Kit snapped. Fuller was everyone's younger brother, fair, beardless, quick to blush, keen to prove himself and, unlike Rains, unsure of his ability. He had about him a touching deference, overawed by almost everybody, like a new arrival in the upper sixth. His most severe swear words were 'gosh' and 'golly'. He was agonisingly short of hours on Hurricanes and only a moderate pilot. They all feared for him.

As Fuller eased back gingerly into formation Kit experienced a wave of pure joy at the thrill of flight. So many boyhood daydreams had brought him to this point: the tales of the early pioneers – Lilienthal, Farman, Blériot, Rolls, Orville Wright teetering into the air at Kittyhawk; the well-thumbed adventure yarns of daring pilots doing battle with the Richthofen Circus over the wasteland of the Somme; little Albert Ball, laying down his violin and climbing into his red-nosed SE5 Scout to take on scarlet Hun Albatrosses at impossible odds; hours and days of constructing flimsy model flying machines from doped paper and balsawood, all doomed to destruction; and, most intoxicating of all, a birthday treat, an excursion to a flying circus run by wild-eyed young men who had survived the war, flying old Avros bought from the Air Disposal Board, each pilot the symbol of Kit's fantasies. The antics of the RAF's aerobatic display team at Hendon in '31, the stumpy little Gamecock fighters zipping through a hair-raising routine of synchronised loops, turns and dives, confirmed that he wanted nothing more than to be at the controls of his own machine, perhaps in the skies of France, facing a gallant enemy, man against man, wheeling and circling, testing for weakness; triumphing, of course, but saluting the fallen foe as he spiralled picturesquely to his death. Except it wasn't like that . . .

In an instant Kit's moment of exultation was gone. He remembered Dinghy Davis trapped in his blazing cockpit, screaming until he flicked off the R/T switch so that no one would hear his agony; German air-crew falling past him, their 'chutes burned or failed, with plenty of time to think about it; the cockpits of the few Blenheims and Battles that made it back to base, running with blood and viscera. No glory in any of it. Ossie Wolf's words came back to him: 'Forget your goddammed fancy tricks unless they get you in position to kill. You're just a gun platform, aerial artillery. Get up, get in, blow the bastard to hell, get out. That's it. That's all.' The blunt American had many theories. To him the conventional closely gathered vic was suicide, 'a nice fat juicy target': better for fighters to spread wide apart in twos, Luftwaffe-style. Then, while still a sergeant, he'd tried Brewster's patience with a relentless campaign to alter the harmonisation of his Brownings: 250 yards was way too far off, he reckoned – 'You're just going to pepper the guy.' The CO had heard something of the sort from a few ultra-keen types he'd come across in other squadrons. 'I suppose you'd prefer 150 yards, Sergeant?' he'd said drily.

'No, sir,' Wolf had rapped back. 'Make it a hundred.' His rank counted against him. No NCO was permitted to tinker with his aircraft in that way. Fly it and fight in it as the manufacturer intended. End of story. By the time his commission came through, the Hun were rolling west and the time for experiments, inspired or insane, was past. He had gone into his last action with his Brownings still converging at 250 yards.

His cockpit luminous from shafts of sunlight spilling through apertures in the cloud, Kit heard again that Midwest twang, brimming with contempt: 'While you're flying round the fucking clouds like Sir Lancelot looking for the Holy Grail down below the Krauts will be destroying civilisation.' Now it seemed that Ossie Wolf, for all his knowledge and experience, had himself been destroyed and no one outside the squadron knew about it, not Bébé, not Hannah, not the man's family. Kit knew it would be the same if he went down. Things were moving too fast for tactful telegrams or phone calls. One moment someone was there and operational, part of the picture, and then they weren't. Maybe later the niceties might be observed: a tidied-up and sanitised account of their passing would drop through someone's door. If not known they'd probably make it up: 'He was last seen pressing his attack though outnumbered ten-to-one.'

Then, urgently, Buster Brown: 'Look out, Huns!'

Veering this way and that, throttling up and back, desperate to locate the threat, several of the Hurricanes came close to collision. Curtis yanked back his stick and pulled himself out of immediate danger. 'Buster, you bloody idiot, what are you trying to do? Kill us all? Location and height, for Christ's sake.'

Brown, so quick to tear a strip off sprog pilots for the least blunder, was mortified. Even he had got the jitters. 'Sorry Blue Leader. Five aircraft to starboard three o'clock below.'

Kit made them out immediately, grey-green paintwork, yellow spinners, big black crosses just to make sure there was no mistake: Messerschmitt 109s, fading across to the right now, maintaining height, looking for trouble too . . . 'Line astern, line astern. We're going right through the middle of 'em.'

The Me-109s saw them coming almost too late, but not quite. They broke away wildly. To his left Kit saw the Hurricane of Kenny Rains juddering to the recoil of his machine-guns. His shot was wide. His quarry rolled swiftly on to its back and dived away unscathed.

The R/T crackled with frenzied exchanges.

'Buster, Buster, break right!'

'Bugger me!'

'He nearly had you.'

'Goofy, one right on top of you.'

'Okay, I've got him.'

'Eddie, look out behind.'

'Christ . . .'

'It's only me.' Fuller's voice, apologetic even in the heat of battle.

Kit cut in: 'Pip, watch your bloody mirror.' He could hear Fuller panting, the quick rasping breaths of someone close to panic.

Then Rains: 'Blue Leader, Blue Leader, break right, break right.'

White streaks of tracer were passing between Kit's windscreen and propeller, inches above the engine cowling. He flicked to starboard, sensing a looming shape closing fast above and to the left. He steep-turned hard and bullets plink-plinked through his fuselage just behind the cockpit. He heard the fabric and metal framework shred. The Hurricane shuddered, stalled and spun. He let it have its head, spiralling down to 15,000 feet. No good. The sod was still there.

As he levelled out, a stream of tracer drifted almost lazily over his tailplane. He pulled the aircraft into the tightest of turns, his vision greying as the mounting G-force pressed the blood from his brain. He eased the stick and his head came up as his vision slowly returned. The Me-109 shot past him, surprised, unable to contain his speed, screaming away into a rising turn. Kit went after him, the Hurricane buffeting in the Messerschmitt's slipstream. They were climbing almost vertically, hanging on their props. Kit saw on the fuselage of the Hun what looked like an insignia. At first he couldn't make it out. Then it became clear: Betty Boop in provocative pose, winking back at him.

Instantly he was hunting man, not machine. He jabbed the gun-button but the Messerschmitt skidded clear and fell away to the right, belly-up, then looped back for a fresh attack. Kit broke left and plunged into a vertical dive missing the 109 by feet. He glimpsed the pilot staring up, anonymous in his helmet, goggles and oxygen mask – any pilot anywhere. On the deck now, moving fast, throttle wide open, fields flashing below, power lines. Christ! Pull up, pull up! Tracer, bloody tracer, chewing at his port aileron. Oh my God, how to shake off the sod?

He pulled into a steep left-hand climb. He could imagine the German licking his lips. Yes, tracer was passing over his head as he flicked over into a violent lunge to the right that threatened to pull the wings off at the roots – crazy with a damaged aileron but what choice had he got? Again he was feet from the ground. If a farmworker had been ploughing the field, he'd have taken his head off.

And there was the 109, ahead now and slightly above, curving into a climb, looking for him, drifting into his sights. A sitter. God, how had that happened? Who cared? As his thumb went for the gun-button a mass of slowly spinning wreckage fell between them spoiling the shot. A Hurricane and a 109, inter-locked and burning, struck a group of poplars by an earthy track with a mighty impact and exploded. In the midst of the inferno the trees flared up like matchsticks. Who the hell was that? Not me, not me . . .

Now, with elegant vortices curling from its truncated wing-tips, the 109 was wheeling at tree-top level over a straggle of woodland. It turned deliberately towards him. Kit held his course, opened the throttle slightly, thumb once more on the gun-button. As they closed head-on, he saw his bullets raking the 109's cockpit area and port wing. The Hurricane was quiv-ering with the recoil of the Brownings and the impact of the German's bullets going God knew where.

He broke right, the German left. He cranked the stick over, waiting for his machine to disintegrate under him. Where was the bloody 109? He half expected to hear the clatter of machine-guns as the Hun closed in for the kill, unseen. But no, the

Messerschmitt was making for home, a ribbon of white smoke trailing from its faltering Daimler-Benz engine. Oil had blackened the windscreen and was streaming back along the fuselage.

In a moment Kit was on its tail. Its pilot attempted some ineffectual evasive moves but, clearly, the machine was not responding. He was doing well to keep it in the air, the man who had chosen Betty Boop as his mascot. Kit hesitated, his thumb on the gun-button: this was akin to murder. Impulsively he throttled up and surged alongside the wallowing 109. The man ignored him. Kit felt a surge of disappointment. Surely after such a fight there should be some sign of . . . what? Respect? Some acknowledgement of mutual skill, that today you had yielded to a better man?

Suddenly, without warning, the 109 veered right on full rudder, its propeller a lethal arc slicing the air yards from the Hurricane's port wing. The pilot had unclipped his oxygen mask and pushed up his goggles. He was shouting, gesticulating, hatred in his eyes. Instinctively Kit snapped right as the 109 fell away, its engine unable to sustain power. But the intent had been plain. Again Kit banked round and locked on to the grey-green tailplane with its detestable swastika. To hell with Betty Boop. The swastika spoke more eloquently for the Hun's beliefs.

As the Messerschmitt straightened up drunkenly, Kit shouted: 'Right, you swine, let's play it your way.' A pause, and then he pressed the gun-button. There was a hiss of compressed air through the breech-block. Out of ammunition.

Cursing, he thought about severing the 109's tailplane with his prop but came to his senses. Instead he pulled alongside the German, gave him a V-sign, rocked his wings and was off. Maybe back in his mess the man would talk of a stupid Englishman who still believed that chivalry in the air was not dead. Maybe it would make him careless and complacent in his next encounter with an Allied machine. But this had been no trial-of-arms between valiant and honourable gentlemen. The German had fought with malevolence, to extinguish resistance, to further the cause of the Reich. It was a lesson hard-learned and not to be forgotten.

The Hurricane was crabbing awkwardly, its left wing dropping. Kit could only keep her level by forcing the stick hard to starboard. The aileron on the left wing hung in tatters, almost off. Wind whistled through a hundred holes near the cockpit. One of the 7.9mm bullets fired from behind had passed through his Perspex hood, nicked the top of the windscreen frame and fallen at his feet. It rattled round the aluminium floor like a marble.

As he nursed his machine back to Revigncourt Kit realised that he had experienced the reality of what he had so often imagined, sprawled in his room at home with his books and models around him. Had this, then, been the dream, this brutal and merciless trial of skill and nerve? He supposed so, but somehow it had been different: terrifying, senseless, ignoble. Aspects of the encounter came back to him as though in slow motion. The adrenaline was draining from him. His mouth was dry, his lips cracked. He was shaking with uncontrollable funk. He knew that only chance had spared him, that even now he could have been frying in a tangle of wreckage in some unseen corner of the Meuse. He saw again the terrible impact of that other Hurricane and the Me-109, fused together as they smacked to earth from 15,000 feet. One of his bods, no doubt about that. But who – and had he got out?

His right thigh was trembling with the effort of maintaining the pressure on the starboard rudder pedal. He rubbed it to get the circulation flowing. His thumbnail snagged on his trousers. He had broken and blackened it thrusting at the gun-button. It was his only injury.

For Ossie Wolf it was a painful progress eastwards – painful because, with each jolt of the half-track on the rough road surface, the Panzergrenadier *Hauptmann* leaned into him, compressing his torn shoulder; painful too because all the ground he had gained with such laborious care, pushing his physical resources to the limit, was falling away minute by minute. Terrain that had taken him hours to negotiate was gone in a moment. The woodland that had concealed the three French tanks was a tangle of shattered tree-trunks and shredded branches, the ground churned to mush. Flame licked between the stumps but what lay within he could not tell. Further on, the burned-out Dornier still rested on its hillside but the impaled heads had gone.

At the point where an obscure track ran off to the right, the bounding Hanomag left the main highway and headed across a flat expanse of *maquis* towards a densely wooded area on rising ground. Wolf glimpsed a white stone signpost with a thin black arrow: 'Bois des Ognons 3' – some pre-war tourist honeypot, maybe. The earth was scored with the tracks of countless vehicles. On the fringe of the wood, heavily camouflaged with branches and leaves, they were parked up: trucks, tanks, half-tracks of many configurations, mechanised units of every kind. Not tourists these but visitors with a more baleful intent.

The Panzergrenadier half-track pierced the darkness of the wood, going slowly now, and emerged into a glade. The engine died. On every side German soldiers were gathered in groups, talking and laughing, jubilant at the ease of their advance, the smell of victory in their nostrils. Ossie was reminded of St Louis; the same buzz of high-spirited anticipation had run round the Busch stadium before a Cardinals game.

In the centre of the glade stood a black Horch 830 staff car. A number of officers were gathered round it, stiff with tension, listening intently, the heels of their boots clicking as they were addressed one by one. The Panzergrenadier *Hauptmann* approached the briefing with noticeable caution, waiting a few paces away until the officers were dismissed. Then he stepped forward and exchanged smart salutes with a young Luftwaffe *Oberleutnant*.

From the back seat of the half-track the *Unterfeldwebel* took the opportunity to drive the muzzle of his Luger into Ossie's spine. 'Now we will teach you some respect, pig.'

Ossie squirmed with agony but bared his teeth in something close to a grin. 'You lousy bum.'

The NCO thought he was pleading for mercy and, satisfied, pushed the Luger back into the holster at his belt.

The Luftwaffe officer regarded Ossie curiously. His English was bad but good enough. 'Bombers?' Ossie stared back at him. 'Fighters, then?'

The Panzergrenadier *Hauptmann* laughed and said in German: 'We have a stubborn one. Quite pointless, of course, but it's the only weapon he's got.'

'I doubt he has information of value,' said the *Oberleutnant*. 'The skies are ours. Their airfields are falling into our hands. Soon his comrades will be fleeing back to their little island.'

'Tell him that.'

Instead the *Oberleutnant* tried the one-flier-to-another approach. He tapped himself on the chest. 'I at least make no secret. For the moment I liaise with the army. But normally, Zerstorer unit. Goering's boys, the best. Messerschmitt Me-110s. A good machine, fast. Too fast for Hurricanes I think.' He noted a sudden fire in Ossie's eyes. 'Ah, you do not agree.' In German to the *Hauptmann*: 'Fighters, I believe. Hurricanes almost certainly. Probably 67 Fighter Wing, a few squadrons only, part of their so-called Advanced Air Striking Force. Rouvres, maybe, or Revigncourt.' He realised that Ossie had understood. 'You speak German perhaps?' Ossie regarded him dumbly.

'He heard you talk of Rouvres and Revigncourt,' the *Hauptmann* said.

'Of course.' The *Oberleutnant* nudged Ossie in jocular fashion, as if they were acquaintances sharing a beer in a bar. 'We surprise you with our information, yes? My friend, in France we Germans are not your only enemies.'

From the Horch staff car behind them came a brusque

command. The Luftwaffe officer hurried across. There was a brief discussion. Then he was back. 'The commander-in-chief wants to speak with you.'

Even at ease on the rich leather upholstery of the Horch, Heinz Guderian's poise and air of authority were unmistakable: he was a daunting presence. Ossie recognised him at once: shrewd eyes in a round apple of a face, oak-leaf clusters at his collar, the Iron Cross at his throat. Architect of Blitzkrieg, champion of the Panzer cause, thrusting fast and deep through enemy lines, this was the man who had ensured victory in Poland for the Reich.

Standing before Guderian, filthy, blood-stained, his uniform torn, Ossie was conscious that he cut a poor figure. The general, splendid in black-leather greatcoat and swoop-crowned cap, looked him up and down. Ossie felt diminished, part of a pathetic sideshow. Despite himself, he came to something close to attention. Christ, what was happening to him? He must be losing his grip. But there was a compelling power about the man. And a general was a goddammed general, after all. He knew he was going to have to give a little. And what had he got to hide? The sons-of-bitches seemed to know all about them anyway.

The Panzergrenadier *Hauptmann* climbed on to the running-board of the Horch to act as interpreter. He grasped the top of the rear door to steady himself. It swung open forcing him to spring clear. Guderian laughed. 'Take care, Herr Hauptmann. There will be plenty more opportunities for me to award you your wound badge.' The word, *verwundetenbzeichen*, rolled off his tongue. He seemed ready for a lighter moment. Ossie wondered sourly if he was part of the cabaret. He also wondered whether Guderian spoke English and hoped to catch him off guard.

As the *Hauptmann* remounted the running-board the general said: 'Is progress still being maintained?'

'Yes, Herr General. Some light resistance but nothing of substance. French armour has performed with courage in certain sectors but they seem disorganised. Prisoners speak of poor leadership and wireless control is almost non-existent. When they want to change direction on the move they must first halt and request fresh orders. Unbelievable! But they are brave.'

The freedom of the exchange convinced Ossie that they had no inkling he understood their language. He chalked it up as a tiny victory.

'Dithering is not unknown among our own ranks,' continued Guderian. 'Even now Generalfeldmarschall von Kleist questions the value of armoured mobility. For him things have gone almost too well. We have gone too far too fast. He cannot believe we are not about to be thrown back. He persists with the belief that the Wehrmacht is the key. My God, how that man loves his infantry. And even the Führer continues to dabble, perceiving threats from the south where there are none.' He broke off. 'I should not talk to you in these terms, my young friend. But you will find that even the patience of generals is sorely tried by their superior officers.'

Guderian turned his attention to the airman by the car. Ossie was staring stolidly ahead, showing no sign of interest in what was being said. For a moment he swayed with fatigue but caught himself. His chin came up, jaw set.

The *Hauptmann* said: 'The general wishes to know your name, rank and number. I urge you to comply.' He seemed almost concerned for his charge. Ossie told him, masking his Midwestern drawl with an accent that was nearly, but not quite, English. He sounded like an extra in a bad Hollywood movie, one of those travesties about fog-filled London and Basil Rathbone chasing Jack the Ripper. The *Hauptmann* looked relieved. It did not suit him to be tainted by a recalcitrant who thumbed his nose at authority, even from the other side. Besides, he had quite taken to the little fellow . . .

'The general believes you to be the pilot of a Hurricane that crashed near here.'

Ossie was disturbed. Maybe they would make the connection

with the downed Dornier, those grinning heads on sticks. And that bastard Diechmann had pocketed his RAF-issue pen with the silken map. He hoped to Christ that Diechmann's trunk had been thoroughly consumed when the Senegalese torched the Dornier's fuselage. He shook his head. 'No, not me.' He pointed at himself. 'Blenheim. Bombers. You understand?'

'How many in your aircraft?'

'Two.'

'Three, surely?' The Luftwaffe liaison officer had moved in close, listening intently, his manner quick and suspicious.

'Two. We were on photo reconnaissance.' The suggestion of a more passive role might get them off his back.

'Where is your comrade?' The *Hauptmann* again.

'I don't know.'

'Did you see him come down?'

'No.'

'We have no reports of a Blenheim landing in this area.' The *Oberleutnant* now, hostile, accusing, also intent on making an impression. Why let this damned Panzergrenadier do all the talking?

'We didn't land, we crashed.'

'We do not believe you. The general says . . .' The *Hauptmann* listened intently to what the general said. 'The general says you have the cut of a fighter pilot. Unmistakable.'

'No.'

'The general says that generals are never wrong.'

'If he believes that,' said Ossie, 'he's going to find himself in big trouble.'

The *Hauptmann* hesitated before he translated the remark. 'Hah!' exploded Guderian. 'Good advice. I will pass it up the line.' The moment was past. The curtain dropped on the cabaret. The General rapped his driver on the shoulder with his baton. The Horch trembled as the engine fired. Troops snapped to attention, saluting as the bulky vehicle bearing Guderian's standard progressed slowly between their ranks and emerged on the road running west, ready to resume the advance.

They put Ossie into the back of a supply truck with a single guard, a big-nosed Wehrmacht private with tiny eyes very close together. He held his automatic rifle crossways across his thighs, his finger toying with the trigger. As Ossie climbed up, the Panzergrenadier *Hauptmann* said: 'Will you try to escape?'

'Would you?' said Ossie.

'No,' said the *Hauptmann*, flatly. 'This fellow has orders to shoot without compunction.'

'Maybe he's going to anyway.'

'No, he will do as he is told.'

'That's what worries me.'

'As long as you do not attempt to escape you have nothing to fear. You have my word.'

'Okay,' said Ossie.

'Maybe you escape later.'

'Maybe.'

'Maybe you fly your Hurricane again.'

Ossie caught himself. 'Blenheim.'

'Ah, yes, Blenheim. Photo reconnaissance, was it not? A pity they should waste you on such missions. You strike me as a fellow who loves a fight.'

'Is that so?'

'Yes, that is so.' The *Hauptmann* slammed and secured the tailgate. 'Well, goodbye. *Hals und Beinbruch.*'

'Huh?' A subtle test even now.

'Break a neck.'

'*Hals und Beinbruch.* I must remember that.'

'You pronounce it well. You have an ear for our language. Yes, a good linguist.'

'*Hals und Beinbruch*,' said Ossie, haltingly this time.

'Not so good,' said the *Hauptmann*, grinning. 'Never mind. You will have plenty of time to study in prison camp.' He stepped back and watched as the truck made for the road, giving a flick of farewell with his fingers.

As dust from the road curled into the back of the truck Gimlet Eyes regarded Ossie intently. The man was aching for him to make a move. '*Hals und Beinbruch*,' Ossie shouted, over the roar of the engine. The guard grunted, nodded, gave a faint reluctant smirk. Good-luck wishes were always welcome, whatever the circumstances. Ossie hadn't meant it like that.

At Revigncourt, making his approach, Kit supposed he was about to die. He'd seen this before: damaged machine wheeling over its home base, the familiar even homely scene below, so comforting to a desperate and exhausted pilot. So close, so close – surely he'd made it . . . surely it was going to be okay. But then the twist. One thing to keep a buggered kite in the air, but how to get it safely on the ground? This was the moment when all the elements of damage got together: the ripped and almost useless aileron that forced him to thrust the stick to starboard and try to keep it there with protesting muscles; the splintered instruments, so vital now, but no longer feeding gen about pressures and temperatures of oil and fuel, which meant the engine could seize at any moment; the altimeter, mute, the needle sunk to zero; worst of all, the hydraulics shot, no sign of life from the pump powering the undercarriage and flaps. For what he knew he had to do, he didn't need wheels: they'd probably dig in and flip him arse-over-tit. But flaps were something else: without their drag he'd be steaming in for a belly-landing too bloody quick by half. Struggling to maintain his grip on the stick with his left hand Kit strained at the hydraulic selector lever with his right, but no good, nothing doing. It was seized, the final ingredient in a recipe for a thoroughgoing bloody disaster.

His voice on the R/T was calm enough. But that was part of the game. They all knew how to play it, although sometimes things happened that forced a pilot to drop the mask. He hoped he'd be able to see it through. He knew now what Dinghy Davis had felt, back in November. He tried to push the image of how it had ended from his mind.

'This is Blue Leader. Good to be home. Get the beers out.'

'Pouring them now, Blue Leader. Have a good trip?' Buster Brown's voice was calm and startlingly clear, his tone just right. Reception from ground control was patchy, often faint as you headed out on a sweep. Now, right over the field, he could have been right there in the cockpit alongside Kit.

'No hydraulics, no instruments, no port aileron. Yes, everything's top hole. Coming in now.'

'Ride of a lifetime, old boy,' said Brown. 'You'd pay a fortune for it at Margate.'

Dipping in over the perimeter Kit gunned the throttle. The Hurricane yawed violently from side to side as he attempted to increase wind resistance and scrub off some speed; more guesswork as the air-speed indicator wasn't registering. His efforts were barely noticeable. He knew he was caught: land like Halley's comet or risk a stall and put a wing in. As he rocketed down the grass runway, sinking foot by foot, the engine seized. The prop slowed, stopped, changed from shimmering silver arc to three motionless yellow-tipped black blades. The wind howled round the cockpit. The silence was profound.

Kit pushed back the canopy. God be praised, it slid back smoothly on its runners, even to the frantic tug of his single free hand. Yes, do it now, before the impact, before the metal distorted with the shock of meeting hard-baked earth. They could get him out or, if he didn't brain himself on the bulletproof glass of the windscreen, he might even manage it himself. If she didn't burn. Ah, yes, burn like Dinghy, the poor bastard. This was just how it must have been. Curious, thought Kit. Was his number really up?

The Hurricane hit the ground with a colossal thump of rending metal. Kit loosed his grip on the controls and folded his arms over his face. The machine lifted into the air, still eager to fly, but gravity clawed it back. It sank and struck once more, longer and harder this time. Again the shriek and scream of tortured aluminium, explosions and conflagrations as the Merlin engine tore from its fireproof bulkhead and fountains of fuel, oil and glycol pulsed from severed piping. The engine somersaulted away, trailing flame, and buried itself in a distant pond. A few ducks protested at the fountain of steam and spray.

Relieved of the weight, the Hurricane's fuselage pulled up into a neat loop, came over the top and dived vertically towards the ground. On the edge of greying out Kit seized the control column, sank it back into his stomach and felt the elevators bite. The aeroplane swooped towards the ground, levelled out with feet to spare and cocked its nose for another try. Too close: the tailplane cracked against the runway, sheered off and embarked on some complex aerobatics of its own. As the control cables were ripped away the stick flew forward, then suddenly back and struck Kit in the gut. Still conscious, he was spinning violently but on his side not fore and aft. His body was straining at his Sutton harness with the lateral G-force as though he was pinned to the centre of a Catherine wheel.

The Hurricane cartwheeled a hundred yards more, shedding both wings on the way. Then it landed right way up in a cloud of mud, dirt and dust. The fire-crew and blood-wagon were alongside in a moment. Buster Brown was there too.

Kit sat in the remains of his cockpit and watched his hands. They were shaking with violent tremors he couldn't control. He found it difficult to breathe. He fumbled for the harness release and pulled the pin. His body fell forward unsupported. He heard one of the ground-crew shout: 'Get him out before the bloody thing goes up.'

'Blimey, mate,' said someone else, 'there's nothing left to burn.'

He felt himself half dragged, half lifted clear and laid on the ground. Doc Gilmour was crouching beside him, loosening his gear, telling him everything was going to be all right, just as he always did, even to the worst cases. Good to hear, though. Kit wondered if it was true. He craned his head to see the kite. The medical officer protested: 'For God's sake, man, keep still. You could have buggered your back.' But Kit had seen enough. The Hurricane had been reduced to a pod. It looked like a Link trainer, just a cockpit, no engine, wings or tail. He thought he'd like to take it home with him as a souvenir, if he ever saw home again. Something to tell the grandchildren, if he ever had any.

Buster was easing himself on to his haunches next to Doc. 'I told you it would be exciting.'

Kit groaned. He tried to think of something suitable to say but his brain felt numb. 'Quite a ride,' was all he managed.

Buster looked across at the pulverised carcass of his machine. 'Don't worry, old boy,' he said. 'We'll soon have it as right as rain.'

Handling him like a new-born baby the medics lifted Kit on to a stretcher and slid him into the ambulance. As the doors closed he shouted to Brown: 'I say, Buster, where's that bloody beer you promised?' That was better – much more the sort of stuff the erks expected. Sure enough it prompted guffaws from the ground-crew. These fighter boys, irrepressible. As the blood-wagon pulled away he heard Buster bawl: 'Sorry, chum, you took so long getting down I drank it myself.'

Doc Gilmour was baffled. In the Nissen hut that served as sick-quarters he took a step back from the bed on which Kit was stretched out naked. The lean, dead-white body, with the prominent ribcage and flat stomach of youth, was a mass of bruises and abrasions but he could detect no significant injuries. He shook his head in disbelief and nodded to Yates, the medical orderly, who moved forward, like a valet, with a fresh uniform on a wooden hanger. 'Courtesy of Flying Officer Brown, sir,' said Yates.

Kit allowed himself to be eased off the bed and struggled into Buster's spare uniform. It was a little too small, tight across the shoulders. His wrists protruded from the sleeves and the trousers hung an inch or two above his ankles. It was comical but he was too weak to laugh. He sat back on the bed and the crotch of the trousers tightened round his testicles. He winced, and Yates said: 'Take it easy, sir. I should lie down for a bit.'

'It's not that, it's . . .' He tugged at the trousers to ease the pressure. He was laughing quietly now, but couldn't be bothered to explain. He sank back, overwhelmed by visions of the prang, the hellish racket of the kite destroying itself around him, the countless blows and impacts as he'd flailed, helpless, in the cockpit. He was astonished to find himself alive. 'So, what's the verdict, Doc?'

'Nothing that three months in a health spa won't put right,' said Gilmour.

'Book me in.' Then he saw that the ward was empty, except for his bed, a small table and a cupboard, its door hanging from a broken hinge.

'We're moving out,' said Gilmour. 'Menneville, north of Reims. I can offer you a choice. Get there under your own steam or go there in the blood-wagon, which I wouldn't advise, given the state of the roads. Anyway, I understand the CO's view is that if your head's still on you're fit for service. You're certainly going to be hellish stiff for a while but that's about it. Stay here for a bit and recover. Are you up to a debrief with Spy?'

'Why not?'

The intelligence officer approached the bed like a man seeing a ghost. 'We had you pushing up the daisies.'

'Where's the CO?'

'Up to his ears,' said Turner. 'You've probably heard we're on the move. A Flight's already gone. The ground-party's just about ready. Your B Flight chaps are standing by for take-off. HQ tell us all the forward fields are getting a pummelling. Intensive bombing, strafing, the usual hullabaloo. Except us. We don't seem to be on the Hun's list. Don't know why. But it can't be too long before they remember us.' He looked at Kit with concern, something close to sympathy in his eyes.

'Incidentally, you don't need to worry about young Fuller any more.'

'Oh, hell and damnation,' said Kit. 'So it was Pip I saw go down.'

'Quite a shindig, I gather.'

'Yes, it was rather.'

'Sergeant Gates saw it all. Fuller wouldn't have known much about it. Barrel-rolled straight into a 109, bang. A real flamer apparently. Amazing it doesn't happen more often.'

Kit stopped himself saying: 'When I need the musings of a wingless wonder I'll ask for them.' Instead, he said: 'Yes, I suppose it is.'

'Can I put you down for anything?'

'No. Well, yes, a 109 damaged.'

'Good show.'

'How about the others?'

'Rains got one, Brown and Knox shared a probable. Not too shabby.'

There was a clatter of flying boots on the lino. 'So, what's all this, then?' The CO stood over him, bear-like, impatient, as usual ill-at-ease when confronted by suffering or injury. He had found his own wounds particularly hard to accept, had fought the Doc's ultimatum about flying, even gone up in his usual machine and tried a manoeuvre or two. Madness, of course: every twist and turn had been torture. His lacerations had opened and his trousers were sticky with blood when he clambered down from the wing. Worse, he had been a gift to any prowling Messerschmitt and knew it. Grounded when he most wanted to lead his men in battle, he focused all of his energy on honing the squadron as a fighting force, more demanding, more cantankerous than ever, fiercely intent on hitting the enemy hard. Kit had long since come to terms with Brewster's callous stance – because, for what they had to do, it worked – his blank refusal to acknowledge weakness or setback. Kit knew he had young sons. He could imagine Brewster hauling them to their feet with bloodied knees, roaring: 'Stop whining for God's sake. You're all right.'

Now Brewster said: 'You seem to be enjoying yourself. Hoping the Hun will bring you breakfast in bed?'

'I thought I might take a turn round the rose-garden later sir,' said Kit. Then, daringly: 'Perhaps I could borrow your stick.'

'You cheeky pup,' said Brewster. He tossed the walking-stick on to the table and perched on the edge of the bed. 'Narrow squeak, I'll give you that. But the Doc tells me you're in perfect fettle.'

Behind him the medical officer gaped. 'Now I didn't exactly—'

'We need you, Kit, need you to be up and about and doing things. I can't have you lolling about here like a wet weekend.'

'Curtis has had quite a shaking sir,' cut in the MO. 'I strongly recommend we keep an eye on him for an hour or two, just to be sure there aren't any complications.'

Brewster purpled. 'Don't be ridiculous, man. In a hour or two we may find the bloody Panzers arriving on our doorstep. That's the only complication I care about. I'll be the judge of this case. Flying Officer Curtis is walking wounded. End of argument.' He turned back to Kit. 'I gather Spy's put you in the picture about regrouping.'

Not a retreat, Kit noticed. 'Yes, sir.'

'You can help me get the ground-party sorted out. Corporal Evans is in Fonteville now, collecting kit from the billets. Liaise with him, round up the chaps who are left and join us at Menneville. There's plenty of transport knocking about.'

'Yes, sir.'

'I gather you got an Me-109.'

'No, sir. Damaged only.'

'Damned good show anyway. Pity about young Fuller. Foregone conclusion, of course. Bloody waste. But nothing anyone could do. Don't brood about it. Press on. At Menneville we'll have a chance to gather ourselves for another crack at the buggers. Then we'll get our own back. They'll find out there's plenty more where that came from.' And he was gone.

Kit pushed himself off the bed and, swaying, watched as it was dismantled, then carried out to a waiting Bedford.

'Told you,' said Doc Gilmour. 'If your head's still on you're fit for service. Did what I could. How do you feel?'

'I don't,' said Kit. 'Not a thing.'

He emerged from the sick-quarters, walking with some difficulty. A hundred yards away Buster Brown and Kenny Rains, in flying gear, were drinking mugs of tea. They saw him and roared. 'Well, bugger me,' said Buster, 'if it isn't the Ghost of Christmas Past.'

'Christ, who's your tailor?' said Rains.

'The CO says I'm okay so I must be,' said Kit. 'Confusing, really. I thought I was dying.'

'You need the CO's permission to die,' said Buster. 'Anyone dying now without the consent of a superior officer is in serious trouble. There's an acute shortage of man-power in all theatres, or hadn't you heard?'

'Anyway,' said Rains, 'there's a certain procedure to follow.'

'That's right,' agreed Buster. 'Victim will die by numbers. Victim . . . one. Victim will stagger a full pace of thirty inches, followed by a short pause . . . two, three . . . then allow the eyes to glaze.' Kenny Rains did so.

'Victim . . . two,' said Buster. 'Victim will slowly sink to his knees, pause two, three . . . then fall on to his back, pause, two, three . . . before lowering his legs, heels resting on the ground, toes at an angle of thirty degrees to his shoulder-blades.' Kenny Rains did so. 'Don't forget the last breath,' he said, from the ground.

'Victim will be allowed to draw his last breath in his own time,' said Buster, 'but only after ensuring that RAF form 4857921 has been correctly made out and the aforementioned breath signed for.'

'Don't forget the death rattle,' said Kenny Rains, brushing himself down.

'The death rattle will be used on ceremonial parades only,' said Buster, 'and never, repeat never, in the presence of any officer below the rank of acting air vice marshal. Finally,' said Buster, 'victims must draw the following from Barrack Stores: wings, pairs, one; harps, untuned, one; clouds cumulus or clouds fleecy, one. Dress at all times loose order, wings at the glide, harps at high port.'

Brewster's office window banged open. He shouted across a distance of a hundred yards: 'When you ladies have quite finished your gossip, perhaps we can get on with the bloody war.'

Kit watched Buster and Kenny Rains hurry off to carry out pre-flight checks, run up their engines and strap themselves into their cockpits awaiting orders for take-off. Overhead, huge formations of bombers crawled across the sky at high altitude with fighter escorts stacked above them in layers. No venturing into Allied air space without protection now. The Hun had learnt its lesson. Not far away the sound of heavy gunfire, not British or French artillery but deeper and more penetrating, tanks maybe, rolled across the farmland which lay bathed in the radiant gold of a perfect summer sunset.

'Swarms of the blighters sir.' It was Jessop, the ground-crew chief, peering upwards.

'They haven't had it all their own way Chief,' Kit snapped.

'No, sir, of course not, sir. I only meant—'

'Forget it Jessop,' said Kit quickly. 'I'm not quite myself at the moment. The CO's turned medico and passed me fit for duty. Can't understand why I feel so groggy.'

The surviving Hurricanes of B Flight crabbed down the field on their widespread undercarriages and turned into wind. The revs mounted, they moved forward and lifted quickly into the air, banking round and heading west into the sun. No wing-waggling this time, no high-spirited histrionics, not even a final pass over the airfield that had been their home for six months or more.

'Sorry I didn't get the kite back in one piece, Chief,' said Kit.

'At least she got you back sir,' said Jessop.

'Yes, a game old bus.' He remembered his pride, an age ago, at Tangmere when they'd assigned him his own aircraft. He'd walked round her in the hangar, inspected her from every angle, patted her flanks as you would a Labrador, even murmured a word or two that he was careful to keep to himself: a secret pact that, together, they would face whatever was to come, look out for each other. Childish but comforting somehow, crediting this cold machine of war with something like a soul . . .

Ossie was taking stock. He sat with his back supported by the wooden panelling of the stable stall, his legs stretched out on the scattering of straw spread over the cobbles that still reeked of animal urine and dung. A German guard peered in and studied the three prisoners disinterestedly, eyes invisible under the peak of his steel helmet. He pointed at his mouth and pretended to chew.

'*Haben sie Hunger?*'

'*Ja, ja,*' said the English corporal.

'*Haben sie Durst?*'

The Englishman looked blank. Ossie said: 'He says, are you thirsty?'

'*Ja, ja,*' said the corporal.

The guard moved away. 'You speak their lingo,' said the corporal. It was not framed as a question, more an assertion. He had been mistrustful from the first, when Gimlet Eyes had bundled Ossie roughly into the stall.

Ossie had said: 'Any of you guys know where we are?'

The corporal immediately demanded: 'What's a Yank doing in the air force?'

Ossie ignored him. Now he turned to the French infantry colonel propped against the wall, coolly smoking a pungent cigarette. 'Any idea where we are?'

The colonel raised an eyebrow and shrugged. 'In captivity?' he said sardonically.

There was a clatter of steel-tipped heels as the guard returned with a companion who placed a tin tray on the cobbles. The corporal regarded the loaf of brown bread, the slices of tinned meat and the bottle of red wine with suspicion. 'What's all this then?'

The colonel bent down, seized the neck of the wine bottle, wiped the mouth on his sleeve and drank from it deeply, his Adam's apple rising and falling in his thin neck.

'Here, hang on, Monsewer,' said the corporal, reassured. 'What about us?'

The colonel lowered the bottle. The wine sloshed back. He had sunk a third of it. Again he wiped the mouth. The corporal held out his hand. The colonel began to pass it to him, then paused and handed it to Ossie. 'In order of superiority, I think,' he said.

Ossie raised the bottle in a mock toast. 'Here's to you.'

'Bollocks to this,' said the corporal. He sprang towards the tray, tore at the loaf with filthy fingers and attempted to fold the crumbling bread around slices of the liver-red meat, cursing as it fell to pieces in his hands. He crammed the fragments into his mouth, glancing first at Ossie, then at the Frenchman, expecting them to react. Their silence fed his confidence. 'I'll take some of that *vino* now,' he said roughly, food spilling from his lips.

'What's your beef, buster?' said Ossie.

The corporal up-ended the bottle, the crimson *vin ordinaire* dripping from his chin and staining his khaki tunic. 'If you want to know the truth,' he said, 'I've had it with fucking officers.' Any suspicions he might have harboured, and all caution, fell away as he was seized by a fit of anger.

'Is that so?' said Ossie.

'Yes, it fucking is. We're attached to this fucking French infantry division, right? The fifty-fifth, bunch of useless fucking reservists. I mean, this General Corap bloke's meant to be in charge with his ninth fucking Army. Seven divisions holding seventy-five miles of front. Even Lieutenant fucking Wilmer thinks it's fucking ridiculous. Doesn't stop him, though. Keen, know what I mean? Gets wind of all these fucking rumours about Fritz massing to the east, infantry, lorries, tanks, thousands of the bastards. None of the Frogs believe it, fuck knows why, so Sonny Jim, he says to us, he says, "We'll nip down, my lads, and find out for ourselves." Which we do. Fucking Wilmer organises a couple of Frog lorries and we set off like the Charge of the fucking Light Brigade. Sure enough, fifteen miles down the road, the country's crawling with square-heads coming out of the fucking woodwork. Lieutenant fucking Wilmer sends me forward to feel out their flank, except there isn't one. They're spread out right across the bloody shop and I walk right into their fucking arms. What do you reckon to that, then?'

'I guess you were fucked,' said Ossie.

The corporal bent and retrieved a crust from the cobbles, brushed it off and crammed it into his mouth. 'Yeah,' he said, with satisfaction, 'that's why I've had it with fucking officers.' Then he narrowed his eyes. 'Anyway, like I said, what's a fucking Yank doing in the air force?'

Suddenly Ossie was on his feet. He seized the infantryman by the collar of his tunic, spun him round and slammed him against the stable wall. The Englishman's skull rebounded from the coarse plasterwork with a crack. He cried out as the wind was crushed from his lungs. Ossie smacked him back into the wall again; once more the crack of the head, a little blood now, oozing from his cranium and trickling down his neck. 'So I'm a plant, you lousy little jerk, is that what you're saying?'

The man was shaking his head, moaning: 'I don't know. Get your fucking hands off me.' Ossie let him drop to the floor and stepped back. 'You big-mouthed sonofabitch, I don't want to hear one more goddammed word out of you. If I catch you blabbing to the Krauts I'll shoot you myself, God help me.' Pain surged through his shoulder but he fought it down. The Englishman was whimpering now, on the ground still, his arms wrapped round his shoulders, his legs drawn up. 'Leave me alone. I ain't told 'em nothing.'

Ossie prodded the prone figure with the toe of his flying boot and the man shrank away. 'Name, rank and number, you bastard. Not a squeak about your outfit or where it was or what you were trying to do. Get that and get that good. And as for what you think of your officers, who gives a shit? Jesus, if we really were fifth column we'd be having a field day here.' He turned to check the reaction of the French colonel. He wasn't there.

Ossie moved quickly to the entrance of the stall. The helmeted guard barred his way. Somewhere, outside, he could hear a rapid conversation and recognised the voice of the French colonel, speaking passable German. He made out a phrase here and there: 'Corap . . . fifty-fifth Division . . . reservists . . . seven divisions spread across a hundred and twenty kilometres of front.' Holy shit. He remembered the Luftwaffe liaison guy with Guderian: 'My friend, in France we Germans are not your only enemies.'

Behind him, in the growing darkness of the stable, he heard a murmur, almost a sob: 'Fucking officers.'

At Revigncourt Kit was hearing echoes too, Spy Turner's casual observation: 'We don't seem to be on the Hun's list . . . but it can't be long before they remember us.' There had been no reason for old Wingless to be concerned, pushing back his owlish specs on his nose, pocketing his well-thumbed notebook, chucking his bicycle on to the back of the Bedford and, a few minutes later, scurrying off with the first group of the ground-party to the refuge of Menneville. But now, as dusk advanced, the lengthening shadows seemed to hide unknown threats and dangers. It was like being a child again, unwilling to mount the stairs and confront whatever horror lay waiting to pounce in the dark.

There were only a few elements of the squadron left now: Brewster with two three-tonners, laden with ground-staff and equipment, and a third, with Corporal Evans, still doing the rounds of the Fonteville billets. Kit was at the wheel of Buster Brown's rusty Alvis 12/50, its stench of oil, fuel and rubber evoking memories of the Brooklands paddock when the only person who threatened your life was you – 'a jolly good giggle'. No giggling now. Kit could barely move. Each jolt and jar pulsed through him like an electrical charge.

Evans was taking his time. He always took pains for the pilots whether they treated him well or not. Kit had heard him once, on the train from Bar-le-Duc, off for a spot of leave in Metz. 'You can't get close to 'em, like. They're different from you and me. They've not been brought up to mix with the likes of us. Some of 'em, I suppose, you could call stuck-up. But they're clever and they're ruddy brave and that's enough for me. We're here to keep 'em in the air, in our different ways, and biffing the bloody Hun. I reckon they're our best chance of stopping the blighters.'

At Brewster's signal the heavily loaded lorries, well down on their springs, creaked and groaned along the cinder track to Revigncourt village, ready to wind their way towards Reims. At the junction Kit pumped the Alvis's brake pedal to little effect and turned in the other direction, to Fonteville and Corporal Evans.

As he pulled the wheel down with his right hand he heard the swelling roar of an aircraft making a low-level pass at full throttle, then another. *It can't be too long before they remember us.* Two Dornier Do-17s swept across the deserted airfield, their machine-guns raking the empty turf. Too late you sods, Kit thought, with satisfaction. He doubted they'd make out the escaping Bedfords as they sank into the valley beyond the main street of Revigncourt where the mist was gathering again.

The Dorniers banked and came round a second time. They'd throttled back, not firing this time, straight and steady. Kit could sense their frustration as they scoured the ground for targets. Then they turned away.

He had backed the Alvis into the shadow of the grove of four great willows, forty feet high, seemingly growing from a single trunk, close to the entrance to the airfield. It had once been a favourite place but on the day Dinghy Davis had died he had experienced there a sense of something ancient, primitive and evil: a sinister presence. Fanciful, perhaps, but he felt it now as he negotiated the bends that descended from the plain to the Meuse valley. He proceeded like an old gentleman, wary of the sports car's brakes and the alarming play in its steering, taking in the whiff of wood-smoke in the air, the pungent country smells. It was much the same as Wiltshire: those rose-fringed byways that threaded beneath the bulk of the Downs. He fancied himself heading Devizes way, perhaps, or north from Marlborough to Lechlade and the Cotswolds.

It was the drone of aero-engines that came to him first, then the chatter of machine-guns; finally, the successive crump, crump, crump of sticks of bombs. The Dorniers were still intent on prey. From Fonteville a fountain of debris rose into the air and fell, fanning out and fluttering, confetti-like. The second Do-17 banked, descended and levelled off for its run. Again a pillar of destruction climbed into the evening sky. The bell in the tower of Saint-Saulve began to toll. A ball of bilious orange exploded above the rooftops; a petrol tank, maybe, something with plenty of fuel on board, something like a three-tonner . . .

The tar of the road in front of the *mairie* was bubbling and aflame. The Bedford, with all their kit on board, was no more now than an assembly of collapsing struts and poles and blackened steel. Its tyres had melted off its rims. With hands from which the flesh had peeled Corporal Evans grimly clutched the thin wire rim of the incinerated steering-wheel, his good Welsh teeth showing startlingly white against his coal-black lips. Quite dead, of course, deprived of oxygen in an instant, gasping, drawing fire into his lungs and expiring in a howling furnace that had seemed to come from nowhere.

Kit coasted to a halt a hundred yards down the road and was sick. The Dorniers made a final pass, assessing the damage for their intelligence reports. A stroke of luck coming across the truck like that – military, I think. The way your bullets caught it, Horst. My God, did it go up! There's a car now. Shall we go round again and pepper its arse? No, enough for today, you fellows. Time to repair to the mess and get some food and drink inside us. Great heavens, but battle gives you an appetite.

The two sticks of bombs had marched through the centre of Fonteville in roughly parallel lines, like an ogre's footsteps. In some places whole houses had been removed, families extinguished as they prepared their evening meal. In others, blast had played its usual quirky tricks, sparing some, felling others in lanes, gardens, working in the fields, peering from a window. All stone dead and not a mark on them.

Madame Bergeret was in the small vegetable plot behind the untouched farmhouse. Clean washing, secured with wooden pegs, fluttered on the line. A crisp white quilt cover that Curtis recognised as his was stained with ruby droplets. The savoury aroma of rabbit, simmering in the old cast-iron pot she always used for stews, wafted from the open kitchen door. He remembered their simple exchange: 'What's for supper?'

'Rabbit.'

'I will try not to be late.'

Had it really been only this morning? The wireless was tuned to music – Chevalier, bold and saucy, the usual nonsense about Parisienne cocottes. The verses, full of life, danced in the air.

Kit could only identify Madame Bergeret's lower limbs, the sturdy legs that had served her so well through a hard and worthy life now decently covered by the long drab skirt, and spread over it, still secured with a neat bow behind her back, her favourite floral apron. Above the waist everything had gone, atomised and dispersed. Bomb or bullet, it was impossible to tell. One of those freakish incidents of war, inexplicable, obscene.

People were gathering in front of the *mairie*. It seemed the natural place. They stared at him, sullen and shocked, but said nothing beyond the barest courtesies. Their expressions seemed to suggest that he and his comrades had failed them. A profound hatred of the enemy swelled in Kit's heart, expanding like a growth, malignant, consuming him. At once everything seemed odious, ruined, hopeless. Was this, then, some kind of apocalypse? Could they prevail in the face of such evil? Would they be required to match deed with deed, denying human thought or feeling? Was that the price? Was it worth paying? And afterwards, if victory came, what kind of world would emerge from the ruins? He did not recognise the man who had woken to the low sun filtering through the shutters of the Spartan room in the farmhouse of Madame Bergeret fifteen hours ago. It was as though he had passed into another universe. He wished he could step back.

In Ossie's stable stall, illuminated occasionally by the yellow beam of the guard's torch, the English corporal sat in a corner, his knees drawn up under his chin. 'I could do with a fag.'

'So ask the guy,' said Ossie.

'That fucking Frenchman. How was I to know?'

'Forget it.'

'I didn't give much away, eh?'

'Just the disposition of the whole goddammed front.'

'They must have known already, surely?'

'Maybe, maybe not.'

'You're not much fucking help.'

'Pipe down, you sonofabitch.'

'How was I to know?' The corporal nodded to himself. 'They would have known already. No harm done, I bet.' He pulled himself on to his feet and called to the guard: 'Oi, Fritz. Over here a minute.' The torch flicked on, bathing the corporal's unshaven face in light. 'Any chance of a fag? You know, cigarette.' He mimed the act of lighting up. The guard regarded him uncertainly, then the light flicked off again. The corporal returned to his corner. 'What do you reckon they're going to do with us?'

'Search me.'

'Prison camp I bet. Might not be too bad. At least we're fucking out of it now.'

'Yeah, that'd be what you want I guess.'

'Too fucking right mate. I didn't sign on for a fucking war. Just wanted a job, me. Learn a trade, they said. Learn to drive, they said. Learn to fucking drive. Stuck me in with the fucking foot-sloggers, didn't they? Fucking cannon-fodder. Just like the last time.' He snorted. 'Yeah, I'm glad to be fucking out of it, all right.'

Somewhere, quite close, there came a burst of fire from an automatic weapon followed by a single shot.

'Fucking hell,' said the corporal. 'I don't like the sound of that.'

A voice came out of the darkness. 'Which of you is the American?'

'Not me mate,' said the English corporal quickly.

Ossie rose to his feet.

Someone moved closer. 'Are you the American?'

'Yeah.'

'I'm from Chicago. You know Chicago?'

'Sure I know Chicago.'

'That's where I'm from.' Again a flood of yellow light from a torch. Alongside the guard stood a Wehrmacht private, an *Oberschutze*, his forage cap thrust through the epaulette on his left shoulder. His hair was fair and cropped short, flat on top in the Prussian style. He was carrying a Schmeisser MP-44 machine pistol.

'You don't look like a guy from Chicago,' said Ossie. 'Or maybe you do.'

'Oh, I'm from Chicago, all right,' said the *Oberschutze*. 'I was raised there. Maybe I'll go back one day. Where do you hail from?'

'Not Chicago,' Ossie said.

'Midwest somewhere,' said the *Oberschutze*.

'Maybe. What's the difference?'

'You'd be surprised. Maybe all the difference in the world.'

'I don't get you, buddy.'

'Buddy, yeah, I like that. I like to hear that. Buddy. Yeah.' The *Oberschutze* was very close now, talking low. 'What's your racket, slugger? I mean, this British air-force stuff? What's your problem? You don't want to believe all you hear about the Reich, all the bad stuff they pump you guys with. We've got a mission, sure. It's no different from the States, but we're talking United States of Europe. That's the deal. What's so wrong with that?'

'You want me to tell you?'

'Listen,' the man's tone was more urgent now, 'we've got no beef with the Americans. Jesus, I'm half American myself. You guys are neutral, for Christ's sake. What are you doing here?'

'I can't answer that.'

'I'm trying to help.'

'Maybe I don't need help.'

'Maybe you do.'

At a snapped order from the *Oberschutze*, suddenly hard and impatient, the guard unslung his automatic rifle and pushed past Ossie into the stable stall, pulling at the English corporal. '*Kommen Sie, kommen Sie.*' The man hung back, unwilling to move. The guard raised the butt of his rifle but seemed reluctant to use it.

The corporal sensed his hesitation and said to him: 'What's going on? Where are you taking us?'

The guard looked perplexed but the *Oberschutze* seized the corporal by the arm, swung him round and helped him on his way with his boot. 'You'll find out soon enough.' He took Wolf by the shoulder and bundled him out of the stable. 'It doesn't have to be this way,' he said.

'Oh, I think it does,' said Ossie. 'With you guys it always has to be this way.'

A deep irrigation channel ran along a stretch of hedgerow a little way from the nearest farm building. Knots of troops watched as Ossie and the corporal stumbled past them, thrust forward by the kicks and shoves of the *Oberschutze* and the guard.

The corporal was beginning to comprehend. His face was white in the darkness, like that of a corpse. 'You can't do this. We're prisoners of fucking war. What about the Geneva Convention? Oh, for Christ's sake, you can't fucking do this. What are you thinking of? We won't do nothing, not now. What harm could we do you? Please, for God's sake, please. I've got a wife and kids. Haven't you got a wife and kids? Think of them, oh, think of them.'

'So it's a tough break,' said the *Oberschutze*, tiredly. 'What do you expect us to do? Order up a Pullman just for two? Quit whining and take it like a man.'

They halted by the irrigation channel. In the bottom, face down in the acrid stream, lay the French colonel. The exit holes of many bullets had punctured the back of his uniform. The corporal was almost silent now, just a barely audible but continuous moan, like the keening of an anxious child. He allowed himself to be pushed a pace or two away from Ossie by the *Oberschutze*. 'We're prisoners of fucking war,' he murmured one last time.

The guard switched on his torch. The light was blinding. The *Oberschutze* was beside him cocking the Schmeisser. The barrel swung up. Ossie felt the wind of the bullets tear the air inches from his body. He was conscious of the English corporal hurling backwards to his right and spinning down into the irrigation ditch with a splash of filthy water. The torch-light was wavering as though the guard was shocked by what he had seen, or maybe he'd had his eyes closed. For a moment it focused on the ground, picking out tufts of grass and pebbles. In that instant two fists hammered into Ossie's chest. He hit the bottom of the ditch head first and surfaced, gasping. The *Oberschutze*, poised on the bank, was shouting over his shoulder at the guard to give him the torch. The man pushed it into his hand, hung back, unwilling to see what lay in the ditch. Again the yellow beam.

The English corporal lay on his back, eyes closed, chin dipping into the water. From time to time a deep breath shuddered through him. The *Oberschutze* looked Ossie straight in the eye, then deliberately raised the Schmeisser and put two bullets into the corporal's chest. He threw the torch back to the guard waiting out of sight.

Then, out of the darkness came the *Oberschutze*'s voice, hoarse, urgent: 'Beat it. Get the hell out. Go. This isn't your goddammed war. Go home. Tell them what I said. United States of Europe. Tell them that.' Then Ossie heard the crunch of gravel as the *Oberschutze* walked away.

As he crawled along the ditch Ossie heard laughter: the *Oberschutze* was restored to his comrades, intent on a beer after taking his turn to do a job none of them looked for.

The volume on a wireless was turned up. Jesus, Lucienne Delyle. The saccharine melody floated across the warm summer air. '*Sur les quais du vieux Paris . . .*'

In an instant Ossie was back in La Vosgienne, the air heavy with tobacco smoke and patrons shooting the breeze, pushing a glass of Kronenbourg around the zinc table, hearing the Champs-Élysées traffic beyond the plane trees; Dinghy, of course, good old long-dead Dinghy sitting beside him, balancing dangerously on the back legs of his chair, scanning the crowd for popsies – always popsies, crazy guy. Other faces too: Kit Curtis pushing his way between the tables, standing over them, angry, accusing, acting like a goddammed English stuffed-shirt. And Bébé, of course, over there, like the first time he saw her with that damned Una Westcott, acting kind of provocative but somehow not like the others, like maybe something special could happen between them later . . . always later.

The Wehrmacht troopers were humming along to Delyle's refrain, a little subdued, maybe thinking how simple it was to solve the problem of three unwanted prisoners, maybe thinking of home; maybe thinking of Paris and unimagined pleasures to come.

Sur les quais du vieux Paris
Le long de la Seine
Le bonheur sourit
Sur les quais du vieux Paris . . .

Yeah, thought Ossie, he'd had himself some pretty damned good *bonheur* on the *quais* of old Paris an age ago, back in '39 . . .

Part two

'J'aime la Drôle de Guerre . . .'

Five

Impossible, it seemed to Kit, that barely four weeks had passed since the squadron had lifted away from its temporary base near Chichester, within sight of the Sussex Downs, gathered itself into four vics and made a final low-level pass over the aerodrome, a valorous sight that raised a cheer from the ground-party and a straggle of relatives and locals who had gathered to wish them Godspeed. Among them, he knew, as he craned his neck for one last sight of the white breakers fringing the English coast, was his father, probably back in the Rolls now, the reliable Barlow feeding the broad steering-wheel through his gloved hands and turning north to Midhurst.

Farve's eyes had brimmed with tears, he remembered, at their final handshake. His father had patted his shoulder tentatively, smiling, swallowing hard. In the harsh late-summer light he looked old and small, not proud but anxious, fearful. Was this the man who had spun so many tales at bedtime from gilt-backed yarns, *For Honour's Sake, For England, Home and Glory, A Victory Won*, yellowing pages interspersed with images of jut-jawed Jacks and Neds battling all-comers, the French, the fuzzy-wuzzy, the wily Oriental so that the English way might prevail? Now he seemed a stranger, feeble in his fusty, formal suit, confronted with the bitter price of duty, the fight for right, his country's role in the world as a force for good, concerned with the welfare of other peoples and other continents gathered under the benign imperial cloak. He believed it all implicitly and this was where it had led him: to make awkward farewells to his boy at a hot, dusty aerodrome beside a fully armed weapon of war.

'Your mother so wanted to be here,' he said.

'Yes.'

'She simply couldn't face it. You know how she is.'

Kit knew how she was. She had never attended Speech Day, 'Darling, it's such a drive and I know how these things go'; had refused to go to her mother's funeral, 'Too upsetting, I can't bear the thought of her stretched out in that awful box'; had never seen him fly, 'So noisy, dear, and dangerous, but I'm sure you're very good at it.' He recalled her parting comment by the staircase in the hall where he had stacked his kit ready for the drive to the aerodrome. 'Now, do be sure to visit the Maierscheldts in Paris, Christopher. I'm dying to have news of dear Karoline.'

'Diana, the boy's fighting a war,' his father had said.

'Not all the time, surely?'

The thin strand of the Sussex coast fell away in the haze. The Hurricanes, so bulky and aggressive on the ground, seemed minuscule and insignificant, held between sea and sky, as expendable as a swarm of insects. Passing in ranks below, the waves of the English Channel thrust shorewards, timeless and unhurried, carrying phantom hosts: Caesar's galleys, the fleet of William of Normandy, the castellated Cinque Port ships of Edward III surging to battle with the Spanish at Sluys, Drake's sea-wolves harrying the Duke of Medina's doomed Armada; Nelson, Collingwood and the rest in their square-rigged 'wooden walls', lords of the ocean. A hundred years later, the multitudes of khaki Tommies, savouring the taste of sea-salt in their faces, bound for the trenches of the Great War and oblivion. Had these warrior generations experienced the same emotions as Kit as he too set out to do battle? He was conscious of an exhilaration, a tingling in the blood, an eagerness to measure himself against the present foe and the valiant who had gone before. He realised he had a role to play, if only a small one, in the making of history. His senses seemed raw, lending a pin-sharp focus to the least action as he manoeuvred the control column or made the slightest adjustment to the throttle lever. But there was also a deadening apprehension, not fear, of course, never that, but a nagging speculation about what might lie ahead. No sense of personal mortality, though, because he knew it couldn't happen to him – perhaps an injury or two, a few light burns, something that might take him out of the conflict for a week or so, nothing more. He imagined the others felt the same, although they didn't talk of it. As they readied themselves for the flight, there had been much joshing, much overloud laughter. Among the grinning faces he had caught one or two off-guard, sombre, bound up in their thoughts. The latrines had been busy before take-off, pilots emerging awkwardly, stricken by the squits and attempting to shrug it off. But nobody thought the worse of them. They understood.

Now, swigging Lanson from the bottle, Buster Brown peered down from the lofty window of Kit's suite at the Crillon and reviewed the turbulent traffic scurrying round the place de la Concorde with an expert eye. 'Put most of those buggers behind the wheel of a decent car at Brooklands and they wouldn't stand an earthly. All twitch and snatch and losing their rag. They'd be over the Byfleet Banking before you could say knife.'

'Didn't the French invent motor-racing?' said Kit innocently, stretched out on the gilded Louis XV bed. His own bottle remained in the ice-bucket and from time to time he refilled his fluted glass with care, savouring not swigging.

'Wrap up Curtis,' said Buster Brown. He wiped his mouth with the back of his hand. 'This is the life, eh?'

'At last a chance to find out how good the Hun really are.'

'I meant all this,' said Buster, waving his bottle at the city outside the window. 'For God's sake, man, don't get too beetle-browed on me. Stop fretting. There's plenty of time for derring-do.'

It was their first leave since the squadron had flown into Revigncourt three weeks earlier and they planned to make the most of it. But first they had to get through this damned interview business dreamt up by the little man from the ministry with his banal chit-chat about political expediency, oiling wheels, keeping things sweet – an obscure language of his own. And Kit had another call to make, the one he had reluctantly promised Mother.

They occupied the suite the Curtis family usually took when they spent a week or two in the French capital. Buster Brown had been impressed by the welcome Kit had received when they arrived: Monsieur Albert, the maître d'hotel, had kissed him enthusiastically, twice on each cheek. The portly Frenchman had been impressed in his turn by the sight of RAF wings on their uniforms. 'Ah, Monsieur Kit, I should have known. You have your eyes raised to the skies where you belong. You are familiar with Saint Exupéry, *Le Petit Prince*?'

'Of course.'

'So you're a little prince?' said Buster Brown, as the wrought-iron door of the *ascenseur* was flung back and they piled in with their sparse luggage.

'That's me,' said Kit. 'Prepare for take-off.' And they lurched up to the first floor where Monsieur Albert fussed and fretted them into their opulent accommodation.

Buster turned away from the window, tapped a Craven A out of its packet, snapped a flame from his silver lighter and, one eye closed against the smoke, squinted quizzically at his fellow pilot. He noted that Kit had removed his shoes rather than soil the counterpane.

'Never had you down as a line-shooter,' he said.

'What?'

'Old Albert and all that Monsieur Kit malarkey.' He paused and took a long drag at the cigarette. 'What did you say your family was in?'

'Tea.'

'Much money in tea?'

'Not bad. How about you? Motor-cars wasn't it?'

'Purveyors of horseless carriages to the gentry.'

'Much money in it?'

'Not bad.' Buster glanced at his surroundings. 'Never stayed at the Crillon though. Decent of you to put me up.'

'Perhaps you should be in tea.'

'Perhaps we should. Is there much to it?'

'Piece of cake.'

'Need a plantation or two, I suppose, and those women in saris with baskets on their backs?'

'Yes, and ships . . .'

'Got to collect the stuff.'

'Factories and offices. People, of course, managers, shop-floor types . . .'

'Tasters. The bods who do the slurping. Got to have the slurpers.'

'Them as well. Then there's distribution, lorries, vans. And advertising, sales promotion . . .'

'It all sounds simple enough. Would you help with advice, once we've sold the garages? I mean, we'd be starting out.'

'Delighted. Always room for more in tea.'

'That's a deal, then.'

'Absolutely.'

'Of course we need to get the current unpleasantness behind us first.'

'Of course.'

'Better to wait until then.'

'Far better.'

'So, beat the Hun . . .'

'And then it's tea.'

Buster Brown exploded: 'What bollocks.' He glanced at his watch. 'Time you went to see this bloody little pen-pusher. I hope your clot of a Yank turns up. He'd properly got the jitters about the whole idea.' He yawned. 'When you get back we'll take in that nightclub you told me about.'

'Le Boeuf sur le Toit.'

'That's the place. I hope it's suitably sordid.'

Kit raised himself from the bed. 'I'm pleased you're interested in tea. It'll give us something to talk about when we're on Readiness.' An exquisite cushion embroidered with gold thread hit him squarely on the back of the head.

The arrangement with CBS was the sort of stunt that nobody wanted; not Brewster, the CO, who abhorred the concept of the flying ace, the individual star who hogged the headlines at the expense of his comrades; not Kit, who had been landed with the job of making sure that Ossie Wolf behaved himself and was appalled by the idea of talking to a civilian, worse, a journalist, for God's sake, about what he reckoned were confidential squadron matters; not Ossie Wolf himself, who had met the suggestion with lowered brow and derisive grunts, then realised, like a trapped beast, that there was no way out.

'Christ knows what they expect of him,' Brewster had said, briefing Curtis. 'All we know is the word's come down that someone somewhere thought it would be a Good Idea to drum up support from the Americans by trumpeting some tosh about our gallant Yankee volunteers. I wish this bloody CBS johnnie the best of luck. Sergeant Wolf is about as eloquent as a brick.'

'I gather he's more voluble after a tot or two, sir.'

'That's really good news,' said Brewster. 'Keep on top of it Kit. I have bad feelings about this lunatic wheeze.'

It was no lunatic wheeze to Rupert Pringle. He thought it an excellent idea. So, apparently, did his superiors in Whitehall. He told Kit all about it from the depths of a leather armchair in the lobby of the Crillon. The chair swallowed him up. His feet barely touched the carpet. He had a childlike smallness about him and a piping voice. Behind thick lenses his prominent eyes darted this way and that, never quite meeting the sceptical gaze of the gangling pilot, who had chosen a lofty perch on a plain, upright chair of some antiquity. Pringle, forced to tilt his head, seemed to be addressing someone on a balcony. 'I envy you chaps,' he said unconvincingly.

'Do you?' said Kit.

Pringle tapped his spectacles. 'Damned eyesight you see. Otherwise . . .'

'Ah.'

'Have you read this?' Pringle removed a newspaper cutting folded into a pocket diary. He passed it to Kit, his expression comically grave.

Kit scanned the report. 'Isolationist sentiments in the United States.' A paragraph had been marked in ink. It quoted Roosevelt addressing Congress. 'The first President of the United States warned us against entangling foreign alliances. The present President of the United States subscribes to and follows that precept.'

'That's what we're up against,' said Pringle.

'I see.'

'Sooner or later the States will realise this policy is wrong. We, that is my people, want it to be sooner. But the Americans aren't making it easy for us with their tiresome neutrality acts. For heaven's sake, they're even mulling over a new one.'

'Where does Sergeant Wolf fit into all this?' said Kit. He was keen to move things on.

'You may not be aware of this but under the provisions of these blasted Acts it's illegal to recruit Americans for the armed forces of so-called foreign countries. Even us,' Pringle added heatedly. 'Not only that, they've made it unlawful for a US citizen to travel anywhere to enlist. The thing is—'

'Can we get to the thing?'

'There are loopholes. We need pilots, trained pilots, and America's stiff with them, chaps who are keen as mustard and want to get involved in this business. The answer is . . . Canada.'

'Ah.'

'It's just a handful at the moment, chaps who've gone north, joined the RCAF and crossed the Pond. But the number is growing and we want more. And, just as important, my people want ordinary Americans to be aware that some of their fellows are not content just to stand by and watch Europe go up in flames. So, the two things are bound up together. First, more pilots, second, encourage America to jump down from the fence.'

'I see,' said Kit. He supposed it was fair enough, when you thought about it. Prod Sergeant Wolf into the limelight, the reluctant hero, and maybe it *would* help the war effort. A mega line-shoot, of course, but no doubt these things had to be done in the name of propaganda. And who was he to judge this odd little man with his artful ploys to influence, even in a tiny way, the outcome of the next Great War? Farve, who hadn't fought in the First, would have said quietly that he was doing his bit . . .

'What sort of cove is this Wolf character anyway?' Pringle was saying. He was struggling to escape from the cavernous armchair like a fly from a web. Kit gave him his hand and heaved him to his feet. Pringle's grasp was limp and damp.

'He knows how to fly an aeroplane,' Kit said.

'Is he an idealist, would you say? You know, firm convictions?'

Now here, thought Kit, is where this particular artful ploy is a bit on the weak side. 'I wouldn't know, to be honest. You should ask him yourself. We'd better get our skates on, hadn't we? The Press Club's quite a trek.'

'Oh, we're not meeting at the Press Club after all,' said Pringle. 'Got a phone call from a Sergeant Davis. It's been switched to a place called La Vosgienne.'

'Who decided this?'

'I'm not entirely sure. It may have been Sergeant Wolf himself. But I don't see a problem. As long as it's a place where we can have a confidential chat . . .'

The noise, light and heat of the La Vosgienne bar, about midway up the Champs-Élysées heading west towards the Arc de Triomphe, was startling after the gloom of the blacked-out city. Outside, as the evening shadows deepened, even the traffic had lost its verve, navigating with unusual caution, guided by head-lamps daubed dull blue and shuttered according to regulations. More daring souls took the inky murk as a challenge and a new sound had become familiar to Parisians: the abrupt crump and tinkle of pulverised metal and glass, followed swiftly by raised voices. It had its amusements, this lightless demi-world; the bars, nightclubs and hotels held a new allure, oases of radiance where normal life could be pursued with almost desperate energy. Cinemas, theatres, the opera played to packed, appreciative houses. But this dreamlike state was disquieting too, when one glanced above the familiar skyline and knew that, even in the depths of this bizarre Drôle de Guerre, where great forces seemed frozen on the brink of war, there lurked the threat of destruction and death, unseen as yet and all the worse for it.

Ossie Wolf had bagged a corner table close to the bar. His uniform jacket was unbuttoned, his tie loosened, his face flushed with Alsace beer. He was balancing himself on the back legs of his chair, pushing against a table leg with his feet. The remnant of a stained Gitane jutted from the corner of his mouth. The sight of Rupert Pringle seemed to spoil his concentration: the chair tilted back a shade too far, then fell forward. His feet hit the table hard and the accumulation of bottles and glasses tumbled over, some spilling on to the floor and shattering. There was a gust of laughter and some ironic cheers but Kit Curtis wasn't smiling. Ossie Wolf watched him push his way between the tables, face twisted with anger. Ossie stayed where he was, tipped back on his chair once more, scrutinising the advancing officer as Dinghy Davis, crouched on the floor, helped the barman to sweep the broken glass into a dustpan.

'What on earth do you think you're playing at, Sergeant?' said Kit.

'I'm not playing. I'm waiting.' Ossie Wolf eased the chair on to four legs, placed his hands on the table and began to drum his fingers rhythmically, coolly meeting Kit's incensed gaze.

'Stand up when you're talking to me,' said Kit, 'and smarten yourself up man.'

Rupert Pringle said: 'I hardly think this place is suitable—'

'Really? I think it's very suitable,' said Ossie, rising slowly to his feet and buttoning his tunic. 'Dinghy and me, we checked out the Press Club. The place is like a morgue and some of the corpses in attendance have big ears. The guy in charge was real curious about why we were there and what this CBS character might be after. Very goddammed curious. The whole set-up stank.'

'It was pretty rum, sir,' said Dinghy Davis. 'You hear all these yarns about careless talk but some of it has to be true.'

'You can barely hear yourself think in this place,' said Pringle, plaintively, overcome by the swell of voices, the groan of an accordion and the pig-squeal wail of a jazz violin, the cries of waiters delivering trays of drinks with a clatter, all overlaid by a dense fug of cigarette smoke, cheap perfume and the odour of hot bodies.

'If we can barely hear then nobody else can,' said Ossie. 'Want to take a beer?'

'I'll take a beer Sergeant. In fact, I'll take two.' It was the CBS man, leathery hand extended, Nordic blue eyes set in a prematurely lined face. He was tall – taller than Kit. Beside him Ossie seemed a pint-sized kid. 'I'm Ed Nielsen,' the journalist said. He shook hands all round. Kit knew the decision had been made for him. He wasn't sure it was such a good thing. Ossie Wolf had won and they both knew it.

At a glance from Ossie Wolf Dinghy Davis quickly dragged two tables together, commandeering their corner of the bar and making space for Nielsen, who pulled off a long white trench-coat and hung it from the bracket of a metal wall lamp. Pringle said: 'Thank you, Davis. You don't need to be involved in this.'

Dinghy looked at Kit enquiringly. He nodded. 'Righto,' said Davis.

Ossie Wolf grunted, deciding not to make a fight of it. 'Catch you later, Dinghy.'

'Righto,' said Davis again. He gave them a thumbs-up, collected his beer and threaded his way carefully through the throng, heading for the only spare seat he could see, on the far side of the bar where two women were talking, one heatedly, the other half listening. '*Excusez-moi*,' he said, and then, very slowly, in English, 'is . . . anyone . . . sitting . . . here?' The older woman stared at his coarse uniform and sergeant's stripes with distaste, pale lips pursed. She ran thin fingers through her dyed black hair, cropped close like a boy's. She said, '*Oui*,' at the same moment the younger one said, '*Non*.' The younger one laughed and Davis did too. She was quite a dish. He plumped himself down.

'Tell me, Sergeant Wolf, how come "Dinghy" Davis?' The CBS man's voice rang with easy authority. His fruity tones were familiar to millions of his fellow countrymen, reverberating from the tinny speakers of wireless sets spread across the States. Ossie Wolf had never heard of him.

'He ditched in the drink.'

'How was that?'

Ossie shrugged. 'Out of gas.'

Kit cut in: 'Got lost in fog on patrol when we were up Le Havre way about a month ago. Took to his dinghy and got picked up by one of our patrol boats.'

'Lucky.'

'Very.'

'Yeah, the guy was George but he's Dinghy now,' said Ossie Wolf.

Nielsen gave him his full attention. 'Tell me,' he said, the sentence rolling from him fully formed, as though from a prepared script, 'what manner of man is it who journeys from the other side of the world to fight another man's war?'

Ossie Wolf grunted – Good grief, thought Kit, he actually flushed.

The CBS man hadn't finished. 'Do you, for example, subscribe to the view that there is something greater than your own life, greatness of soul, perhaps?'

'I wouldn't know about that,' said Ossie. He stared across the bar and saw Davis enjoying himself with the young woman. Her head was thrown back and she was laughing, eyes closed, dark hair long and glossy, shining in the lamplight. It moved delicately around her shoulders as though stirred by a gentle breeze. The older woman's expression was fixed and sullen, almost hopeless.

The CBS man backed up a little. 'You know what this is about, Sergeant?'

'Tell me again,' said Ossie Wolf.

'Murrow, Sevareid and the boys at CBS, well, we have a certain influence and we feel we should do something about you fellows from the States who've joined in on this thing.'

'Uh-huh.'

'Tell the folks back home they've got some heroes over here, men of courage and principle who see the whole world opened up to barbarian conquest and have chosen to throw in their lot with the forces that oppose the enemies of civilisation, who are ready to fight side by side with them whatever it takes, even their lives.'

'Do you prepare this stuff or does it come natural to you?'

Nielsen tried again: 'I guess you're sick of seeing your country procrastinate while Europe implodes.'

'Well—'

Pringle said quickly: 'Naturally my people believe that the United States must be given time to make up its own mind about the right and proper course to take. It is a matter of consultation, deliberation and policy. But, of course, time is not necessarily on our side. That's why, Sergeant Wolf, your views and beliefs as an individual, the motives that set you on this path have such significance for the man in the street, who may, in his turn, help to shape the very policies we're talking about.'

'Uh-huh.'

'Roosevelt warned against entangling foreign alliances,' said Nielsen.

'Yeah, I heard that.'

'How do you feel about it?'

'How do you think I feel about it?'

'At a guess I imagine you'd think it wrong.'

'I guess you'd be right at that.'

Nielsen reached behind him, pulled a bottle of Kentucky bourbon from the pocket of his trenchcoat and signalled for four whisky glasses. 'You're aware that if we run a piece we won't disclose your name, in the interests of state security and your own personal safety?'

'Yeah.'

'Doesn't make it any easier, huh?'

'Not really,' said Ossie, eyes fixed on the Jack Daniel's in the centre of the table. 'I'm just here to fly an airplane, fight a war. Me, I don't want to be portrayed as anything special. I'm just a guy who always wanted to be a combat pilot. I leave politics to the goddammed politicians.'

'Not your favourite species, then?'

'They're the feeble bastards who've allowed this sorry mess to happen, no question.' Ossie glanced at Pringle, who was biting his little fingernail. He could see the man wondering how the interview could get worse. Explanations and excuses would be needed in Whitehall, not good on his dossier . . .

'I'm not alone in hating all this line-shoot crap,' said Ossie. 'The CO hates it most of all. Why single out a guy when the whole team's pitching?'

'Line-shoot, huh?' Nielsen grinned. 'You're turning into an Englishman, Sergeant.' Carefully he passed round hefty slugs of bourbon. 'Tell me, how do you get on with the British?'

'Fine, just fine.'

'And how did you get on with the Spanish?' The question came abruptly and Nielsen's mellow tones had a sudden edge. It was plain he had grown tired of Sergeant Stonewall, Ossie thought, had decided to muss things up just a little, see if he couldn't provoke the man into saying something he might be able to use. 'And don't tell me the Spanish were fine for Christ's sake,' he added.

It was a bum move and Ossie Wolf glowered at him. Nielsen switched to Kit. 'Tell me,' he said, 'I'm interested. How conscious are you guys of what you're doing? Is it just personal, proving yourselves in some way, or do you believe, like Horace, that it is a sweet and honourable thing to die for your country?'

'Horace who?' said Ossie.

Kit cut in. 'First of all, Nielsen, none of us expects to die. It may happen to some of us or even all of us, it may not. It's beyond our control so we don't brood about it. Now, this business of honour. Well, who can deny there's honour in standing up for what's right? Perhaps you should stress that in your report. Maybe it'll make a difference, strike a chord where it matters, wake up some people in Washington. But it's also a more narrow thing, a personal thing. It is for me, anyway. I've been brought up in a certain way, in a certain society, with certain beliefs. I just hope I match up. It's the Greek notion, isn't it, that holds that whatever you've done in your life, if you end badly it counts for nothing? Well, I'm resolved to do my damnedest to make sure that doesn't happen to me and I know all the chaps feel the same. Perhaps above everything I believe we have a duty—'

'You mean the British?'

'If you like, yes – a duty to resist evil—'

'A duty to whom? The Empire? Or is it broader than that?' Before Kit could respond the CBS man turned back to Wolf. 'Are you involved in this from a sense of duty, Sergeant? Is that what took you to Spain?'

'A boat took me to Spain. After that, stuff happened. But I

saw what happened there and I aim to get even. In my book Fascists are vermin and that's why I'm here, a rat-catcher. It's as simple as that.'

'So, no crusade, no quest for honour, no sense of duty?'

'No,' said Ossie flatly. 'I don't care about me. When I was a kid I got stuffed full of all that crap about the Fatherland—'

'Your family's German background, yes, I read the briefing notes.'

'Yeah, well, I took it all in, all that stuff about *Heimat*, what it should mean to me, what I owed it and what I owed the family. Me, I was confused because I reckoned I was American, period. Third generation for Christ's sake! How long does it take before you can kick off ties to the old country? But for a time, too long, I went along with all the bullshit about the golden age of the greater Germany to come: duty, honour, belief in a certain way of life, all those words and phrases that seem so simple and screw you up. Yeah, I was taken down that road good. But then I wised up.'

'What did it take?'

'I realised it was the wrong road, one of those big highways going nowhere or maybe to hell. I'd gotten wrong directions.'

'You appear to have a lot of hate in you, Sergeant.'

'Hate's what it's going to take,' said Wolf, with a glance at Kit. 'Guts won't be enough.'

Suddenly Nielsen was on his feet. 'Tell me, Sergeant,' he said, 'your time in Spain. Clearly you were with the Communists. I'd like to explore that.' Without waiting for a reply, he shoved the Jack Daniel's across the table. 'Help yourselves to a slug or two boys. I'm going to take a leak.'

'Screw you,' said Ossie under his breath, slightly slurred.

'Cut that out Sergeant,' snapped Kit. 'And lay off the liquor.'

Pringle sat back in his seat with a low groan. 'Good grief, what is the man going to take away from this?'

Kit said: 'Listen to me, Sergeant, I'm ordering you to stop playing games and get your finger out. None of us likes this circus but we're here to do a job and the sooner you give this chap what he wants the sooner we can all get on with our leave. Do you understand?'

'I guess.'

'I said, do you understand?'

'Yes, I understand . . . sir.'

It was the first time that Ossie Wolf had seen Kit Curtis sore. For a moment he sensed a tenuous bond with the Englishman: he was stirred by his display of spirit, more heated than might have been expected from his usual calm indifference to whatever life threw at him – that goddammed stiff upper lip, the lofty assurance that only he and his kind knew the rightness of things. The smug, complacent bastard.

Nielsen was back, reaching for the bourbon and noting that the others hadn't touched it. Wolf said: 'So we're heroes, right? How do you figure that? We've not seen hide nor hair of a Hun so far.'

'When you hear my piece you'll all believe you're heroes.' Nielsen paused. 'Tell me, son, why aren't you an officer?'

Ossie looked at Kit and opened up, some. It was the same difference, he told him. He flew the same airplane with the same object in mind. Maybe ranks weren't so important. In Spain, for a time, the Republicans hadn't had ranks. It was a window, kind of, on what might have been; everyone pulling in the same direction, men, women, peasants, the bourgeoisie, no one setting themselves up to be any better or worse than anyone else, a kind of trust in the man or woman beside you. And everyone having a say about the way things should go, no big cheese throwing his weight around.

'Don't disappoint me, Sergeant. Don't tell me I sniff an idealist under that gruff exterior?'

Ossie shrugged. 'That's your call. All I know is it seemed to work, for a time at least. There was a common purpose, an alliance—'

'An alliance of enemies,' said Nielsen.

'As it turned out, yes.' Wolf took a slug of Jack Daniel's, drained the glass and poured another. 'But in the beginning who could have guessed how things would pan out? I knew a guy in Barcelona in 'thirty-seven. He'd seen what the Nationalists were prepared to do to their own countrymen so he reckoned he'd have a shot at stopping them. This was no callow kid. He'd seen action with POUM at the front near Huesca.'

'POUM?'

'Partido Obrero de Unificación Marxista.'

'Marxista?'

'Yeah, Marxista. A breakaway outfit, not big at all but going back to the roots, not Stalin's way. The way the POUM guys saw it was that opposing Fascism with bourgeois democracy, as they called it, was trading one form of capitalism for another. They had it that the only real answer was worker control.'

'You were with POUM?'

'Yeah, I was. By accident really. That's the way it was back then. You got a problem with that?'

'I'm not paid to have a problem with anything I'm told, Sergeant, I'm just a plain old reporter. This guy in Barcelona . . .'

'Okay,' said Ossie. 'At the start, he told me, it had all seemed clear to him, the rights and wrongs. He believed in the cause. But when Málaga fell to the Fascists there was talk of treachery, divided aims, all kinds of crap, and the alliance started to fall apart. This guy came close to being shot by some of the other factions he'd fought alongside only weeks before. That was where idealism got him and thousands like him. The whole damned thing got muddled.' He made circles on the marble table-top with the whisky-wet base of his glass. 'It was a gift to the goddammed Nationalists. We handed them victory on a plate. And, you had to admit, those bastards had it right. Wars are about killing, any way you can. Whoever kills most wins. Forget that, get swept up in goddammed dreams of Shangri-la, and you lose. This guy in Barcelona finally realised that.' He was speaking fast, stumbling over his words, more voluble after a tot or two.

'Seems you knew this fellow well,' said Nielsen.

'Pretty well.'

'So, Spain, an experiment that failed,' said Nielsen, 'yet you still cling to a few of the old beliefs.'

'Such as?'

Nielsen reached out and touched the stripes on Ossie's tunic. 'These.'

'Could be I'm a sentimental jerk. Maybe it's simpler. Maybe it's just me I want to be responsible for.'

'That's a bunch of maybes,' said Nielsen. Silence. 'Tell me, how's your family feel about all this?'

'I wouldn't know.'

'Are they proud of what you're doing now?'

'I told you, I wouldn't know.'

'Level with me. Were they the influence that sent you down that wrong highway, your so-called highway to hell? Let's face it, son, follow that route and you could have wound up fighting for the other side. Maybe your family would have preferred it.'

'They see only the Fatherland. They don't choose to see the Nazis. They want Germany to be strong, no matter what. The family doesn't figure with me any more, hasn't for years. That suits me fine – and them. We lost touch a long while back and it's better that way.'

'So, they don't know where you are or what you're doing?'

'Not unless you tell them.'

'Only if you want it, Sergeant, and it doesn't sound like you do. You've got my promise you won't be identified in any piece we may do.' Nielsen took a slow, contemplative mouthful of bourbon. 'Tell me, Sergeant, these rats you're so dedicated to exterminating. You realise, of course, that some of them might turn out to be your own people – relatives, folk who share the same lineage, grew from the same stock?'

'Sure I've thought of that but, like the rest of that wonderful nation, they've gone along with this thing, swallowed all the bullshit, been suckered into yet another war. They had a choice but they never learn. Who knows? Maybe they'll win, maybe they'll lose. Whichever way the dice fall it's going to be a goddammed disaster for everyone, including them.'

'Maybe you've been suckered, Sergeant. You changed routes, sure, but it could be said you were suckered in Spain. You've admitted as much. And here you are again, caught up in someone else's war when you could be back home flying folk to Acapulco and living the high-life as a hot-shot pilot.'

'Maybe I *am* a sucker,' said Ossie, quietly. 'You know what? I don't care. I'm doing what I'm doing and that's it, that's all of it. You're trying to get me on the couch like some goddammed shrink. Well, I guess that's your racket and I've gone along with it because I've been told to. I'll give you this, though. Seems to me, the way things have been moving, the issues are clearer right now. Sure they may get muddled, maybe like they did in Spain. Who knows what kind of world we're moving into or going to be left with? But I talked about choice a moment ago and it's a choice we're all going to be forced to make eventually, even those folks with their heads in the sand back in the States. It's either that or lie down and let Hitler and his gangsters stomp all over us. I'm just a guy who happens to have made that choice sooner, that's all. I want to be in on the start.'

'Do you believe the Allies will prevail?'

'Maybe. We're making all the right noises, but noises don't scare anyone. We seem to have convinced ourselves it's all going to turn out okay, sitting on our butts on the Maginot Line. You want to know the truth?'

Across the table Pringle craned forward, clearing his throat and making signs that he felt the interview had run its course.

Ossie ignored him. 'I'll tell you the way I see it. I think the Allies, and particularly the French, are still reeling from the last show. I don't think we're prepared for what's coming our way. I don't think we can even imagine it. For the Reich, Spain was just a rehearsal. They tried out a lot of stuff they're going to use on us. Everything that happened there is going to happen here in spades, like Poland. The only response is hit 'em quick and hit 'em hard. It's all they'll understand. Defence is no longer enough. You can build all the bunkers and dig all the trenches you want, but you'll just be rolled over by tanks and flown over by airplanes. Dead meat. A guy named Patton has it right. He says the only thing to do when a sonofabitch looks cross-eyed at you is to beat the living hell out of him right then and there.'

Nielsen was nodding. 'Interesting.' There was a long silence, broken by the scratch of his Parker on the notebook. Then he slipped it into the inside pocket of his jacket and carefully screwed the top back on to the fountain pen. The others watched him in silence. It seemed the CBS man had got enough to warrant a bottle of bourbon on expenses. He turned benign, avuncular. 'Tell me, Sergeant, I don't fly, what kind of experience is it to pilot a Hawker Hurricane?'

Ossie Wolf, on firmer ground, brightened. 'Swell. One helluva machine. Outperforms anything in the States. Remember, I had more than two hundred and fifty hours on all types of airplane, all kinds of flying, all weathers but, boy, the Hurricane can whip 'em good. And whoever talks about British red tape is talking up his ass. Once you showed 'em you had the goods they bought. They got us across the Pond from Canada quicker than a knife, bypassed all the elementary stuff, straight into operational training. That was a day, believe me, when I finally got to climb into a Hurry.'

'That's great,' said Nielsen, not really listening, scanning the bar, 'that's really great.' They shook hands all round. 'I wish you well, boys, I really do.' He jerked a thumb at the blackness that awaited him outside. 'Hey, someone threw a switch on the City of Light.' Pringle was the only one who laughed. 'Yup,' said the CBS man, 'someone threw a switch on the City of Light all right.'

'I'll see you out,' said Pringle, like a nervous curate escorting a bishop. He was talking with some animation, waving his hands, as they vanished through the door of La Vosgienne. It was plain that for Ed Nielsen he might as well not have been there. The journalist had got what he came for.

Una Westcott cast a sour eye over the porky figure of Dinghy Davis, noting the receding hairline with a touch of scurf, the droplets of sweat standing on his brow, the protruding crimson ears, the thick neck bulging over the blue shirt collar. When he laughed, which was distressingly often, his purplish lips, so like the nozzle of an infant's balloon, parted to disclose crooked yellow teeth. He was wholly repugnant, Una thought, yet Bébé could not resist holding out a few hoops for him to jump through. It was too cruel but, then, what else could one expect of the tantalising Anna Dubretskov? It was, she knew, part of her capricious charm, the ability to toy with emotions, to raise up and cast down at will. With Bébé at her side, the world had seemed to Una a wondrous place, delirious in its beauty and potential. At others Bébé would slide a blade deep into her heart and twist it until Una could not tell whether she was screaming with pain or ecstasy. All she knew was that she was screaming.

Dinghy Davis was laughing now. He seemed to believe he was doing well with this magical creature. Bébé was guessing his age – difficult, because he was neither young nor old, just plain, porcine and slumped in front of them like a sack of beet.

'Thirty-five,' said Bébé.

'Fifty,' said Una Westcott, almost to herself but waspishly.

Davis looked stung. 'Twenty-eight,' he said, but added, 'You're right, of course. A bit old compared to the rest of the chaps. I was in the air force when Pontius was a pilot.'

'That is so funny,' cried Bébé, but Davis didn't notice that her eyes were dead. A slim, delightful arm curled round his neck. He quivered with pleasure and attempted to take her by the waist but, in some mysterious way, found her beyond his grasp, though so close that her perfume was in his nostrils, heady and intoxicating. She stared at Una, mocking and coquettish, pleased that their difficult conversation had been interrupted by this lumpen Englishman with his naïve expectations of what the fabled city might have in store for him. She knew that Una Westcott was waiting for an answer. She also knew her reply. She did not know how she would tell her because somewhere, almost unacknowledged, she still retained a spark of affection for the odd American woman, with her hunger for love, gaiety and the arts, who was about to lose everything she valued.

'My God, *chou*,' said Una in French, 'surely we've slummed enough?'

'Darling, don't be so dreary,' said Bébé.

Una stifled a sob. 'Don't be cruel to me, *chou*. Please.'

'What's up girls?' said Davis. 'Afraid I haven't got the lingo.'

'It is the Drôle de Guerre,' said Bébé in English. 'My friend finds it very sad. *Moi, j'aime la Drôle de Guerre.*'

'My friend.' Was that all she had become? Una Westcott felt she was going mad. For days she had been waiting for Bébé to respond to her plan. But every approach had been brushed aside impatiently, almost with spite. Once, Bébé had been unable to suppress a gasp of laughter, as though she had derived a thrill of pleasure from Una's misery. It was more than a week now since the Philadelphian had sat Bébé down in the quai des Grands-Augustin apartment, fashionably white in the manner of Syrie Maugham, and told her: 'You know I've been thinking of leaving France?' Bébé had stared back at her, mute, with the fixed glare of a prison mug-shot. 'I want you to come with me.' Still the unreadable stare. 'It was the devil's own job getting tickets. First they offered me the *Normandie*. A French boat, for heaven's sake, and the Atlantic crawling with U-boats. Then my father pulled some strings.' Una knew she was filling a void and prattled on: 'The *George Washington* leaves for Southampton and New York in a week. It's not going to be comfortable.

They're cramming two thousand passengers into half the normal space. But it will be safe. They've even painted the stars and stripes on the deck in case of German aircraft.' She had moved across to the motionless figure poised beside the Léger sculpture, fashioned from old bicycle wheels. She caressed Bébé's neck. 'You always talk of opportunities, *chou*. What greater opportunity could I offer you?'

'And my mother?'

'Oh, come now, I know how you regard your mother. Still, perhaps she can follow later. Yes, I could make arrangements.'

'I'm not sure I could leave, not sure at all,' said Bébé, coldly. 'I feel . . . I don't know what I feel. Perhaps that great events are going to unfold, that all the old ways are going to be pushed aside. Everything is new, unknown . . .'

'Fearful.'

'Is that so bad necessarily? You talk of opportunities. What opportunities might there be in a world turned upside-down? Are we not at the centre of things? And how can you think of fleeing to America when you love all this so much?' Bébé had waved her slender hand at the vivid colour blazing from the whitewashed walls of the studio room: the Bonnard, the little Daumier, the big nude by Valloton. On every side were exquisite objects: an enamelled ceremonial cup by Fabergé ranged beside a collection of jewelled imperial eggs, Gallé vases, lamps and fabrics from Morocco.

Outside, Una knew, lay the prospect from the Île St-Louis to the Tuileries, bathed in that peculiar, distinctive pale light that always made her swallow hard. God, yes, she thought, it was too perfect. Of course Bébé was right. How could she leave it all, her reason for living, her friends, this divine city, the art and culture, her existence for almost twenty years? She remembered the miraculous sense of freedom when, at last, she had found herself among her own kind, unjudged, unjudging, indulged, desired even . . . the crazy days, the passion and foolery, faces crowding in, warm and loving. And Bébé's face, the face of a fallen angel – this damned kid she was so mad for. It didn't make sense. It was illogical, ridiculous. She had an intellect, didn't she, an analytical and perceptive mind? Everyone said so, everyone except Bébé, who dismissed her as *folle-à-lier*, mad as a hare, fit for a strait-jacket, and she was probably closest to the truth. She said to Bébé: 'I'm thinking of returning to America *because* I love all this so. I fear for France. It has suffered so much. Can it really suffer again? I couldn't stomach the Boches, in Paris, destroying and corrupting everything around them, those blond, pig-eyed farm-boys with their bulging bellies and empty heads, led by psychopaths and egomaniacs.'

'You're very gloomy,' Bébé had said. 'France is strong and, besides, we are not alone.'

No, mused Una Westcott, contemplating Dinghy Davis now, as he guffawed with pleasure at Bébé's playful ripostes, we're not alone. We have this little man and others like him to protect us. Men without a shred of malice in them, men like eager children who look on this mess as a game and worry that it will all be over before they've had a chance to test themselves. Yet was she right? Even as the thought came to her, she heard the Englishman confessing to an apparently fascinated Bébé that he had joined the air force to learn to fly. 'I mean, blimey, when I signed up as an apprentice, just a kid, how was I to know there was going to be a war?' So he had grasped reality all right, understood what price he might have to pay. Perhaps she was wrong. Perhaps some, or even many of them, knew it but would never admit it, least of all to themselves, hiding whatever fears they might have in an outward show of insouciance and high spirits.

She winced. Bébé was putting on quite a show, totally believable of course: apparently fascinated, hanging on every darned word, fixing the podgy Englishman with those dark, promising eyes. And the poor mutt didn't see through it. He thought he was the most interesting and attractive fellow in the place, was probably wondering why nobody had told him so before. Until

114

another airman clapped him on the shoulder and said: 'Jesus, Dinghy you're boring these dames stiff. Let's beat it to Pigalle.'

Una Westcott had seen the man coming, pushing his way unsteadily between the tables, the rising cigarette smoke eddying behind him like some cheap effect in a flea-pit melodrama. A different proposition this one, with his bruiser's nose, thick, tight-curled thatch and pugnacious chin. There was something of the gladiator about him, a cocksure swagger, a brutish air. Such men had paced the arena, winning freedom with their swords. He was drunk but in control, and his gaze, when it fixed on her, was knowing and disdainful.

'You go,' said Davis. 'I'm sticking around.' He stood up for a moment, swaying.

'You're wasting your time, you cock-eyed mug.'

'What are you getting at?'

'On your horse,' said Ossie, and gave him a none-too-gentle shove towards the door. Instead Davis fell back into his seat, grinning foolishly. 'I realise,' he said, 'that I am somewhat inebri- ineb – blotto. Staying put for the present, thank you very much. Why don't you take a pew and say hello to the ladies?' He placed a horny hand on the older woman's arm, oblivious to her shudder. 'Allow me to introduce a fellow American.' He waved a paw at Ossie and knocked the woman's Balkan Sobranie from her lips. The cigarette fell to the filthy floor in a shower of sparks. The girl gave a shriek of laughter, then covered her mouth with a kid glove, eyes shining. Ossie was transfixed. It was as if he was looking at her for the first time.

Her friend extracted another Sobranie from her Tiffany ciga- rette case, flicked her lighter and breathed out smoke in Ossie Wolf's direction. 'American?'

'St Louis,' said Ossie, reluctant to be drawn in. He was still staring at the girl.

'Philadelphia,' said her friend.

'Son of a gun.'

'Just fancy.'

'Tell me,' said the girl, 'Philadelphia, it is very near St Louis?' She pronounced St Louis in the French way, giving it an exotic air.

'A million miles away,' said Una Westcott.

Across the bar Kit watched Ossie Wolf reach over for a spare chair, spin it back to front and slowly lower himself down, like a cowboy easing on to the saddle of a bronco about to be loosed from a rodeo pen. He had positioned himself, Kit noted, next to the pretty one, cutting out poor old Dinghy who was looking glumly at the grim article with the severe bob. By now Rupert Pringle had returned, his face drawn and thoughtful. He had watched as Nielsen was swallowed up in the murk of the blackout, rather wishing he could be swallowed up too.

'Do you want another drink?' said Kit helpfully, pushing Nielsen's almost empty bottle of Jack Daniel's across the table.

'Another?' said Pringle. 'I haven't touched the stuff all evening.'

'Perhaps you should try it now.'

'What I need is a good strong cup of tea. You don't suppose . . . ?'

'Not a chance.'

'I asked you what sort of cove this chap was,' said Pringle, in an accusing tone.

'I told you,' said Kit. 'He knows how to fly an aeroplane.'

'How these characters slip through the net I wouldn't know,' said Pringle. 'Someone must be screening them. I mean, what we have here is a drunken, foul-mouthed, Communist sympathiser, with German antecedents, quite possibly insane, whose entire purpose in life is to kill the Hun.'

'Well, Nazis at least,' said Kit. 'But, yes, if you put it like that it does sound a dodgy concept. Who was the clot who dreamt it up?'

'Me,' said Pringle. He seized the bourbon. 'Can I borrow your glass? I think I'd prefer to share yours.'

'Did Nielsen give you any clues?' said Kit. 'How he thought it went? Perhaps it wasn't so bad. Our trusty sergeant certainly sounded off. You've got to give him that.'

'You mean how we're all going to be rolled over by tanks and aeroplanes? "Dead meat", I think, was the phrase. Yes,' said Pringle, 'that was just the sort of thing I was after.'

'I see what you mean,' said Kit. 'Ah well, perhaps this sort of show isn't such a brilliant wheeze after all.' He tried to sound regretful.

'I wonder if CBS would agree to suppress the report?' said Pringle.

'Unlikely old chap. They bought us a bottle of bourbon.'

As Pringle took a tentative sip of Jack Daniel's and started to cough, Kit noticed that the older of the two women was on her feet, moving swiftly towards the door. Her face was screwed up, her hands clenched tight against her chest. He wondered what Dinghy Davis might have said to her, but dismissed the thought – Dinghy was a decent fellow who knew how to behave. Ossie Wolf, then. But the American was absorbed in the striking girl who seemed, for a moment, awfully familiar. Kit knew that face, he was sure of it. He had met her somewhere – daft not to remember such a cracker. Where could it have been? He knew she was French without hearing her voice. No Englishwoman moved like that, so profoundly feminine, so elegant yet provocative, her gestures and expressions so delicate and disarming. She was confident of her beauty, understood its effect on those around her, men and women, and did not look, as an English flirt would, for reassurance in their faces. She was the kind of woman, thought Kit, who had always known she aroused admiration, lust and envy, and how to deal with those emotions to her advantage.

He said to the barman: 'Tell me, Monsieur, who is the young woman with my comrades over there?'

The man snorted. 'I do not know her name, *mon copain*, but I do know that your friends are hunting a rabbit that only looks like a rabbit. She comes here sometimes with *la mangeuse améri-caine*.'

'*Mangeuse?*'

'Ah, *oui*. Madame Westcott. You know of her?'

'No.'

'Surely everyone knows of her? *Très riche*, a friend to all artists, moves within a certain circle, unusual in her tastes.'

Dinghy Davis was saying: 'Was it something I said?'

'Huh?' said Ossie Wolf.

'Old Una shoving off like that.'

'What did you say to her?'

'Nothing. Well, I asked if Bébé here was related – you know, her niece or something.'

'You prize jerk,' said Ossie. He turned to Bébé. 'You reckon she'll be okay?'

'Who knows? But probably, yes,' said Bébé carelessly. 'She is moody, that one. She is also unhappy because she must go back to America very soon. She believes this war will turn out bad. She is sad because she asks me to go with her and I must tell her no.' She paused, then added in a smaller voice: 'I have not told her yet.'

'Why would she want you to go with her?' said Dinghy Davis. 'You're French.'

Bébé ignored him. 'So,' she said, arching a perfect eyebrow, 'you are off to Pigalle. Is that the best you can do?'

'What you got in mind?' said Ossie.

'I am sure that young officer over there would have far more original and amusing plans for the evening.'

'I doubt it,' said Ossie. Sonofabitch, he was just moving in on this quite possibly bent but alluring peach and she was recruiting goddammed Fauntleroy over there. Jesus, and he'd been working out how to dump Dinghy . . .

'Why don't we ask him?'

'I don't think that's such a great idea.'

'Tell me,' said Bébé, 'who is the little man with him?'

'That's his butler,' said Ossie.

'He's nice.'

'Who? The butler?'

'No, your officer. A very correct English milord.'

'He's that all right.'

'I think he should join us. Ask him to come and share his amusing plans.'

'You ask him, why don't you?'

'*Eh bien*, I will. Why not? I find you moody also. I grow tired of moody.' She pouted like a child and moved away with the smooth grace of a mannequin at a fashion show. To Ossie she presented a rare image: he imagined her beauty must be an affront to every woman in the place and an object of desire to every man. But, hell, he was forgetting . . .

'Thanks for muscling in like that,' glowered Dinghy.

'Still sore, slugger?' said Ossie. 'Wise up. It's you she's crazy about.'

'Do you think so?'

'No.'

For Kit the resemblance was startling: more comely, of course, curved where Hannah was angular; the eyes alive, challenging and amused, not cast down and demure and uncertain; the mouth broader, fuller, the white teeth a touch more prominent. She was smaller too, not quite to his shoulder, while Hannah was tall, and stooped a little to distract the eye from her breasts. As Bébé leant forward to speak, her blouse, tiny top button undone, fell loose and Kit knew she was aware of where his eyes were resting. He felt a flush of guilt. No reason to, of course. No suggestion of an understanding between him and Hannah, even though it was Mother's dearest wish. Nothing more than friendly warmth that went back to when they were tots together on those long shared holidays in Torquay or Antibes with their families regarding them sentimentally, speculating about what future might await them, as they skipped among the waves.

Bébé extended her hand. 'Your friends said you might like me.'

'They're not friends, exactly . . .'

'They also say you have amusing plans.'

'Really?'

'Shall I go away?'

'No, no, of course not.'

'Shall I sit then?'

'Please do.'

'You are *très gentil*, a very correct English milord.'

'I'm afraid not. Just an ordinary chap.'

'No, you are not ordinary.' Bébé glanced at Pringle, gathering papers into his briefcase. She said softly: 'He is ordinary. I want you to send him away.'

Kit laughed. 'Don't be ridiculous.'

Pringle said: 'Don't worry about me. I'm leaving anyway.' But still he looked hurt.

'Look, I'm sorry,' said Kit, 'but it's impossible. I'm meeting someone. I'm late already.' He checked his watch. Buster would be kicking his heels in the Crillon lobby. He couldn't let the chap down. 'Perhaps another time. My next leave.'

'She is more beautiful than me?'

'He, actually.'

'Ah,' said Bébé, tapping her nose.

'Nothing like that,' said Kit reddening. 'He's a fellow pilot.'

'What of it?' said Bébé. 'I have heard of you English and your preferences. Don't concern yourself. All is understood in Paris. No need to be ashamed. You understand, I think, that I also enjoy variety and follow whichever way life takes me. It is amusing, no?'

'Not amusing, no,' said Kit. 'I don't think this conversation is going anywhere.'

'You find me boring?'

'Not you. Playing games.'

'You are dull,' said Bébé. 'A dull English milord who does not like women.' She got up and began to walk away. Then she turned: she had a startling smile. 'But games. I understand the English like games very much. Perhaps there is a game you do not find boring.'

Kit laughed reluctantly. 'Perhaps there is.'

'*À bientôt.*'

'Goodbye.'

Pringle broke into his thoughts. As Bébé walked away, he said acidly: 'I've had just about enough of fighter pilots for one day. What you characters get up to is your own affair, of course, but I sincerely hope you save something of yourselves to do a bit of fighting when the time comes. You do realise that's what it's all about don't you?'

Kit turned on him. 'I don't need any advice from you, Pringle. Just shove off and keep us out of any more daft schemes that come into your head.'

The ministry man placed his briefcase on the table. He swallowed hard, once, twice, gathering himself. 'Look I'm sorry, Curtis. Stupid of me. Things seem to have got on top of me today. Bit of a nightmare really. Lots of explaining to do. Actually, I appreciate your help. And I'm quite wrong, of course. You fellows deserve every bit of relaxation you can get, even that crazy American. I know we can all rely on you—'

'That's right,' said Kit tersely. 'You can, and tell them that from me. And here's a bit of advice for you and your people. Keep the blasted press johnnies away and let us get on with it. We know what we're doing and we'll give a good account of ourselves – don't have any doubts about that.'

'No,' said Pringle. He paused by the door, jostled by customers, his dark City coat tugged to and fro by their passing. He seemed unwilling to leave the light, the cacophony of voices and the swirl of mediocre jazz. He raised his hand. 'Good luck,' he said.

To Kit the evening seemed suddenly ugly and depressing, a shapeless, senseless procession of unrelated scenes and situations, none of any significance or importance. This bloody Phoney War . . .

'*Vous avez terminé?*' A waiter with a rough southern accent swept in and began to clear the mess of glasses and bottles from the two corner tables, which he pushed apart. It was as though the meeting with the CBS man had never taken place, as though Nielsen, Pringle, Ossie Wolf and Dinghy Davis had never existed; and, although Kit remained uncertainly by the bar, as though he had never existed either. He wondered if in, say, a year none of them would exist, except Pringle, of course, and Ed Nielsen, who might mention their passing in one of his broadcasts. Fresh customers swiftly seized the vacant seats. The sergeant pilots had already left, presumably with the girl who so resembled Hannah. For a long time she lingered in his mind.

Six

On the broad sandstone steps of the Fonteville *mairie* Kit watched Ossie Wolf and Dinghy Davis disappear into the shadows of the slumbering village, heading for their billets. They were still sniggering over some joke like unruly urchins. Or maybe it was one of their adventures in Paris. If the hair-raising accounts he had overheard on the train were to be believed there were plenty to choose from. But it was probably all hot air – no doubt they had ended up, like the rest of them, in a bar somewhere nursing a final unwise drink and wishing the time away, eager to get back to business.

'The bloody Boeuf sur le Toit,' said Buster Brown. 'Not all it's cracked up to be, old boy.'

'No,' said Kit. 'Sorry about that.' In a perverse way they had felt affronted by the studied affectations of the crowd there: it seemed paltry and superficial, not fun at all. They found themselves on the sidelines like aged military relics muttering, 'Don't they know there's a war on?' Their uniforms were almost an embarrassment and the brittle hedonists at the discreet tables and on the close-packed dance floor a reminder of that other world, honing its weapons of war.

Buster had said: 'I think I'll cause a sensation. I'm going to dance with someone of the opposite sex.'

'Damn,' said Kit. 'I was hoping you'd save the last waltz for me.'

They tottered out soon afterwards, back to the Crillon, where Albert found them a gramophone and Buster lowered the needle on to his newly acquired record: Lucienne Delyle and 'Sur Les Quais du Vieux Paris'. Savouring chilled Lanson they played it until they knew the words by heart. In time it would become, for Kit at least, an instant evocation of that pause in history, both bitter-sweet and brimming with menace.

'Well,' said Buster, the outline of the *mairie* sharply silhouetted against the sky, 'I'm buggering off. Shut-eye calls.' For moments Kit could hear him quietly humming the song's refrain, then the sound faded and died away. Soon he would stumble back to his own billet and Madame Bergeret, with her bizarre hot bricks. He wondered if any of the other chaps were treated to hot bricks. He'd never know – it was too ridiculous to mention.

On some freak of wind Kit picked up the growl of the Bedford lorry that had collected them at Bar-le-Duc station, stuttering through the gears on the stiff climb up the winding lane to the aerodrome at Revigncourt three miles away. The smell of autumn was strong now, that acrid blend of damp earth and leaves, wood and coal smoke drifting from the cottage chimneys, sheep and cattle hunched against the hedgerows to escape the sapping drizzle. Yet the sky was clear. He remembered cycle rides on nights like this, exploring the Wiltshire Downs with Hodges and Dawson-Smith, guided by the Plough, making their way reluctantly back to college after some expedition or other, to Silbury or Avebury or East Kennet, past the ancient barrows and standing stones wreathed in mist and Iron Age forts where they fancied spectral warriors strode the ramparts. And here the Plough still glittered in the ink-black night sky, occasionally obscured by drifting cloud but always emerging, unchanged, unchanging.

At the Gare de l'Est there had been brief hilarity when the members of the squadron met up once again: extravagant claims of successes with women, how many beers they'd downed, how little sleep they'd had in forty-eight hours. A few first-timers had taken in the sights, the Eiffel Tower, Sacre Coeur, even hanging about uncertainly outside flea-bitten bordellos in Montmartre where they agreed they didn't want to catch something and sidled off with plaintive cries of '*Attendez*' floating after them. At the terminus, fatigue clawed at their spirits and the yarns fell away. No one believed them anyway.

Kit alone had arrived in Paris with a chore to accomplish – perhaps not such a chore because he had always been fond of the Maierscheldts but the duty call he had promised to make had come on top of Brewster volunteering him for the CBS shenanigans. Still, he had obediently made his way on Saturday morning to the rue du Faubourg St-Honoré to meet Maurice Maierscheldt at the appointed time. On the telephone, Maierscheldt had apologised that he would be alone: his wife and Hannah were involved in the final stages of mounting some ambitious retrospective of stained glass produced by the works in Nancy. 'However, *mon cher* Kit, I understand you are stationed not so far from us there so, no doubt, you will find your way to see us all in due course. For the moment, though, you will have to make do with me.'

But even he was absent: he had left an apologetic note with the sullen concierge, explaining that some crisis with the exhibition had arisen that demanded his immediate return. The concierge tut-tutted at the ill-luck of it. He was desolated, he told Kit with a mendacious smile. *Quel dommage.*

Damn and blast, thought Kit. He could hear his mother now: 'Yes, I imagined it would be too much to ask. Of course, I quite understand you must be frightfully busy with all your other more important interests. No, don't explain. It's all too tiresome. More and more one has to carry out the simplest tasks oneself.'

In the corridor of the train to Bar-le-Duc Kit had come across Ossie Wolf, leaning on the window bar smearing away the condensation with a brawny hand and glaring out at the flat plains of Lorraine streaming past in a darkening blur as they rattled eastwards. The man was slow to make room for him.

'I lost track of you at La Vosgienne, Sergeant,' said Kit.

'We'd just about drunk the place dry. Went looking for a new waterhole.'

'I meant to say, you did an okay job with the CBS chap.'

'Only okay, huh?'

'Yes, only okay. Your views on our allies didn't go down too well.'

'Says who?'

'Says our friend Pringle mainly.' Finally Ossie Wolf straightened up but Kit didn't push past him immediately. 'I was interested to hear about your experiences in Spain.'

'Is that right?'

'Yes, I didn't know.'

'Why should you?'

'That's right, why should I?'

'I mean, what do I know about you?'

'See you later, Wolf.'

'Yeah.' He caught Kit's arm. 'Tell me, what did that dame have to say for herself?'

'Which dame?' said Kit, knowing very well. 'Oh, her. She wanted me to treat you all to the Folies Bergère.'

'No kidding?'

'Yes, very much kidding, I'm afraid. Actually, I haven't got a clue what she was after, but she looked like trouble to me Sergeant.' Kit looked him straight in the eye. 'Was she?'

'Nothing I couldn't handle,' said Ossie.

At Bar-le-Duc the pilots tumbled out of the station and told Corporal Evans to turn off the Bedford's engine and join them as they knocked up the patron of the Hôtel de la Gare and convinced him to open the bar. He took it in good part and, with the usual hearty '*Vive la France, Vive l'Angleterre, à bas les Boches*', popped a bottle or two of cheap champagne. Dinghy Davis farted hugely after his first glass and said: 'Well, if the Hun doesn't get me cirrhosis will.'

'They ought to bottle that, Davis,' said Buster Brown, holding a handkerchief over his face, 'and drop it on Berlin.'

Corporal Evans, emboldened by his first encounter with fizz, said: 'Had a bit of a jolly have we, gentlemen?'

'Too right Corporal,' cried Dinghy. 'A toast, chaps.' He held up his glass. 'Here's to the hero in our midst.'

'Who's the hero?' said Evans.

'Sergeant Wolf,' said Dinghy. 'Star of scrage and steen.'

'Stage and screen,' said Buster Brown.

'That's what I said. But wireless first, yes, 2LO calling, 2LO calling.'

'Jesus, Dinghy,' said Ossie. 'Put a goddammed sock in it.'

'Just like the Yanks to play the bloody hero,' said Buster Brown.

Ossie Wolf rapped his glass on the bar so hard that the stem broke. He was on his feet and thrusting his face into Buster Brown's. Brown pushed him away impatiently but the American came back on him.

'That's out of line Buster,' said Kit. 'Absolutely out of line.'

'Very possibly, but I have an excellent excuse.'

'Oh? What's that?'

'I'm pissed.'

Dinghy pushed himself between the antagonists, Ossie Wolf shaking with resentment and Buster Brown leaning back on his stool and waving away the American as one might brush away a fly. He was grinning hugely. 'Don't get into such a bate old boy. It'll shorten your life. Have another drink, for God's sake. We're all heroes here. *Patron*, another bottle of this disgusting brew you have the cheek to call champagne.'

'No,' said Kit, 'we're calling it a day before someone lays you out cold.'

'And who's going to do that may I ask?'

'Me, if necessary. Move.'

Buster Brown stood up, adjusted his battered service cap with some dignity so that it shielded his eyes from the lights, which seemed suddenly unpleasantly bright, and proceeded with an excess of care out of the door and across the car park to the Bedford parked in front of the station. On the short journey to Fonteville he and Ossie Wolf found themselves sitting side by side.

'Hey,' said Buster eventually.

'Something eating you, buddy?'

Buster nudged the American hard in the ribs and his teeth showed white in the darkness. They both laughed long and low. Close by, Kit relaxed.

Now, still relishing the silence, he headed away from the Fonteville *mairie*, down the rue de L'Église towards the straggle of squat buildings that comprised the raggle-taggle Bergeret farm. Almost immediately, despite the hour, a light in the hall answered his tentative knock. Madame Bergeret had been waiting for him.

'Madame, I'm sorry . . .'

'Ah, Monsieur, you are safely returned.' She scurried off into the cavernous kitchen and returned with a tray. 'Your bricks.' She shivered dramatically to suggest the extreme cold that called for hot bricks in his bed.

'Madame, you should not trouble yourself,' said Kit as though to a penurious aunt who insisted on costly fruitcake for a favourite nephew.

Madame Bergeret puffed out her cheeks dismissively. 'It is a small reward for what you give us, Monsieur. Besides, it is pleasant to look after a man again. It makes the house feel . . . alive once more.' Then she turned him in the direction of his room at the back of the farmhouse and gave him a gentle push. 'My child, you smell as though you have been enjoying your-self in that wicked city. What time in the morning?'

'Three,' said Kit. 'The lorry will collect us at half past.'

'Sleep well,' said Madame Bergeret, closing his door. Her voice came softly from the corridor. 'Enjoy the bricks.'

*　　*　　*

In the bare, icy room of the clay-walled peasant house, close by the church of Saint-Saulve, Ossie Wolf had no such comforts. He turned and twisted under the meagre quilt, damp with perspiration despite the chill. He was in that drowsing state in which dreams and reality blend: the bark of a dog or the whine of a sudden gust of wind around the eaves became part of his turbulent visions. There were distant clatters and bangs, too, as Monsieur Paturel complained to himself about the cursed airmen who had descended on his village and disturbed an honest man's slumbers. Ossie did not reckon Paturel was an honest man: he was sullen and hostile, resentful of having an Allied pilot foisted on him, fearing reprisals if the Boches came; and he had that shrewd eye for the main chance possessed by many country folk who scratch a living from the soil. Ossie detested the slippery bastard, a tyrant to his shadow of a wife and brutal with his beasts. But Paturel was of the real world and, for the moment, Ossie was in a land of fantasy . . .

He seemed to be on the Champs-Élysées but drifting, not walking, and the street-lights were strung down the broad avenue like pearls, their glow reflected on the face of the girl beside him. Kind of weird, he thought, no blackout now. A rod of brilliant light poured from a spotlight, picking out the obelisk in the place de la Concorde. They were gliding through traffic, cars, vans, trucks and buses, all with headlights ablaze and horns sounding a crazy serenade. They were passing through a gold-leafed gate into the Tuileries but even here lamps lit the gravel pathways and lanterns twinkled among the trees. Ossie and the girl made no sound on the gravel, which he found disturbing, until he remembered they were drifting not walking. He felt himself guided gently into a darker place, hedged around with sweet-smelling box. They seemed to hang in the air with the subtle scent. She was looking up to be kissed. He felt her small cold hand on him, his urgent response and the thrill of fulfilment, her lips on his and her tongue in his mouth . . .

He was awake. Sonofabitch, had it really happened like that?

Something had. He touched his lips as though the touch might tell him. He felt bleak, disappointed and alone. Somewhere outside Paturel was bawling at his animals or at Madame – impossible to tell: the tone was the same. Ossie could see it was growing light. He reached for his watch – three fifteen. He lay back, fully conscious now, and thought of Paris. It was true what they said, then, about Ed Nielsen's goddammed City of Light. Something had touched his shrivelled soul there. He remembered the girl's shining face as they stood round the corner from the Gare de l'Est where the guys were assembling to catch the train back to Bar-le-Duc. His heart had been pounding like a high-school virgin on his first date.

'Maybe I can see you next time Bébé.'

'Next time?'

'Next time I'm in Paris.'

'Maybe, yes.'

'How can I find you?'

'Oh, you will find me.'

'No – I mean where do you live?'

'Paris is very small. You will find me.'

'This is crazy, not telling me where you live.'

'Yes, isn't it? Goodbye.' She kissed his cheek.

'Yeah, *au revoir*.'

And in an instant she was no longer with him and he was just a guy on his own in a foreign city waiting for a train. Crazy. But then, as he knew now, things happened in the City of Light . . .

Seven

Thursday, 2 November 1939

It looked at first like a Blenheim at high altitude, 20,000 feet or more, crawling westwards, a streak of white vapour marking its course against the thin ice clouds of cirrostratus. A dazzling halo radiated from the sun and forced the B Flight pilots, at Readiness and suddenly on their feet, to shield their eyes as they craned their heads to identify the lumbering machine. On the gramophone Gracie Fields was shrilling 'Wish Me Luck As You Wave Me Goodbye'. Kit shouted to Dwyer, the duty corporal: 'For God's sake, get that woman to put a sock in it.' The needle was snatched up with a hiss and a scratch and they could make out the distant oscillation of the aircraft's engines.

'It's not a bloody Blenheim you know,' said Buster Brown. 'I reckon that's a Hun.'

Now Kit's keen eyes could discern the machine's light blue belly, the long-nosed fuselage with its distinctive pencil shape, the twin-finned tailplane, even a suggestion of bold black crosses beneath the wings. 'You're right by God. I think it's a ruddy Dornier.' It was the first enemy aircraft they had seen.

Brewster had bustled across from his office. 'What's the flap about?'

'Dornier we think, sir. Looks like a reconnaissance flight.'

'Well, don't stand there thinking about it Curtis. You and Brown go and get the bugger.'

131

They ran for their machines, dragging on their flying gear. As usual the ground-crews had parked the Hurricanes nose-into-wind and run up their engines periodically to keep them warm. They were quickly airborne, mouths bone dry, going through their cockpit drill, trying to stay calm, and eagerly scanning the sky for their quarry. At 3,000 feet they lost sight of him, cursing with frustration, gun-sights on, gun-buttons set, ready to go, ready to go at last. Then they picked him up again, still on a westward course but lower now, dropping to 18,000 feet. Their Merlins on boost-override they climbed to intercept him, coming in from astern with the pale sun behind them. Buster was rocking backwards and forwards in his cockpit, urging on the Hurricane as though he was riding a horse. His goggles were still pushed up on his forehead. Kit could see his eyes dancing above the oxygen mask. He asked himself whether he was ready to kill.

A fly had become trapped in the cockpit. It zoomed dizzyingly around Kit's head, terrified, as he tried to crush it. Occasionally, it settled somewhere out of sight; then, as he relaxed, it would flash back into frenzied activity bouncing off the canopy and the instrument panel, then jinking away as he slapped down with his gloved open palm, always missing. Finally it landed, fleetingly, on his right knee and he squashed it with an oath. It was full of blood. He brushed it away. Was it such a simple matter, then, this business of taking life?

Cloud had built up as the two Hurricanes swept further west, gaining on the Dornier, which throbbed through the thin atmosphere absorbed in its scrutiny of the hostile landscape, unaware of a more immediate threat closing fast. Then, clearly following its flight plan, the bomber banked gently to starboard, towards the distant haze hanging over Verdun, still ignorant of the British fighters. Hunted and hunters dipped through broken cloud, thin sheets of stratus that obscured the ground far below. The Dornier pilot put his machine into a gradual shallow dive to regain his view of the Allied positions and, in that fraction of time, was lost to his pursuers. Kit was flying blind. He snapped his R/T send button. 'Where are you, Buster?'

'Dunno.'

'Don't hit me, dammit.'

'Okay.'

It was the last that Kit heard from him until they met up later in the day. He pushed forward on the control column and barrelled out of the cloud cover in a steep downward curve. To his astonishment the Dornier was dead ahead but slightly below, its port flank turned towards him, perhaps a thousand yards away. He threw the Hurricane into a vertical turn to starboard and momentarily blacked out, the G-force tearing at his eye-sockets. He was yanking the controls in frantic and violent movements, forcing the machine into an attack position from below, instinctive actions dictated by some distant element of his brain. But the pilot of the Dornier, alerted at last, dived away almost vertically. Lazy trails of glowing tracer, like fireflies, streamed from its mid-upper 7.9mm MG-15s. The Hun gunner had an eye all right. In a luminous stream the tracer was tracking Kit's descent and working closer, closer, not fireflies now but zipping past like lethal steel hornets until he crossed its path and felt the machine shudder with the impact of the bullets. There was a curious *pit-oom* and the cockpit filled with engine smoke and dust that had come up from the floor. Hot glycol plastered his goggles and there was oil on the windscreen. Christ! He was on fire!

He thrust back the hood and, gripping the sagging control column with his left hand, seized the securing clip of the Sutton harness with his right. Then he realised there was no fire. He sank back into his seat. He was down to 2,000 feet but level. He pulled off his useless goggles and scanned the sky. He expected to see the Dornier sweeping in for the kill but there was nothing: it had vanished. He checked his instruments: the cluster of dials on the starboard side of the panel had taken damage – the needle of the oil-pressure gauge was rising and falling wildly, fragments of metal had shattered the compass, penetrated the rate-of-climb and turn indicators and taken out the radio. But the kite was still flying, he knew where he was and resolved to have a good go at getting her back. He snapped the guard on his gun-button to safe and then it struck him that he hadn't fired a shot.

Twenty miles to the north of the airfield Kit realised he wasn't going to make it. He was losing oil pressure rapidly: streams of fluid were flowing back over the port wing. A line must have ruptured. If the engine seized it would almost certainly catch fire. The radiator temperature gauge was off the clock. Immense waves of heat were sweeping back over him. The dogged Merlin began to miss a beat here and there. If he lost all power now, at a thousand feet, it would be catastrophic. He had lost his chance to throttle up, make height and jump for it. He realised that quite possibly he was about to die and felt oddly resigned to it. Below, the countryside was a confusion of small fields with straggling, sturdy-looking hedgerows and many trees, but then, as he dipped a wing, he glimpsed to starboard a single, larger area, a meadow almost, beside a winding stream that reminded him of Wales. The ground climbed, gently at first, towards a jumble of dwellings gathered round a square-towered church on the edge of the escarpment. There was no time for an exploratory pass. It would have to do.

By now the machine was increasingly reluctant to respond to the controls, yawing violently as though the tailplane had also taken some damage; perhaps an elevator jammed or shot away. Juggling the throttle, rudder and what little elevator movement still remained, he turned into wind. Wheels up or down? Down it was. From what he had seen he reckoned a three-point landing was on: just plop her down and redeem himself a little. He throttled back as much as he dared, mixture rich, pitch lever to fine, 140 m.p.h. on the air-speed indicator, flaps down, 85 m.p.h. now, holding off and holding off, level with the tree-tops, now below them, everything quiet except for the burble of the Merlin and the whine of the slipstream round the open hood. At any second he expected the sore-pressed engine to cough and die; then 64 m.p.h., stick gently back and she stalled gently: a perfect three-pointer. The Hurricane was barely moving now, rumbling and bouncing to a halt and then it dug a wheel in on soft ground and neatly somersaulted on to its back.

Kit hung upside down from his straps. The top of his leather helmet was touching the grass. So many chaps had died like this in training – heaving a sigh of relief, snapping their Sutton harness and breaking their necks. In the distance somewhere he could hear cattle bellowing; then approaching voices. The raw country smells mingled with the stench of escaping oil and petrol. The shattered Merlin was ticking like a bomb.

An aged peasant was crouching beside him, astounded, shouting over his shoulder. Kit hung there, waiting for the Hurricane to explode. A second man appeared with a spade and began to dig methodically as though he were preparing a trench for potatoes. A third peasant pulled away the earth with his hands, excavating a space below Kit's head and shoulders. Somehow they supported him as he freed himself from his harness. He took his weight on the palms of his gauntlets flat on the grass and eased himself down, twisting and writhing through the tiny gap, scrabbling free on his hands and knees.

The peasants, their torn work-clothes plastered with mud, crowded round him, clapping him on the back, laughing. He thanked them politely, then pulled away and walked round the inverted Hurricane. It was thoroughly peppered, the fuselage behind the cockpit riddled, and a gaping hole in the shredded port elevator he could have put a leg through. The undercarriage stuck up jauntily, the struts and wheels undamaged. The Frenchmen tried to raise him on their shoulders but he resisted and walked a little apart from them, occupied with his thoughts, towards the nearby hamlet where more villagers were gathering. At the *mairie* of Les Charmontois, watched by a curious crowd, he phoned for transport.

By the time the Bedford arrived with Corporal Evans at the wheel he had downed a glass or two of *vin rouge* to toast unspecified acts of heroism and was somewhat the worse for wear. The rough red wine softened the pain of failure: the first real show and he had let himself down, the others too. Oh, yes, for good reasons – that damned freaky cloud cover, the anxious moments when it seemed he must collide with Buster and he had taken his eye off the ball, the ill-chance that the Dornier crew included a skilful pilot and a gunner who knew his stuff, and the undercarriage digging in like that – but who cared about excuses?

He walked back down the hill to the stranded Hurricane with Corporal Evans, flattening a path through the rustling grasses of the soft meadow.

'Good grief sir. Bit of a mess, isn't she? What was it? That ruddy Dornier?'

'Yes, that ruddy Dornier.'

'Flying Officer Brown made it back all right sir,' said Evans. 'Seems you lost track of each other in all the excitement.'

'Something like that,' said Kit. He could imagine the chit-chat and speculation running round the squadron.

'She'll take a bit of getting out,' said Evans, circling the wreck. 'I'd better get it sorted.' He started back up the hill.

'Get some camouflage netting Corporal,' Kit shouted after him. 'She may be salvageable and we don't want the Hun finishing her off.'

'Don't you worry about that sir,' said Evans. 'The main thing is you're all right.'

A lump rose in Kit's throat. Such an ordinary remark, uttered with hardly a thought, but he felt absurdly grateful.

* * *

At Revigncourt something was up. The pilots were standing around their aircraft in small, animated groups. They were boisterous, loud, and there was a high pitch of hilarity that suggested something special had happened. The ground-crews, too, were shouting and laughing, pushing and pulling at each other like children in a playground. As Kit climbed down from the cab of the Bedford the CO came out of his Nissen hut, with Spy Turner scurrying behind. 'Give Spy a thorough rundown Kit. I gather the Fordson's gathering up the battered remains.'

'I'm afraid she's almost certainly a write-off sir. I thought I'd got away with it and then a wheel dug in.'

'I've heard all about it. You should have gone for a belly landing, boy or, even better, a brolly-hop. I can always replace aeroplanes but I don't want to lose my pilots. Next time, jump.'

'Yes sir.'

Brewster slapped his arm. 'Don't look so despondent. Give Spy the gen and get yourself a drink.'

'What's all the fuss about, sir?'

'Our damned Yankee downed a Dornier. Spy's been quizzing him. Get anything out of him Turner?'

'Just the bare bones.'

'He's opened our score anyway,' said Brewster. 'Now we're in business.'

In his small office Turner carefully recorded Kit's terse account of his flight in blue ink on a buff form and placed it in his out tray.

'What happens now?'

'Nothing old boy. You don't get a bill for the aeroplane or anything like that. We'll find you another one.' He paused. 'Just jolly bad luck that's all. On the other hand,' he said, 'you could say it's jolly good luck that you lived to tell the tale.'

'Sounds as though the luck's all with Sergeant Wolf.'

'Not much luck involved there, I'd say. He was already in his cockpit, all strapped in and the engine nicely warmed, just waiting for something to happen. Sure enough, this Dornier comes stooging west at twenty thousand, same as yours. Seems the Hun never learns. Naturally Wolf gets the drop on everybody, beetles off without orders, absolutely typical of course, and downs the blighter. Simple as that. He was back in twenty minutes, demanding a Kronenbourg.' Turner glanced at Kit curiously. 'I say, he's in your flight, isn't he?'

'Yes.'

'You'd better congratulate him then. One up to B Flight, eh?'

'Absolutely.'

'Get your skates on,' said Turner, 'and you can join in the fun.'

'What fun is that?'

'We nabbed the Dornier pilot. Came down by 'chute just this side of Fonteville. Straight in the ruddy river. The locals were getting ready to stick their pitchforks in him but we got there just in time. Seems quite a decent cove. We're giving him a little supper before the French whisk him away.'

'What about his crew?'

'No news of them. They jumped all right. They're probably in the bag by now. Actually,' Turner added, suddenly serious, 'you should know, as Wolf's flight commander, that he's being distinctly sticky about this whole business.'

'What whole business?'

'Sending the Hun on his way with a few celebratory drinks inside him.'

'Sticky how?'

'He refuses to attend.'

'On what grounds?' said Kit.

'Well, the way he put it to me,' said Turner, 'was that earlier this afternoon he'd been out to kill the man and if he turns up for this shindig he might well be tempted to finish the job.'

'I can understand why he'd say that.'

'You surprise me Curtis. I had you down as a different sort of fellow.'

'For God's sake, I didn't say I agreed with him. I said I could understand why he'd say it.' Then: 'Sorry, Spy. Rather an eventful day.' He stood up. 'I'll talk to Wolf, see what I can do. No promises, mind. You know how he is.'

'Oh, yes, we all know how he is. But still, he's opened our account. You've got to give him that.'

'Yes you've got to give him that.'

Kit found Buster Brown playing cricket. Someone had just started a makeshift game to let off steam. The Kiwi Eddie Knox was hammering Dinghy Davis for six after six. Every minute or so Buster would scamper into the long grass looking for the ball: a six-seamed Dukes that Brewster used as a paper-weight. He shouted to Kit: 'I can find the ruddy ball but I couldn't find you.' He threw it back to Beaky Parker, who was keeping. It skimmed in, just over the stumps, slapping into Parker's gloves.

'Good throw,' said Kit.

Buster stretched out on the grass, selected a blade and began to chew the stem. 'I hear you've written off your kite.'

'Can we change the subject?'

'Wheels-down landing in a Froggie boggie. Bit bloody risky.'

'A meadow, actually,' said Kit. 'What's the score?'

'No idea, old boy. Not sure we're even keeping one. Anyway, about you going arse over tit—' There was a bellow from Dinghy Davis. Buster leapt to his feet and rushed to a skied ball. It fell through his fingers to an ironic cheer. 'Bugger.' He was panting, droplets of sweat trickling into his eyes from his hairline.

'Have you seen Wolf?' said Kit. 'I want a word.'

'You might not get one back,' said Buster. 'Anyway, no, he seems to have made himself scarce. Odd type, our colonial cousin.' He spat out fragments of chewed grass. 'Sorry we got ourselves in a bit of a muddle by the way.'

'That's all right. Damned cloud.'

'Yes, bloody cloud.'

Kit found Wolf attending to his machine. Two LACs were carrying out refuelling from a towable bowser. A corporal armourer was feeding belted .303 ammunition into the starboard wing magazines. Ossie Wolf watched, leaning against the ammunition trolley, constantly offering advice and suggestions. The airmen seemed to take it in good part, grinning and laughing in easy exchanges.

'I gather you've done B Flight proud,' said Kit.

'B Flight?' Ossie said. 'Len, careful with that feed. Take it nice and easy feller.'

'Okay Ossie,' said the corporal.

Kit was struck by their relaxed tone, the casual use of Christian names. 'A damned good show Sergeant. I just wanted—'

'Yeah, okay,' said Ossie. He shouted to the armourer: 'That's the way Len. Nice and easy does it.'

'You've probably heard,' said Kit. 'Flying Officer Brown and I weren't so lucky.'

'Luck had nothing to do with it.'

'No,' said Kit. 'That's what Spy Turner told me.' He walked slowly round the Hurricane. There wasn't a mark on her, apart from the paintwork aft of the exhaust stubs, blackened in the usual way, and black streaks of cordite running back across the wings from the recessed muzzles of the Brownings. The crew hadn't replaced the gun patches yet. 'Did the Hun loose off at you at all?' said Kit.

'Oh yeah.'

'Anything come close?'

'Nope.'

'I understand you're not joining our little party,' said Kit at last, trying to keep his tone light, leaving the American a chance to change his mind, climb down from his damned ivory tower.

'That's right.'

'May I ask why?'

'I'm not a hypocrite I guess.'

'Perhaps you'd prefer us to put the fellow up against a wall and shoot him.'

'Perhaps I would.'

Kit realised that the airmen were listening. He took Ossie by the elbow and moved him out of earshot. 'I can't order you to attend but I think it's a pity.'

'Are you done?'

'Yes Sergeant. Allow me to add that I think your conduct is reprehensible.'

'Noted,' said Wolf.

The reception for the German pilot fell flat. He spoke no English and seemed suspicious and wary, bemused by the jollity around him. His face remained set; he accepted only a single tumbler of wine mixed with water. He was correct, cold and remote and one by one the pilots lost interest in him and talked shop among themselves. Only Brewster, Kit and Spy Turner continued to make the effort.

The German came from Bad Ems on the Rhine. Kit had been there, rowing for Marlborough, and there was a momentary spark of interest. But it passed as quickly as it had come, leaving the man nervous and distracted again. Kit imagined he was trying to come to terms with losing his aircraft and crew, struggling with suffocating guilt, trying to rewrite in his mind the pattern of events, thinking of what he might have done for things to turn out differently; emotions that left no room for the relief that he had survived. Kit could identify with that. And it certainly left no space either, he thought, for light-hearted celebrations with a hutful of strangers who, only hours before, had been eager for his death. So different, the reality, from Kit's Great War yarns in which RFC aces toasted a monocled Prussian baron in vintage Mumm.

Now the German was pointing at the absorbed pilots and asking something. It became plain that he wanted to know who had shot him down. Perhaps in identifying and assessing his foe, Kit speculated, he might be seeking to come to terms with his defeat. Brewster made excuses as best he could. No one could bring himself to admit that the man who had brought him down still wished him ill. But somehow the German seemed to sense it, became sad and thoughtful. To their alarm tears started in his eyes.

'Good God, man,' said Brewster impatiently, 'get a grip.'

Kit hurriedly passed him a clean handkerchief. He seized it and blew his nose loudly, sniffed several times, then recovered himself and stood straighter. 'Get a grip,' he repeated. '*Ich verstehe nicht.*'

'Just as well,' said Spy Turner. There were smiles now at the German's comic English.

'War no good,' he said.

'You started it, old boy,' snapped Brewster.

'*Ich verstehe nicht.*'

'No,' said Brewster. 'Neither does anybody else.'

It was a relief to them all when the prisoner chose to remove himself to Brewster's office and wait for his French escort there. As he moved to the door there was a feeble attempt at camaraderie, a handshake or two, a slap on the back. '*Auf wiedersehen. Danke.* War no good.'

'You're right there chum,' shouted someone. 'You should have thought of that earlier.' There was a burst of laughter.

'Probably just as well that Wolf wasn't here,' Brewster said. 'Where is the bugger?'

'Out for the count on his bed,' said Turner.

'Rum, Spy, bloody rum. Still, as long as he knocks down Hun I'm not complaining.' He looked at Kit. 'Glad you made it. I'd hate to have to write a note to your mother.'

Kit imagined her opening such a note, could see Agnes Hobbes bringing it to her at the satinwood writing-table by the oval window overlooking the Lutyens pond. She would scan it quickly, deciding whether she was interested or not. And then? Would she colour and weep? Or would she compose her features into the face of a grieving mother, then sally forth to find someone to tell?

Eight

Saturday, 18 November 1939

Leave came round every three weeks or so, depending on Brewster's needs and mood, proper leave, two or three days to wile away in Bar-le-Duc, Metz or Nancy if funds were tight, or Paris if they weren't. Since the day Ossie Wolf had bagged his Dornier the weather had closed in, constant rain and poor visibility, the river valley flooded, the cattle wading in dun-coloured water, even the streets of the village threatened. There was mud everywhere, spattering clothes and dragged into dwellings, the household animals stiff with it. The higher ground of Revigncourt escaped the floods but was swept with high wind and enveloped in racing clouds. No flying, not for them, not for the Hun. After the jubilation of the squadron's first victory it was an anticlimax.

Late on Friday evening the Chemin de l'Est service from Bar-le-Duc had trundled without stopping through the Station Pantin and across the viaduct spanning the intersection of the rue de Flandre and the porte de la Villette, then tackled the multitude of points guiding it to its destination against the buffers of the terminus. Its wheels screeched and rattled in protest and the passengers were rocked against each other as though by some seismic force. There were smiles and amused apologies. The old woman seated across from Ossie Wolf cradled her reed basket of brown eggs covered with a blue check cloth and said: '*Comme un tremblement de terre, Monsieur.*'

144

'*Oui, Madame,*' he said, not really understanding but guessing her meaning.

She nodded and turned to stare out of the window. She had a stiff neck and, Ossie reckoned, a hard life. They were passing huge locomotives gasping in sidings, belching steam and hauling open trucks or carriages darkened for the blackout. The glow of flames glimmered from the cabs where coal-crusted crews in singlets and scarves, peaked caps worn back to front and topped with goggles in the manner of old-time racing drivers, spun brass wheels and thrust fuel into bellowing furnaces with steel shovels. Occasionally they vanished in huge wafts of white and grey steam and it was hard to believe they were still there. It reminded Ossie of the stroll he had taken round the base a few days back, seeing the parked-up Hurricanes fading into the mist, everything running wet, his breath showing with the cold. Hard to believe the fighters were still there.

The city was dank and chilled. Dinghy Davis wanted to pop in for a Pernod at the Bar Pom-Pom just round the corner from the Gare de l'Est in the rue d'Alsace. He had heard about Pernod from Eddie Knox, who had told him that when you drank it you knew you had had a drink. He wanted to try it on this leave. Ossie pulled him past. 'For Christ's sake, Dinghy, lay off the Pernod. Sink one and in five minutes you'll be thinking about killing yourself.'

They checked into the Hôtel Villemin opposite the small green park in the rue du St Recollets, shabby but adequate. The *patron* remembered them from last time. He greeted them cordially and asked for their news.

Dinghy opened his mouth. Ossie shot him a glance and Dinghy shrugged. '*Rien?*' said the *patron*. '*Vraiment?*' He shrugged too, as though befuddled by the Drôle de Guerre. So many forces gathered on the border and no one had anything to report. Perhaps even now the politicians would realise the folly of it. Then everyone could return to their homes, including the two English pilots with their brave wings on their breasts, their excellent machines and no one to fight except maybe *les poules*.

They took separate rooms, not like before, washed, shaved and clattered down the gloomy staircase into the box-like lobby, where the *patron* sat behind the desk in a cloud of cigarette smoke. He told them of a little place down by the canal St Martin, quite close by, where the dockers and barge crews ate, a *menu simple*, plain and tasty cooking, like roasted lamb and haricot beans or chicken in a casserole with garlic and herbs, filling and cheap, with baskets of bread and jugs of *vin rouge* included in the price. That night it was *pot au feu*, Alsace-style, with light dumplings made from the marrow of beef bones. Good, yes, very good, as the *patron* had said it would be, and after a selection of cheese and *tarte Tatin*, coffee and Armagnac the pilots felt warm, full and satisfied. A pleasant fatigue crept over them as they ambled slowly back to the Villemin along the tree-lined quai de Valmy, with the canal like a spill of ink on their left and water swirling and gurgling in the unseen depths of the locks. Near the hotel Dinghy said: 'You know what? I think I'm ready for that Pernod now.'

'Don't be a mug.'

'That's the trouble,' Dinghy said. 'I am a mug. A happy mug.' He continued on, a little shakily, leaving Ossie by the hotel door. The *patron* had heard them and peered out.

'I'm coming in,' said Ossie.

'*Eh bien*,' said the *patron*, standing back and holding open the door. '*Un bon repas?*'

Ossie nodded absently. 'Hey,' he called.

'What?' said a distant voice.

'I got plans tomorrow.' He heard Dinghy stop, turn and listen.

'I thought you might have.'

'Yeah, I'll catch you some time, tell you what's cooking.'

'Don't mention cooking.'

'Go easy on the Pernod.'

'Okay. You know what?'

'What?'

'You should stop me. I might decide to kill myself.'

'Goodnight, you mug.'

'Goodnight, Daddy.'

And Ossie went up the few steps into the hotel, past the *patron*, climbed the dark stairs and unlocked the door of his room. He was asleep in minutes, his uniform thrown over the pine chair beside his bed. He began to dream of searching for the girl down streets that seemed to be Paris streets but weren't quite. There was something screwy about the way they twisted and turned and always brought him back to the Hôtel Villemin where Dinghy Davis was waiting for him on the step and saying he was ready for a Pernod.

At about seven thirty Ossie went down to the small breakfast room and drank cheap orange juice, ate two croissants with apricot jam and worked his way through a jug of black coffee. He was on his own: Dinghy's snores had reverberated along the narrow landing with the regularity and power of a foghorn.

The city was awash with a meagre golden light and water from the street-cleaners' trucks. The filth of the night before was being swept down gutters, into drains and out of sight as Paris prepared for another day. But the weather quickly closed in and it began to rain again, but lightly, not enough to dishearten the determined walker.

Ossie knew where he was heading. The *patron* had told him how to get there, working west along the rue de Chabrol and left down the rue La Fayette and right into the boulevard Haussmann, then straight ahead. Couldn't have been simpler. Except he took a left, not a right, and found himself crossing the boulevard Poissonnière way south of where he ought to have been. After a stretch, though, things became familiar. He could make out a statue of some kind, gold like the morning light, a dame astride a horse and bearing a banner. Bébé had pointed it out to him when they had come out of the Tuileries into the rue de Rivoli. He looked at the statue now, the Maid of Orléans, armoured, martial, tough-looking. Maybe all Frenchwomen were tough, not soft and indulged like their American sisters who had never known war or its effects. Bébé had steel in her for sure.

The equestrian statue stood in front of a decent-looking hotel partly hidden by the pillars of a stone arcade. The Regina ran to five storeys, the lead roof topped by a gallant tricolour, stretched in the wind like the one borne by Jeanne d'Arc. Inside, there was a grey and cream check-tiled floor, elaborately carved wood and gilded chandeliers dripping with Italian glass. It was the right kind of place for Bébé, Ossie thought, not the flea-bitten Villemin with its matchwood furniture and Dinghy rattling the thin partition walls. Maybe he'd check in, find the money somehow or sweet-talk the pretty girl at the desk, use his uniform, his nationality, to cut himself some credit; everyone in Paris seemed to believe all Americans were millionaires, even Bébé. Maybe he would take a room, but not right now. Still, he sauntered in, asked for the tariff and came out with a fancy brochure.

He carried on down the rue de Rivoli and walked up the Champs-Élysées to La Vosgienne. He was early trade and they were still wiping the place down, but he wanted time with the guys behind the bar. It was too cold to sit outside so he squatted on a stool and ordered café-crème. There was only a handful of customers hunched over their morning fresheners, some foreigners, Americans mostly, and a uniform or two, red-eyed survivors of a heavy night on the town who maybe hadn't even made it to bed.

He recognised the man who clunked his coffee on the marble bar, slopping it into the saucer, but there was no recognition in return.

'I was here about three weeks ago.'

'Ah, *oui*?' The disinterest was slick and professional.

'We sat over there, a group of us. A journalist, Monsieur Nielsen, American. He seemed to be well known here.'

The barman stuck out his lower lip and shook his head,

looking down at the glass he was wiping with a grimy cloth. Ossie placed a ten-franc note on the saucer with the bill.

'Nielsen?' said the man. 'Yes, perhaps.'

'There were also two women,' said Ossie. 'One American, name of Westcott, the other French, younger. They sat over there.' He didn't give Bébé a name. At this time of day, talking to this clown, Bébé sounded absurd: it was a night-time name. But it was the only name she'd given him.

The barman stared at the saucer and Ossie placed a second ten-franc note with the first. 'Ah, *oui*, perhaps I know them, the old one, anyway. Sometimes they amuse themselves by rubbing shoulders with *la foule*.'

'Je ne parle pas français.'

'Of course you don't. It is part of the English charm. *La foule*, it means the vulgar, the ordinary, my clients. You.'

'I'm American,' said Ossie working a fist out of sight. At Nick's Place in downtown St Louis he would have dragged the guy across the counter by his ears and worked him over in the parking lot, except you didn't mess with anything to do with Nick. Instead he said quietly: 'I lost their address.'

'*La mangeuse* gave you her address?' The man seemed surprised.

'*Mangeuse?* What the hell is that anyway?'

'Ah, what should it be, Monsieur? A woman who eats.' The barman laughed at some joke he didn't share.

'The address was somewhere round here,' Ossie said.

'No,' said the barman, performing to type and delighted to correct him. 'Far from here. Left Bank.' He laughed again. 'They like it down there.' He was very amused. 'Your American friend has a reputation. She is one of the monuments of Paris.'

'The Left Bank?' said Ossie. 'Narrow it down a little, feller.' He held a third ten-franc note between his fingers.

'I don't know,' the barman said irritably. 'The quai des Grands Augustins, somewhere there. Ask anybody. She is known, that one.'

'Write the names down. You know I haven't got a brain in my head, like all your clients.' He moved the banknote in his fingers. The barman went for a pencil and scrap of paper by the till. He wrote down the names, his tongue in the corner of his mouth. Good at numbers, not so hot on words, thought Ossie. The man passed over the piece of paper and reached for the banknote, but Ossie twitched it away and replaced it in his pocket. 'Twenty is plenty. Buy some lessons in treating folks nice.'

The barman launched into rapid French, snatching up the twenty francs before Ossie could change his mind. Ossie caught the gist. 'Go chase yourself,' he said.

He didn't feel like walking any more so he picked up a taxi that set him down on the south side of the Pont Neuf. The sky was black behind the bulk of the Palais de Justice on the Île de la Cité. The waters of the Seine were running high, fast and brown with soil leached from thousands of hectares of flooded farmland to the north-west where the river wound its course from the coast at Le Havre. The town had been the squadron's first sight of France two months before and Kit Curtis had done an okay job that day, leading B Flight as the outfit swept low over the town in salute. He really was an okay guy, Ossie had to admit, when it came to stuff like that. But, Christ, the man was so damned English, brainwashed, even: his way, the English way, the only way. There were weaknesses there along with strength, and they would be punished cruelly when the Phoney War stopped being phoney.

Wolf soon located Una Westcott's place on the quai des Grands Augustins. The barman at La Vosgienne had been right. The woman seemed to be as well known as one of the monuments of Paris. The first passer-by Ossie stopped knew exactly where she could be found; several others slowed, hearing the name, and contributed anecdotes and opinions about her that he couldn't understand. She seemed to arouse much amusement.

The apartment was on the top two floors of an old François 1er house on a corner of the *quai* and a narrow street with a dirty name plaque leading to the Quartier Latin. There was nobody home. Ossie descended the serpentine stairway and dug out the concierge, a squat old biddy with the suggestion of a moustache, who was feeding a bunch of cats with last night's leftovers. She gave a dismissive puff of breath. '*La belle* Westcott, *elle est rentrée en l'Amérique.*' So she'd gone. He had overheard a little of what had passed between Bébé and Una Westcott that night in La Vosgienne; she'd meant it, goddammit, but had Bébé gone too? Now the concierge was jawing about some darned *comtesse*. What the hell was that? A countess? A *comtesse russe*? It was just a jumble of words, made no damned sense. He gave it one last shot. 'Bébé. *Vous – vous connaissez Bébé, Madame?*'

'*Oui, oui, la Comtesse Dubretskov.*'

'*Non, Madame, Bébé. Elle est jeune, une jeune femme.*'

'*Oui, oui, la Comtesse Dubretskov. Elle est ici mais pas à présent.*'

'Still here? She remains here now, today? Not gone away? Not gone to America, Madame?'

'*Non. Elle demeure actuellement ici, Monsieur.*'

Then Ossie heard the door to the street bang open and voices speaking English. Bébé looked round the door of the old girl's quarters. 'Madame,' she began, and saw Ossie. 'Oh, you. You are a detective?'

'I needed to be,' said Ossie.

'What do you want?'

'To see you.'

'Why?'

'Crazy, I guess.'

'Yes, very crazy. I cannot talk with you now.'

'So, you're a countess?'

'Yes.'

'A Russian countess. On the level?'

'Yes. It is of no importance. Paris is full of paupers with empty titles. Prince Dishwasher, Count Street-sweeper, Princess Femme de Chambre.'

'You're no pauper.'

A lofty English voice said from the hallway: 'Who on earth are you talking to, darling?'

'Nobody,' said Bébé.

A tall woman was waiting by the foot of the stairs, smartly dressed in the style of an English countrywoman: tweeds, sensible brogues and a broad-brimmed green felt hat. 'Well, say goodbye to nobody. I need a pick-me-up.'

Ossie came out into the hallway and the woman looked him up and down. She had an imperious air. Bébé made no effort to introduce them. The woman sighed. 'Bébé, you're the limit.' She held out her hand. 'I'm Kitty Bannister,' she said, as though it should mean something to him.

'Hi,' he said. He gave her his name.

'Wolf,' she said. 'How appropriate – how wonderfully appropriate. A Russian wench being pursued by a wolf.' She gave a sardonic laugh. 'Darling, I'm gasping. And I'm dying to see what you've done with the place.'

'Well,' said Bébé, 'goodbye.'

Kitty Bannister was starting up the stairs impatiently.

'Is that it?'

'What do you want?'

'I've told you what I want. This is my leave. I thought I'd look you up.'

'Well, you have. Goodbye.'

'Oh, for God's sake, darling, please don't keep poor Kitty dawdling so,' called the English woman halfway up the stairs.

'You can reach me at the Regina. Do you know it?' said Ossie.

'Oh, yes, I know it.'

'You can reach me there.'

'Why would I want to?'

'I don't know. I thought maybe you would. Like I said, crazy, I guess.'

'Yes, very crazy.' She hesitated. 'The Regina . . .'

'Yes, it's very nice there.'

'I know. Well, goodbye.'

'So long, Countess.'

'You are dismissed,' Bébé said, with a slight smile. He thought a lot about that smile later, reading into it whatever he might have been hoping for but seeing things he didn't want to. Jesus Christ, he was going loopy. He stepped out into the light and hailed another taxi. He was going to track down Dinghy Davis at the Hôtel Villemin but he changed his mind. He tapped on the glass partition and told the driver to head for the Regina.

Nine

By now the pilots had come to expect, when they rose each morning, the freezing mists and veils of thin, penetrating rain that drifted over the Meuse, blurring the outlines of the fields, woodland, small hidden valleys and shivering villages, and lending the landscape the appearance of an early photographic plate by Niépce. No flying again, no bloody flying. But this morning: 'My Heavens, my child, it is as though the world has been reborn.' And despite the hour, Madame Bergeret threw back the curtains in her glacial kitchen and stretched out her arms towards the golden light with the rapture and delight of a girl.

A heavy frost encrusted the countryside, blue-white like a fresh snowfall, the crystals shimmering in the rising sun. Gathering by the Bedford outside the Fonteville *mairie*, the pilots drew the crisp, invigorating air into their lungs. Their breath hung in the still atmosphere, undisturbed by the slightest hint of a breeze.

The lorry made its way slowly out of the village and crossed the Ornain where ducks and moorhens were thrashing gilded sprays of water with their wings as though delighting in the magical dawn. The pilots were silent, thoughtful, not contemplating for once the hazards that might lie ahead but thinking back to days when attics were searched for skates and toboggans, when sensible hats and woollen scarves were dug out of drawers and fun was to be had.

As the sun climbed above the low ground mist towards the ice-blue sky its rays pierced the woods round the airfield perimeter. What had been black bulks of dripping vegetation were now revealed as individual trees, their bark catching the light. Between them, rabbits, squirrels and pheasants threw up the rotting leaves questing for food. Above, rooks and crows, jackdaws and pigeons wheeled as though in mockery of dogfights yet to come. Yet higher, a brace of buzzards circled majestically on thermals. The countryside teemed with unsuspected life. Thousands of animal prints criss-crossed the runways and near Dispersal moles had created a midget Alpine range, each summit topped by its own crisp frost-cap.

On the bend of the lane from Fonteville, where it climbed the incline beyond the canal de la Marne au Rhin and skirted the heights of the Revigncourt base, Kit had a favourite grove of trees, or tree: what at first appeared to be three or four grey willows rising forty feet or more apparently grew from one base. Was it really a single specimen or had four saplings simply merged into one trunk? Kit wasn't interested in knowing: he wanted to preserve the almost spiritual significance the willow grove held for him, to leave undisturbed an enchanted place. Now, as tendrils of creeping fog softened the outline of the grove, its almost sinister aura was enhanced by the parasitic clumps of mistletoe, clinging to the branches. For a moment the willow grove was caught in a blaze of light: a vivid blend of gold and silver flickered up and down the serpentine trunks and everything was touched with glinting, luminous frost.

'Sod me,' said Buster Brown, pushing his service cap on to the back of his head as they piled out of the Bedford. 'What a brilliant bloody morning.' The sparkling weather seemed to have had an effect on the CO too. Brewster was in an ebullient mood, stumping back and forth in his heavy boots, blowing on his hands and rubbing them together vigorously. He gathered B Flight together. 'Right, chaps, perhaps this morning we can tempt the Hun to come out and play. I want you to do a sweep along the German border and try to draw the buggers out. Go over as high as possible. Twenty-seven thousand feet should do it, so check your oxygen. And if you run into trouble make sure it's over our territory. You'd look bloody silly if you were taken prisoner.'

With pre-flight checks completed, the early shift usually snatched a nap, brooded over a cup of tea, skimmed through dog-eared copies of *Lilliput* or did the lavatory tour, all the while watching the clock until they received the order for take-off. Kit took particular care in going over his new Hurricane, flown in fresh from Hawker Siddeley's factory at Kingston during a brief break in the weather a week or so before. It was still unfamiliar, a little stiff on the controls, down a touch on power and less nimble than his old machine which, dragged from its meadow at les Charmontois by the Fordson tractor and deposited under camouflage netting by the perimeter fence, was waiting to be cannibalised.

Brewster had taken him aside after the briefing. 'How's your new toy?'

'Excellent thank you sir. Smells like a brand-new Bentley.'

'To hell with its smell. How does it go?'

'Okay.'

'Only okay?'

'It'll be fine.'

'Don't settle for second best, Kit,' said Brewster. 'Get Flight Sergeant Jessop to drive those erks until they get it precisely to your liking. It's your life at stake, not theirs.'

Now, over at Readiness, something was going on. Dark figures appeared to be cavorting outside the hut, eccentric shapes against the dazzling sunrise. Beyond, the ground-crews still fussed and fretted over the Hurricanes, poised like half-glimpsed beasts.

As Kit made his way across, the collar of his sheepskin Irvin high round his neck and ears, he saw a creature stranger than the rest, a character drawn by Rackham for a tale of the Brothers

Grimm. It hooted, yelped and slapped its knees. A tall hat with a wide brim wobbled on its head. Around its throat hung a disc of concertinaed paper, in the style of an ancient ruff. A black cloak hung over the flying jacket and trailed across the frozen puddles. It was Dinghy Davis.

Curious ground-crew were drifting across now, to join the gleeful pilots as they crowded round a bemused Ossie Wolf and cheered on the leaping Dinghy, who saw Kit and shouted: 'Ah, our noble leader. What day is it today?'

'Thursday.'

'Right but wrong. It's more. It's Thanksgiving Day. The day when our colonial cousins celebrate their humble origins even when far from home.' A number of the pilots pretended to weep. 'The day when the Pilgrim Fathers, champions of the Puritan faith, crashed into Plymouth Rock.' Now Kit understood the broad-brimmed headgear fashioned from paper and glue; one fragment, pasted upside-down, proclaimed, 'The Hun Is Not Deaf' – even the CO's office was not safe from light fingers.

Ossie Wolf was grinning reluctantly, head bowed, acknowledging the piss-take. He'd been caught nicely. 'Thanksgiving? Hell,' he said, 'I don't know what any of us has got to be thankful for.'

To a roar of approval Buster Brown appeared, carrying a large cardboard turkey. 'I bagged this bugger dropping propaganda leaflets over Reims,' he cried. 'Answers to the name of Doctor Gobbles.'

'Speech! Speech!' demanded the pilots, as the turkey was thrust into Wolf's hands.

'Well,' said Ossie slowly, 'I've heard a lot about the great British sense of humour and now I know there isn't one.'

'Shame! Shame!'

Ossie inspected the cardboard bird. 'All I need to know from one of you hot-shots is how to fly this bloody thing.'

It was enough. To roars of approval the company came to attention and Dinghy led them in an erratic rendition of 'The

Star-Spangled Banner' with much puffing of cheeks and misplaced oompahs. Then Goofy Gates, who had liberated a metal rod from the fitters, set off at the head of a rag-tag parade round the Readiness hut. From time to time he hurled the twirling rod high into the air, like the leader of a marching band, and cries of protest rose from the straggling mob behind him as it fell dangerously among them.

Kit stood back, content to let the foolery unfold without him. In less than an hour he might be leading some of these men in battle. Ossie Wolf had detached himself from the crowd and was looking on too. He was still cradling the cardboard fowl.

'A good crowd, the best,' said Kit.

'Yeah,' said the American. His voice was flat.

Kit wondered why the man disliked him so much. It was plain in the way he held himself, tense and stiff, ready to move off. 'How did your leave go Sergeant?'

'Fine. The usual.'

'Is Paris ever just the usual?'

Ossie propped the turkey against his legs and folded his arms against the cold. 'Maybe not.'

'You're flying Blue Two, Sergeant. Remember what the CO said about oxygen. Make sure the chaps have got the message.' Without waiting for a reply Kit walked away quickly to double-check his laid-out kit. He amused himself by feeling a stab of satisfaction at beating Ossie Wolf to it. It was a game that two could play – kids' stuff, but satisfying.

The procession was over, the pilots were quietening. Buster Brown cranked up his Lucienne Delyle record. There were groans of protest. 'Please God, Buster, not again. Doesn't old Lucy ever cheer up?'

Kit quickly raised the needle and put the disc aside. He reckoned the chaps needed a dose of something bracing. George Formby twanged his way into action, chirruping some rot about sitting on a mine on the Maginot Line. It didn't strike him as funny – in fact, the fatuous jollity made his blood run cold –

but it seemed to fit the bill. Even Buster, at first pretending to sulk, began to sing along.

Thirty minutes later Control came on the phone from Reims and they were in the air.

At 27,000 feet B Flight had made its height over Metz and banked east for the German border. Kit sat taut in his harness. Usually the apprehension and tension left him as soon as they were in the air. Today was different, yet the sky was clear. The throb of the Merlin, the Brownings armed and ready, poised at the push of the gun-button, his sense of oneness with the aircraft, instinctively guiding, correcting and anticipating its every move: none of these gave him the usual reassurance that he was in control. Odd: conditions had never been better. He should have felt comforted by the knowledge that they had the advantage of any Hun who might materialise, in height and visibility.

The prospect laid out before them was staggering. Confronted by such beauty he experienced the same old compulsion to daydream. The boffins said it was lack of oxygen, but Kit thought there was more to it than that. It was a kind of denial that, in such surroundings, horrible things could happen – a weakness that had to be fought. He turned his attention to the treacherous sun, now climbing fast towards them. Then, in the far distance and 5,000 feet below, he detected tell-tale streaks in the atmosphere.

'Look, there's China,' said Dinghy Davis over the R/T, his voice muffled by his oxygen mask. He was still in high spirits after the success of his Thanksgiving stunt.

'Radio silence,' snapped Kit. He glanced to port at Blue Two. Yards away Ossie Wolf's machine jinked and twitched in the thin atmosphere. The American was glaring straight ahead, goggles up. Then he looked across at Kit, as though he had sensed his scrutiny. He jerked his head towards the distant condensation trails. Kit nodded, twisted in his harness and caught Dinghy's eye. He got a jaunty thumbs-up; no hard feelings. Kit shook his head violently. No, not that, you idiot. He jabbed his gloved

159

finger forward and down, once, twice. He saw Dinghy's eyes widen.

Finally he flicked on his R/T. 'We have some trade. At twenty thousand I'd say.' He shielded his eyes with his hand.

The Hurricanes were trailing black smoke now, all at full throttle in a shallow dive. Almost imperceptibly the outlines of two lumbering aircraft revealed themselves at the end of milk-white condensation trails, heading west.

'Heinkels, a brace,' someone yelled.

'Yes, they're Huns all right,' said Kit. They could make out the conical glassed-in noses, the twin engines with bright yellow spinners, the canopies on top of the fuselage shielding the gunner: Heinkel 111s. Surely they'd been spotted by now. But no, they held their course.

Briefly Ossie was back with the Dornier, his first kill. Then he had waited for a sign that he had been seen. But it had been intent on its task, had only realised he was there when he raked the fuselage from stem to stern. The port engine had exploded immediately in flame and the crew had known it was all over. Two had taken to their 'chutes immediately, but the pilot had waited a little longer, stabilising the Dornier, which was blazing nicely, before he appeared at the hatch. Ossie had zipped past close as the man tipped himself into space.

B Flight banked and came in from the sun. 'Line astern,' Kit shouted. Instantly Ossie Wolf drew in behind him with the rest of the flight. They had a 5,000-foot advantage. At last, too late, the Heinkel crews saw them and the green-grey bombers split, one left, one right. Kit could imagine them screaming to each other over the intercom.

'Echelon starboard.' The Hurricanes spread out fanwise. 'Going down.' At three hundred feet Kit had the lead Heinkel in his sights. It filled his screen. He jabbed his gun-button. Nothing. And again. Nothing. He flashed below the bomber and tracer followed him as he went. He flicked the Hurricane on to its back and into a dive. Tracer bullets hummed through his starboard wing. He checked his gun-button. It was jammed. He recalled it being stiff when he'd loosed-off some practice rounds on a test flight. Oh God, another cock-up from the paragon, the man so eager to set an example, so quick to keep the chaps in line. They'd all be flummoxed, unable to believe he'd missed. How could he have missed? A sitter by all that's holy.

Safely out of range he pulled up in a half-loop, rolled out of the top and pushed hard on the gun-button. It resisted, then yielded: several hundred .303 bullets chattered into thin air.

Following Kit Curtis down, Ossie Wolf had no such problems. It was like a filmic rerun of his first victory. The fire from his Brownings chewed its way through the Hun's tailplane and tracked a murderous course along the fuselage and into the cockpit area. Instantly the bomber flipped on to its back and fell away in a sheet of black smoke and flame, shedding its tailplane and starboard wing and spinning, fast and flat, before exploding at 10,000 feet. For the other B Flight pilots it was their first experience of violent death in the air. Momentarily they were startled by its swiftness and brutality. Then radio silence went to hell, crackling with excited cries as they sped after the remaining Heinkel, veering hopelessly eastwards.

'He's mine, he's mine,' screamed someone. That was Davis.

'Don't hog it Dinghy. Give us all a chance.' Buster was ebullient as ever.

'I've hit him! I've hit him! Strikes all over the sod.'

There was desultory return fire from the Heinkel before Dinghy's Brownings did their work. The propeller of the port engine stopped. Then the starboard prop seized and the bomber dipped into a steep dive, a torrent of flame tracking its descent. Dinghy went after it. Kit shouted over the R/T: 'They're goners Davis. Don't waste ammunition.'

As Dinghy continued to press his attack the Heinkel blew up in his face enveloping him in a wave of fire and flying shards of metal. Five hundred feet below Kit swung his machine to avoid the falling wreckage. A German airman plunged past him, struggling, the silk canopy of his parachute vanishing in a puff of flame. He must have been crouching at the hatch when the bomber went up.

B Flight was hooting with triumph. Two kills in a matter of minutes.

'Boy oh, boy,' said Ossie Wolf. 'Dinghy, you gave it to him good.'

Dinghy's voice came back muted, strained. 'I've taken some damage. I don't know whether it's anything to worry about.'

Ossie manoeuvred himself alongside. 'Can't see anything, feller. Just a little smoke up front.'

'What colour smoke?' said Dinghy. They were down to 15,000 feet, could see each other clearly in their cockpits. Dinghy's face looked white. He had unclipped his oxygen mask and was chewing his lips with tension.

'Blackish, greyish,' said Ossie.

Kit drew level on Dinghy's port side. 'Everybody else, beat it back. I'll stick with Davis and escort him home.'

Instantly Ossie Wolf chimed in: 'Permission to remain on station.'

'Return to base,' said Kit. 'No damned arguments Sergeant. Get down on the deck and re-arm pronto. There may be more of the swine.'

For thirty seconds or so Ossie Wolf continued to fly straight and level. Then he took both hands off the controls, gave Dinghy a double thumbs-up and dropped away to join the others.

Kit said: 'Keep me in the picture, Davis, there's a good chap. It's going fine but we don't want you ending up in some Hun holiday camp.' The levity was false and sounded it.

'It's not just damage to the kite,' said Dinghy. 'I've taken some shrapnel up the arse.'

The trailing smoke was more apparent now. Dinghy had

pushed back the hood and it was streaming from the cockpit area too. 'I think the elevator and rudder cables are buggered, but maybe I can get her back.'

'What do the instruments say?'

'No instruments to speak of,' said Dinghy. Now he was losing height, ten thousand feet, eight, six. By degrees the Merlin's power was fading as red-hot damaged components sheered, seized and failed.

At five thousand feet Kit decided: 'Get out of there Davis. You're safe enough here.' He remembered Brewster's words: *I can always replace aeroplanes but I don't want to lose my pilots.* He said again, more urgently: 'Davis, get out now. That's an order. Don't try to be a hero.'

'Not possible, Kit.' It was the first time Dinghy had ever used Kit's name. He was grunting with pain. 'I'd never trust the old brolly again after that dip in the briny. And I'm afraid I don't feel much like walking just now. No, I think I'll motor home.'

'How much control do you have?'

'Very little,' said Davis. 'Lucky I'm a brilliant bloody pilot.' At 3,000 feet, with agonising slowness, they crawled towards Revigncourt.

At the aerodrome B Flight had landed. Still in their flying kit the pilots had gathered in a small group by the runway, at a distance from the blood-wagon and the massive six-wheeled fire-engine with its three thousand gallons of foam. They were scarcely recognisable as the practical jokers of a few hours earlier or the gleeful band who had downed two Heinkels with such practised ease. Only Ossie Wolf had turned away, leaning on the tailgate of the three-tonner, tracing a meaningless pattern in the mud on the wooden boards.

Dinghy managed a model approach, flame mingling with the smoke and eating into the fuselage. The wheels didn't come down. A belly landing then. He was busy in the cockpit, battling for control. Kit said: 'Easy does it Davis.' Stupid. Should have been a black joke. Something laconic: Don't damage the kite, we'll make you pay for it. The sort of thing that means, 'You'll be okay, of course you'll be okay, and tonight we'll take a beer or three in Bar-le-Duc.' Five hundred feet now. God, this was unbearable . . .

But surely Dinghy had got it right? Agonised and fearful, splinters from the incendiary bullet searing into his buttock, the ground coming up fast, perhaps too fast, the Hurricane rocking, yawing, dipping below tree level, very close now, down a little, closer still; yes, even so it seemed that Dinghy had got it right. 'I don't think . . . you're going to . . . witness one of . . . my best . . . landings.'

Then the engine cut, the Hurricane faltered and nosed down, losing its buoyancy, no longer floating but falling. It struck the runway with the force of an express train and the cockpit was engulfed in a belch of flame. Kit, still in the air, could hear Dinghy screaming: 'Oh God, oh God, oh God.' Then silence. Even in his agony Dinghy had turned off the R/T. The Hurricane was cannoning towards the perimeter fence, spinning on its axis in lazy circles. As it slid it spouted fuel, leaving a trail of flaming grass to mark its course. Dinghy had not used all his ammunition. The bullets hummed and howled into the sky like fireworks. To Kit, leaping from the cockpit of his machine before it had stopped rolling, it was like the final act of the Thanksgiving buffoonery dreamt up by the man who was being consumed by fire before his eyes. In a distant copse a multitude of rooks clattered into flight, cawing with alarm. From the inferno the metal-tube skeleton of Dinghy's machine began to emerge. A huddled black shape could be seen in the cockpit, now still thank God . . .

Within twenty minutes A Flight was in the air. Brewster judged it better that way. The pilots dipped in salute over Revigncourt where the smouldering remains of the Hurricane were quickly doused and dragged away.

At four in the afternoon a monstrous fog-bank rolled across the countryside, curved over the hillsides and sank into the valleys with startling speed. The world became nebulous and indistinct. In this changed world Kit found himself by the willow grove. He didn't know why. Perhaps he expected the venerable trees to impart some primitive message of continuity, of hope. But something else whispered among the leafless branches, a murmuring of despair, a vague malignancy, an echo from a distant time, dark, cruel and baleful. It was always a quiet place but now the silence was oppressive and unnatural. Eager to get back to the others Kit found it difficult to retrace his path. He stumbled into gullies, tripped over tussocks. Somewhere he could make out the yellow glow of headlights. He heard the engine of the three-tonner ticking over, ready to return to Fonteville; conversation, low, joyless. He called out. Someone shouted in response. He didn't recognise the voice.

Something brushed past his legs. He stepped back, startled. The object tumbled towards the silent Hurricanes then stopped, trapped by a tail-wheel. Kit bent to pick it up. It was Dinghy's *Mayflower* hat, in pieces now, sodden, falling apart. He let the remnants drop and it lay on the grass like a card-and-paper mole-hill. But on its crest was no crisp frost cap. It was hard to believe there had been a frost at all.

Ten

Apart from brief visits to Bar-le-Duc Kit Curtis hadn't taken any appreciable leave since October. He'd had the chance but always turned it down. He didn't explain why and the other fellows, moving up the roster, didn't ask. Only Brewster pressed him to take a break. 'You're doing nothing here boy,' he said. 'Go and kick your heels somewhere convivial.'

It was true enough. Since the brief spell of combat and the squadron's first successes, the Luftwaffe had seemed reluctant to engage, turning for the safety of their lines at the first sight of British fighters taking to the air and climbing towards them. The lull gave them plenty of time to think, to brood. The CO did his best with hard-pounding games of rugger on the rock-hard ground, a tournament with teams drawn from every rank. It kept Doc Gilmour busy: nothing serious – abrasions, cuts, blackened eyes and bloody, even broken, noses. Brewster was in the thick of it as referee, roaring encouragement and oaths, lashing raised backsides in the scrum with his Acme Thunderer. There were cross-country challenges too: men staggered along stony tracks through frozen woodland, shallow ice-topped streams and over hoary pastures, watched by bony cattle sheltering from the cutting gales, and an occasional bemused local. And when the snows came the so-called Cresta Run de Revigncourt involved descents of hair-raising inclines on bobsleighs improvised from bed-boards.

166

Kit drove himself hard in these contests and, if he was leading a team, its members even harder. To them, trying to their utmost, his zeal seemed out of place. There was a swell of resentment that added to the frustration of being grounded week by week. Confounded by Kit's raw desire to win, even Buster Brown said: 'For God's sake, Kit, what's eating you? We'll all be laid up before the Hun can have a proper go.' Only Ossie Wolf stayed silent, matching Kit stride for stride on runs and always at his shoulder, tackling uncompromisingly on the rugger pitch, rising from one bruising encounter after another, always ready for more.

Brewster acted. 'Kit, I'm ordering you to shove off somewhere and enjoy yourself, there's a good chap. You're getting on my nerves and everybody else's.'

'Am I? Why?'

'Look, give yourself a break. Perhaps you'll know why then.'

'I'm perfectly all right.'

'I don't agree and neither does Doc Gilmour. Is it the Dinghy Davis business? You have nothing to blame yourself for there.'

'I'm not with you sir.'

'You've had a pretty rocky start to things, one way or another. You need a change of scene while you've the opportunity. I'm sick of hearing that someone else has pinched your leave.'

'It's not a question of pinching sir. I'm happy to give the chaps a chance.'

'Don't be such a bloody prig Kit,' said Brewster. 'And don't think you've got to take things on your shoulders. That's my job.' He hesitated. 'I don't know if you think you've failed the squadron, me or yourself in some way. If you do, forget it. Believe me, I'll be quick enough to tell you if I think you're wanting. You've got nothing to reproach yourself for so snap out of it man. You've got a nice new kite, B Flight's got two victories to its credit and you're leading a grand bunch of chaps.

What more could you want?' He lit a cigarette. 'Don't you know some people in this neck of the woods? I seem to remember someone called Nancy.'

Kit laughed reluctantly. 'Nancy the place, not a popsy. Friends of the family. Yes, I owe them a visit.'

'There you are,' said Brewster. 'Problem solved. Now, get out of here and don't show your face for three days. And give my regards to Nancy.'

It had been like a pre-war jaunt, motoring east towards Nancy, alone at the wheel of Buster's Alvis 12/50. The CO had probably been right. Perhaps he had let everything get on top of him. There was nothing more he could have done for Dinghy Davis, absolutely nothing. But as he drove the images crowded in on him: the meadow rising to meet him at Les Charmontois and holding off, waiting for the engine to die, as it had for Dinghy a few weeks later; the battle on Thanksgiving Day, the damned gun-button jamming and tracer flicking around him as he hurtled past the Heinkel; and Dinghy, that charred form crouched at the centre of a tangle of red-hot metal surrounded by a ring of fire. A shock ran through the car as the nearside front wheel thumped the verge.

Closer to Nancy, Kit came across occasional columns of *poilus* sauntering nonchalantly in the direction of the front. One, led by a well-mounted officer in expensive boots, marked its entry into a small town with flying standards, beating drums and those harsh French bugles shrilling out 'La Sambre et Meuse', a martial echo of Bonaparte's legions. It was all very stirring and raised the spirits, but for how long? In the faces of the troops Kit thought he saw doubt and uncertainty. We must prevail, mustn't we? Surely?

Otherwise the route was largely deserted. The village houses were shuttered and the bars generally closed. He pressed on, amusing himself by working the throttle and sliding the rear wheels of the protesting Alvis on the slick *pavé*. Buster would have been proud of him.

He drove right up to the front of the Maierscheldt house, boldly placed on the west side of the place de la Carrière in the centre of Nancy. It was an extraordinary concoction. At the entrance to the square stood two palaces, and within, ranged on either side of an avenue of plane trees, rows of venerable houses. To the south, through a triumphal arch erected for Louis XV, lay the place Stanislas and beyond it reared the twin towers of Nancy's baroque cathedral. To the north, graceful colonnades flanked an oval space leading to the Palais du Gouvernement and the bosky pleasures of the Parc de la Pépinière. In surroundings of such antiquity, beauty and elegance, the Maierscheldt house was an adventure, an uninhibited reworking of Gothic themes interwoven with art-nouveau inspiration in the birthplace of the movement.

It was Maurice Maierscheldt's good fortune – and also his influential position as an *industriel* – that when fire laid waste to a Renaissance villa in the place de la Carrière he had been well placed to acquire the plot, secure the various permissions, despite protests from traditionalists, and commission Lucien Weissenberger to produce a pinnacled extravaganza that, to his mind, not only celebrated the city's heritage of art and culture but also his personal success as a pre-eminent *maître-verrier*. His own designers produced the rich stained glass, Prouve the exquisite interior decoration, Prudhomme the organic and tortuous wrought-iron, Gruber the ceramics; in fact few among his peers had not contributed to the creation of Monsieur Maierscheldt's daringly handsome house.

In the cool, echoing salon Karoline Maierscheldt talked of girlish escapades at the École Internationale in Thun. Kit found it difficult to imagine his mother as the scampish Diana, the architect of so many hare-brained scrapes under the sharp noses of the stiff, earnest teaching staff. 'So very Swiss,' said Madame Maierscheldt. 'So very starchy, my dear Christopher, you can't imagine.' She began once again the tale of the pretty blue sailing boat on the lake, the old fishermen in the punt and the glorious youth in the skiff who had pulled Diana and her from a watery grave. Her eyes filled with tears of amusement and nostalgia. 'The dreadful war seemed so far away to us, like a battle on the moon or Mars. So hard to believe that, as we enjoyed those wonderful days, so many boys were dying.'

Hannah, dreamy and abstracted, leant against the silk-papered wall, feet extended, back straight, pale arms at her sides, palms flat on the green-blue floral wallpaper. Her head was inclined, as though in submission, and her dark curls tumbled round her shoulders. 'I'm sure Kit doesn't want to hear this Mama,' she murmured.

'Oh no,' protested Kit. 'Please continue.'

Karoline smiled. 'Always the English gentleman, Christopher. Hannah is right, of course, and you have heard the tale before.' A pause. 'But there is great pleasure in the telling.'

'For me,' said Hannah, pushing herself away from the wall and walking to her mother's side, 'Thun was not such a paradise.' She rested her hand on her mother's shoulder.

'Perhaps the school had changed,' said Madame Maierscheldt, covering Hannah's hand with hers, 'although to me it appeared much the same. Perhaps you did not work hard enough at making friends – special friends, I mean. Perhaps . . .'

'Perhaps, perhaps,' said Hannah. 'Perhaps the *école* never was a paradise, Mama. Perhaps your Diana simply made it appear so.'

'Ah,' said Madame Maierscheldt, thoughtfully. 'Perhaps.'

Later, strolling quietly beside the dark waters of the Meurthe, Hannah said: 'The first time we met as children, Kit, you told me you were going to the big boys' school. You were very serious about it.' The air was chilled and an occasional fish disturbed the surface of the river as tendrils of mist fingered their way between the banks. The great bells of the cathedral sounded across the *parc*. Back in the place de la Carrière preparations were being made for dinner and Monsieur Maierscheldt's return from the factory.

'Good heavens,' said Kit. 'That would have been in, what, twenty-seven? You can't have been more than three or four.'

'Three,' said Hannah. 'You don't remember. How odd. I remember it so well.'

'I remember going to big boys' school.'

'We'd come to stay with you at Tea-leaf Towers.'

'Oh, good Lord, yes.' He grinned. 'How Mother hated the locals calling it that. Farve couldn't care less. In fact, he thought it rather funny.' He took Hannah's hand, experienced a momentary fondness for her, then let it go again.

'It was good of you to drive all this way,' she said.

'I wouldn't have dared not to. You know what Mother's like. But of course I wanted to come,' he added, 'on my own account.'

'What an elegant liar,' said Hannah, laughing. 'Yes, we find ourselves here simply to please our mothers.' She gave him a playful push. 'If you had come earlier you could have admired our wonderful exhibition, my exquisite designs, and lied about them also.'

'I understand you have great talent, Hannah.'

'It is always easy to become a designer if your father owns the firm. But, still, Le Maître seemed to think I had ability. You know of Léger?'

'No, I'm afraid not.'

'I must confess I was proud that he seemed to believe in me. But, of course, he would have had no interest, had it not been for my father's position. Privilege is two-edged, is it not?' She pushed her hand through her hair. 'Tell me,' she said, 'were you, like me, always conscious of how our dear mamas watched us when we found ourselves together on those holidays? How they hoped?'

'I think so, yes.'

Hannah slid her arm through his. He felt its warmth. Quite

like sweethearts, he thought, but that was not enough. Almost as though she sensed his reaction, she said: 'Wouldn't it have been perfect for them if it had worked?'

'For you and me as well, perhaps.'

'Perhaps.'

'You're very lovely Hannah,' said Kit, not really knowing why. He turned her towards him. She seemed very small as she lifted her face. My God, he thought, she was so like . . .

'And you,' she said, 'are very handsome.'

'We make a handsome couple.'

'Not a couple,' said Hannah. 'Handsome, yes, and lovely, yes, if such an elegant liar is ever to be believed. But a couple, no. How convenient it would all have been, my father retired and you in his office with a black waistcoat and a big belly looking forward to lunch, and me with my designers creating beautiful things.'

They turned in the direction of the place de la Carrière. 'Is it so very horrible, Kit, this war in the air?'

'It's barely started yet but, yes, it's pretty ghastly.'

He told her a little but not too much. He didn't talk about Dinghy Davis at all. He said, well, yes, he was a little afraid. Well, not afraid exactly but apprehensive, concerned about letting the others down, of not proving up to it. He described his landing at Les Charmontois, the impromptu fête thrown for him by the villagers, and made it seem much lighter than it really was. He didn't talk about the way he had seen the German air-crews die.

'Are the others, your comrades, as good as you?'

'Oh, I'm not so good.'

'But Papa understands you are among the best in your squadron. Exceptional. This he heard at Hendon.'

'I've learned there's more to fighting than being handy at the controls,' Kit said. 'When there's someone out to get you, your fancy air-show routine doesn't necessarily mean a damned thing. When I first went up, in the University Air

Squadron, the instructor said I was a natural. Duck-to-water stuff. Rather went to my head.' He grunted. 'We've got a little American fellow in our squadron. He's a decent pilot, nothing special, but what I've learnt from him is that fighters are simply aerial artillery, airborne gun platforms. You can pretty well forget your loops and stalls and fancy tricks unless they help you get in position to achieve the kill. Mostly they don't. It's more a matter of selecting your prey, getting in fast and out faster. We lost a man, our first, two weeks ago. He forgot that.'

'It sounds horrible,' Hannah said. 'Not at all like those adventures you used to tell me of years ago, those gallant pilots like chevaliers of the heavens. Your little American is no chevalier.'

'No, but he's proved it works,' said Kit. 'A Heinkel and a Dornier.'

'And you, Kit? Where does this leave you?'

'Alive and learning. The longer you live the more you learn. Mostly you learn from your mistakes. But I don't know how much time we've got. The weather is on our side but there's no doubting Boche intentions. Come spring, when they turn up in force, it's going to be quite a party.'

Arm in arm once more, they left the gathering shadows of the parc de la Pépinière. They looked a romantic pair, content in each other's company as they prepared for Karoline Maierscheldt's anxious quizzing about where they had been and what they had said as she tried to perceive behind their eyes what might become of it all.

Over an elaborate dinner laid out in the dining room, with its tiled frieze of seagulls taking flight over a raging sea, Maurice Maierscheldt said that this accursed war was a devil of a nuisance, a barrier to progress, an insult to the intelligence, a return to the Stone Age.

Kit had been shocked by his changed appearance. Once fresh-faced, corpulent and cheery, full of energy and original schemes that, to a growing boy, had seemed wild and exciting, he was fat in an unprepossessing way and bald with crusty sores on his scalp. His views had always been trenchant, even exaggerated, and he had amused himself by challenging Kit's romantic illusions of swashbuckling gallants and stirring adventures. His views were still trenchant but no longer tempered by a wry twist of the mouth. The firm, he said, had not been prospering. Again it was this damned war and he was clearly in the wrong business. He should throw it all up and go into armaments so that more fools could murder each other and the whole affair come to a conclusion. Then he, and others like him, could resume the serious matter of industrial growth.

Kit felt the heat grow within him. 'I'm probably one of your fools,' he said, laying down his knife and fork, his plate half cleared. To his father, Maierscheldt had always been an honest buffoon; to his mother, a vulgarian with the Midas touch. The most golden of his gifts, she used to say sadly, was Karoline.

'You may dispute this, my dear young friend,' Maierscheldt protested, 'but you are simply a victim. We are all of us victims of giant forces beyond our control. Nothing changes, all is the same.' He took a gulp of red wine too good to be gulped, waved the glass wildly and showered spots on to the fresh white linen. 'Two hundred years ago in the Judengasse, in Frankfurt-am-Main, the Maierscheldts were victims along with the rest. There was oppression and tyranny on every side – Jews were allowed no movement outside the walls of the Judengasse, only a certain number of marriages each year and denied the right to buy property in the city. So we left, abandoned everything, established ourselves here, in Nancy, and began again. We felt we were French, but what then occurred? The Germans came. They came in 1870 and again in 1914. Overnight we found ourselves Germans once more. Now it may happen again. If it does not, if the Allies prevail, then God be thanked. If the Boches succeed, I pray that our German heritage will save us.' He was talking loudly now, and it occurred to Kit that here was a man frightened out of his wits. Knowing this, he inwardly forgave him.

Karoline Maierscheldt had been pulling at her husband's sleeve, her face flushed. Now Maierscheldt cried: 'I'm told I have offended you, my poor boy. If so, I apologise.' Then, more quietly: 'I am not myself these days. I am not the fellow I was. I lived for possibilities. I was eager for the days, the months, the years to come. Everything seemed possible. Yet now, well, now I fear the dawn, I fear for France, I fear for the world. Most of all, I fear for my family, my friends. I strive to remain hopeful but it is hard. No, it is impossible.'

On the landing outside Kit's room Hannah touched his cheek. 'You see things clearly, Kit. He is a good man but he is in despair. You were always fond of him. I know you forgive him now. He was never one to bear uncertainty. He is used to choosing his own path. Now it is chosen for him.' She pressed her lips softly to his cheek and was gone.

Kit had intended to remain with the Maierscheldts until Sunday evening. The next morning, however, he made his excuses. 'I must get back.'

'When you return to England,' said Karoline, 'be sure to give Diana my fondest love. A kiss from me.'

Walking to the Alvis, Hannah said: 'They are like sisters, our mamas. No, more than sisters.'

'Yes.' He hesitated. 'I sometimes think your mother is the only person in the world for whom mine has a shred of fondness.'

Hannah halted. 'Oh, Kit, that is a terrible thing to say.'

'Terrible how?'

'That you suggest your own mother has no fondness for you or your father or anyone except—'

'It doesn't matter.'

'It matters a great deal.'

'Not to me.'

'You don't mean that.'

'I'm afraid I do. It might have mattered once but not any more. Actually, I pity her. She always seems alone and lost – bitter, even. You said that privilege has two edges. So it is with her. She has everything, yet it counts for nothing. She detests her life and those around her. When your mother talks of her, it's as though she's speaking of another person, a stranger.'

'But why? What happened?'

'What didn't happen, perhaps. I don't know. Life is baffling, isn't it, so different from what you've been led to expect?'

Maurice Maierscheldt hurried out of the house bearing a small wooden crate, its lid nailed down, containing half a dozen bottles of Heidsieck. 'For you, my dear Christopher, to toast your squadron's victories. Now you have your wish, to be among heroes. You were always a brave little fellow.' He placed the crate on the passenger seat of the Alvis. 'I fear I have driven you away.'

'Not at all.'

'I regret that on this occasion I have been unable to show you the factory. We still produce many beautiful things.'

'Hannah spoke of them. Perhaps next time.'

'Of course. Or possibly we will meet in Paris. I was sorry to miss you there. I will buy you dinner at Maxim's, you and your comrades. It will be better than a tonic.' He lowered his voice. 'Perhaps these tales from the Reich are exaggeration, propaganda. One must hope. Even if the worst occurs, perhaps things won't be as bad as we fear. It is not so much for myself, you understand, but I cannot bring myself to contemplate what might lie in store for Karoline and Hannah.' He forced a thin smile. 'But one must remain an optimist, no?'

'Of course,' said Kit. He could think of nothing to add, nothing that would provide any comfort.

Hannah was waiting by the car. On the first-floor balcony Karoline Maierscheld was waving, smiling. 'Goodbye,' said Hannah. She kissed her fingertips and placed them gently on his lips, like a blessing. 'To me you are a chevalier still.'

Kit clambered into the Alvis and started the engine, looking straight ahead through the stone-crazed dirty windscreen.

Eleven

Wednesday, 20 December 1939

For three weeks operations had been stifled by low cloud, fog and snow until, at last, the sky lightened a little. The breath of the men clearing the runways was white against their crimson faces as their bodies warmed with the heavy labour. They sang venerable Great War songs: 'It's A Long Way to Tipperary', 'Roll Out the Barrel', the usual old chestnuts. They bawled the verses as their fathers had before them. It was good to have a purpose once again. Muffled and gloved, the ground-crews also busied themselves on the Hurricanes, running up the engines to keep them sweet in the Arctic temperatures, and Brewster readied the squadron for patrols the following day, if conditions continued to improve.

It seemed a long time now since Dinghy Davis had died. The pilots caught themselves forgetting and felt guilty.

Flight Sergeant Jessop and his men had noticed a change in the B Flight commander since his leave. He still drove himself and them as hard as ever, even when there was nothing more to do than check what they had already checked a thousand times, but it was the way he did it that had altered. The technicians were proud of their abilities, and criticism bit deep. Jessop knew that efficient relationships weren't built that way, that inevitably a pilot would not secure the best service from a demoralised crew nervous that he would constantly find fault. And it was well known that Flying Officer Curtis seemed to lack confidence in his fitter Corporal Taggart and in Gray, the rigger, cross-questioning them repeatedly over the smallest details, his manner cold and pedantic. But now he was easier in himself, not so stiff and starchy, bit less of the stewed ruddy prune, almost human. Jessop found it hard to imagine, but perhaps he'd had home comforts of the warm and womanly kind. Or maybe that prang at Les Charmontois had shaken some humility into him.

'Is the kite D/I'd, Flight?'

'Yes sir,' said Jessop, promptly. He produced the daily inspection form for Kit to sign. It already bore his own, Taggart's and Gray's signatures. Kit didn't sign it straight away, as many would. He paced slowly round his fresh Hurricane, inspecting the control surfaces, testing the movement of the rudder and elevators, trying each cowling button with a sturdy screw-driver to make sure it was fully home and secure. Taggart and Gray looked at each other. 'Quite like old times,' said Taggart.

'Thanks chaps,' said Kit. 'It all seems fine.'

'Not quite like old times,' said Gray.

'I'm going to take her up Flight.'

'Bit marginal sir,' said Jessop, squinting skywards.

'It'll keep the Hun away while I check out your tweaks. We're probably going to be back in business tomorrow. I need to be sure everything's top hole.'

Kit cleared his flight plan with a sceptical Brewster and began to prepare for the flight. The word had got about. Buster Brown came across, clapping his arms round his body. 'You're a prize bloody clot, Kit. It could close in on you at any moment.'

'Oh, I don't think so. Definitely brighter.'

'That's what my old man used to say on holiday in Wales. Never stopped us going home four days early. Well, send us a postcard.'

'A postcard?'

'From wherever you land. It probably won't be here. Just make sure it's not sunny Rhineland.'

A few paces away Ossie Wolf was leaning against the fuselage of Kit's aircraft, studying the toes of his flying boots. He was shrugged deep into his Irvin jacket, which was zipped to the neck, and had a sheepskin hat with the ear-flaps pulled well down. His eyes were hidden behind anti-glare Ray-Ban Aviators. He was clicking a syncopated rhythm with his tongue behind his teeth. He waited for Buster to leave. Then: 'I hear Strasbourg is kind of neat.'

'Neat?'

'How far do you reckon it is from here?'

'I don't know Sergeant. Two hundred miles, two fifty.'

'You ever been there?'

'Yes.'

'Worth the trip?'

'If you're planning a leave, Sergeant, you're too late. Or hadn't you heard? They evacuated the place in September, all those towns and villages along the border. Shifted the entire population. It's a ghost town.' He corrected himself. 'City.'

'Yeah, I heard that. Should be quiet then. No tourists. I was considering checking it out today.' He pushed the sun-spectacles on to his forehead and looked Kit straight in the eye. 'You know, head east awhile. A fair bit east.'

'Strasbourg.'

'Yeah, Strasbourg way. Maybe a little further, even. I hear the country's grand round there.' The American shifted his weight. 'I was thinking. You've been there. Maybe you could show me around.'

'You won't see much from the air in conditions like this.'

'Oh, I guess we might find something of interest.'

'What have you in mind?' Kit was playing for time, conscious that this was a moment on which a great deal might turn. Was the man suggesting what he thought he was suggesting? He might be wrong, of course. Maybe he was genuine – simply wanted to tag along for company, safety in numbers, catch a glimpse of a masterpiece of medieval architecture marooned in no-man's-land. He caught himself. Come off it. That was as likely as Brewster taking up embroidery. His instinct was to send the American away with a flea in his ear.

'What have I got in mind?' Wolf was saying. 'Nothing specific, but something might turn up.' He pushed himself off the fuselage and rubbed his hands. 'But maybe you wouldn't want that.'

Kit was back at the swimming pool at prep school, trembling on the tip of the highest board, reserved for seniors who knew how to dive, the prefect Groombridge taunting him: 'But you said you could do it, Curtis. You're not scared, are you?' Then he had jumped. Now he jumped again. 'You understand, Sergeant, it's only a test flight . . .'

'Oh, sure.'

'Very well. You still need to clear your flight plan with the CO.'

'I'll square it with him. Like you say . . .'

'It's only a test flight.'

'Yeah.'

'I'm taking off in ten minutes.' He wanted to make clear that he was going with or without the other man, that it was all the same to him, that as far as he was concerned it really was just a test flight.

'Okay.' Ossie adjusted the Ray-Bans and started to walk away.

'Sergeant,' said Kit. 'Why me?'

'Why not? Anyway, I figured you might like to get one back for Dinghy.'

Ah, now it was out in the open, no mistaking that. And still Kit didn't say what he knew he should.

'Dinghy rated you, you know,' said Ossie, offering a nugget to tip him over the edge.

Kit recognised it for what it was. 'Oh, really?'

'Yeah, he always was a cock-eyed mug.'

He watched the American disappear in the direction of Brewster's Nissen hut. Even now it was not too late to call him back and abort the flight. But he said nothing. After all, the CO was perceptive. He'd see through Ossie Wolf soon enough, understand his real intentions. And Brewster might even approve of a show of fighting spirit when things were so damned dull. Besides, the chances of coming across any opposition were pretty well nil. As far as Kit was concerned, it was a matter between Brewster and Wolf, nothing to do with him. His own objective remained the same: to stooge around for a while making sure the kite behaved itself. Nothing remotely wrong in that – common sense, no possible blame attached. He knew he was lying to himself but at that moment it didn't seem important.

After the long, dull days of nothing it was a welcome sound, the bellow of two Hurricanes throttling up and pounding down the runway, streams of slush flying from their tyres. Everyone stopped to watch. On each aeroplane, almost simultaneously, the wildly spinning wheels lost contact with the ground and the Dowty hydraulic rams eased the undercarriages to their in-flight position between the centre-section spars. Kit snapped the R/T. 'Dicey.'

'Icy,' said Ossie Wolf.

Brewster watched them go, his chin thrust upwards, chewing his pipe. 'Who's that taking off with Kit Curtis?'

'Sergeant Wolf,' said Spy Turner.

'What's he think he's ruddy well playing at?'

'He came looking for you, sir.'

'He didn't look very hard. I was in my bloody office.' Brewster spat out fragments of tobacco. 'What was his excuse?'

'Test flight sir. Something to do with a vibration at about 250 m.p.h.'

'He must think I was born yesterday.'

'Unlikely, sir, or he might have bothered to find you.'

Brewster grunted. 'Do you think they're after what I think they're after?'

'Curtis seemed genuine,' said Turner. 'I can't speak for Wolf.'

'Wise of you Spy.' A fierce chew on the pipe-stem. 'Well, I suppose you can't expect to keep these chaps down indefinitely.

I'll give Kit Curtis the benefit of the doubt, but remind me to give Wolf a bollocking when he gets back.' He grunted. 'If he gets back.' He shot a glance at the two fighters climbing away strongly at five hundred feet. 'Let's hope he manages to trace that tiresome vibration.'

'Oh, I think he will sir,' said the intelligence officer. 'He's probably found it already.'

The Hurricanes levelled out at eight hundred feet on a westerly course just below the cloud base, which ran like an inverted sea, flat and grey, to the horizon. The land of the southern Meuse streamed beneath their wings, the black outlines of towns and villages, remote farms, clumps of forest and woodland stark against the muffling blanket of snow. There was little traffic on the roads, mostly military, moving slowly and staining the air with exhaust fumes that drifted across the frozen farmland. In the enclosed fields knots of cattle stood in the lee of hedgerows, the snow flattened by their hoofs and criss-crossed with hay pitched off horse-drawn carts. A herd would take fright at the passing of the British fighters, the beasts scattering across the crisp pastures, then forgetting their alarm and straggling slowly back to their feeding ground.

It was good to be flying again. The power of their machines passed through the bodies of the two pilots; they felt at one, components of flesh and blood directing a beast of steel and alloy, wood and fabric, trembling with the force of thrusting through the air at 300 m.p.h., immune to harm, secure in their sense of wielding deadly force. Kit tried his Brownings. No problem now with the gun-button. The Hurricane faltered briefly with the force of the recoil.

They were many miles from Revigncourt now, had been in the air for perhaps five minutes, when Kit said: 'How's that vibra-tion, Sergeant?'

'Seems okay. How's your kite?'

'Seems okay. Bit early to tell.'

'We got lots of time.'

'Ready for a spot of sightseeing Sergeant?'

'Sure thing.'

Kit began a gentle bank to starboard and, maintaining height, they turned east.

They came in over Petite France, the old tanners' district of Strasbourg, where ancient mills leant on each other, shoulder to shoulder, in a maze of tortuous streets and tiny bridges spanning canals running off the river Ill. They throttled back and swept in low over the cathedral, Notre Dame, its pink-red Vosges sandstone glowing even now in the dull light, too swift to glimpse the great rose window at the centre of the western façade but taking in the Gothic spire that had dominated the Alsace landscape for five hundred years, more lace than stone, Hugo's delicate marvel. Kit remembered climbing the tower as a youth with Hannah Maierscheldt. Together they had counted aloud the 505 steps to the gallery, 350 feet above the ground, where Hannah clung to him and refused to look down at the place de la Cathédrale. There, the music from the orchestras outside the restaurants and cafés rose up to them like the echoes of a vanishing age. They had skipped down, Hannah laughing at her fear, and collapsed, panting, at a table outside the Maison Kammerzell where they drank chocolate to the strains of Franz Lehar. They had been natural together then, like siblings.

Now it was as though the city were dying, if not dead. A few official vehicles scurried about the streets but otherwise all life had gone. Strasbourg, the crossroads of Europe, awaited its fate, meek and mute, its architectural treasures exposed and vulnerable to whoever cared to take possession of them, as though they had been judged valueless, not worth fighting for. Or perhaps the pragmatic French were unwilling to see their Gothic jewel reduced to rubble, like the doomed cities of the Somme two decades before. To Kit, at least, it seemed that the brass-hats and politicos had got it very wrong, their strategy suggesting that even now, so soon, they were prepared to yield to the forces of the Reich. By offering no resistance it was as though the coalition had already lost a battle, falling back before a spectral army advancing through the deserted streets of Strasbourg.

Suddenly, without a word on the R/T, Ossie Wolf throttled up and pulled away north-east. He headed across the canal du Rempart where it ran down to join the racing waters of the river Ill, and gained height over the place de la République. The cloud base was low now, even shrouding the crown and cross on the tip of the cathedral spire at little more than four hundred feet. As Kit climbed quickly to formate on the American's starboard wing they found themselves flitting in and out of nebulous masses of vapour, as thick as any London special, yellowish and heavy with undischarged snow. There was no communication between the pilots, verbal or visual. Consciously now, Kit was allowing events to take their course. It was not wise or responsible: a simple command was all that was needed and Wolf would be compelled to obey. But, by God, it was electrifying, barrelling towards Hun territory like this. At last – yes, finally – this was an adventure worthy of the name. With their Merlins on full-throttle and vortices curling from their wing-tips the two Hurricanes charged for the German border four kilometres distant.

They crossed the Rhine south-west of Baden-Baden and banked to starboard, heading south, swooping over and round the high ground of the Schwarzwald that flashed below, mimicking the Alps with its mantle of white. Contrails were streaming from the Hurricanes' wing-tips, flurries of snow and hail striking the windscreens, the moisture running back along the hoods. Soon they picked up a significant road running north and south, freshly salted and busy, a route from Karlsruhe, maybe, dropping down to the Swiss border. Too fast to see, they grinned at the idea of German motorists slowing and gaping up at British fighters playing fast and loose in the sullen skies of the Fatherland.

Kit was first to pick up the cluster of buildings familiar to any pilot anywhere in the world: hangars and admin blocks set on a wide, flat expanse of open country on the outskirts of a size-able town close to a road junction. To the north-west they could make out the tell-tale signs of a major city, the atmosphere heavy and livid with purplish industrial smoke. Stuttgart – yes, it had to be. Which meant the town below was Freudenstadt where, before the war, different hosts had marched, hikers heading for the forests and hills of Baden-Wurttemberg before returning at night to gorge on Schwarzwalder Kirschtorte and cherry schnapps. He knew this because he, too, had walked those hills.

As they throttled back, closing on the airfield at little more than three hundred feet and banking steeply round the perimeter, they picked out a single high-winged twin-cockpit aircraft in black-green camouflage with black crosses on its flanks, warming up on the Tarmac. Behind it, two more were parked, their two-man crews moving around them. They were tactical reconnais-sance Henschel Hs-126s, effective and fast, despite their antique look, the graceful parasol wing with its central notch reminis-cent of a Great War fighter. By the hangars, also parked, were half a dozen twin-engined Messerschmitt Bf-110Cs, the first they had seen, which served as escorts to the Henschels on their reconnaissance missions; no one in evidence. It was all very peaceful and well ordered. The scene reminded Kit of a diorama at the Science Museum in South Kensington, so neat, so normal. It seemed criminal to attack but things had gone too far to pull back now and, anyway, wasn't this what they were here for?

'We may have only one chance at this,' Kit said. 'Follow me down.' He ran his eyes over the engine instruments and altimeter. That was a joke: they were almost on the deck. Gun-sights on, range and wing-span indicators checked, just time for a final finicky adjustment to the airscrew control, gun-button set to 'fire'. That damned gun-button. Would it fail him again? 'Attacking, attacking,' he said over the R/T, fighting to suppress his excitement.

He came round in an almost vertical turn to face the taxiing Henschel, so close to the ground he expected to put a wing in at any moment, then levelled out, the tips of his propeller blades only feet from the runway. Ground fire had opened up from sandbagged anti-aircraft-gun emplacements spread round the airfield, the cones of flak trying to keep pace with the Hurricane in its high-speed pass at 330 m.p.h. His peripheral vision noted them somewhere in a recess of his brain but his focus now, through the gun-sight, was the Henschel 126 teetering crab-wise into the air, its single radial BMW power-plant at peak revs. His bullets tore it apart and it fell back on to the Tarmac in flames. He pulled up and banked round, staring down at the fire and smoke pouring from the wreckage. At that moment he had no thought for the men inside. He was suffused with a thrill of satisfaction.

In his pass, moments later, Ossie Wolf took out the two remaining Henschels in one sustained burst as the crews ran for cover. Over by the hangars one of the Me-110s began to move; then another. These guys were on the ball, a crack squadron. But Ossie was moving low and fast, skidding and jinking to avoid the flak. He made a wide sweep, still hugging the ground, and came in from a fresh direction. His bullets raked the runway. The leading 110, still in contact with the ground, veered violently to the right, lifting its starboard wing and heaving up on to one wheel, then thumped back down and slid across the snow-crusted grass. Its undercarriage collapsed and, helpless, it hit a concrete bunker almost end-on, shedding its tailplane, then slewed to a halt in a shower of earth and debris. Dense black smoke billowed from its Daimler-Benz DB-601s and the propellers were bent back over the nacelles. Before it stopped moving the cockpit hood flew open and the pilot and gunner threw themselves clear.

By now three more 110s were airborne, rising quickly towards them. Kit said: 'They seem rather peeved.'

'Ain't it the truth?' said Ossie Wolf. They turned for home, pursued by the trio of Messerschmitt-110s.

Kit knew they were fast machines, at almost 350 m.p.h. marginally faster than a Hurricane. And the nose armament was deadly: four 7.9mm MG-17 machine-guns, each of a thousand rounds each, and twin MG-FF cannons, with 180 rounds apiece. They had good range too, 530 miles, more than enough to take them to Revigncourt and back if they felt the need; a nice test of their determination. But they had lost critical time getting into the air and Kit knew that 110s were slow to attain maximum speed. Then, if it came to a scrap, their wide turning circle made them vulnerable to a well-handled Hurricane – that was what Brewster had told them and he wasn't prone to shooting a line. Finally the weather would play its part. Me-110s were most dangerous diving from high level for a single attacking pass before breaking away, but that was not the name of the game today with low cloud and lousy visibility. Overall, as they powered for the border, Kit felt the odds were in their favour.

Wing to wing, the British fighters recrossed the border south of Strasbourg with Molsheim below and Nancy dead ahead. Above their heads the unbroken mass of cloud was almost black now, the air veiled with vast sheets of falling snow. They found themselves straining to detect the slightest fluctuation in engine note, their eyes fixed on the three critical instruments on the panels by their right knees: oil temperature, oil pressure, radiator temperature, the infernal trio. Behind them another infernal trio appeared to be making up the distance between them.

'The bastards are gaining,' said Ossie Wolf. It was plain they would be engulfed before they reached Nancy.

'I know it.'

'We're going to have to take 'em on.'

'Looks that way.'

'What's the deal?'

'Throttle back a little.'

'Huh?'

'Throttle back a little and close up. Keep me in sight and when I give the word climb like hell.'

'Got you.' Wolf had instantly perceived the plan.

They eased their throttles and the white needles of their airspeed indicators, pin-sharp against the matt-black backing plate, quivered and wound back. The Messerschmitts, running abreast and level, were closing fast now but not quite in range. In the external rear-view mirror clamped to the top of his windscreen Kit watched them come. It was quite a sight. Then, an instant before flashes of gun and cannon fire began to appear on the nose-cones of the 110s, he shouted: 'Go!' He judged it to the second. The two Hurricanes shot upwards into the cloud-base and vanished.

On balanced throttle with Ossie's wing-tip barely visible behind and to his right, Kit's eyes flicked from the artificial horizon at the top of the instrument panel – its indicator stabilised after rolling wildly as the Hurricane turned on its back – to the altimeter below and to the left. Inverted, the Merlins had faltered as usual, then picked up as the angle of the dive out of the loop steepened. Kit sensed the Hurricanes were feet apart but now, outside the cockpit, he could see no sign, just cloud as dense as smoke from a pyre of burning tyres. 'Still with me Sergeant?'

'Try losing me.'

The dive became vertical and the Hurricanes thundered into clear air, control columns hard back as they emerged below and behind the 110s and opened fire. Ossie Wolf yelled: 'Got you, you sons-of-bitches!' The Messerschmitt on the right fell away, its starboard engine pouring flame. At the same moment Kit's bullets struck the lead 110 in the cockpit area as it pulled up vertically to gain the safety of the cloud. It came over on to its back and dropped into a flat spin. A single figure fell clear but there was no sign of the man's parachute opening and the struggling form was lost against the featureless white of the countryside below. The surviving 110 screamed round in a vertical turn that threatened to pull its wings off and dived for home.

For a long moment nothing was said. Kit was soaked in sweat. His breath was coming hard and fast as though he had just completed a cross-country run. His hands were trembling on the control column. He began to laugh. My God, he thought, my God, what a party. It was not what he said. He intoned into the R/T: 'Nicely done, Sergeant.'

'Yeah. Who said fancy flying was dead?'

'Not me.'

'Must have been some mug.'

'I think that's enough test flying for today. The CO's waiting for our report.'

'Jesus Christ.'

'Exactly.'

Kit had always found landing in difficult circumstances satisfying. Normally he would have welcomed the chance to deal with a single available runway made still more hazardous by a layer of drifting snow, a capricious crosswind and a shortage of fuel: it represented an interesting challenge, an opportunity to demonstrate his flying skills to anyone who cared to watch – perhaps, most of all, to himself. It was a question of deeds, not words. In line-shoot sessions in the mess he usually nursed a beer in a corner and limited himself to a few sparse comments on others' yarns: 'Really? Good grief.' But often someone, usually Buster Brown, would turn to him as the squadron's most proficient pilot, a Hendon ace no less. 'Kit, remember that time . . . ?' And Kit, with every show of reluctance, would confirm the details of the incident, curbing Buster's more purple passages and modestly acknowledging that that was how it had been. Secretly he supposed his position was that of the ultimate line-shooter. But now, as he performed a tightish circuit of Revigncourt, turning gently all the way down to get a clear view of the runway round the long snout of the Hurricane, he did not want an audience. He was keen to get down, out of the cockpit, into the CO's office and get the damned thing over with. He was going to have to come clean. No point in trying to bluff it out with a man like Brewster . . .

He three-pointed it, applying just the correct amount of right rudder to counteract the torque. She didn't pull to port an inch, sliding quickly to a halt on the slush. He taxied in and shut her down, snapped his harness and unbuckled, then unplugged his helmet and climbed out on the wing. Yards away, Ossie Wolf was doing the same. Spy Turner was slapping the blackened holes in the canvas gun patches on the wings of Kit's machine. 'No problems with the Brownings, then?'

'None.'

'That was the longest test flight in the history of the squadron. Where the heck did you go? Berlin?'

'Pretty well.'

'The CO wants to see you immediately. You're to speak to nobody until you've talked to him. That goes for Sergeant Wolf too. I'll take your reports after that.'

'Very well.'

Buster was there, and Goofy Gates and Knox, all the B Flight crowd. To Curtis, they were a blur of curious faces shooting questions he barely heard and didn't answer. Jessop had forced his way through, trailed by Gray and Taggart. 'Everything okay sir?' Kit gave a thumbs-up and an approving nod.

Ossie Wolf came over, pulling off his flying helmet and unzipping his Irvin jacket. His eyes were wide open, almost protruding, the pupils dilated. Kit thought he looked slightly mad and felt alarmed that he had been flying with the man. But, then, maybe he looked slightly mad too.

'Fancy flying.'

'Yes.'

'That was one hell of a manoeuvre.'

'Yes.'

'We were lucky there.'

'Earlier too.'

'Boy we hit the bastards good.'

Kit turned away. He found the edge of hatred in Wolf's voice disturbing. For the first time he thought about the German crew burning alive in the Henschel he destroyed; the man whose 'chute had failed, with plenty of time to think about it. He was freezing in the keen wind, yet wet with perspiration. The situation, everything that had occurred, seemed suddenly unreal. He was also aware of a curious sense of fellow-feeling towards the American and confused by it. Instantly he felt the need to distance himself. He said: 'Good show Sergeant. Excuse me. The CO wants to see us. I'm on first.'

'Just you?'

'Just me.'

'What are you going to tell him?'

'What do you think I'm going to tell him?'

'I don't want you taking the rap. I muscled in.' Ossie hesitated. 'I guess I got you into a position where you didn't have much choice.'

'I had plenty of choice Sergeant. I didn't have to go along with a damned thing. The flight was my responsibility and the decisions were mine. I could have aborted the affair at any time.'

'Yeah, I guess you could. Why didn't you?'

'Let's put it down to temporary insanity.'

Ossie Wolf gave a rare, crooked grin. 'Well, there's no denying we had ourselves one helluva duck-shoot, didn't we? The CO will have to give us that.'

'Don't try to pull the wool over his eyes,' said Kit. 'Just stick to the facts and let him come to his own conclusions.'

They walked across to the Nissen hut. Nothing more was said. Brewster came out of his office. 'Park yourself with Spy Turner, Sergeant, I've got things to say to Flying Officer Curtis. I'll call you when I need you.' He closed the office door. Kit reached for a chair.

Brewster said: 'I'd prefer you to remain standing.'

Kit stiffened. 'I want to make it clear, sir, that I take complete responsibility—'

'Oh, spare me the selfless heroics, Kit, for God's sake. What the bloody hell do you think you were playing at? Jessop tells me you've got bullet-holes in your aeroplane. Some test flight!

192

I want the truth now, just the facts, no excuses, self-justification or flannel.'

Kit described the flight in the baldest terms. It was difficult to make it sound matter-of-fact but he did his best. He was vague only about what had impelled them to overfly the German border, making no special mention of Ossie Wolf's part. Brewster was quick to notice. 'Tell me, are you aware that Sergeant Wolf took off without my authorisation?' Kit's face provided the answer. Brewster said: 'It doesn't make much difference, as far as you're concerned. It's what happened once you were in the air that baffles me. What in Hades were you thinking of?'

'Perhaps we weren't. Thinking, I mean.'

'Is that all you've got to say?'

'Yes sir, that's it.'

'Sit down, boy.' Brewster began to fill his pipe from his tobacco pouch, tamping down the shreds with an empty .303 cartridge case he kept on his desk. 'Three Henschels and a brace of 110s.'

'Yes, sir.'

'I suppose you and Wolf think that makes everything all right.'

'No sir. Not at all.'

'Don't try to kid me, Kit. Of course you do. Let's face it, it's your only hope.' He lit the pipe, sucking noisily as the match flared and caught. 'I've got news for you, boy. It's one thing to go up hoping for trouble. It's another to go actively looking for it over enemy territory against unknown odds. That's self-indulgent, irresponsible and totally bloody stupid. You could have cost me two Hurricanes, for God's sake. My only consolation would have been getting shot of two idiots who seem to think they're fighting a private war.'

'Yes sir.'

'Yes sir, yes sir. I believe you chaps think you've been pretty bloody clever don't you? Don't answer that.' Brewster stood up and glared out of his window, taped against bomb-blast. It was snowing heavily now, the flakes fine, dry and dense, caught in a keen east wind; the runway on which Kit and Ossie Wolf had landed only thirty minutes before was piled with sculpted drifts. 'I believe I know what's gone on here. I will not tolerate weak leadership, woolly thinking or reckless escapades out of the pages of a comic. I'm thoroughly disappointed in you. I don't want schoolboys out here, Kit. I want men.' It was the worst thing Brewster could have said. Kit felt close to choking. 'I expect far better from my flight commanders,' said Brewster. He turned round, his face grim. 'However, I'm not prepared to risk the reputation of this squadron for the sake of a couple of out-of-control imbeciles without a brain between them.' A lengthy pause. 'The fact remains that I authorised your flight. We will draw a veil over whether or not Wolf also got my okay. Conditions were bad, you lost your bearings, encountered enemy opposition, took the necessary action and got away with it. All you can be accused of is piss-poor navigation. Do you understand what I'm saying to you?'

'I think so, sir,' said Kit.

'"Think so" isn't bloody well good enough. I'm going out on a limb for you on this. God knows what HQ will say about two of my most experienced pilots apparently getting lost like raw cadets up for their first solo. Given the outcome, they'll probably smell something distinctly fishy. But never mind that. They'll have to accept my word and I can take care of myself. Understand that I am only prepared to take this course of action because I'm damned if I'm going to risk making us a laughing stock in Group or compromising morale at this stage in the war. I want that crystal clear.'

'Yes sir.'

'They call this the Phoney War, Kit. It isn't a phoney war. It's deadly and it's serious and when the action really starts we will win only by fighting together. It's not your war, or Sergeant Wolf's. It's our war. Now, send in Wolf.' As Kit reached the door Brewster said: 'You accounted for two Hun. That was well done. But I don't expect you to make anything of it. I know that bragging is not your style so you shouldn't find it too difficult. Stick to that principle and hold your tongue. Otherwise I'll come down on you like a ton of bricks. And one more thing.'

'Yes, sir.'

'I'll be recommending Sergeant Wolf for a gong. Given the circumstances, as they'll be presented to Group, it would be difficult to do otherwise. Nothing for you, of course. Officially you were only doing what's expected of you. Officially.'

'Yes, sir.'

'You've got some ground to make up Kit,' said Brewster finally, not unkindly. 'I'd like to think you're up to the task. Convince me. For the time being B Flight is still yours. But step out of line once more . . .'

'I understand.'

'Make sure your damned American understands it too. I have no doubt you've underplayed his role in this sorry mess. The bugger needs sitting on good and hard. Harness that aggression, Kit, get it under control. If you succeed he might be of some use to us. If not, he's a liability and we're better off without him. Now, send the sod in and let me start the process.'

Twelve

Sunday, 24 December 1939

It had been arranged that Ossie Wolf would take his three-day Christmas leave in Paris and spend some time with Bébé Dubretskov. How much time he didn't know because she wouldn't say. But he did not get his Christmas leave.

He got permission to use the telephone in the Mayor's office in the Fonteville *mairie* to tell Bébé he could not meet her. The phone in the apartment on the quai des Grands Augustins was answered by the Englishwoman, Kitty Bannister. 'Who? Oh, for heaven's sake, don't mumble. Say again? Oh yes. A moment.' He heard her call: 'Darling it's your little American wolf. He sounds frightfully glum.' She laughed. He could hear Bébé laughing too as she came to the phone. He told her about the leave.

'No matter,' she said. She seemed about to hang up.

'Is that all?'

'What more do you want?'

'I don't know.'

'Then how should I?'

'I don't know. It's just it's been a while . . .'

'Is it so long? Not so long, I think.'

'Maybe not. It seems a while to me.'

'So you think of me, then?'

'Sure I think of you.'

'You think of me when I came to you at the Regina?'

'Yes.'

'Did they send the bill to your rich papa?'

'Yes.'

'And did he pay?'

'I didn't hear he didn't. I'd reserved the same room again. I thought you'd like that.'

'That room made me feel like a whore,' said Bébé.

'Jesus, you never said that.'

'Why should I? It was amusing for me. We enjoyed ourselves, I think. *Eh bien*, I have to go.'

'Okay,' said Ossie. He hesitated, trying to keep the disappointment out of his voice. 'Hey, I'm sorry about the leave.'

'No matter,' said Bébé again. Then, casually: 'Why was that anyway?'

'I can't tell you.'

'Ah, you don't entrust me with your confidence,' said Bébé. '*Je suis désolée*.' It was said lightly but with an edge, as though she was taunting him.

He was sore, and it showed in his tone: 'Well, maybe we can meet next time I make it to Paris.'

'As you wish.'

'I wish,' he said, but the telephone had gone dead.

Ossie Wolf could not explain his feelings. He felt like a grade-school punk pining after his first crush. There was nothing about this woman he should like. And yet she came into his thoughts again and again as he half slept in his glacial cell in the Paturel farmhouse, a fantasy so tangible and vivid that gradually the dreams became more real than reality. She was wonderful in his dreams: he delighted in the scent and feel of her. Her naked shoulders curved forward, her breasts rose and fell with each breath, trembling as she moved her position. Her thighs were firm about his hips and he was big with desire. She leaned forward and her body passed over him as she guided him to where she wanted him. He buried himself in her and in his senses. She ruled him in this, where he had always thought himself the ruler.

Her fingernails incised his skin. He imagined many things; he imagined her with women. She slid away from him and down, and he entered her, and for a time there was nothing else. All this occurred in a dream-world room with rich furnishings and low, golden lights. He supposed it must be the Regina. Afterwards he watched her as she bathed. She took pleasure in the way he looked at her, and performed small, arousing acts that brought him to a peak once more, and he was in the warm, milky water with her, their bodies sleek and squeaking against the enamel of the hot tub as they wrapped their limbs round each other. He knew they had experienced something like this but not entirely; the phantasm and the real woman had grown to be one so that, in the periods of time he had to consider such things, she was constantly in his thoughts.

Now he walked down the lane to his billet with the Paturels. The cold was numbing. The smell of wood-smoke was in the air and Fonteville appeared deserted, the only sound a dog yapping, tied up in a yard someplace. Beyond the church Ossie saw an old woman, no teeth, blue headscarf, floral pinafore showing under a heavy coat, ankle socks. He knew her by sight. She ignored him. This, too, was a woman . . .

Ossie had known many women. His first, at fourteen, had been in a whorehouse in downtown St Louis, Hot Marie's, not far from the Mississippi levees where the steamboats once moored. His cousin Boyd had fixed it up. They'd gone there in the Packard full of hooch. He'd been given Glennis, heavy-set with gold teeth and whiskey-breath. 'Reckon you're man enough to handle my tail, honey-lamb?' she'd said, and opened her legs. He reckoned he was and he did all right. Glennis told him so. And after that he wanted more, his mind full of white, heaving flesh, grunts, cries, a swell of sensual pleasure and money changing hands. It was as impersonal but satisfying as lighting a cigarette, like the time in the dugouts on Mount Aragon, guarding the approaches to Huesca. One of the female militia, the one with the swinging walk and challenging eyes, had murmured simply: 'Yes, comrade?' And they had given themselves, each alone in their thoughts, on the limestone scree strewn with boulders where the wild rosemary grew. Afterwards Ossie had straightened his clothes and stumbled back to the line, leaving her on the hillside calling after him, '*Visca POUM*,' her eyes closed and her white teeth showing.

Ossie was aware that all this set him apart from his fellows. He was puzzled by it. In the Roxy in Nancy, or Les Fleurs Bleu in Metz, the English would indulge in a dance or two with the pretty demoiselles angling for a drink, but the evening always ended round a table crowded with empty glasses, swapping black jokes about horrific prangs, fantasising about what they would eat on their next leave or hooting with laughter at nothing more than Buster Brown falling off his chair. Seeing his blank face they would cry out: 'That's the trouble with you Yanks. No bloody sense of humour. Get the beers in, there's a good chap.'

At the end Ossie was rarely there. The French officers, chic in their army and air-force uniforms, left first. He never saw one drunk or even, as the guys would say, merry. The Frenchmen were attentive, amusing and great dancers. They did not lurch, stagger or belch in a partner's face. They identified their quarry early on and provided her with whatever alcohol she wanted, strong and in large amounts. At ten or ten thirty they would depart quietly, so early that often the girl would reappear, freshly made-up, and resume her place at the bar.

Such appetites were rare among the English. There was plenty of chat and a flurry of mild flirtation when the chance arose but usually it led nowhere. A pat on the buttocks of a Petty pin-up as they left on patrol was the nearest most pilots got to intimate relations. They characterised the Frenchmen as dodgy types and guffawed as they made off with their prey. But Ossie detected uncertainty in their banter, the bravado of those who hadn't done it yet, whose knowledge of women was limited to sisters, or sisters of buddies. He kept quiet about his own appetites, which, until now, had been raw, urgent and quickly satisfied.

With Bébé, though, it was all unknown, fresh, disturbing, and nagged at him. It was true: there was nothing about the woman he should like yet he was crazy for her, and it had been a bad moment when Brewster denied him his leave.

'But I was kind of fixed up, sir.'

'Then unfix it.'

It had been a rocky session, something like those times with the Old Man when he'd started off about the goddammed family, and duty to the Old Country, and how he owed his future to what had gone on in the past – about Cousin Max in his damned red Albatros Scout with Jasta 12, tradition and honour, glory and sacrifice. The worst thing was that he'd swallowed the stuff whole until he'd arrived in Burgos in the spring of '37 with the rest of the so-called tourists, the only American, and found out how it really was.

But Brewster did not deal in abstractions. In the English way the big words were unspoken. His points were brief, brutal and left no room for argument. One more chance . . . one more chance: balls it up and that was it. No more gung-ho gambles with valuable aircraft, no more evasion of orders, no more shrugging aside the responsibilities that came with rank and the privilege of being selected air-crew in the best damned air force in the world. And finally, oh, yes, you're being recommended for a gong – a medal, you idiot. Now, get out of this office and use all that spare time over Christmas to think about what's been said.

Ossie let himself into the Paturel place and clattered down the timbered hallway to his room. The stink of damp was almost tangible. Old Paturel banged open the kitchen door, releasing a waft of boiling cabbage. He saw who it was and slammed the door. Ossie let himself into his room and lay down on the bed, still in his Irvin jacket and flying boots. He thought about Brewster. Well, hell, whatever the guy said, he'd still got himself two goddammed Henschels and a couple of 110s. And then there was the Heinkel when Dinghy had bought it, and the

Dornier back in November, the squadron's first success. Jesus, six kills and Brewster was bawling him out. The hell with him – the hell with all of them. He knew why he was here, even if the rest didn't. A long time back he had decided he was as good as dead already and before it happened he was going to take as many of the Fascist bastards with him as he could. But who knew how long he'd got?

He wondered how his father had reacted to the bill from the Regina. Since Spain he had communicated with the Old Man only once. 'Spain didn't work out. Heading north.' Now he'd been landed with an invoice from a fancy Paris hotel without an explanation. That would have thrown him, but he'd have paid. He always did. It was the honourable thing to do. Ossie could imagine him, stiff-necked, his heavy face set like stone, Hindenburg's *doppelgänger*, in his oak-panelled office in the Wolf Building that sprawled like a Disney castle over eleven blocks of St Louis real estate; good German beer had been brewed there for a hundred years, beer the Old Man said sold itself, had no need of childish advertising gimmicks. He had sniffed with disdain as Busch built refrigerated railcars and shipped its output beyond the local market; he had refused to contemplate non-alcoholic product lines to counter the impact of Prohibition, and when the crash came in '29 he'd found himself left with a mockery of a once-formidable brewing empire, catering for a dwindling pool of yesterday's tastes and yesterday's consumers. When they were gone, there would be little more than air in the vats. Each crisis had been met with a blank refusal to believe it was happening, couldn't be true. Just as the Great War could not be judged a defeat for Germany because the military had been on the brink of victory only to be betrayed by the politicians. And Ossie had gone along with this too, believing, always believing. Believing in Spain and what the Old Man told him he ought to do in Spain: tradition, honour, glory, sacrifice, all those big words again, and gathering overall, like a mighty storm-cloud beyond the horizon, swollen with menace and growing, always growing, the Fatherland moving relentlessly towards its destiny.

'Happy Christmas,' said Ossie Wolf aloud. Then shouted: '*Joyeux Noël.*' There was a clatter down the hallway, Paturel's voice: '*Quoi? Qui est là? Qu'est-ce que vous dites?*'

Ossie called out: 'Happy Christmas, Paturel. *Joyeux Noël*, you miserable bastard.'

'Ah, *oui*,' said Paturel reluctantly. '*Merci, Monsieur. Joyeux Noël.*' The door banged and he went back to his cabbage.

Thirteen

Sunday, 31 December 1939

On the morning before the New Year celebration at Chapelle-sur-Marne someone took a shot at Brewster as he stumped from his office towards the big Humber with Corporal Evans at the wheel. He was bound for the Bignet château, the largest grand house in the district, to meet the mayor, the organising committee drawn from the surrounding towns and villages, and Mesdames Hortense and Stephanie Bignet, who were insistent that their invitation should extend only to officers. Brewster was equally firm that it should include all non-commissioned officers, air-crew or not. As Spy Turner observed, the difference of opinion did not seem enough to warrant an unknown marksman taking a pot-shot at their CO but they all knew there was more to it than that.

The bullet struck the door jamb a foot from Brewster's left shoulder, pierced the woodwork and ricocheted down the corridor, tore through a number of greatcoats hanging from hooks, then fell on to the linoleum and spun to a halt. Titch Baker, the AC2 admin clerk, picked it up curiously and dropped it because it was still hot.

The crack of the rifle, echoing across the runways after a moment's delay, helped them pinpoint the spot in the woodland on the far side of the airfield where it had been fired, but nothing was found; no carelessly discarded cartridge case, no tell-tale cigarette butt, just flattened grass and leaves where someone had lain between two beeches. Sous-lieutenant Trochu, the Armée de l'Air liaison officer, examined the bullet and said it had probably been fired from an 8x50mm Berthier, standard weapon of French infantry but, given the accuracy, quite possibly an MAS-36 model of recent issue and even then not in great numbers. '*C'est une devinette singulière n'est-ce pas?*' It had been an admirable shot, he added, from a distance of more than 1,500 metres. But he professed himself perplexed as to why anyone would want to do such a thing. Perhaps it was a joke, he suggested, no more than New Year's Eve high spirits . . .

The replacement for Dinghy Davis had arrived. With a decent number of hours on Hurricanes Pip Fuller was fresh from operational training at Little Rissington. He had passed out well, rated above average and eager for combat. He regarded anyone who had seen action with awe, particularly the top-scorers, Carter and Wolf, around whom a certain air of mystery hung. Buster Brown was merciless. Kit Curtis's absence over Christmas was due to a special investiture at Buckingham Palace, he told Fuller. The King had cut short his visit to Balmoral to award Kit a knighthood, tapping his shoulders shortly after breakfast on Boxing Day. For a few pleasurable moments Pip Fuller believed him. But such teasing was rare and generally he was indulged. He had not been touched by the sour taste of fear and his coltish enthusiasm was refreshing – reminded them of how they had been when they'd first arrived in France. Now, in the early evening, he climbed into the Alvis and squeezed between Kit and Buster Brown, like a youngster off for a treat with his uncles.

They took the winding lane that descended the hill from Revigncourt to Chapelle-sur-Marne, making good progress on the packed snow. Buster worked at the wheel and talked of road races at Donington, Brooklands, Montlhéry. He had raced an Aston Martin at Le Mans in 1938. He drove well, fast, smooth, confident, his feet dancing on the pedals, his hands holding the steering-wheel in an easy, sensitive grip. Then he slowed. Through the clinging fog, on the straight, featureless route beyond Ponthiou, they glimpsed what at first appeared to be a shattered tree-trunk rearing from the verge, shorn of its branches. Gradually it revealed itself as a stone column narrowing in sections towards the top like the shaft of an umbrella and crowned by an insignificant concrete urn. The pilots piled out of the ticking hard-used Alvis, vaulted a wall, crunched across a gravel surround and mounted a shallow flight of steps. Kit alone had French. '*À La Gloire des Combattants de Chapelle-sur-Marne, 6 avril–11 septembre 1914. Inauguré 6 aout 1939.* Good God,' he said, 'they only put this up five months ago.'

'Bloody marvellous,' said Buster Brown. 'Instead of thinking about the last war they should be concentrating on this one.'

'Daladier was here,' said Kit. 'And General Orly. Quite a shindig.' He scrutinised the inscription once more. 'The Battle of the Marne. Before the trenches. When the war was still fluid.' He looked around him. 'Great cavalry country.'

Reading over Kit's shoulder, Pip Fuller said: 'To the memory of the officers, under officers and soldiers of Provence and the coast of Nice. I say, what must they have made of this God-forsaken country?' He looked around him. 'An uncle of mine died in the Battle of the Marne. I remember my father saying it was a turning-point.'

'It was for him, poor sod,' said Buster.

'After the Marne everything got bogged down,' said Kit. 'Half a million dead. The Huns thrown back. Everyone dug in from here to the Channel coast.'

'Do you think it's going to happen like that this time?' said Fuller.

'Not a prayer,' said Buster Brown. 'It's all opened up with the war in the air and the Blitzkrieg stuff. Look at what happened in Poland – those bloody Stukas and Panzers.'

'I think we can hold them,' said Kit. 'The BEF is raring to go and we mustn't underestimate the French. What did Marshal Foch say? "My centre is giving way, my right is falling back, situation excellent. I am attacking."'

'When did he say that?' said Buster Brown.

'Anyway,' said Kit. He climbed back into the Alvis.

Despite the passing of a hundred and fifty years the Bignet family was still regarded locally as a nest of commoners and opportunists who thought themselves better than others. At the time of the Revolution, the grand houses of those who fled the mob had been sold off as *bien nationaux* to those fortunate enough to have money without the stigma of aristocratic descent. The Bignets, pig-farmers for generations and famously careful with their cash, chose unexpectedly to purchase the château built and formerly owned by the Duc du Chapelle, who had success-fully escaped to Naples in time to perish in a cholera epidemic.

For the Bignets, it proved a faltering step on the social ladder. The peasants and farmers sneered at their attempts to elevate themselves to the bourgeoisie. The bourgeoisie and those aristos who survived the Terror chuckled at what they considered the fatuous posturings of a family impertinent enough to aspire to the trappings of wealth and privilege only to be betrayed and made foolish by its lack of grace, style and breeding. It was quite unfair. At first the Bignets had made their way with some success. One of their number had attended the Sorbonne and entered the law, to be appointed to a senior position in the Ministry of Justice. Another was the best cadet of his year at the École Militaire, rose to become a marshal of France and served with distinction in the Crimea. A cherished daughter sang *Traviata* to the approval of discerning opera-goers at La Scala. Many married well. But none of these and other achievements changed opinion around Chapelle and its environs that the Bignets were jumped-up social climbers who should have stuck to their pig-sties and what they knew.

Through the generations the Bignets appeared to become worn down by the constant ridicule. It was as though, gradu-ally, they gave up, stopped trying. No Bignet shone in any sphere. Their fortunes dwindled, their marriages grew less propitious or failed, then ceased altogether. The great château crumbled, the drives and parks, barns and stables gradually fell to ruin. Finally only two sisters remained in the shell of the still elegant château. Mesdames Hortense and Stephanie Bignet remained aloof from those above or below them on the social scale for fear of reproof on either side. And as they considered no one their equal their lives became solitary and lonely, except for a few hours on Christmas Eve when, unaccountably, local urchins were permitted to roam the state rooms and corridors in search of tangerines, wooden dolls and tin-plate clowns – some throwback to a happy memory treasured by Hortense. Or when they sensed a broader duty to open the doors of the Château du Chapelle, as now: to mark the passage of time into a new and ominous decade.

Brewster had quickly settled the issue of which of his men should or should not be on the invitation list by threatening to boycott the affair. After much puffing of cheeks and raising of eyebrows the sisters Bignet, encouraged by the anxious mayor, could only accede.

The various cars and trucks, military and civilian, mustered by the squadron mingled with local Renaults and Citroëns, battered and smart, a saucy Delahaye and even an ancient Darracq on the half-moon drive in front of the château's portico, with its Greek columns and massive wood and iron doors that crowned flights of steps that swept up from left and right. The visitor, entering the château at what would normally be first-floor level, was invited by the architect to pause on the balcony and admire the parkland laid out before him, with the twin red-brick gatehouses and lofty wrought-iron gates marking the entrance half a mile away. Now the shabby prospect emphasised the estate's transient fortunes.

Drinks were on hand in the tumult of the reception hall. 'No bloody beer,' said Buster Brown, gulping indifferent champagne. Around them, almost laughably spruce, their comrades struggled to be polite, marooned in a sea of Gallic faces. Kit saw Ossie Wolf slouched in an Empire chair by a towering bookcase, alone, abstracted, insouciant as ever. As he watched, the mayor, majestic in his tricolour sash, sailed across, bowed deeply to the American and presented his plump wife, who launched into a torrent of enthusiastic and incomprehensible French. Ossie rose reluctantly to his feet and the mayor moved just as swiftly away, leaving him with his wife. Kit took mean enjoyment from watching the American nod and grin, in his crooked oh-shucks way, shuffle his feet and look for a means of escape. Nearby, the other NCOs, Knox, Goofy Gates, Flight Sergeant Jessop and the rest, had gathered in a defensive knot, ill-at-ease and talking low, fiddling with their ties and sipping doubtfully at their champagne.

To a lacklustre ripple of applause the Bignet sisters descended the noble oak staircase, steadying themselves with trembling hands on the gilded banister as the steps creaked alarmingly beneath their bird-like weight. At Kit's elbow a small, dapper fellow with *pince-nez*, a local-government official perhaps, remarked to his companion: 'It occurs to me, my dear Mourat, that we find ourselves at such fêtes out of respect to this house rather than for those who, at present, occupy it.' There was no thought in the man's mind that the English officer could understand him. Such things were not possible.

'Still one must concede that the family Bignet are even-handed in their readiness to make the place available for such functions,' said the other. 'I recall just such a bun-fight for the Boches in 1916.'

'From what one hears perhaps there will be again,' said the first. He sighed. 'In some situations we are all required to be pragmatists.'

Kit moved away. Here and there he glimpsed the dark blue uniforms of l'Armée de l'Air. Half a dozen pilots had been enlisted by the mayor to represent the squadron of Morane 406s and Curtis Hawks at St Dizier in the interests of *entente cordiale*. Buster Brown was in lively conversation with a tall French pilot with crow-black hair combed straight back and recent burns to his nose and cheeks. The pale area round his eyes, which had, no doubt, been protected by his goggles, contrasted starkly. He gave no explanation.

'Here's some luck,' Buster said. 'Meet Johnny Balbec, the bloody nuisance who sat on my arse in his Bugatti for three hours at the Sarthe in thirty-eight and beat us on the index of performance.'

The Frenchman shrugged. 'What do you expect with your English lorries?' He looked at Kit. 'Are you also a reckless fool?'

'My father was a car man,' said Kit. 'Knew Parry Thomas. Used to help with the timekeeping. Never raced himself. Rather lost heart after Pendine. For me, though,' he added, 'it's always been flying.'

'Another province of reckless fools,' said the Frenchman. 'But all pilots are heroes now. What valiant gods of the air we are – and the women, my heavens, the women. Though this,' he touched his face, 'inhibits them somewhat.' His fingers were also burned.

In the ballroom long tables had been set for dinner, the light from cream beeswax candles in elaborate antique holders glinting on silver cutlery and condiments laid out precisely on crisp white linen. From the wall drooped the Union flag and the French tricolour, crossed.

The feast came as a sensory shock to the squadron, grown used to its daily fare of bully-beef, potatoes, hot tea and cheap alcohol. Each course, which offered many choices, was not only good and rich but the portions were on a giant scale. *Pâté de foie gras*, truffles, *choucroute*, trout and pike, pork in many guises, eccentric and suggestive sausages that resisted the knife, tarts of flaky pastry made with meat and onions, cheese after cheese, some with red and white currant preserves, others flavoured with aniseed, fennel and cumin; all kinds of cakes, preserved fruit and sweets; wine, bottle after bottle, red and white, drawn from regions with disturbingly Germanic names: Ammerschwir, Sigolsheim, Bergheim, Guebwiller. And beer, yes, God be praised, strong beer from Strasbourg, Champigneulles and Metz. No one could say that the family Bignet, grudgingly supported by the community and its various commercial and political enterprises, had not laid on a memorable repast. The CO said as much in his stumbling speech.

'Happy to be here in your time of need . . . historic alliance . . . shared history, admittedly not always on the same side . . .' laughter, cheers and glasses beaten on the table by his young pilots '. . . mutual resolve to smash the common enemy . . . what pleasure to join with you on this magnificent occasion . . . I call on every member of my squadron to stand and propose a toast . . . may we stand firm, shoulder to shoulder and prevail. *Vive la France!'* The address, written by Kit, was greeted with enthusiasm, despite a wry smile and a wince or two as Brewster murdered the French language.

The mayor of Chapelle-sur-Marne spoke in the same vein but for longer. He saluted the brave allies of the Royal Air Force who fought in the skies over hallowed earth where their fathers had fought before them. Right and reason would prevail. The vile Boches would be driven back. This was a struggle that would involve every French man and woman, every person in the room. All would be called upon to fight, if necessary to the death for the honour and glory of France, for the survival of civilisation. God was on their side. He would not fail them. He had ordained a savage winter to provide the coalition with still more time to prepare. When the Boches came, they would be met with merciless force. The mayor, perspiring with patriotic fervour, concluded with only mild compliments to Mesdames Hortense and Stephanie Bignet for throwing open the Château du Chapelle – he made them sound almost like caretakers – then cried the obligatory, '*Vive la France, vive l'Angleterre*' – a storm of applause and cries of 'Bravo' – and signalled for the digestives to be served without delay.

Kit, warming an Armagnac, passed close to Monsieur Pince-nez. 'I confess myself surprised, Mourat,' the diminutive official was saying, 'that our esteemed mayor should nail his colours quite so firmly to the mast.'

'I sincerely hope,' Monsieur Mourat responded laconically, 'that some of his more colourful reflections will not be laid at his door, should we find ourselves in unfavourable circumstances.'

'Indeed,' said Monsieur Pince-nez, and they smiled at one another in perfect accord.

Many of the guests remained lolling at the disordered tables in the ballroom, bubbling with lively conversation. Others moved away to distant parts of the huge château, curious, inquisitive or intent on amours. Somewhere a gramophone was being cranked into service. Arletty began to trill 'Coeur de Parisienne'. Outside the ballroom a group of pilots, English and French, were simulating dog-fights with the Luftwaffe, their hands executing the universal language of aerobatics. Ossie Wolf had been cornered by the mayor's wife. She liked him – she liked him very much. She reached out and touched his face as she talked and talked, and he did not understand a word. She was laughing like a young girl. Perhaps he reminded her of an old beau. Perhaps it was because he was American and she had visited the cinema too often. Close by, three locals were listening to what was said, glancing at each other and smiling thin, contemptuous smiles.

Kit walked over to him. '*Pardon, Madame*. Sergeant, *je veux vous parler. C'est très important.*'

'Huh?' said Ossie Wolf. The mayor's wife was piqued and rocked her head from side to side impatiently, sighing through pursed lips.

'*Je vous en prie, Madame,*' said Kit. The woman sighed again, shrugged her shoulders and moved away, a picture of studied indifference, looking for her husband.

'Worried the *entente*'s too darned *cordiale*?' said Ossie.

'I thought you might be, Sergeant.'

'Maybe I was at that. So, what's so important? Am I being scrubbed?'

'Hardly. I hear you're in line for a gong.'

'I don't want a goddammed medal,' said Ossie. 'Can't you stop it?'

'Out of my hands,' said Kit. 'Tell the CO you don't want it.'

'I tried that.'

'What did he say?'

'I think he told me to bugger off.'

'That sounds about right.' Kit noticed that the three locals were closer now, listening. 'We seem to be arousing some curiosity.'

One of the trio, gaunt and stooped with big, grease-stained hands, said awkwardly: '*Pardon, Messieurs.* Please do not misunderstand. Naturally your presence here is of interest to us. Revigncourt is an excellent *terrain d'aviation*, is it not?'

'Not bad,' said Kit.

'Very suitable for your Hurricane machines.'

The pilots said nothing. The gaunt man said he was the *garagiste* of Chapelle. He told them he was a *cycliste de course* of some repute, had finished well in the Tour de France but never won; always the wrong team or ill-luck with the conditions. His companions said it was a great pity. The *garagiste* asked if the squadron had been successful in shooting down the dirty Boches. The pilots said nothing. The *garagiste* hoped they had. He understood the Hurricane was a formidable aeroplane and more than a match for the German Messerschmitts; more manoeuvrable, it was said. His companions said they had heard that too. The pilots said nothing. The *garagiste* said it was clear the English squadron was of the finest but there had been rumours of accidents and perhaps losses. Surely it could not be true. The pilots said nothing. The *garagiste* told them what a privilege it had been to talk to such gallant allies and have an opportunity to express his admiration.

'Thank you,' said Kit.

'*Vive la France, vive l'Angleterre*,' said the *garagiste*.

'Sure, *vive* everybody,' Ossie said. He watched the Frenchmen move away slowly, talking animatedly. 'That is one helluva nosy guy.'

'I'm not sure we're entirely among friends,' said Kit.

It was dense night under the château's portico. No light escaped from the interior. Leaning on the stone balustrade, Kit made out the shapes of trees and distant lakes. The air was fierce with cold. Shrieks and calls of beasts and birds echoed through the woodland. He found it odd to be standing beside the silent American. He felt they each had something to say but did not want to be first. Stupid . . .

'Good leave Sergeant?'

'Cancelled.'

'I didn't know.'

'Bad boys don't get leave. Some bad boys. Now, why would the CO make an exception?'

'You'd better ask him.'

'Looks like I've got to ask the guy everything now, even permission to wipe my arse.'

'Admit it, Sergeant, we were absolutely out of order. We had it coming.'

'Even so, I reckon we did pretty good.'

'The CO gives us that. Have you got a cigarette?' Kit lit up, his face orange-yellow in the flame. 'I've got a lot of ground to make up. So have you.'

'I thought we were here to kill Hun.'

'So we are. We're also here to do as we're told. Like Brewster said, we're not fighting a private war.' He squinted at Ossie Wolf through the cigarette smoke. 'Am I getting through to you, Sergeant?'

'Maybe so.'

'I pleaded temporary insanity. What was your excuse?'

'I didn't offer one. I told him I wasn't the kind of guy who only flew when there wasn't a cloud in the sky. I've always made it my business to go up when everyone else is making goddammed excuses.'

'He must have been tickled.'

'It's what I know,' said Ossie, 'the code I was taught by guys flying mail out of the old Robertson hangars at Lambert Field where Charlie Lindbergh got his break. You remember when Lindbergh dropped in on France that time? He asked what kind of man would live where there's no daring. He didn't reckon to take foolish chances but he also reckoned you achieve nix not taking any chances at all.'

'You knew Lindbergh?'

'No, before my time. But they were all Lindberghs at Lambert, tough cookies who knew what made a pilot.'

'They taught you?'

'Yeah. My old man wanted me to fly and I was happy to go along with that, all right. We had flyers in the family, a cousin, Max, who did stuff in Europe.'

'What kind of stuff?'

'Now we're getting to it.'

Back in the château there were whoops and cries. Midnight came and passed. For all the assumed jollity it was curiously muted, the arrival of 1940. A few of the pilots struggled through 'Auld Lang Syne' but it didn't catch on. French and English became lost in thought, their expressions grave.

A shaft of brilliant light illuminated the parkland briefly as Buster Brown and Balbec came out of the house through the big doorway. Behind them, unsteady on his feet, was Al Miller. The heavy door thudded shut behind him. 'Bloody hell, who put out the lights?'

'*C'est drôle,*' said Balbec. 'I am told that my good friend Al is a weaver and see how he weaves, even on the ground.'

'I'm no friend of yours,' said Miller. He descended the steps to the park with some dignity and was violently sick in a bed of rhododendrons.

'A perfect conclusion to a delightful evening,' said Balbec.

Behind him the doors of the château were thrown back but the lights had been dimmed. People were beginning to leave. Guests stumbled on the steps, laughing and shouting farewells. Car doors slammed, reluctant engines turned over, caught and fired. Exhaust fumes drifted into the château's salon. Miller had taken off his tunic and was sitting on it by the rhododendrons, watching the activity. 'That idiot is going to die of exposure,' said Kit. He went down, pulled Miller to his feet and pushed him back up the steps into the warmth of the château.

In the doorway Miller brushed past Brewster, hurrying to the Humber. His instinct was to salute but his hand only got as far as his chest. He wiggled his fingers in familiar fashion. 'Jolly good speech, sir. Excellent command of the language.'

Brewster glared at Kit. 'Make sure this man gets back to his billet.'

Kit tumbled Miller on to a Louis Philippe giltwood sofa where he settled himself comfortably and began to snore, head back, mouth agape. He looked disturbingly dead.

In the hallway Monsieur Pince-nez, the sardonic Mourat and the *garagiste* were absorbed in conversation. The mayor of Chapelle-sur-Marne stood nearby as though uncertain whether to join them, his tricolour sash creased and stained, no longer splendid. His wife twisted a silk scarf in her hands. She looked as though she had been weeping. Beyond, on the magnificent staircase, the Bignet sisters returned to the shadows step by painful step.

Kit found Buster Brown standing by the burbling Delahaye of Johnny Balbec. The Armée de l'Air pilot, seated at the wheel, extended his hand. Kit could feel the burn tissue. Balbec jerked his head at Buster Brown. 'You are certainly brave to permit yourself to be driven by this crazy fellow,' he said, in English. 'You should know he fell asleep on the Mulsanne at a hundred and sixty kilometres an hour.'

'Until I was disturbed by your bloody headlights coming up behind me,' said Buster.

Kit said: 'It's not the driver I'm nervous about, it's his car. It doesn't seem to have any brakes.'

'Who needs brakes?' said Buster Brown. 'A throttle is all that's required. And don't be so critical. This old bus may be yours one day. I've left it to you in my will.' He grinned. 'Don't you remember the adj handing round those bloody blue will forms at Tangmere? I thought you'd like the old bus.'

'Good God,' said Kit.

'Why so shocked, old boy? I suppose you've paused from time to time to weigh up our chances? Best to leave things neat and tidy, I say. Pity about poor old Dinghy, though. Never thought he'd be the first. I'd left him my golf clubs – he was always droning on about what a piss-poor game it was, played by stuck-up snobs. I liked to picture his face.'

Balbec said: 'Perhaps you are too gloomy, my friend. It is possible the situation in which we find ourselves might resolve itself sooner than we imagine.'

'Really?' said Buster. 'How do you make that out?'

'I remain unconvinced that the Boches are committed to total war in Europe. It will be too destructive for them, for everyone. I believe they will pull back, negotiate. If this is not so why else would they permit this Drôle de Guerre to drag on so?'

'The weather might have something to do with it,' said Kit. 'Or hadn't you noticed?'

'Please understand, I do not mean to arouse your English sensibilities. I simply state the situation as I perceive it.'

'Not too bloody helpful, Johnny,' said Buster. 'Do the rest of your chums share similar views?'

'Forget my remarks,' said Balbec. He attempted to make light of it. 'The French and the English rarely see matters from the same perspective.'

'I hope to God you don't speak for the French,' said Kit, and to Buster Brown: 'Al Miller needs a lift. He can take my place. See him back to his billet, there's a good fellow.'

'Well,' said Balbec, 'goodbye.' He did not meet their eyes again. He blipped the throttle of the Delahaye. The exhaust was jarring and discordant as he sped away between the trees towards the estate gateway.

'Damn and hell,' said Buster.

'How did he get his burns?' asked Kit.

'Oh, put a wing in doing a slow-roll at low level to celebrate five hundred hours on fighters, stupid sod.' In the darkness Buster was tossing the ignition key of the Alvis from hand to hand. He dropped it and bent down, groping around in the gravel. 'Do you reckon he's typical in any way?'

'God knows,' said Kit. 'I hope not. Perhaps Stuffy Dowding was right.'

'Isn't he always? But about what particularly?'

'Oh, wasting our resources on someone else's battle, leaving our home defences weak when the Hun attack.'

'Bloody Balbec says they won't. Attack, I mean.'

'You don't believe that, do you?'

'No.'

'Neither do I.'

'Did you have a good leave?'

'No.'

'Neither did I. They don't know what to say to you, do they?'

'No. Christmas at home. I just wanted to get back here.'

'Me too.'

'Funny that.'

'Bloody odd.'

'I'll rustle up Miller.'

'Jolly good.'

'Well, cheerio.'

'Yes, cheerio.'

The Rolls had been waiting for Kit outside the ticket office at Midhurst station. 'Decent journey, Mister Kit?' Barlow took his kitbag and placed it carefully in the boot of the silver and blue 20/25 coupé.

'Mind if I drive, Barlow?'

At the end of the long blue bonnet the silver lady flew gracefully down Bepton Road and right into West Street. At the junction Kit slowed. There was no traffic. Christmas Eve was a family time even in the midst of war. Otherwise why was he here? The Rolls began to move again, very slowly now, down South Street, halting with a whisper of brakes outside the Spread Eagle. The façade of the old coaching inn seemed distressed and shabby, its windows dirty and criss-crossed with bomb-blast tape, the brasswork on the black front door unpolished. At this hour, late afternoon, the place stood closed and, even across the street, gave off that stale aroma of yesterday's ale. But soon Sam Abrams would open up and fill the place with gentle light. The buzz of gossip would swell and fill the bars, glasses would be drained and drained again, tobacco smoke cloaking everything with a distorting haze to lend the scene a timelessness: any evening, any year, any century stretching back five hundred years.

'I learned to drink there, Barlow,' said Kit. 'Or how not to.'

'Shall I knock up Sam, Mister Kit? He wouldn't want to miss you.'

Kit shook his head, engaged gear, and the Rolls slipped smoothly away, south towards Cocking, then right, crawling down the twisting lane to Linch Down. The sky grew big. By the twin elms the white-painted gates stood open and the Rolls passed silently up the drive to the house.

Kit let himself in. In the hallway, on the sycamore card table, Farve's Nativity scene was set out, exactly as Kit remembered it, year by year, each Christmas from his infancy: in the centre the mirror-pond surrounded by cotton-wool snow, the Holy Family carved in wood, struggling breast-high in the fluff, Jesus pink and tiny in a straw crib, the three kings, one without a head, lead cattle, sheep and collies with the one-armed shepherd known as Silas, half a dozen pigs, ducks and geese, a red-faced farmer – Old Ben, as tradition had it – bigger than the rest, made to a different scale, unexplained giraffes and elephants, a lion, two tigers and the chipped green crocodile known as Tim. Every year the grey Tricker's of St James's shoebox with 'Nativity' pencilled on its lid came downstairs from Farve's dressing room, to be laid out in just this pattern. From the drawing room Diana Curtis called: 'Arthur, is that you?'

'No, Mother, it's me.'

Agnes Hobbes looked out from the kitchen door at the end of the hall. She called over her shoulder: 'It's Mister Kit, sir.'

Farve appeared, holding a mug of tea. He liked to spend time taking in the warmth of the kitchen range, deep in one of the yew and elm Windsor chairs, watching Agnes prepare the evening meal and listening with half an ear to village gossip with Ben, the Airedale, at his knee. Tea was spilling from the mug. He steadied it and put it down on a bookcase. He seized his son's hand, his grasp flaccid, changed, and held it for a long moment, searching Kit's face. 'So pleased, so pleased.' He bit his lip, composed himself, managed a smile, nodding at the Nativity. 'The same old crowd.' Ben was leaping round the hallway, panting with joy, drooling on the tiles.

From the drawing room Diana Curtis called: 'Christopher, is that you at last? Where on earth have you been? We've been expecting you for ages.' She came out into the hall slowly and offered her cheek for a peck. Farve was adjusting the position of Old Ben, a tremor running down his fingers. 'The rector called for sherry yesterday,' she went on. 'He positively goggled at your father's seasonal travesty. I'm sure it's sacrilegious.'

'Four hundred years ago Farve would have been burned at the stake,' said Kit.

'Do you think so? Yes, I'm sure you're right.' She noticed the mug on the bookcase. 'Oh, for Heaven's sake, Arthur, you're ruining the walnut with your damnable tea.'

Kit followed his mother into the drawing room. A jigsaw of Stubbs horses was set out on a tray, almost completed. 'What news of Karoline?' she said. 'I have to ask. You never write.'

'I did write Mother. I motored over to Nancy.'

'Oh yes, I dimly recall. A few brief lines. All well?'

'I think they should get out while they have the chance. Things don't look good for Jewish folk.'

'Personally, Christopher, I think all we hear about Germany being down on the Jews is vastly overstated. It's just one of Hitler's whims. Besides, Karoline is Catholic, like me. I don't think she's ever seen the inside of a synagogue. In the early days there was even talk that Maurice would convert but he became too occupied with chasing money.' She looked thoughtful. 'I suppose that might be his Jewishness coming out.' She raised an eyebrow. 'Anyway, this is by-the-by. Surely there's not the remotest chance of Germany succeeding? The Maginot Line is impregnable, isn't it? And our forces are so great. Every day the newspapers are full of it. Confidence is high.' She looked at him reprovingly. 'I'm surprised you indulge in such defeatist talk.'

Kit's father had been listening by the door. 'Anything is possible, Diana. Kit knows the situation better than us. And if he's right, if the danger is so great, then it's only sensible that the Maierscheldts should think about getting out while the going's good.'

'Oh pooh,' said Diana. 'Maurice is practically a Hun himself. And the man doesn't look remotely Jewish, not like some of them. Even if the Germans got as far as Alsace I'm sure they wouldn't bother with him. I mean, really, why should they be interested in a little man who makes household goods? Although, of course, one has to admit that the Germans are frightfully methodical and, if the stories about the Jews *are* true, then I suppose there is the remote possibility that they might cart him away.'

'Cart them all away,' said Farve. He turned to Kit. 'You should talk to them, Kit, urge them to leave France now, come here if need be until we can find something for them. They're among our oldest friends, after all.'

'Oh Arthur, be sensible,' said Diana. 'The prospect of accommodating Karoline and Hannah is one thing. But the thought of Maurice turning up on our doorstep is too ghastly for words.'

Later, after dinner, served by Agnes Hobbes – chicken, roast potatoes, stuffing, bread sauce and a blazing Christmas pudding – Kit found himself alone in the drawing room with his father. His mother had retired early, a migraine coming on. She had asked only one question about the squadron. 'Agnes tells us she saw a newsreel in the cinema the other day, those vulgar little Crazy Gang people entertaining the troops. Do they drop in on you?'

'No Mother. The Dorniers paid us a visit but they didn't stay long.'

'I'm not familiar with the name.'

'It doesn't matter. They weren't terribly funny.'

Kit told his father something of what had passed in France, rather vague, dismissive, short on detail, nothing to make him anxious. He was aware that he felt profoundly indifferent about attempting to explain the inexplicable. Farve's hand, as he listened and fondled Ben the Airedale's ears, trembled uncontrollably. For the first time Kit noticed that the left side of his face drooped and that his lips there were still and twisted. 'Farve, are you entirely well?' he said.

'Not entirely, no. They picked it up when I got myself checked for the Local Defence Volunteers. High blood pressure or some such. Then, bother me, a week or so later things went a bit haywire. Since then I'm afraid the business has rather gone to pot, as far as I'm concerned. Haven't been to town for ages. But I'm never sure how much I'm needed, these days. They all seem to get on perfectly well without me. You'll have a lot of sorting out to do, my boy, when this business is over.' The Airedale looked up at him, uttering querulous whimpers as though he had understood every word. 'But I'm all right now, aren't I, Ben?'

'Why didn't you let me know?' said Kit.

'Hardly any point my boy. You've got enough on your plate.'

The next day Kit left and took a room at the Savoy. He told them he had been recalled early. His mother said, 'Oh yes?' and gave a small cry of pleasure as she found the elusive piece that completed the stallion's ear in her jigsaw. His father swallowed and gazed at him for a long time, his sagging mouth giving him a desperate look. 'Of course,' he said. 'Of course you must go.' Kit did not explain how the news had reached him: there had been no telephone call, no telegram. For Farve, he knew, no explanation was required.

At the Château du Chapelle, a little after midnight, the gathering had largely dispersed. Kit woke Al Miller on his Louis Philippe sofa in the salon and thrust him into the Alvis between Pip Fuller and Buster Brown. Then he walked over to the Bedford. The tailgate was still down. He pulled himself up. Everyone stopped talking. Flight Sergeant Jessop said: 'Not going back in the Alvis sir?'

'Flying Officer Miller not feeling too well sir?' In the darkness someone sniggered.

Kit eased himself on to the bench between Jessop and Ossie Wolf. Around him cigarettes glowed. There was a stench of alcohol, the occasional burst of coughing, prolonged farts and groans of protest from those nearby.

'How do you think it went sir?' It was the voice that had asked about Al Miller.

'Who wants to know?'

It was Goofy Gates. His voice changed: he tried to sound as though he really wanted to know how it had gone.

'I hope you all said thank you for having me,' said Kit. 'They laid on quite a spread.'

'A lot of us think it was a dodgy old do,' said Gates.

'I wouldn't know about that,' said Kit. 'Now, if you don't mind, I'm going to get some shut-eye.' He tipped his service cap over his eyes and pretended to fall asleep, and the sleep became real, in spite of the Bedford lurching, bouncing and squirming its way through the freshly falling snow to Fonteville.

As the lorry slid to a halt, Ossie Wolf gave him a jab in the ribs with his elbow. The others were pushing past them, jumping down and heading for their billets. 'End of the line,' the American said.

Kit had been dreaming. He was sitting in the wreckage of a Hurricane cockpit waiting for it to explode. He heard a movement on the shattered wing beside him. He called out: 'I can't move.' There was panting, puffing, a commotion and two paws appeared on the side of the cockpit. Ben the Airedale started licking his face. He woke up, startled and amused.

'Some dream, huh?' said Ossie Wolf. 'Was she a honey?'

'She was a he actually and he was licking my face.' The single bell in the tower of the church of Saint-Saulve tolled one-thirty. 'It was my dog, Sergeant, our dog from home.' They dropped down on to the gravel of the square. Ogley, the driver, checked them in his mirror and sped away. The American slapped his hands together and rubbed them.

'Goodnight Sergeant,' said Kit.

'Hey,' said Ossie Wolf, 'I never got to finish what I started saying back there.'

'Back where?'

'Back at the Château. I need to square things with someone. I was getting round to stuff.'

'What sort of stuff?'

'I need to square things and, Christ knows why, but you seem to be the only guy I can talk to now Dinghy's gone.'

'Talk to about what?'

'About what happened in Spain.'

'Believe me, Sergeant,' said Kit, 'we know all about what you did in Spain.'

'Not all,' said Ossie Wolf. 'Not even Dinghy knew. But somebody's got to know so I can get things right with myself.'

'Got to know about what?'

'I saw it all, the way it's going to be. Spain was just a single ring in a three-ring circus. But now the whole show is heading our way. I know it. I saw Guernica.'

'Everybody knows about Guernica,' said Kit, harsh, dismissive. He was tired and impatient to be alone.

'How could you know about Guernica?' Ossie Wolf said. 'You read about it, sure. The difference is, I was there. I saw it all. It was market day. Everyone had come into the square. The church bells of Santa Maria were ringing. And then the airplanes came, the bombers and the fighters. They dumped fifty tons of high explosive on those poor bastards in the space of three hours. The place went up in flames. We killed a third of the population. Sixteen hundred people dead or wounded.'

'We?'

'We,' said the American. 'I was flying with the Condor Legion.'

Fourteen

Monday, 1 January 1940

Inside the church of Saint-Saulve the temperature was glacial. The cold struck to the bone, rendering Kit breathless as though it were freezing the air in his lungs. He sat down in a pew, slippery and green-blue with damp. In the tower he could hear the creaking and ticking of the clock. Ossie Wolf found his way into the vestry and came back with a paraffin lamp. He struck a match, the wick sputtered and caught. The crude carving of the Gothic font was picked out in relief. Something scratched and scurried in the depths of the nave. Ossie Wolf said: 'This is a heck of a place for a confessional.' His voice reverberated round the building, the echoes dying away in the timbers of the vaulted roof.

'Is that what this is?' said Kit.

Ossie hesitated. 'Level with me. Have you done things that, even when you were doing them, you knew were wrong but you didn't bother to think about it too much?'

'I imagine everyone has.'

'I'm talking about stuff that maybe seemed small and unimportant, going along with someone else's ideas because it was easier that way, then finding yourself led into something that wasn't small and unimportant at all. Something that's really lousy.'

'Oh, you mean the little matter of flying for the Fascists?'

'I'm getting to that.' Ossie Wolf was pacing the aisle, the

steel-tipped heels of his service shoes rapping the tiles. 'But that's not all of it.'

'For God's sake man,' said Kit, 'sit down.'

Ossie slid into the pew in front of him. He faced away, staring down the length of the church at the big window, with plain glass, not stained: when the Germans had come to Fonteville in 1916 they had used the saints' heads for target practice.

'It seems to me,' said Ossie, 'that whenever we bad-mouth people we don't understand it's kind of a small betrayal. Like the blacks in the States. Like the poor bastards in the bread lines in the depression. Like the people of the Left in Spain. Like it is now with the Jews. There are plenty of folk around who've got it in for the Jews, not just the Fascists but ordinary folk who reckon in their own quiet way that the Jews had it coming, that it's not their business and are simply glad it's not them.'

Kit heard his mother's voice: *Maurice became too occupied with chasing money. I suppose that might be his Jewishness coming out.* He said: 'Where is this taking us, Sergeant? It's a little late for a lesson in morality, in every sense.'

'I'm saying it's the mugs of the world who allow the little things to go by, and grow and grow, then get unstoppable. And I'm just such a mug, in spades.'

'It takes more than gullible mugs to produce a Hitler.'

'Does it?' said Ossie. 'Jesus, man, there's nothing a mug likes better than someone telling him what to do, what to think and what not to think. So they go along with all the big words and the grand plans, and it's all made so easy for a guy like Adolf, haranguing a million suckers all eager to be part of his thousand-year wet dream, not a voice of dissent among them. No question, every time some character gets up on his hind-legs and starts sounding off about duty and honour, patriotism, the Fatherland and, yes, the Empire, this is good and that's bad, love this and hate that, watch out, buddy. You're heading down a one-way street with a brick wall at the end.'

'For God's sake Wolf,' said Kit, 'you can't equate the British Empire with what's going on in Germany.'

'We've all been used,' said Ossie. 'Gone along with situations, stayed silent instead of speaking out because life was easier that way. And we all share a responsibility for what's coming now because we placed our trust in people who did nothing when something might have been done and, yeah, sat in pavement cafés and made cheap cracks about the Jews or the blacks or any soft target to get an easy laugh. Like at high school, ganging up with the other guys to make life hell for the fat boy, the cissy, the egghead who loved to study. Maybe we even said you had to hand it to this guy Hitler, he had a lot of sound ideas and look what he'd done to put Germany back on its feet, that perhaps a lot of the horror stuff was just the newspaper boys hyping it up.' Ossie turned round and looked at Kit. The light from the lamp was behind him, his face in darkness. 'Or maybe we never thought about it at all, reckoned it was all a great game, the ultimate test, a chance to prove we were men. Warriors, heroes, knights of old reborn but mounted on a goddammed Hurricane instead of a trusty charger.'

'Meaning me?'

'If it fits,' said Ossie. 'For you and guys like you it's black and white, good against evil, and you're loving it, you're happy to be here. It's what your background and education prepared you for. You don't consider what's got us into this mess, what's gone before, when words might have worked and we didn't have to press a gun-button to stop the bastards.' Kit was silent. 'Don't get me wrong,' the American said, 'I've seen the way it is with you. You're not the guy who started out, that day we flew from Tangmere. You've seen the way it really is. You're beginning to understand, like I began to understand in 'thirty-seven when I pitched up in Burgos with the rest of the Nationalist volunteers, a gold-plated sucker with a head stuffed full of nonsense. A lot of you guys think I wound up in Spain because I cared. But I was there because I didn't give a flying fuck and thought it would be a hoot. I was brainwashed good. I'd gone along with everything the old man told me – tradition, family, the fucking Fatherland. And goddammed Cousin Max flying his Albatros Scout through a kid's brain year after year so that I wound up wanting to be like him and never thinking twice.'

'This is all very lofty Sergeant,' said Kit, 'but it's one thing to be naïve, another to fly for the damned Fascists. You've assembled a pretty powerful argument about how it's everybody's fault, not just yours. I don't go along with that. The fix you found yourself in was down to you. You had a choice.'

'This is all about choice,' said Ossie Wolf. 'You had a choice on that little trip to Strasbourg. Nobody gets it right all the time.' With a thud and a grinding of metal the clock mechanism in the tower above their heads groaned into action. The clangour of the bell sounding two was shocking in the silence. Ossie waited for the resonance to die away. Then he told Kit Curtis about his time in Burgos.

Ossie had never been to Europe before. He picked up the *Bremen* at the docks in Lower Manhattan, travelling in style, the youngest first-class passenger on the old super-liner built by Norddeutscher Lloyd to bring the Blue Riband back to Germany. When they docked he made his way to Spain by rail, through Germany and France, taking his time, amazed by the antiquity of it all. Everything had been arranged for him in Burgos, through his father's office in St Louis, but the Nationalist authorities took their time to process him and for the first week seemed wary of him, the only American despite his German background. They were keen for him to understand the official line, that he was just a tourist like the rest of the volunteers. But finally the word got round about who he was and he found himself shipped out to the Condor Legion airfield where three squadrons of Junkers Ju-52s were being readied for a mission. At first they would not disclose the target, but then they decided he could go along for the trip and he met his pilot, Claus Diechmann, smiling, always smiling, and trembling with anticipation.

Diechmann told him: 'Prepare for an interesting afternoon, my young friend. We are to attack Guernica. You are fortunate. This is a fine introduction. But stay firm. Don't waste your pity on these Reds and Jews. It is well known that the town is a bolt-hole for rebels. If they choose to hide among the people, so much the worse for the people. That is the responsibility of the Republican swine, not ours.'

They gave Ossie special treatment. Alone among his batch of volunteers he was ushered across to the Hispano-Suiza staff car of Hugo Sperlle, who had come to watch the bombers take off – Sperlle, heavy-set, brutal-looking, monocled, a caricature of a German major general. The commander of the Luftwaffe's Condor Legion descended from the open vehicle with some difficulty, bowed stiffly, and shook the young American's hand. He studied his face intently. 'So,' he said. 'Yes, very like the valiant Max. You should know that I had the honour to serve with your cousin in Albatros Scouts. He was my section commander in Jasta 12. I saw him go down. That day he took three Englishmen with him. How sad that he did not live to see the new-born Luftwaffe in action. Though, of course, we are all Spaniards now.' The officers around him joined in his laughter.

He questioned Ossie about his flying. 'Hardly enough hours to put you at the controls of one of our machines, but in time we will provide you with plenty of experience. I realise that you must be eager to do what you can for the Fatherland but be patient. You are now part of the greatest training programme in the world.' He clapped Wolf on the back and chuckled, blue jowls quivering, monocle winking in the mellow spring sunshine. 'Our families have always had a mutual respect,' he said. 'The Wolfs and the Sperlles – we brewers must stick together. It is what makes the world go round. Beer and war, war and beer.' Again, a general burst of laughter.

'Present my compliments to your father,' said Sperlle. 'I met him towards the end of the war when he visited from America, shortly before your cousin fell in action. Max held him in high regard.' He mounted the running-board of the Hispano-Suiza and sank back on the bull-hide upholstery. His elegant adjutant congratulated Ossie on being accorded an unusual honour. Ossie could not recall saying a single word, but a nod, a smile and a display of youthful determination were all that was required. He was not surprised that his father had never mentioned Sperlle. In those days the fat general would have been a slim *Leutnant*, far too insignificant for the old man to waste time on. Ironic that now the burly Sperlle was Goering's choice to lead the Spanish adventure into which the old man had pressed his son; the adventure designed to further the interests of his beloved *Heimat*, so often in his conversation even after a lifetime in the United States. The old bastard would have been impressed.

The destruction of Guernica started with a single Heinkel 111 bombing the centre of the city. The air-raid shelters were inadequate and many people rushed to the open fields, where they were strafed by fighters. An hour later, a little after five in the afternoon, the three squadrons of Junkers Ju-52s arrived from Burgos. The carpet bombing, using high explosive and incendiaries, was carried out in twenty-minute sequences. It lasted for two and a half hours. Guernica burned for three days. More than one and a half thousand people died.

From Claus Diechmann's Junkers, droning unopposed over the carnage, bombs gone, Ossie had seen a taxi packed with women and children lurch down a dusty road towards a bridge that spanned a gorge. The dust trail had given them away. Diechmann banked, dived down and the machine-guns opened up. At first the car kept going but when the driver was hit it veered this way and that, then struck the parapet of the bridge and tumbled, as though in slow motion, into the gorge below, spilling bodies as it went. Diechmann and his crew laughed as though they were watching the Keystone Kops.

Landing at Burgos, the stench of the burning city still pervading the interior of the Junkers, Diechmann and his comrades were in the highest spirits. They shouted with excitement and ran from bomber to bomber recounting their exploits.

Hanging back, Ossie lowered himself through the hatch and shrugged off his borrowed flying kit. He felt unclean. He headed across the runway, between the control buildings towards the main gates of the airfield. As he walked he was met with cheery greetings and lively questions about the raid. He made no reply and a few of the men paused and stared and watched him hurry away. Two weeks later he was in the Lenin Barracks in Barcelona offering his services to the Republicans.

The officers of the militia appeared impressed with him. 'Ah, an American. You see? Support for our cause is becoming universal.' They did not question him too closely and recruited him with some enthusiasm: 'A pilot, wonderful! We have a great need for pilots. We have more aeroplanes than men who can fly them.' But Ossie's flying skills were never tested. One time, towards the end, it seemed he might get to take up one of the Soviet Polikarpov 1–152 bi-planes but typically it came to nothing in the chaos of retreat. Instead he bore a rusty rifle he never fired in the hill-top trenches around Huesca. It was by chance he had found himself in POUM, the fighting force of anti-Stalinist socialists. He found it hard to tell one faction from another.

Then the Camballero government fell and the pro-Communist Negrin took its place. The cleansing began. POUM was denounced as Trotskyist, even Fascist in disguise. A fellow militiaman he knew, an American who had lived for a long time in Japan, was accused of being a Japanese spy. At first it was taken as a joke but no one smiled when Vincent was put before a Russian firing squad and shot. The executions became general and the cauldron of political conflict moved far beyond the comprehension of a kid from St Louis. Finally he resolved to save himself and, hidden in a huge truck of oranges driven by three Frenchmen, he made his way to the French border, then to England.

Ossie was lodging in a cheap hotel in Paddington when he learnt from the wireless that the United States government had denounced Americans who fought for the Republicans: they were premature anti-Fascists, said Washington. After that, as the weeks passed into months, he drank too much good Scotch whisky and ate too little bad English food while the Spanish Republicans went down before the final Nationalist onslaught as Western democracies watched. He got into the habit of taking the Bakerloo line to Piccadilly Circus and heading north into Soho where he settled on a basement bar in Frith Street and fell in with a crowd of small-time spivs, chisellers and easy women who were excited by his accent.

One evening, Big Don, the owner of the bar, showed up with a blackened eye. He'd been supporting Mosley at the British Union of Fascists' rally at Earls Court. He said he'd laid into the fucking Reds and Jew-boys good, showing his bruised knuckles with pride. Ossie blackened his other eye and Big Don's guys worked him over with fists and coshes and Ossie didn't go out much for a while. He began to lay off the Johnnie Walker and thought about flying again: the newspaper headlines were grim and he could see where things were heading. He took another tube ride, further west this time, to Holborn and walked down Kingsway to the RAF recruiting office. They were curious about his cuts and bruises and asked how long he'd been going short on food but he passed his physical for the Volunteer Reserve, was allowed to skip elementary flying and went straight into ten intensive weeks of service training at Kidlington. He got his wings, no trouble, declined a commission, for reasons he kept to himself, and after six weeks' operational training proved himself a competent, aggressive pilot, good enough to be assigned to Hurricanes.

'And now,' he said to Kit, 'I guess you've got another choice: whether I stay in this show or you arrange for me to get the bum's rush.'

'Did you sign anything in Burgos?'

'No. They talked about it but I'd lit out before they could get round to it.'

'I can understand now why you were so reluctant about that CBS party. I wonder if General Sperlle listens to the wireless. Your family must.'

'Nielsen promised they wouldn't use names.'

'That's true. The trouble is, you're making a bit of a reputation for yourself. Even in line for a DFM. I understand that Goebbels and his crowd are pretty hot on putting two and two together. And your father sounds no fool. Let's face it, things could get sticky. And not just for you.'

'You think I should level with the CO too?'

'I don't know. On the face of it you've done no more than any other idiot would in the same circumstances.'

'Gee, thanks.'

'And you got out pretty quickly when you saw the way things were.'

'Hey, am I in the clear with you?'

'Not entirely, no. But there were plenty of people in my neck of the woods who were convinced that the Right was right for Spain, feared the Communist threat, Soviet domination. They've all gone back into the woodwork now of course. The trouble is, you haven't gone back into the woodwork. You're running around as large as life, ready for someone to swat.'

'Maybe CBS won't broadcast Nielsen's piece,' said Ossie. 'Maybe they could be asked to kill it. Reasons of security, something like that?'

'Maybe you could ask the CO not to give you a gong. Maybe you could change your name to Donald Duck.' Kit stood up. 'Look here, Sergeant, I'm not entirely out of sympathy with you. I'm prepared to accept that you've told it to me straight. I think the squadron would be poorer without you. You talked about choices. Here are some more. We can try tackling this head on, come clean with Brewster and leave the decision to him.'

'You know the guy better than me. What do you think he'd go for?'

'I think he'd kick it upstairs, let the brass-hats decide. He doesn't always play it by the book but he's bound to on this – he'd have to, to protect his own backside. He's already gone out on a limb over the Strasbourg stunt. He'd put in a good word for you, of course, but whether it would make any difference, I really don't know.'

'You said there was a choice.'

'Yes. The other option is we keep our heads down and hope it never comes up.'

'We?'

'Did I say we?'

'Yeah, you said we.'

'Well,' said Kit, 'I am your flight commander after all.'

'You'd be laying yourself on the line.'

'I suppose I would.'

'So you're saying we keep mum and trust to luck?'

'I suppose I am.'

'I sure appreciate that.'

'I hope you do, Sergeant.' Kit started down the aisle, then paused and turned. 'Actually, there's something you can do for me in return.'

'Sure.'

'When you're on the ground, toe the blasted line, show willing, drop this damnable disrespect for authority. It's childish and diminishes you. And in the air follow, don't try to lead until you put those rings on your sleeve. I was a chump, an absolute prize clot, to let you get away with that Strasbourg party. I don't deny I was as eager for a bit of action as you were, but we were lucky as hell. Try the same thing with Pip Fuller, Gates or Knox and you might not be so fortunate. You wouldn't just have Guernica on your conscience.'

'Yeah, I guess you're right.'

'Stop guessing Sergeant. I expect your firm assurance on this.'

'Okay,' said Ossie, 'you got it.' He followed Kit out of the church. 'There's something you can do for me as well.'

'Oh, yes? What's that Sergeant?'

'For Chrissakes, when there's nobody else around stop calling me goddammed Sergeant.'

It was three hours into 1940. It looked the same as 1939. They knew it wasn't. They wondered, as they walked to their billets, if they would see 1941.

Part three

'I see a blue man falling.'

Fifteen

Saturday, 11 May 1940

It was four hours since Ossie had crouched in the ditch by
the bodies of the French infantry officer and the English
corporal, four hours since he had heard laughter as the
Oberschutze who hailed from Chicago clicked the safety catch
of his hot Schmeisser MP-44 machine pistol, returned to his
comrades and the volume on a wireless set had been turned
up. Lucienne Delyle. '*Sur Les Quais du Vieux Paris.*' Four
hours since Ossie's thoughts had flown back to La Vosgienne
with Dinghy, long-dead Dinghy sitting beside him and Kit
Curtis pushing his way between the tables, angry, accusing;
Bébé with that damned Una Westcott, provocative, like maybe
something special would happen later. Four hours since he
had been snapped back to reality by the Wehrmacht troopers
beyond the ditch humming to Delyle's refrain, thinking of
Paris and pleasures to come.

> Sur les quais du vieux Paris
> Le long de la Seine
> Le bonheur sourit
> Sur les quais du vieux Paris . . .

Yeah, and four hours since he'd reflected that he'd had himself
some pretty damned good *bonheur* on the *quais* of old Paris an
age ago, back in '39 . . .

Now he carried on along the ditch on his belly, pushing through nettles and reeds, gasping with the effort and trying to suppress the noise of the gasps, his open mouth taking in gritty liquid, pungent with the ordure of beasts and whatever else the goddammed peasants spread across their God-forsaken hectares. He pictured again the hunched forms of the Frenchman and the Englishman, blood, piss and faeces running into the mud round their bodies but a long way back now.

He risked raising his head above the bank. A few hundred yards away a thin new moon rose behind a copse of sessile oak, its feeble light glimmering through a tracery of branches. The ditch curved to the right and Ossie kept the moon behind him, to the east, as he worked his way, yard by yard, further west.

An oppressive silence hung over the countryside, as though the machine of war had paused for breath. It seemed to magnify the slightest sound marking his progress; the suck of a flying boot pulling out of mire, the splash and wash of water where the channel deepened, the grunt of pain and an involuntary curse as he stumbled into it and lost his footing and fell, or half fell, his fingers clawing into the earth of the bank, jarring his shoulder, still numb but working fine. It made him think about the *Feldwebel*: the schoolmaster with the fat wife, the comfortable home and the small heads bent over arithmetic books; the schoolmaster who knew about playground misfortunes and how to pop a shoulder joint back into place, and had died under the machetes of the Senegalese *tirailleurs*. Ossie was clumsy with cold now and birds rose, as he moved towards them, with a clatter of wings and strident calls of alarm that made him wince with apprehension. But as he put distance between himself and the Wehrmacht platoon he sensed he was increasingly alone in this wilderness of farmland, and as dawn lightened the sky his confidence grew.

There seemed to be no roads nearby, just tracks providing access to the fields for horse and plough. He struggled up the bank and out of the ditch that had sheltered him. He felt exposed, vulnerable, half expecting an abrupt command, the crack of a rifle shot. The sun was warm on his back as he began to walk, forcing himself to move briskly. He was very hungry. It was good that he thought of food: maybe he would get back, after all. Maybe he would find the guys, fly again. Surely it would happen that way. He'd been through so much, endured, survived. Surely he would get back. Everything pointed to it, like Fate or luck or even God willed it that way. And then he walked harder and faster because he wanted to stop himself acknowledging that such thoughts didn't mean beans and he still had one hell of a way to go through hostile country crawling with Krauts and even now he could find himself dying in a ditch with a bullet-hole in his gut like the poor bastards he'd left behind him in that stinking ditch.

The sun had real heat in it now. Where it had been a friend, now it was an enemy. He drank deep from any puddle or pool he came across, however foul.

About noon he became conscious of a distant murmur, a faint disturbance, like a river running over shallows, that grew more distinct as he hugged the shelter of a dense hawthorn hedge. He made out cries and calls and the burble of occasional engines: the phut-phut of a motorcycle, the deeper note of automobiles and trucks. He'd known all along that the country was crawling with Krauts and now that vicious trio, Fate, luck or God, seemed about to play a lousy trick on him. One of those damned little Henschels, flying low and heading south at no more than three hundred feet, seemed to prove that he was about to find himself in the bag once more – maybe for keeps this time. He flattened himself against the hedge and thorns pierced the material of his filthy uniform.

The spindly reconnaissance machine banked and began to circle an area about two miles away. It looked sensitive to the controls, wavering in the wafts of hot air rising from the ground. There was no sense of urgency about its manoeuvres and no hint that the crew anticipated a threat from whatever lay below. An inner voice told him this was significant. Finally the Henschel's engine note deepened and it turned north-east, then climbed away, pin-sharp in its blue-grey camouflage, the pilot and observer clearly visible in their open cockpits under the notched parasol wing. They were nervous now, heads tilted upwards, sweeping the skies for the first hint of an attack from above and out of the sun. And then it was gone, lost against the wooded hills on the horizon, still flying low, hugging the ground with a tale to tell of . . . what?

Suddenly it was clear. He was going to find out. He was sick of running. He despised himself for cowering in stinking mud and water like a cornered rat. He sensed that whatever lay beyond the fields two miles away was either the end of it all or the start of something, maybe a fresh opportunity. He'd been lucky so far. Why should that change now? Okay, he felt bad about getting down, brooding about what a raw deal he'd got. But he was still free and in with a chance. He'd gotten weak – just fatigued, he guessed – but he'd wised up now. And he'd liked the way the Henschel crew had scanned the sky, frightened of being bounced by a guy like him. Anger and frustration washed over him and he wanted to be back in the cockpit of a Hurricane, coming in from the sun with throttle set just right and squeezing out a nice deflection shot on the gun-button, no more than a two-second burst, and seeing that juicy little Henschel fold up and take its intelligence report to the grave.

He stepped out from the shelter of the hedge and began to walk, taking long strides, savouring the freedom. He felt a new strength in him. He thought: I don't give a flying fuck for anyone. And he laughed and said it aloud: 'I don't give a flying fuck for anyone.' He was at peace, walking towards the distant murmur, the faint disturbance like a river running over shallows; a low sound that rose and grew with each stride. He was ready to meet it, whatever it turned out to be.

The child was crouched by an off-shoot of the irrigation ditch. She wore a green smocked dress that matched her eyes and tan sandals with metal buckles. Her hair was fair and curled, not French-looking. She was about four. She was picking ox-eye daisies with small, delicate fingers, snapping the stems close to the ground. She looked up and saw him on the other side of the stagnant stream, standing against the sun. She shielded her eyes but her expression did not change. After a moment she started picking daisies again.

Ossie said: '*Bonjour, Mademoiselle,*'

'*Bonjour, Monsieur,*' the child said in a sing-song matter-of-fact kind of way without looking up. She stood up and began to walk away, not because of him but because she had enough daisies. In the distance he heard a woman calling. He could see they were approaching a road. Dust was rising above the trees. The noise of traffic and people was quite loud now. A woman was running towards them through the long grass that grew beside the road. She gathered the child into her arms and stared at him defiantly, shouting something in French. He shrugged and tried a grin to show he didn't understand and was not a threat. The woman and the child regained the road and were swallowed up in the human stream. The child was still holding the bunch of daisies.

A bizarre collection of contrivances crawled along the road, all heading in the same direction. Decaying farm carts dragged from barns after decades of neglect, timbered wagons pulled by heavy horses, traps with exhausted ponies between the shafts, even a horse-drawn coach. Between them wove automobiles and trucks, groaning wrecks from the turn of the century or brand new – Benzes and Darracqs, Citroëns and Renaults, Panhards and Talbots, with grinding gears, wailing brakes and horns. Every conveyance was stacked high with treasures from homes where they had lain for generations; treasures with no value except to those who owned them, but a shred of normality in a frenzied world. Occasional *poilus*, a cavalry motorcyclist in khaki canvas coveralls and, here and there, an officer slumped in the back of a staff car. Ossie chose not to talk to them. He knew what they would say.

And anyway, he was largely ignored. Some glanced at him but saw he posed no danger and dismissed him. He waved down an old man with a white moustache on a black bicycle; he rode with his knees stuck out, panniers over the rear wheel and a bulging rucksack on his back. He did not want to stop and almost fell. Ossie caught him and pushed him upright, still in the saddle. He said, in his bad French: 'What is happening here?'

The old man spat into the dust. 'We are evacuating.'

'Who told you to?'

'Who knows? Perhaps the mayor. It is always the mayor.'

'And where are you going?'

'Perhaps Verdun.' The old man spat again. '*Ils ne passeront pas.*' He gave a short and bitter laugh. 'Perhaps I will lay my bones at Fort Douaumont after all. *Les sales Boches.*' He thrust away Ossie's arm, pushed at the pedals and gained a little speed and teetered on down the road.

Ossie reckoned Verdun sounded okay, a decent-sized city and in the right direction. Maybe the trains were still getting through to Bar-le-Duc. For sure he'd be able to telephone from there, tell the guys he was still alive, maybe even get picked up before the place was overrun. He joined the shuffling column of people walking, bent under the weight of cases, bags and sacks. Even the kids were carrying stuff, their faces stained with dirt and tears. Occasionally the effort would prove too much and the precious burdens were dumped at the roadside.

Beside the road, close to a small lane running north, a granite milestone said 'Fromezy'. Ossie asked a heavy-set fellow in blue work-clothes, sitting high on a cart, and holding the leather reins easily between cracked paws: '*Monsieur, c'est . . . uh combien . . . de kilometres Verdun?*'

'*Qui êtes-vous?*'

'*Je suis un aviateur anglais.*'

'*Ah, oui? Un aviateur sans avion?*'

'Huh?' said Ossie. He was falling back from the cart. The man turned in his seat: '*Dix kilometres de Verdun.*' Ossie didn't thank him. The guy had cracked some gag he didn't understand and he wasn't in the mood for gags.

The child with the ox-eye daisies was standing at the edge of the road, leaning against the trunk of a poplar. The daisies were a little limp. The woman was bent over the engine of a tiny car, steam rising around her. She put out her hand to unscrew the radiator cap. Ossie shouted out: 'Hey! No! Don't do that. Stop. *Arrêtez!*'

She raised her head and said, in English: 'Are you shouting at me?'

He came up beside her. 'Let it cool down first, lady. You'll burn yourself to hell.'

'I cannot wait,' said the woman. 'We must not fall behind.'

'Unless you wait you won't have a damned automobile.'

The child pushed herself off the trunk of the tree and moved closer. '*Je m'appelle Cécile.*'

'Hi,' said Ossie. He pointed at himself. 'Ossie.'

'Hi,' repeated the child. '*Mes fleurs.*' She handed him one.

'Yeah. I saw you pick them.' He took the flower, then handed it back. '*Pour vous.*'

'*Merci, Monsieur,*' said the child.

'Ossie.'

'*Ah, oui,* Ossie.' She pointed to the wings on his tunic and said something in rapid French.

The woman said: 'She wants to know what those are.'

'Wings,' said Ossie.

The woman translated for her daughter and the child spoke again. The woman said impatiently: 'She wants to know if you can fly.'

'Not at the moment,' said Ossie.

245

The woman sighed. 'You are English?'

'Yes,' he said. It was easier that way.

'An English pilot?'

'Yes.' He anticipated the next question. 'I was shot down yesterday.' Christ, only yesterday? 'I'm heading back to my squadron.'

'To fight again?'

'I sure hope so.'

'What is the point? We are beaten. Better to accept it and come to an agreement. The German are not barbarians. This is Europe, after all. And they are too strong. We cannot resist.' She looked at her daughter. 'What kind of world awaits her now?'

'I don't know,' said Ossie. 'But it's something we can't allow the Boches to decide.'

'So you and your comrades will continue to fight?'

'Yes.'

'It is hopeless. It will only make things worse.'

'Worse than this?'

'It is hopeless. We will never agree.' The woman paused. 'How long must we wait?'

'For what?'

The woman smiled faintly. 'For the radiator to cool.'

'Not long,' said Ossie. 'What the hell kind of automobile is this anyhow?'

'A Dixi. You should not laugh. It has brought us from Luxembourg.'

While they waited for the radiator to cool the woman told him that the day before, in Esch-sur-Sure, they had been woken by rifle and artillery fire. She and her husband had seen Germans in the forest behind their house and French soldiers firing at them. The authorities ordered the people of Esch to evacuate and head south-west for France. Her husband had taken the Delage and their son Guillaume. They became separated on the road and she hadn't seen them since. At first Cécile had asked for Gigi and Papa but now she had stopped. She seemed almost happy, even when German aeroplanes were flying over and dropping bombs on nearby targets. Children were unfathomable. The noise of bombs and cannon seemed to follow them as they travelled south.

At Bouligny they had hidden in woods, which were full of others hiding. The woman and her daughter had been compelled to share some of their food with those less prepared. In the morning they had seen parachutes falling from the sky and the sound of big guns was very loud. Instead of following the main route to Verdun through Étain, with many French soldiers in retreat, they had set off across country on this minor road, winding through obscure villages and hamlets, Gondrecourt, Hermeville and Grimaucourt-en-Woëvre. The column grew as more and more of the population became frightened by tales of military collapse and reports of the advancing Boches. Some German planes had come down low to look at them but they had not been attacked. There were stories that on the main route to Verdun civilians had been bombed and machine-gunned. Surely it could not be true. Why would the Germans do such a thing? When Ossie told her they would, he could see that she did not want to believe him.

He checked the radiator and released the cap. The woman gave him an enamel jug and he and the child found some water in a pond about two fields away. The Dixi fired up immediately. The woman leaned out of the driver's window to hand him half a baguette and some slices of sausage in greaseproof paper. He thanked her and stepped back to watch them go. There was no room for him in the car, which bulged with expensive leather suitcases and travelling trunks. A label on one showed palm trees and the promenade at Nice and bore the name of the Hôtel Negresco. Also the family's name, Docteur et Madame Legrandin and an address in Esch-sur-Sure, Luxembourg. The child stared at him from the front seat. 'Goodbye, Cécile,' he said. '*Au revoir.*' The child did not reply.

The woman moved the gear lever and the car lurched forward. She did not say goodbye either or look in her mirror to see him again. He wondered how the child had become separated from her mother when he had come across her picking daisies and if the woman would find her husband and her son.

He found himself a lift on the running-board of a commandeered Renault van. It was driven by a *poilu* in a steel helmet. He had buttoned security patches on his coat collar, folded back to conceal his regimental number. It struck Ossie as a waste of time. Two more infantrymen, without weapons, and some women and children sat in the back.

'The Boches, they came at us in great force,' shouted the *poilu*, through the window. 'Tanks, Stukas and behind them infantry like a sea of grey. What could we do?' Ossie had known the talk would go like this.

'This is a good route,' cried the *poilu*, 'this is a very good route. Between Bouligny and Étain . . .' He drew his finger across his throat. 'Tell me,' he demanded, 'you killed Boches with your machine before they brought you down?'

'Some.'

'Some? Ah, *oui*, we killed some also. But, of course, some is not enough. *En vérité nous sommes dans un pot de chambre, dans la merde.*' Ossie understood that all right. He shrugged. The *poilu* was satisfied. He took it to mean what he wanted it to mean. 'What is your destination?' he yelled.

'Bar-le-Duc,' Wolf said.

'At Verdun we leave you then. We go directly east to St Menehould and Reims. There we will regroup.'

'Really?'

'No not really. No one knows what is happening. All control is lost.'

They dropped him in the northern suburbs of Verdun – they

did not want to be drawn into the centre of the city. Ossie asked directions to the station. Bar-le-Duc was only thirty minutes south by rail. It seemed that everyone had gotten the same idea. He couldn't get to the ticket office and folk were fighting for the phones. As he pushed his way back through the lobby he heard a railway official saying that the station at Bar-le-Duc had been bombed. If Bar-le-Duc, why not Verdun? A wave of fear ran through the crowds. A woman was screaming, separated from her family. Ossie stood uncertainly by the entrance. A plaque on the wall told him that the body of the unknown soldier, killed at Verdun, had been shipped out of here in 1920 to be interred at the base of the Arc de Triomphe. '*Mort pour la patrie*,' said the inscription, but Ossie reckoned the poor anonymous sucker hadn't had much say in the matter.

On the other side of the forecourt loomed the art-nouveau bulk of the Hôtel de la Gare, grim with memories of grieving fathers and mothers, wives, daughters, sons, and girls not widowed because they had never married, come to see where Gaston, Henri, Marcel, Jean and little Louis had got themselves blown to bits in Butcher Mangan's push to recapture Douaumont, Vaux or Le Mort Homme or any other scrap of territory worth a thousand lives a metre.

Ossie walked across the forecourt to the hotel. The doors were padlocked. Through the diamond-shaped stained-glass panels he could make out a muddle of papers on the reception desk. Some had fallen on to the tiled floor. He pressed the brass door-bell, which echoed through what seemed a hundred storeys. He peered inside again. On the desk beside the papers stood an antique shellac telephone, candlestick-style, the receiver dangling on a brass bracket beside the mouthpiece. Was it still connected?

On an austere iron bed in a bare, chilly upper room in the house of Father Roland Dumouriez, adjacent to the church of

Saint-Saulve in Fonteville, Kit Curtis was still sleeping and the *curé* was growing concerned for him. He had already conducted mass twice, first at six, then at eight, and the spiritual care of his parishioners, weeping and shivering in the pews as they mumbled their way through the liturgy, was foremost in his mind. But, still, the boy had slept for fourteen hours and had resisted every attempt to rouse him. The priest looked down at the English pilot. The face was unlined and at peace, but marred with purple-yellow bruises and contusions that stretched from jaw to temple.

Dumouriez knew that yesterday, before the German bombers came to Fonteville, the Englishman had crashed at the Revigncourt field. Had some latent brain injury induced a coma? He put his thin hand on the boy's shoulder and shook it gently.

The young man started, opened his eyes and stared at the priest. For a moment he seemed perplexed, uncomprehending, but then his expression cleared. Inwardly Dumouriez gave thanks to God.

Kit attempted to sit up, cried out, 'Oh, Christ,' and fell back. '*Excusez-moi, Monsieur le Curé.*' Dumouriez smiled. He poured some water from a flask into a tumbler. Kit drained it and the priest gave him another. He wiped his mouth and fell into perfect French. 'Madame Bergeret.'

'She is at rest,' said the priest.

'And Evans? Corporal Evans?'

'They are all at rest. We have employed the *mairie* as a *mortuaire*. Everything is at it should be – as far as it can be.'

'All?'

'Twenty have died and fifteen more have been removed to the hospital at Bar-le-Duc. Only one is missing, Emile Paturel. No trace of him has been found. Madame Paturel is taking it bravely.' Dumouriez moved over to the door, the empty water flask in his hand. 'You must be hungry.'

'Yes, extremely,' said Kit. He could hear the clatter of pans downstairs and the smell of cooking was in the air.

'Old Madame Hourticq,' said the priest. 'Since her husband died two years ago she serves as my *domestique*. It is an arrangement that suits us both. I will see what she is preparing for dinner.'

'Dinner?'

'Certainly.'

'What time is it then?' said Kit, voice rising. 'How long have I been asleep?' He began to get up, but his legs were weak and he sat down again, rubbing his face.

'First you must eat,' said Dumouriez. 'Then you may concern yourself with what you must do and where you must be. The war, my young friend, will wait for you. Be assured of that.' His expression was sorrowful. 'I will bring you warm water to wash. Rest now while you may.'

On the mantel above the empty fireplace a small clock showed six. Evening then. Kit knew that at some point he had been running from house to house, helping to drag the injured from the wreckage of their homes, joining a chain of villagers with buckets trying to quell the flames. The memory came to him of an old man pinned beneath the roof beams of a barn, calling to God as the blaze consumed him; horses tethered in the centre of an inferno, insane with terror; the kitchen, that lay open to the air and the dead woman at the pine table, her head fallen forward on to the potatoes she had been peeling. There had been rescues, miraculous survivals, cries of relief and joy as familiar faces were recognised through the clouds of acrid smoke. He had seen the *curé* in a dozen places, working quickly, dispelling panic, sometimes offering prayers for departed souls or thanks for those who had been spared. It had resembled a nightmare by Bosch, figures silhouetted against dancing flames, the air ringing with cries of horror and despair, the sky red-gold with the reflection of the conflagration. Then his vision had blurred, and he had fallen backwards on to hot embers. He was

251

pulled up and dragged away – he supposed to here, the priest's house, where he had been overcome by sleep. Guilt swept over him.

The *salle à manger* was dark and sparsely furnished: an ugly mahogany table from the turn of the century standing slightly askew on cabriole legs, assorted dining chairs of similar vintage and, against the wall, a bow-fronted sideboard, its veneer marked with the imprint of hot plates and wet glasses. The only decoration was a selection of religious prints, hung very high and crooked, the Virgin and Child, the Virgin and Child, the Virgin and Child, and Saint-Saulve himself being martyred in front of the cathedral of Saint-Étienne in Metz.

The bent figure of Madame Hourticq tottered in with a weighty cast-iron casserole. Tears ran down the creases of her cheeks and dropped with a hiss on to the hot lid. She did not like to serve the food: she felt it was not God's will that they should eat at a time like this – a little bread, perhaps, and a sip of water but not more. She would not, could not join them. She wanted them to understand that she had prepared the stew, cubed beef steak with carrots, olives, herbs and diced bacon, before the attack by the accursed Boches. At that she caught herself and begged Monsieur le Curé's pardon for the imprecation, crossed herself and lifted the lid of the pot. The rich aroma almost made Kit retch, but the food was good and wholesome, and he felt fresh strength run through him as he and Father Dumouriez ate, locked in thought. Finally they had done and Madame Hourticq cleared the table.

Kit pushed back his chair. 'Father, it is extremely important that I use a telephone. I must report.'

'Of course. We have no telephone here but in the *mairie* . . .' The priest's voice faded. Both men remembered the bodies laid side by side in the principal meeting room.

In the mayor's office, to his mild surprise Kit raised the HQ of the Advanced Air Striking Force at Reims without much difficulty. 'Jolly good show,' said the admin officer mildly when Kit told him he was still alive. 'Oh, bad show,' he said when he told him about Corporal Evans. Kit could hear his pen scratching, noting the details. It was a mundane sound and oddly reassuring; it spoke of order and business-as-usual. Perhaps the situation was not so critical after all. The man's voice was calm and unflurried. 'Well, make your way back to your squadron as quickly as possible, there's a good chap.'

'Are they still at Menneville?'

'As far as I know, old boy. Just a sec.' There was a rustle of papers. 'Yes, still there, just north-west of Reims. Have you got transport?'

'Yes.'

'I should stick to the roads if I were you. The Hun are giving the railways a proper pasting.' The admin officer paused. 'Where did you say you were again?'

'Fonteville.'

'Fonteville, yes – quite close to Bar-le-Duc. Funny that. We had another call not so long ago. Could have been from one of your chaps. Stuck in Verdun. Not too far from you. Brolly-hop, apparently. Looking for a lift. Couldn't help of course. Just told him what I've told you, to make his way back as best he can. Perhaps you could keep an eye open in case he makes it to your neck of the woods.'

'Did you get his name?'

'No. Bit of a flap on. But he sounded like one of yours all right. Hurricane got knocked down in a bit of a party yesterday. Been making his way across country. Pretty decent show. Think he was phoning from the station. I imagine he'd be jolly pleased to see you and, candidly, if he's operational, we can do with all the pilots we can get. Up to you, of course. Possibly wiser if you press on and rejoin your chums. At least you won't run the risk of being nabbed yourself. As I say, your decision. Good luck old boy.'

Kit's thoughts flew back to November, his prang at Les

Charmontois when he'd tried that insane three-pointer on that damned meadow and written off the kite, Brewster bellowing: 'I can always replace aeroplanes, boy, but I don't want to lose my pilots.' He tried to remember who hadn't made it: Beaky Parker, Ossie Wolf, Pip Fuller – God, the list was growing. But who might be kicking his heels at the station in Verdun? If he was kicking his heels and hadn't already set off across country. But what a thing if he found this type and restored him to the bosom of the squadron. It seemed like a risk worth taking, what Buster would call a jolly good giggle. How long would it take him to get to Verdun? Well, not so long if he got his skates on in the Alvis. He saw himself reporting to Brewster: 'Two for the price of one sir. Remember what you said? You can always replace aeroplanes but . . .'

Father Dumouriez was waiting in the hallway of the *mairie*. He looked up expectantly. 'You were successful in getting through?'

'Yes, thank you. Please thank the mayor for the use of his telephone.'

'I'm afraid that is not possible.'

'Damn.' Again Kit flushed at the oath.

The priest patted his arm. 'I think we may be permitted a malediction or two. You, Madame Hourticq, even myself. It is very difficult to acknowledge the spirit of forgiveness at such a time. May God fly with you my son.'

'Thank you. And please thank Madame Hourticq. I'm afraid I enjoyed her meal.'

The village stank of smoke and death. Kit climbed painfully into the Alvis. The engine churned, coughed and came alive. The headlamps shone dim yellow, worse than useless, but the sky had cleared and the moon was rising. He turned the heavy motor-car towards the river and headed for the winding climb towards the flat expanse of Revigncourt, where pleasant evening breezes eddied across the empty runways. Only Father

Dumouriez watched him go. At the crossroads in the centre of Revigncourt village, where the road ran right to Vitry-François then followed the eastern bank of the Marne to Chalons, Épernay and Reims he turned left and began the gradual descent to Bar-le-Duc where, he knew, the Voie ran north to the ill-fated city of Verdun.

Sixteen

Sunday, 12 May 1940

At about one in the morning, in the vicinity of the railway station at Verdun, it began to be said that the Boches were drawing close. The rumble of their tanks had been heard to the south, advancing up the Voie Sacrée close to the *citadelle* where the road became the avenue du Mort-Homme and took a dog-leg swerve over the railway line. People shouted back and forth: 'The Boches are here! The Boches are upon us!' Fear struck the multitude like a bolt of lightning. Those who had arrived in hope of a train to safety and found none had sunk to the ground, exhausted. Now they rose, gathered together their goods and moved once more, fanning out through the streets of the city. New arrivals, straggling in from the north, halted, turned and pushed against the tide of their fellows. 'The Boches! We are encircled. We are lost. Go back! Go back!'

The noise of the vehicles was loud now: the distinctive clatter of steel tracks on *pavé*, the bellow of powerful engines, the whiff of acrid exhaust fumes carried on the south-westerly breeze. Three large, shadowy half-tracks, each drawing an artillery piece, swept round the bend in the avenue du Mort-Homme and curved left into the station forecourt. Figures jumped down and regarded the scenes of panic around them.

Ossie pushed through the crowd. Three Regiment d'Artillerie UNIC light artillery tractors stood in echelon, tiger-striped in khaki and black camouflage, engines still ticking over. Behind each was hitched a big-wheeled 75mm field gun. There was a wave of relief and some laughter among the refugees who had not been quick enough to flee the forecourt; shouts of derision at those who had been panicked into believing that the Boches could possibly have advanced so far – what gullible clowns, what faint-hearts, *quel potronnerie*! People drifted back to gather round the twenty or so artillerymen.

'Where have you come from?'

'We cannot tell you.'

'Where are you going?'

'We cannot tell you. Here, take a cigarette. Take a pack. Share them around.'

'Be warned, the Boches are hard on our heels.'

'*Vraiment? C'est bon.* Our petrol is getting low.'

The group's colonel, grim-faced and tall in a long khaki greatcoat, stood near Ossie. A beige woollen scarf was looped around his neck, the ends tucked through his dark tan leather belt. At his waist on the right was a bulky leather holster, on the left a square map-case. A cane was tucked beneath his arm, his mark of command. In his right hand he held a silver flask, the hinged lid open. Beneath his cap, forage-style and set square, his eyes were grey and hard. He looked tough, like his men. He noticed Ossie, took in the uniform with a swift, professional glance. '*Hein! En retraite, Monsieur Royal Air Force?*'

'*Non,*' said Ossie. 'Shot down.' He mimed a diving aircraft with his hand. 'I return . . . to fly again.'

'*Ah, oui?*' The colonel held out the flask. '*Vous avez détruire des Boches?*'

'*Cinq.*' The flask contained fine brandy, smooth and aromatic. Ossie took a mouthful and handed it back, nodding at the 75s. He said, in English: 'You intend to use those?'

'Certainly,' said the colonel, assuming the language easily. 'What else are they for?' He snapped the cap on to the flask and pushed it into a breast pocket. 'Worthless against an enemy dug-in or fortifications, of course, but against troops in the open . . .'

He held his fingertips to his lips and blew them. 'I hear we may expect many troops in the open. I look forward with keen anticipation to peppering their backsides with the little steel balls of our shrapnel rounds.' His mouth twisted wryly. 'Bizarre. I cannot escape Verdun. I was here in 'sixteen, a private first class with a *régiment d'infanterie*, railing with the others about the men of fifty who directed us up the chemin de l'Abattoir to the front. As we passed them we bleated like sheep to show our feelings. I expected to die at Verdun. When Fate dictated otherwise and I survived I was surprised. But now I realise that Fate did not say when.' He pulled off his cap and wiped his face with a silk handkerchief. He wore his hair *en brosse*, crew-cut and bristly. 'I no longer have beliefs, Monsieur. Twenty-four years ago they preached the gospel of *l'attaque à outrance*, attack to the death. Today we have the Popular Front and Blum – defence, defeatism and that damned Maginot Line. Between them France reels from one disaster to another.' He turned his grey eyes to the three UNICS and the angular outlines of the sinister 75s. 'We are only one group of three from St Dizier. I mustered the best. The others . . .' He shrugged. 'My comrades share the same philosophy. War is simple, direct and ruthless. We are here to fight and, if necessary, die. To my generation honour is a dirty word but perhaps we can burnish it a little, even now. At least this time we have the opportunity to choose our ground and our weapons. And the more of them we kill, the fewer of us will die. Simple arithmetic, my friend.'

A sous-lieutenant presented himself and saluted smartly. 'We are encountering certain difficulties mon Colonel.' He looked doubtfully at Ossie but the colonel waved to him to continue. 'It appears the people do not approve of our presence here. They believe it will attract the Boches when daylight comes.'

Somewhere a voice was raised, shrill and accusing: 'There are women and children here. Do you think only of yourselves?'

In the semi-darkness a man exclaimed roughly: '*S'il vous plaît, Madame, allez-vous faire foutre.*'

The colonel laughed and called out: 'That is no way to address a lady, *Caporal* Bulat.' He replaced his cap and pressed something into Ossie's hand. It was the flask. 'In popular fiction this would undoubtedly stop a bullet. Here's to your sixth victory, *mon ami*.'

The engines of the artillery tractors started up and the mood of the crowd lightened; there were even cries of approbation and a few half-hearted cheers.

Ossie watched the UNICs go, then walked back into the scene of desolation that was now the Hôtel de la Gare. The hotel, so silent and aloof, yet still intact when he had forced the door to the main entrance and telephoned HQ at Reims, had long since been invaded, its interior a ruin as people ran from room to room, seeking food, drink, clothing and anything of value. A boy emerged from the kitchens with an enamel saucepan, waving it above his head and calling to his father, who was in the salon using a screwdriver to prise from the wall a gilt-bronze light. An old woman was coming down the staircase carrying a framed print of a winsome child dressed for skating in a snowy landscape.

Ossie went into the bar and sat down on a torn plush settee. He had saved a slice or two of the sausage that the woman from Esch-sur-Sure had given him and a little of the bread. He ate carefully and slowly. He was in for a long walk and did not know when he would eat again. He brushed the crumbs off his filthy uniform.

Outside the sky was lighter and through a window he saw a motorcycle, weaving between the knots of refugees. It stopped in front of the station and the rider eased himself off the saddle stiffly and pulled the machine on to its stand. He had a big square of material over the lower part of his face to keep out the dust. When he removed it, Ossie knew him at once. Well, son-of-a-gun, he thought. The call he'd made to Reims must have worked. It was Kit Curtis.

* * *

The motorcycle, a hefty Alcyon 350 with dull gold fuel tank and mudguards, had been 'borrowed' by the two French riflemen Kit had come across stretched out under the porch of the little church beside the road at the village of Naives-Rosières on the Voie Sacrée. He had pulled up in the Alvis, little more than five kilometres from Bar-le-Duc, knowing it was hopeless to try to make further progress against the surging crowds of refugees. It had still seemed possible as he crossed the twin courses of the l'Ornain and the Canal de la Marne in the centre of Bar-le-Duc, even though smoke and flame rose from the bombed ruins of the railway station to his right, but as he turned north he found himself overwhelmed. He sat at the wheel, the ignition turned off, trying to think of a solution. He hated to fail. The riflemen had looked at him curiously. One shouted: 'Where are you bound?'

'Verdun.'

'Why do you go to Verdun?'

'That's my business.'

The man's eyes narrowed. 'There is nothing at Verdun, only Boches.'

'Already?'

'Probably.'

The riflemen, a corporal and a private, had become separated, they said, from their platoon during the withdrawal. They got to their feet and came to look at the Alvis. 'This will not take you to Verdun,' said the short corporal.

'I know,' said Kit.

'You need a machine like ours.'

'Yours?'

The corporal grinned. '*Bien sûr*, we are soldiers intent on restoring ourselves to our unit and simply claimed right to posses-sion. Fortunately the owner was a patriot. He understood.' The private gave a coarse guffaw. The corporal said: 'Is it difficult to drive, your English automobile?'

'No.'

'Can you master a motorcycle?' Kit said nothing and the

corporal tried again: 'You would make good progress on our machine.' He held invisible handlebars and rocked from side to side, then made sinuous movements with his right hand. 'No obstacles for a machine like ours.'

Kit knew he was right. 'How much petrol do you have?'

'*Complet*, Monsieur. Well, almost.'

Kit straddled the motorcycle and kick-started the engine. It seemed to have been well maintained, emitting a throaty roar. He checked the controls carefully. All moved smoothly. He nodded, sealing the exchange. The corporal gave him a filthy scarf to wrap round his face. The private took out a knife and cut the string securing a folded greatcoat to the black-tubed luggage rack behind the single triangular seat. 'My arse is full of gratitude,' he said. He climbed into the Alvis and sat down, smirking, fiddling with the switches on the dashboard and jiggling the gear-lever. Kit revved the throttle of the shuddering Alcyon and eased in the clutch.

The corporal stood back, arms folded. 'Be sure the Boches do not pop you off the saddle for a little target practice,' he said.

In the darkness and against the flow of refugees Kit made slow but steady progress along the route that had been Verdun's life-line in 1916. Two million French soldiers had passed this way, and half a million had not returned. The road, barely seven metres wide, ran along the crest of a causeway with gentle wooded hills rising from meadows on either side. The doomed *poilus* of twenty-four years ago, packed into Renault lorries that ran day and night or trudging from the rail terminus at Bar-le-Duc had been treated to a beguiling final glimpse of the beauties of the country for which they were about to be sacrificed.

As he rode through the night it occurred to Kit that those who dreamt of honour, glory, deeds of arms and believed in nationhood and empire were no more than the tools of men with broader, darker dreams that threatened to swallow the world unless millions stepped forward to be slaughtered.

* * *

Ossie Wolf walked across from the Hôtel de la Gare and stood by the Alcyon 350, the exhaust clicking as it cooled. It had already attracted interest: three or four men had gathered round it and one placed his hands on the handlebars. He was stocky and powerful, his round head set deep on his shoulders, face dark with stubble. He watched Ossie approach, regarding him with small suspicious eyes, as though he had already established a claim to the machine.

Kit Curtis came back out of the station, scanning the faces of the crowd. He saw the group of men standing by the Alcyon but for the moment did not notice Ossie. He pushed his way to the bike and, with some deliberation, positioned himself on the saddle. The stocky man gave way reluctantly, sullen and watchful. Ossie was at Kit's shoulder. Still he had not noticed him. 'What'll it do, mister?' said Ossie.

Kit turned sharply. 'Christ where did you spring from?' He dismounted and they shook hands, surprising themselves.

'My airplane, at fifteen thousand feet.'

'You mean aeroplane.'

'There you go,' said Ossie. 'Jesus. Say, would you be looking for me?'

'If you're the chap who ordered a taxi from Reims.'

'Boy,' said Ossie, 'that's what I call service. I was just about to carry on hiking. So the guys in Reims tipped you off?'

'Something like that,' said Kit, 'although they didn't have your name. I happened to have time on my hands, you know how it is, so I said I'd pop across.' He yawned. 'Reims weren't too keen, of course.'

'Shoot. Does that mean I owe you one?'

'Looks that way, I'm afraid. Actually, I thought it might be Pip or even Beaky. I should have known.'

'Beaky's dead for sure,' Ossie said, 'but I didn't know they'd got Pip Fuller. No big surprise.'

'So, what's your excuse?' said Kit.

'Dornier. I had him cold but he knew his stuff. You?'

'An Me-109. Also knew his stuff. Got back to base a bit shot-up but made a balls of my landing.'

'Tough titty.'

Kit described what had happened at Fonteville, after the last ground party had abandoned the Revigncourt field and headed for Menneville, about Corporal Evans in the Bedford and Madame Bergeret and Monsieur Paturel.

'So they got old Paturel?' said Ossie. 'Well, there's a sunny side to everything I guess.'

'Let's make a move,' said Kit.

Ossie tugged at the metal luggage-rack. 'Am I expected to sit on this?'

'Well, if you're going to be choosy . . .'

Ossie jerked a thumb at the Hôtel de la Gare. 'If the goddammed peasants haven't stripped the place bare there might be a remnant or two I can use for padding. I'll even treat you to a drink.'

Kit started up the Alcyon and rode over to the hotel. Ossie followed on foot. The stocky man with the stubble watched them, moving slowly in their direction. Ossie did not like the way he moved, as though he had some plan in mind. At the entrance to the hotel he unbolted the second of the large front doors and swung it back. Kit had just pulled the bike on to its side-stand. Ossie kicked it off again, 'Let's get this baby out of harm's way.' He dragged it up the steps into the lobby, steered it into the ruined bar, heaved it on to its stand and sat down once more on the torn settee.

Kit stretched out beside him. 'Where's that drink you offered me?'

'Here,' said Ossie. He opened the silver flask and passed it across.

Kit took a short sip, then a longer one. 'I've always detested brandy.'

'Don't force yourself.' Ossie took the flask and put it back in his pocket.

'So, Menneville,' said Kit. 'Should be a nice ride. I gather the countryside is lovely Saint Menehould way.'

'Have we got enough gas?'

'Oh yes.'

'How long to get to Reims?'

'A day, perhaps, with things as they are. Depends on . . .'

'Yeah,' said Ossie. 'Depends on . . . What the hell day is this anyway? I'm losing track.'

He got up and went to the bar. Glass covered the floor, crunching underfoot. He selected a knife-like shard, went to the settee and hacked into its upholstery. When he had enough he bundled it into the semblance of a cushion and secured it to the bike's luggage-rack. 'I guess we'll both do stints as arse-end Charlie,' he said.

There was a scuffle in the entrance lobby and the stocky man appeared in the bar doorway with his friends. He was smiling.

'Mount up,' Ossie shouted. 'Move it!' He sprang into the saddle and kicked the engine into life. He gunned the throttle and the noise in the enclosed space was startling. He felt Kit's weight thump on to the bike behind him, his hands on his shoulders. Ossie toed the gear-pedal upwards into first and they surged towards the crowd at the door. He kicked out at the stocky guy as they passed, catching him in the groin. The impact threw the bike off balance and it swerved dangerously but Ossie caught it and got it back under control and the Alcyon vaulted the few feet from the front door of the hotel on to the forecourt, compressing the suspension on to its stops. Right in front of them two women were pushing a hand-cart. Ossie threw the bike into a slide, the back wheel kicking out to the right. He stabbed at the ground with the heel of his left foot, and they passed the women in a long curve, missing them by a few feet. Ossie gave a cowboy whoop, then Kit was bellowing in his ear and pointing towards the avenue du Mort-Homme and the route that would take them west towards Reims and the squadron's new base at Menneville.

* * *

They made slow progress, crawling mile by mile with the column of refugees that choked the highway. Kit was up front, his second spell, when they came down an incline near the hamlet of Somme-Suipe and saw the crosses standing in the small walled enclosure at the roadside, backing on to a field of young wheat. There were two kinds: in one section, white and carved from stone, and in the other – divided from the first by a low brick wall – black iron. There were trees near the gated entrance to the enclosure and in the heat the shade looked good. A few refugees had had the same idea. Children lay asleep under the shelter of the branches, but the adults dozed, constantly alert for signs of the Boches.

'We'll take a breather,' said Kit He kicked the gear lever into neutral and killed the engine. Small stones rattled on the mudguards and the brakes squealed as he pulled up by the entrance gate. At once the refugees began to rise to their feet, helping the older ones and shaking the children awake. They regarded the two pilots with something close to fear. Kit walked across to them and began to speak in rapid French, his expression open and eager. They peered up at him with faces of stone and began to move away.

Ossie looked across at Kit and shrugged. Then curious he went through the small gate into the cemetery.

He walked slowly along the lines of white stone crosses. The dead here were American. 'Well, I'll be damned.' Every man had died in 1918, at the butt-end of the war: Elmer Harvey, 20, Private, 309 Infantry, Wisconsin, killed 7 October; Earl C. Marshall, 22, Private, 353 Infantry, Kansas, 14 October; Lester E. Lambert, 21, Private, 60 Infantry, Texas, 2 November; Willie Hunt, 18, Private, 370 Infantry, Tennessee, 10 November. Christ, the day before the Armistice was signed. One raw deal, Willie. Ossie wondered what kind of guy Willie Hunt had been. 'Hey Willie boy, get your arse over here. We're sailing to La Belle France. Haw-haw, we're going to get us a piece of those juicy gals from Gay Paree my boy, you just see if we don't.' And

Willie had wound up here, on a bend in the road three thousand miles from home.

Ossie looked across the wall at the black iron crosses on the other side, and moved towards them. Karl and Otto and Claus and Friedrich and Helmut and Joachim, name after name, all mothers' sons. All of an age with Willie and his pals . . . all from this regiment and that division and falling on this day or that day to a bullet, or drowned in the bottom of a bomb crater, or caught in a trench by a flame-thrower or suffocated in a cave-in laying mines under the enemy's position. So many ways to go. That's the one thing they gave you; plenty of choice as long as they were the ones to choose.

Back at the bike Kit said: 'I say are you all right?'

'Sure,' said Ossie. 'Just been saying hello to Willie Hunt from Tennessee.'

Beyond Somme-Suippes, Ossie at the controls now, they turned off the main route into Reims and headed north-west on empty lanes, passing through deserted villages where beasts stood abandoned in the fields. At the sprinkle of buildings that made up the hamlet of Cussy-le-Mont they came across a small farm not yet pillaged. The doors were chained and padlocked. Cattle were bellowing in the meadows and a few chickens and ducks that had somehow escaped having their necks wrung by fleeing peasants were scouring for scraps in the yard. A dozen cats ran forward, tails erect. The pilots did not break in but found, behind the farmhouse, a cherry tree bearing good fruit, beds of lettuce and strawberries. Ossie watched where the chickens went, a low wooden shack, and followed them inside. He came out cradling fresh-laid eggs. They cracked them and poured them into their mouths raw, gagging a little. The fruit and lettuce cleansed their throats and they took long draughts of spring water from a tap in the yard.

'We could hole up here for the night.'

'It's early yet,' said Kit.

It was then that they heard the growl of aircraft very high. About thirty Dornier Do-17s were visible through the wisps of cirrus with an escort of perhaps fifteen Me-110s. There was a distant chatter of machine-gun fire. Half a dozen unknown fighters pierced the formation but did not break it. They climbed to attack again, meeting the diving 110s head-on.

'Hurricanes,' said Ossie.

'Yes,' said Kit. 'Come on, chaps, lay into the sods.' As the Dorniers held to their course the cloud grew a little thicker. It became difficult to make sense of the mêlée. Then, spinning and in flames, a single machine fell through the clouds: a Hurricane. Then another, diving almost vertically and smacking into farm-land about four miles away.

'Could you make out any 'chutes?' said Ossie.

'No. Let's make a move.'

The cats followed them down the track to the lane, mewing, until the noise of the motorcycle was lost in the thunder of more bombers passing overhead. Not far behind, beyond the rising hills towards Verdun, the noise of the Luftwaffe was joined by the thud of heavy artillery.

As dusk came on fuel ran low. Kit could feel the Alcyon light-ening and eased the throttle, keeping the revs down, staying in top gear. Ossie on the pillion shouted: 'Do you know where the hell we are?'

'Of course. There's a great little pub just round the corner. Wonderful ale. We'll put up there for the night.'

'Thank Christ for that. I was beginning to worry we might be lost.'

At the next crossroads a sign to the right indicated Rethel, but nothing about what lay ahead or to the left. 'Rethel's way wrong,' said Ossie. 'We're looking for the main highway from Laon just north of Reims. Menneville's beyond that a little to the west, smack bang on the Aisne.'

'I know where bloody Menneville is, thank you,' said Kit. 'I just don't know where we are right now'

They rode on expecting the engine of the Alcyon to die at any moment.

Then Ossie cried out: 'Hangars. There, against the trees.'

'Good God,' said Kit. 'I rather think you're right.'

Near the three hangars, but positioned well back against the cover of the woodland, were twin-engined French reconnaissance machines, Potez 63.11s, the tricolour roundels of l'Armée de l'Air on their flanks.

A barbed-wire fence ran round the perimeter of the airfield. Kit pulled up on a bend short of the gates where two guards, carrying rifles with fixed bayonets, were moving slowly back and forth. They heard the Alcyon's engine ticking over and slipped their rifles off their shoulders, staring hard down the road, jumpy with their fingers on the triggers.

'Why do you have to look so damned Aryan?' said Ossie. 'Slump down a little.'

Kit shouted.

'*Camarades, nous sommes deux pilotes de chasse anglais. Nous voudrions voir votre commandant.*'

'*Avancez!*' came a voice hoarse with tension.

They were escorted to the commandant's office by a lieutenant who was probably twenty-five and looked forty. He wore the wings of a pilot on his *vareuse*. His eyes were red-raw. From time to time a tremor started up on the left side of his face and he suppressed it with a quick movement of his hand. He finished smoking a cigarette as they passed in front of the silent Potez 63s and immediately lit another.

'How many aeroplanes have you?' said Kit.

'Today eight,' said the lieutenant.

The commandant was at his desk on the telephone, speaking with heat to someone in a supply depot, telling the man he was an imbecile, that for refusing to deliver spare parts unless the requisition was made in the correct manner and on the correct forms, the whole damned depot would tomorrow fall into enemy hands. Meanwhile, his squadron, the eyes and ears of the French army, on which its whole strategy depended, found itself with aircraft unfit for service and pilots unable to fly. The exchange ended inconclusively. Eventually he replaced the receiver and, with a glance at the RAF men, issued some brief orders to the lieutenant, who lit another cigarette and left. 'Break it gently, Dorance,' the commandant called after him.

Kit explained something of their situation and the commandant listened carefully, chewing the inside of his cheek. 'I can give you little cheer,' he said. 'I do not know how it is with your people but within my squadron it is now a matter of spirit over intelligence. We continue to be operational because that is our role until instructed to do otherwise. Unfortunately our radio communications are a joke. The army telephone system has virtually ceased to exist and we receive only garbled orders for reconnaissance and support, which we carry out to the best of our ability. Many of the sorties are unrealistic against the odds we face but we persevere. We – those of us who survive – submit our reports but who knows how the situation has changed by the time they arrive on someone's desk at Division Headquarters? Meanwhile we continue to go out in the morning and some of us come back, to hear that l'Armée de l'Air is nowhere to be seen and is taking no part in holding the Boches. That is the story the army tells us: "We have never seen a French aeroplane." Thus we return, if we do return, from our patrols with holes in our machines put there by our own forces because, they say, any aeroplane must clearly be a Boche.' The commandant was silent for a moment. Then he said: 'We have lost the battle for supply. You heard how it is with us – I saw little point in pretence. The Potez is an admirable design but without spares perhaps half stay on the ground and the others—' He broke off. 'My crews have two enemies, the Boches and the machines. The tally is not good. Can you imagine, my friends, how many we were only days ago?'

'No,' said Kit.

'Twenty-three machines,' said the commandant, 'three men to a machine: pilot, observer, gunner. Sixty-nine men. Today, eight machines and twenty-four men. That is why,' he said, with a rueful smile, 'you find me less than my normal amusing self.' He stood up. 'I'm afraid the mess is also less than amusing at present but at least you will eat well. That is one of the great attractions of being a pilot, is it not? You are always home in time for tea.' He held the door open for them adding: 'Well, perhaps not always.'

Seventeen

Monday, 13 May 1940

The red-eyed lieutenant of l'Armée de l'Air buckled himself into the pilot's seat of the Potez 63.11, and called up his observer and rear-gunner on the intercom. His hands still trembled on the controls but his voice was calm enough. '*Vous pouvez m'entendre?*' His crew responded promptly. It was plain that they knew each other well.

Lieutenant Dorance bent his nicotine-yellow fingers around the throttle levers and ran up the twin Gnome-Rhônes. The ground-crew gave him a final wave and started back for the hangars where more machines were being prepared for the first sorties of the day.

'*Prêt à partir?*' said Dorance. The observer and the gunner said they were, and the Potez began to move. Dorance turned into wind, an almost imperceptible breeze from the south-west, and took off. He had to allow for the extra weight of the two RAF men stretched out in the nose of the machine alongside the observer but this was a luxury, an easy trip, heading away from the front line where flak, German and French, would rise to meet them in deadly, hypnotic streams; where, later in the day, he and his crew would resume their normal routine of skimming across the enemy positions at 400 k.p.h. at a height of fifty feet in the name of intelligence, already out-of-date by the time they landed.

He was glad the commandant had been so insistent about

restoring the Royal Air Force pilots to their squadron at Menneville, and delighted that the task had fallen to him. He knew that he would die soon but this little trip gave him a few more hours or even days before he joined the boys who had already gone. He remembered one of the RAF fellows, the tall one, in the mess at dinner making some remark about his plans for when the war was over. Dorance had said politely, 'I believe it wiser we consider ourselves already dead.'

After less than fifteen minutes in the air the Potez put down at Menneville. In that brief time Kit and Ossie covered almost fifty kilometres, close to the distance they had travelled from Verdun to the Potez base in twenty-four hours. The flight had passed too quickly for Dorance but he valued every moment: it had been like his peace-time flips with l'École de l'Air when his only goal had been to earn the *brevet de pilote*, the first step on a path that had led him to this unimaginable point.

From the air the aerodrome at Menneville showed no sign of activity, just a collection of deserted-looking buildings close to a large but obviously empty hangar. Dorance assumed his passengers knew what they were about. He taxied slowly towards the hangar and braked to a halt, keeping the engines running and constantly checking the sky for an Me-109 on a free-hunt. However, the odds were fractionally better here, and beyond the perimeter the prospect of the vineyards running down to the valley of the Aisne, the hills green and the river blue as the sky, belied the existence of that other world to which he would soon return.

The RAF men came into the cockpit. They thumped him on the back and gave him thumbs-ups. They were smiling and seemed happy, shouting words he could not make out through his leather helmet with its earphones. He realised that because of their position in the nose of the Potez they did not know that the Menneville field was deserted. There was no way to soften the blow. He shouted: 'I could see nothing, absolutely nothing, as we descended. Your squadron is not here as far as I can see.'

The tall Englishman who spoke excellent French translated for the other, the one who, after much wine, had told him he was an American volunteer.

They lost their smiles. They talked urgently to each other, then came to a decision. '*Je vous remercie*,' said the one who could speak French. 'We have no choice. Please leave us here. Thank you again. You have saved us many miles at least. *Bonne chance*.' The stocky American fumbled in his pocket and pulled out a silver flask. He held his thumb and forefinger against it to show it was a quarter full and pushed it into Dorance's hand. 'Cognac,' he said. '*Le mieux*.' Then he and the Englishman ducked down and made their way forward to the port hatch, just below the pilot's cockpit where they clambered out on to the wing and slipped to the ground. The Potez was quickly gone, the red-eyed Dorance contemplating his next sortie. Although it was tempting, he did not drink from the silver flask: he owed it to his crew to preserve his edge.

Ossie stood with the palms of his hands on his head, his fingers interlocked and elbows jutting. It eased the pain in his damaged shoulder. Near the hangar, in the centre of a circle of scorched grass, stood the blackened skeleton of one of the squadron's three-ton Bedfords. 'They were here all right,' he said.

Kit inspected the wreck. The stench of petrol hung in the air. 'Probably us. Brewster wouldn't have left it for the Hun.'

'Why did they skedaddle so fast?' said Ossie. 'Dammit, we should have checked with Reims last night.'

Menneville still had the semblance of a normal community: shops and cafés open, a church bell ringing, people in the streets, even children in the school. From the *boulangerie* in the main square, ringed by plane trees, where old men were playing *boules* on the sandy gravel, came the fragrance of the morning's baking. Kit and Ossie found themselves walking through the town without purpose, other than thinking about their next move. They said nothing to each other, going over the options in their minds. The Potez crews had lent them soap and razors and helped them clean their uniforms, but with Kit's face a patchwork of blue and yellow bruises and Ossie's fractured nose now a bilious purple, they aroused distaste and suspicion. From the doorway of the *boucherie* a voice called: 'Why does the Royal Air Force desert France in its time of need? Why do you leave the door open for the Boches and expect l'Armée de l'Air to do your fighting for you?' The man was careful to stay out of sight.

Ossie moved towards the door, bunching his fist, but Kit pushed him ahead. 'I'll treat you to a drink this time.'

They sat down at a metal table on the cobbles outside the Café des Allies in the rue de Chevaliers where the fourteenth-century houses leaned towards each other as though exchanging secrets. It was gloomy under the shadow of the houses and cool. They waited a long time to be served.

'If the Boches get here,' said Ossie, 'these guys are going to have to change the name of this place.'

'You think they will get here?'

'I'd say it's beginning to look that way, wouldn't you?'

Kit pictured Wehrmacht officers sitting where he was now, those damned braided caps tipped over one eye, the red-striped breeches, the polished boots, their voices, very loud, ringing round the enclosed space. He imagined the service would be quicker. Finally, and without a word, their order was taken by a morose youth scratching himself with a hand thrust inside his shirt. The beer arrived in chipped tumblers, with a scrawled bill on a china saucer. The youth wanted to be paid immediately but Kit ignored him. At least the Alsace brew was good, very strong and rich in hops. Ossie quickly drained his glass, tipping it high to catch the last drop of froth. Then he said: 'So, what's the plan?'

'You tell me,' said Kit. 'I know we can't stay here.' He peeled off a ten-franc note from the roll of a hundred the commandant had pressed upon him as they prepared to board Dorance's machine, picked up the china saucer with the bill and went inside the café. A brown Bakelite wireless with yellow dials stood on a shelf behind the bar. An information bulletin was reporting encouraging news from the front. The German invaders were being held at Sedan, thanks to the heroic pilots of l'Armée de l'Air destroying the bridges across the Meuse; no mention of the Blenheims and Battles of the Royal Air Force. The Maginot Line was performing magnificently, the invaders hurling themselves against its impregnable fortifications in vain. It was admitted that the railway network had been bombed in certain areas to the east, which explained the suspension of some services, but little was said about casualties and nothing of the thousands of refugees being swept west from the border. Ossie had heard the crackle of the wireless and was leaning against the door. Accordion music resumed and a man with wild, uncut hair and prominent dark eyes seated by the window, said: '*Moi, je pense qu'on est foutu.*' He wore the blue overalls of a peasant, and although his observation was not cultured his accent was.

'What's he say?' said Ossie.

'It's his personal opinion we're fucked,' said Kit. He told the man by the window: '*Monsieur, nous n'avons pas perdu la guerre jusqu'à maintenant.*'

The man rose to his feet. He was holding a glass of milk-white absinthe. He took a final gulp and replaced it on the table next to a small jug of water. 'Perhaps. I sincerely hope you are right, Monsieur. I perceive you are English. I compliment you on your French but may I also urge caution? It is well known that the English can barely speak their own language and in these times, when people leap their own height at the sight of their shadows, your fluency might cause undue nervousness.' He smiled sardonically. 'I see also that you are airmen. Have you parked your aeroplane outside?'

'No,' said Kit. 'It is parked, and none too neatly, beyond

Verdun.' He was content to allow the man to believe that he and Ossie shared a machine.

'It is bad there?'

'Not so good.'

'Where are you bound?'

'Who knows? Perhaps Reims.'

'Ah, you are wary of my questions. Rightly so. But I would not advise Reims. My sister lives there. All is confusion and dread. The aerodrome was bombed on Saturday. A hundred Boche bombers they say. The railway junction was also destroyed. The population is gripped by terror. I do not blame them but I scorn the chiefs who have brought us to this. My name is Loeb, by the way.' He banged on the bar counter with his knuckles.

They heard a newspaper cast down and the morose youth appeared from behind a shabby curtain with a cigarette in his mouth. Loeb insisted on paying for their beers as well, after checking both bills with exaggerated care. He said to the waiter: 'You'll forgive me for being so careful, Lucien, but you and I know your arithmetic was always abominable.' He threw down the money and some of the coins fell to the floor. The waiter, still silent, regarded him with something close to hatred but did not pick them up. Loeb said: 'Gentlemen, I have business in Soissons, which, I understand, has so far escaped the attentions of the Boches. You are welcome to join me. From there you could make your way to Paris, possibly by train. The line remains open, at least for the moment. I suspect it might suit the Boches that way.'

Kit told Ossie: 'He's offering us a lift to Soissons. It seems Reims is a shambles. We may not find anyone there who can help if you understand me.' He meant Wing.

'Yes,' said Ossie.

'Soissons, then?'

'Sure. Looks like the only game in town.'

Together they left the café and walked the short distance to the main square, where Loeb unlocked the door of a hard-used Renault truck, roughly daubed in matt-blue paint with vegetables piled in the back. The waiter had come to the end of the rue de Chevaliers. He watched as they climbed into the cab and drove away.

At the wheel of the truck Loeb said: 'I used to work there.' He pointed at the schoolhouse with its separate entrances for boys and girls. 'Lucien, the little charmer, was one of the first to tell me that his father did not want him taught by a Communist Jew. In that alone he was advanced. I told him he was unteachable by anyone. I told his father also.'

'How did he take it – the father, I mean?' said Kit.

'He arranged for me to lose my job. *Il fourre son nez partout.* The café is merely one of his interests. He exercises great influence, the bourgeois *fils de pute.*'

'Yet you patronise his café and remain in this town?'

'It amuses me. Petty, I know, but I have few entertainments these days.' He tapped out a cigarette from a Gauloise packet so that it projected an inch or two and offered it to Kit, who shook his head. Loeb pushed it between his lips, returned the pack to his pocket, then lit up with a match struck deftly against the roof of the cab. 'There was plenty to raise a smile in 'thirty-six,' he said, 'when the factory occupations began after the Popular Front got in. My God, how the damned bourgeoisie trembled in its shoes to find itself saddled with a prime minister of the Left. "Rather Hitler than Blum" was the motto then. Well, now it appears they are about to get their wish. We shall see soon enough how it suits them.'

Kit said: 'Perhaps it will suit those like Lucien's father very well indeed.'

'So it is said, and even now people are cautious of their dealings with him. He tells everyone this war is unnecessary, that it has been wished upon us by the Communists and the Jews – the Communists because of their defeat in Spain and the Jews because they are being hunted down everywhere. And no one dares to disagree, other than me.'

'You take a great risk,' said Kit.

'After Spain it seems a little thing,' said Loeb.

'You were in Spain?' said Kit. He looked quickly at Ossie but he was asleep, mouth open, head jolting with the movement of the truck.

'Oh, yes, it was the natural thing. With my job I also lost my wife and child. She chose not to support me. Her family had been against me from the start. We knew each other as children and married in 'thirty-two. At first her people regarded my leftish views as a joke. With the election of Léon Blum it became less amusing. The Right began to unite and gather strength, and speak of people like me as the Red menace, the enemy within. So I found myself alone, no job, no wife, no family, no ties. The struggle in Spain was the obvious move.'

Kit sensed that Loeb had spoken these words many times before, his eyes alight in the same way, his voice thick with emotion. He was saying: 'It was wonderful in the beginning. We burned money in the little villages of Aragon – said we would abolish it altogether. The only wisdom was derived from the earth, the peasants, those who can tame nature. Those who did not work with their hands were corrupt. Labour should be respected, unearned wealth shunned. All was love and brother-hood, the war and the revolution inseparable. But then it began to be said, by the Stalinists most of all, that first the war had to be won and only afterwards could we make the revolution. And their view of the revolution was not that held by the people. The masses were backward, they said, saturated with democratic illusions, not ready for a true socialist revolution, only for a democratic one.

'The squabbling factions – republicans, socialists, Communists and anarchists – finally destroyed the unity, the revolutionary energy of the working class. And at the end, when Barcelona was yielded to the Nationalists without a fight, nobody was ready to give up his life, nobody was prepared to defend it. Can you credit that? And this from forces who had not so long before believed that if a position had not been taken by the enemy a revolutionary had no right to consider it lost. The war was not won by Franco,' said Loeb. 'It was lost because the people were betrayed by their leaders.' He sat back at the wheel and blew out his cheeks. 'And so it is again. The Boches advance through a divided continent and the questions are the same. Who is ready to give up his life? Who is ready to fight?'

'I am fighting,' said Kit. He jerked his head at Ossie. 'So is he. So are countless others, French, Dutch and Belgian, as well as English. There are many brave men among our ranks who are determined to hold the Boches.'

'I hope you are right, my friend,' said Loeb, 'but tell me, why do you fight? What kind of better world have you in mind? Is it what we fought for in Spain, for love and brotherhood and a fair reward for honest toil? Or to preserve the status of the Right, the bourgeoisie?'

'Your talk of love and brotherhood, of burning money, noble peasants taming nature with their bare hands, those dreams died quickly enough when faced with the reality in Spain,' said Kit. 'Have you not learnt? Now we are compelled to fight because we detest oppression, dictatorship and the will to dominate the world. But after that we must have order, and for me that means democracy. It may not be perfect but it's the nearest thing we've got to a system that works.'

Suddenly Ossie spoke: 'I'll tell you what I'm fighting for. I'm fighting for the little guy. Kind of simple but it fits in a frame.' He yawned and winced as he moved his shoulder. Then he leaned forward and looked at Loeb, whose face was set and angry as he clasped the big steering-wheel, eyes running from the cigarette smoke.

'Hey, *camarada*,' Ossie called across. '*Como le va?*'

Loeb was astonished. '*¡Dios mio! ¿Usted habla espagnol?* You fought in Spain?'

'*Eco, hombre,*' said Ossie. '*Tien un cigarillo?*'

Loeb lit a cigarette, puffed it a couple of times and handed it to Kit, who passed it to Ossie. Ossie said, in rough-and-ready Spanish: 'So, what outfit were you with?'

'The Confederación Nacional de Trabajadores,' said Loeb. 'And you?'

'POUM – and that's lucky. We got along with you CNT guys. Where'd you serve?'

'Mostly I worked in editorial at *La Voz Leninista* but before that I was a militiaman in Huesca.'

'No kidding? I was on the Huesca front. What unit?' Loeb told him.

'No,' said Ossie, 'don't know it.'

'My people fought with their hearts,' said Loeb, 'but always with the same result. We would attack and suffer great losses, overwhelm the Fascists and hold the positions, but then their cursed aviators would arrive and bomb us out. We never saw our own machines. It was towards the end that we began to hear on every side "*Fuera los extranjeros*" and we foreigners knew it was time to get out. Also the Stalinistas had denounced the so-called Trotskyists and militants died before the firing squad. All was corruption and madness and ambition. I returned to this miserable town in March last year to live my life in a small way, by my own labour and selling my produce where I might, enjoying the petty amusement of being *une épine au pied* for the Lucien and his type.' Then he said defiantly: 'But I do not regret what occurred in Spain. It was magnificent, a magnificent illusion.'

The matt-blue Renault truck was on a long straight stretch of dirt road approaching an incline where pine trees crowded in on both verges. It was trailing a plume of dust, through which burst a black Citroën Traction Avant, travelling fast, its driver working the horn, the car sliding as it passed and cutting in to the right. It went out of sight round the bend at the top of the incline. Ossie said: 'That looked like that little punk Lucien.'

Loeb dropped down a gear to make the gradient. The truck slowed and as they approached the crest they saw the Citroën parked by the trees on the right and two men near it. One was the waiter, Lucien, the other bull-like with thick black hair curled over a low brow. He wore a singlet stained with blood and rubbed his hands like a wrestler preparing for a bout. He stepped boldly into the road and held up a fist.

'*Pare el camion*,' said Ossie. The Renault halted at a slight angle, turned away from the man in the road. Ossie opened the passenger door a little, dropped down and rolled unseen into the shallow ditch. Then, bent double, he ran for the shelter of the woods to the right. The man in the bloody singlet did not advance towards them.

He remained in the centre of the road, arms folded now, mouth twisted in contempt. He was calling to them but they could not make out the words, only that he wanted them to get out of the truck and come to him. They stayed where they were.

'Come to us, Monsieur le Boucher,' shouted Loeb. 'What is it that you want?' He said to Kit: 'This specimen is Lucien's uncle. He boasts that he makes sausages of Communists and Jews.'

'We passed his shop in Menneville,' said Kit. 'He gave us the benefit of his opinions.'

The butcher waited for a few minutes, then turned and marched back to the Citroën. He reached into the back of the car and pulled out a leather gun-case, unbuttoned the top flap and removed a two-barrel shotgun, broke it, took orange cartridges from his trouser pocket and inserted them into the chambers, then snapped the barrels shut. Behind him Lucien was fingering a pistol, hanging back a little.

The butcher began to advance down the road. He was sweating, damp stains showing on the front of the singlet. The waiter was a dozen paces behind. They could hear the butcher now. 'This is your time, you Jewish bastard – *connard*, dirty Communist, stinking corrupter of our children. Now you help the English cowards who desert their posts while Frenchmen stand betrayed by filthy Reds and Jews who brought this war upon us. We have no argument with the Boches. We will deal with scum like you, then unite with them. They are our brothers.' He raised the shotgun and discharged both barrels. The windscreen of the truck dissolved into a thousand fragments, showering Loeb and Kit as they threw themselves cross-wise on the seat. Some pellets pierced the metal of the scuttle and Loeb yelped with pain as, though spent, they still had force enough to penetrate his chest.

The butcher reloaded as he walked. He was in no hurry. He was enjoying himself. He did not want it to be over too soon. He was close now, by the driver's door. Kit knew how it would be: the door wrenched open, the butcher pulling himself up on to the running-board, angling the barrels of the shotgun down, perhaps treating himself to a moment or two before he pulled the triggers, taking it all in so he could describe it to the family later.

Then, from outside, came the sharp crack of a pistol and the rattle of the shotgun falling to the ground. The butcher had fallen against the cab of the Renault, screaming. A fat-fingered hand felt for support on the sill of the window, thick with blood. There was another shot and they heard the butcher's body slide down the mudguard and on to the road.

'Okay,' said Ossie Wolf. 'It's over now.'

The butcher was flat on his back in the dirt, arms and legs outstretched, felled like one of the beasts he dismembered in the shed behind his shop in Menneville. There was dust in his curled hair, giving it a ginger hue. He was still breathing and his eyes were open, glazed and uncomprehending. Ossie knelt down beside him, cocked the neat 7.65 military model Savage automatic, placed the barrel in the butcher's left ear and squeezed the trigger. The spout of blood reached the grass bank on the other side of the road.

'My God,' said Kit. Loeb's face was grey.

A hundred yards away the waiter, also on the ground, rose, groaning, and reeled towards the Citroën. He fell into the driver's seat and tried to start the engine, but he had flooded the carburettor by pumping the throttle too hard and the engine wouldn't fire.

Ossie applied the safety catch on the pistol and handed it to Kit. 'Keep that. It should be useful.' He bent down, picked up the blood-spattered shotgun and checked the chambers. He took two more cartridges from the butcher's pocket, removed the expended rounds and slid fresh ones in their place. Then he walked up the incline to the Citroën and loosed both barrels, almost instantaneously, into the head of the waiter as he sat, frozen, the window wound down, at the wheel of the Traction Avant. The trunk of the youth, for his head had ceased to exist, sank out of sight.

Ossie came back down the hill, moving coolly, businesslike. Kit and Loeb fell against the sides of the truck, as though dissociating themselves from what he was doing. Ossie pulled at the arms of the dead butcher and said to Kit: 'Jesus, man, give me a hand here.' They dragged the cadaver to the Citroën and bundled it into the back seat. Ossie threw the shotgun in after it then walked quickly back to the Renault, where Loeb was being sick. '*Callate, hombre,*' said Ossie. '*¡Las cerillas! las cerillas.*' He was snapping his fingers with impatience.

He snatched the matches, found a length of cotton waste in the cab of the truck, soaked it in petrol from a spare can in the back with the vegetables and returned to the Citroën. He undid the cap of the fuel tank and pushed the material down the nozzle. Then he struck a match and applied it to the cotton waste. As the flames took hold the handbrake burned free and the car rolled a few feet across the grass and bumped gently against the pines, which caught with a roar like a furnace door being opened.

Ossie said: 'I'll drive.' He grinned. 'You said that little creep was lousy at sums. He should have told the fat guy there were three of us.' He told them how he had worked his way quickly through the woods, emerging behind the Citroën and had come up behind Lucien and leaned around him before he knew what was happening and had taken the little automatic from his flaccid grasp and struck him down with the butt. Then he'd gone after the butcher. 'Fats was shouting at you guys fit to bust and didn't hear a thing. *Un vero cabron.* Now, where the hell are we heading?'

'Tell him to keep following the signs to Soissons Sud,' Loeb said to Kit in French. 'The railway station lies that side.' It was as if he no longer wanted to speak directly to Ossie even though they shared a common language. Blood had worked its way through his plaid shirt and blue overalls but the wounds were slight. He worked at extracting the pellets himself – like small black seeds lying just below the surface of his skin – and threw them from the window, as though trying to throw away the memory of what had happened at the crest of the rise close by the pine woods.

It was crowded at the railway station but not impossible. Kit purchased two first-class single tickets to the Gare de l'Est. The train was due in five minutes and said to be running on time. He walked out to the truck where Ossie and Loeb were waiting. Still they did not talk to each other though standing close. 'Right,' Kit said. 'We'll be on our way.'

'I am at a loss,' said Loeb. 'What do I do now? I cannot go back.'

'What's he say?' said Ossie.

'He says he cannot go back. He is at a loss.'

'Brother,' Ossie said seriously to Loeb, who could not understand, 'the speed the Boches are moving, a burned-out Citroën with a couple of stiffs on board won't raise an eyebrow. Jesus, those bastards were out to kill you – to kill us all. Don't waste time thinking about them. They had it coming.'

'Don't bother to translate,' said Loeb.

Kit shook Loeb's hand. Loeb looked at the ground. His jaw

was working as though he was chewing something but there was nothing in his mouth. He folded his arms, hands flat under his armpits, hugging himself as though chilled to the marrow. There was something he wanted to say. He was finding it hard. 'Those men,' he said finally, 'Lucien and Émile.' So, the butcher had a name. 'They were my wife's people, God forgive me. How could we have come to such a thing?'

For a long moment Kit could not think of anything to say. Then: 'They were out to kill us, kill us all,' he said. 'What else could we have done? It was the only way.'

'Lucien was a boy,' said Loeb. 'I knew him as a child. He seemed uncertain . . .'

'He was there,' said Kit, 'and armed.'

'It was the manner of it,' said Loeb, 'the manner of it.' He began to weep.

Ossie did not know why the teacher wept. But he spoke to him softly now in Spanish: '*Adios, camarada*. Go west, keep heading west. You can grow your damned vegetables anywhere.'

The two pilots heard the train approaching. Loeb, still weeping, got back into the Renault truck with its shattered windscreen and started the engine. He drove off without looking at them again.

'Jesus,' said Ossie, 'for a guy who claims he saw action at Huesca he acts real squeamish. No wonder the goddammed Fascists won.'

Eighteen

Tuesday, 14 May 1940

Was it only yesterday evening, Kit asked himself, that they had
come into the Gare de l'Est on the 16.50 service from Soissons
to find the grey city touched with green? All seemed as usual
for a Paris spring, tender leaves breaking on the trees, buds
bursting on the horse-chestnuts and the air heavy with pollen.
Outside the cafés, the Closerie de Lilas, Le Dôme and La
Rotonde, the tables had been put out and were filled with the
usual crowd absorbed in conversation. Couples, heads together,
moved slowly along the banks of the Seine. In the taxi from the
station Kit took in the busy streets, the bustle of the shops, the
queues outside the cinemas on the Champs, the strollers in the
Tuileries, the sheer normality of the scene. 'Look,' he said to
Ossie, 'the real world.'

They had first encountered this disturbing ordinariness when
they boarded the train at Soissons. There, the rail service
appeared intact, not bombed to ruins like Bar-le-Duc, Joinville
or Reims. The train had drawn in only three minutes late, smart
and clean, its uniformed attendants brisk and efficient. Even
the first-class seats had not been fully occupied although the
carriages were crowded. And as they had pushed their way
along the corridor to their compartment Kit had noticed
another empty seat beneath a small sign: '*Réservé pour les
mutilés de la guerre.*' No one had chosen to sit there, although
in the corridor many were old and weak, clutching at the

286

window bars for support as they gazed at the passing countryside.

And yet, on the crest of the road from Menneville to Soissons, there was another world entirely, where the bodies of Lucien and his uncle Émile continued to melt in the red-hot glow of the Traction Avant beneath the burning pine trees; a world where death lay in wait behind every rise in the ground, every wood and ditch, every turn in the road, every deserted building, village and town and, in the sky, behind every cloud and shaft of sun. Even as an unchanging Paris passed before him, Kit knew that brutal reality was advancing upon it, like the darkness when the sun goes down.

At the Crillon the maître d'hotel, Albert, made no comment on their appearance, asked no questions. Instead he was profuse in his apologies that the suite normally taken by the Curtis family was unavailable, the hotel remaining unaccountably busy. But he could offer Monsieur Kit and his companion two excellent adjoining rooms on the third floor. He escorted them there himself and unlocked the doors and gave them the keys. When he had gone Ossie came into Kit's room. 'This is swell.'

'Good. I should get some shut-eye if I were you. I'm going to try to raise the British Embassy, see if I can get some sense out of someone, try to fix something up for tomorrow.' His manner was cool and precise. There remained a distance between him and the American since the business of Lucien and his uncle.

Kit wanted to forget the image of the young waiter's face as he had sat frozen at the wheel of the Citroën, watching Ossie stalk towards him with the shotgun.

Ossie was secure in the rightness of what he had done, but did not know how to help this damned dreamy Englishman come to terms with it. But he had come up with nothing, nothing at all. And, back in his own room, sleep overcame him.

At a little after ten thirty in the morning, in a discreet corner of the Hôtel Crillon's *petit salon*, Rupert Pringle poured tea from a white china pot. There were three cups on the silver tray in front of him but for the moment he was on his own. He added milk from a matching jug and stirred in two spoonfuls of sugar. As he raised the cup to his lips he heard the metallic clang of the lift doors in the lobby. Fernand, quick and dapper, who had run the *petit salon* for years, hurried forward as Kit appeared at the door. 'Ah, Monsieur Kit, this way.' He showed him to Pringle's table.

'Hello, Pringle,' said Kit. He shook hands with the ministry man and sat down, flinching as his spine touched the back of the chair. He was wearing a double-breasted civilian suit with a white shirt and a dark blue tie.

'Good Lord,' said Pringle, 'you look a bit second-hand.'

'Really? I thought it fitted rather well.'

'I mean your face.'

'It's *à la mode*, purple and yellow. Haven't you heard?'

Pringle put down his cup. 'I'm afraid I started without you. I hope you don't mind.'

'What is it?'

'Tea.'

'I can see that. What sort?'

'Oh. I don't know. Indian, I think.'

Kit lifted the lid of the pot. 'Earl Grey.'

'I forgot you know about tea,' said Pringle. 'Would you like some?'

'Rather. No milk, no sugar.'

'Oh dear,' said Pringle. He poured the tea and passed it to him doubtfully. 'One *faux pas* after another.'

'I see you're picking up the language.'

'Well, as a matter of fact . . . oh, you're joking.'

'Only slightly,' said Kit. 'Sorry, my humour's a little rusty. It's good to see you again Pringle.'

'Is it?'

'Absolutely. You're a fixed point in a chaotic world.'

'Oh,' said Pringle. 'Good.' He sipped his milky tea. 'So, you and Sergeant Wolf have been rather going through it.'

'No longer Sergeant. Acting Flight Lieutenant. His commission came through in February.'

'Oh yes,' said Pringle. 'I rather think I heard that. Wasn't sure I believed it, though. Such a bolshie fellow, always ready to pick a fight.'

'Quite useful in a war of course,' said Kit.

By the entrance to the *petit salon* voices were being raised. Fernand was in dispute with a stocky figure dressed in a brass-buttoned blazer and flannels. Kit went over. Ossie Wolf was saying: 'Well, nobody told me I need a damned necktie to get in here.'

'That's all right, Fernand,' said Kit. He touched his own. 'Perhaps you could find something suitable for my companion. We're tucked away in the corner over there.'

'What do you think of my get-up?' Ossie said. 'Seems they heard I was an RAF officer. Not too fancy?' He was aiming to lighten things up.

'No,' said Kit. 'It's fine.'

'You don't think the nose kind of spoils the effect?'

'I doubt anyone will even notice it.'

Pringle stood up as they approached. 'Good grief, Wolf,' he said, 'what on earth happened to your nose?'

'You remember Pringle,' said Kit. 'He's here to help us out.'

'Is that right?'

'Yes, indeed,' said Pringle. 'We thought it wiser to have the briefing here. Things have been a bit leaky at the Embassy lately. Jolly disappointing to think you can't trust people at a time like this. I imagine you must have encountered antagonism from certain elements of the population yourselves.'

'Two guys tried to blow us apart with a shotgun just yesterday,' said Ossie.

Pringle laughed. 'Really? A shotgun? Yes, I see.' He glanced at Kit. 'So what did you do?'

'Killed them both.'

'Killed them both,' said Pringle, still laughing. 'Of course you did. Tea?'

'You've got to be kidding,' said Ossie. When Fernand came across with a red and grey tie he ordered a *bière de garde*. After a minute or two an elderly waiter brought it, a little unsteady on his feet.

'Some *garçon*,' said Ossie to Kit.

'May I get anything for you, *Messieurs*?' said the waiter. The flesh around his eyes was scarlet and hung loose. They shook their heads and he shuffled slowly away.

Pringle told them how it had been when Kit telephoned the British Embassy from the Crillon. 'At first everyone thought it was some kind of ploy – you know, fifth-column trickery, that kind of thing. Luckily I caught your names. It saved a lot of going round the houses. Communication with your HQ in Reims has been a bit rocky lately so we contacted your squadron to tell them you're both all right.'

'What did they say?'

'I understand your CO took the message. I think it was on the lines of "Tell them to get the lead out", something to that effect.'

'Where are they now?' said Kit.

'Louvins, just south-east of here. Pretty little place. We'll arrange transport.'

'When?'

'Whenever you want. I shouldn't be in too much of a hurry. You both look as though you could do with a bit of a break.'

'I imagine the chaps in Louvins feel just the same way. We'll leave tomorrow.'

'If you're sure.'

'Absolutely.'

'Early afternoon then. Your uniforms are promised for lunchtime, delivered here, of course. Marvellous little tailor chappie near the place des Victoires. Assures us they'll look like new. He'll pick up the civvies he loaned you then. Afraid we had to take a stab at what suits.' He shot a glance at Ossie. 'Or doesn't.'

'Funny guy,' said Ossie. 'You crease me up, Pringle.' He waved to attract the attention of the waiter and ordered another Trois Monts. When it arrived the old man placed the glass on the table with the faintest flicker of disapproval. Ossie didn't miss it.

'Oh, yes,' said the waiter, absently, 'and Monsieur Pringle is wanted on the telephone.'

It was a very quick call. Pringle was back in minutes. 'Got to dash, I'm afraid. Bit of a panic on.'

'What kind of panic?' said Kit.

'Can't say.'

'Oh, you can tell us,' said Ossie. 'We're on the same side, remember?'

'Well,' said Pringle, reluctantly, 'I suppose it'll be common knowledge soon enough. The Germans are breaking through at Sedan.'

'Start burning the papers,' said Ossie.

'Not funny,' said Pringle. 'Not funny at all.'

'Who's joking?' said Ossie.

Running his finger round the inside of his collar Pringle said to Kit: 'Let me know if there's anything more I can do. You know where to reach me.'

'Hey, Pringle,' said Ossie, 'before you hit the road, whatever happened to that slice of CBS bullshit you got me mixed up in?'

'Never used. Didn't find favour with the powers-that-be. Are you surprised?'

'So it was all a goddammed waste of time.'

'You could put it that way,' said Pringle. 'Whose fault was that, do you suppose? Goodbye Curtis. We'll confirm a time for the car tomorrow.'

When the ministry man had gone Kit said: 'I suggest you lay off Pringle. He's only trying to help.'

'Those guys,' said Ossie. 'They've had it so easy. They hardly know there's a war on. It's kind of an abstract thing for them, shooting their mouths off round a table, pins in maps on walls, statistics about this, directives about that, plans and policies that mean shit, and always the politicos with their sticky little fingers screwing things up. Now they're about to find out what it really means, assuming, of course, they stick around, which I doubt.'

The waiter started to clear the table. He was clumsy and knocked over a cup that still contained a few dregs. The cold tea spattered on to the carpet around Ossie's feet. He swore, stood up, swore again and brushed at his trousers as though he had been drenched. The old man stammered apologies. He appeared close to tears. Kit helped him clear away the mess. Ossie watched, still cursing. 'For God's sake,' said Kit, 'it was an accident, man. Leave the poor old chap alone.' Even in this microcosm of the so-called real world, this place of comfort and plenty, of courtesy and quiet conversation, small acts of cruelty could occur, careless and savage, spreading misery and despair.

'What's your problem?' said Ossie. 'The guy's got little enough to do.'

'Guy?' said Kit. 'He's not just some guy. He's a man of sixty, seventy, still working. Has to. A man who's lived a long, hard life.'

'Yeah?' said Ossie.

'When he comes back,' said Kit, 'take a look at him.'

'What's to see?' said Ossie. 'The guy doesn't know what service is.'

'Look at his hands,' said Kit. 'His knuckles are swollen. Arthritis. Must be painful. His legs are bowed and his back is bent. So many years on his feet in a hundred hotels before the army drew the younger ones away and he found himself with a chance at the Crillon. Have you noticed his cuffs?'

'His *cuffs*?'

'The cuffs of his shirt-sleeves have been mended with great care and skill to make the shirt last just that little bit longer. Did he do it himself or has he a wife, an old seamstress perhaps, who still wants her husband to do her and the Crillon credit?'

'You're killing me,' said Ossie.

Kit persisted: 'Here is a man who's old and ailing, struggling to keep it all together after a lifetime of work because he has no choice. Isn't he one of the very fellows you're always sentimentalising about, someone who's always done his best but needs looking out for, someone to stand up for him and fight the bigger battles, protect him from those characters round that table you talked about, the politicos, the megalomaniacs who hold other people's destinies in their hands?'

'Jesus,' said Ossie. 'What brought this on?'

'I'm ordering you to leave him alone,' said Kit.

'Ordering me, huh?'

'Yes, Flight Lieutenant, ordering you. You're acting, I'm the real thing. For heaven's sake, man, you could be flying again in a couple of days. Save your aggression for the Hun. And while we're about it, cut out the beer as well. This could be our last chance of a breather in Paris for a very long time. I don't want it ruined by a pissed, belligerent Yank. You're here as my guest, remember?'

'Okay,' said Ossie, 'okay, okay.' The alcohol had hit him and he felt distinctly rocky. He wanted to get this damned Englishman off his back. Since yesterday it hadn't been too rosy between them. The guy didn't understand the nature of these things, the way it was when it came to killing on the ground, the way it had always been. The realities of death in the air were hidden away, contained in a flaming cockpit or at the core of a white-yellow explosion or glimpsed as a distant man-shape tumbling towards the earth. On the ground, as it had been in Spain, you watched the life go from another man's eyes, his entrails spill from the wound you had inflicted; you heard the crunch of his skull as you swung your rifle butt, saw the spray of his brains and blood across your boots. The Englishman would never understand such things: he stayed aloof, waging a war that was also a game in which, it was hoped, the best man might win. For all his guts, thought Ossie, the guy was soft. But he knew he had to bring this to an end. He tried to look regretful. 'Okay, maybe you're right. Maybe I'm out of line. Maybe it's yesterday that's getting to me. Those boys had it coming but I didn't like to do it.' Hell, he didn't give a shit about the Frenchmen. They'd asked for it and they'd got it good. But he laid it on thick. 'Yeah,' he said, 'it's bad when you have to do a thing like that.'

'Really?' said Kit. He didn't seem convinced.

'Look,' said Ossie, 'in a situation like that you have to move fast. You make a plan and you stick to it. That's how it was in Huesca. When it's like that it's them or you. Those boys made the first move so they had it coming. Yeah, they had it coming, all right.' He didn't look regretful any more, not a bit.

Kit went back to his room, took off his shoes and sat on the bed then lay down, legs drawn up, arms crossed on his chest. He felt isolated, alone, abandoned. He was reminded of the man they had uncovered in just this attitude during that long summer of his final year at Marlborough. He had arranged to remain in his chill study on the narrow court between Upper School and the museum block and cycled each day along the Avebury road to the dig at the long barrow at West Kennet. Inch by inch the archaeologists had revealed with their trowels the skeleton, its knees beneath its chin, and the hot sun warmed the bones after two thousand years. But the heat and light had no effect. The man, whether chieftain, thane or serf, remained unknowable and unknowing, the world into which he had emerged irrelevant to whatever existence he had led. And so it seemed now to Kit, as he lay with his knees drawn up to his chest on the brink of consciousness, his brain thronged with a kaleidoscope of faces, voices and incidents, some recent, others distant but all fading, almost forgotten, as he slipped away and felt that this must be like dying.

At four in the afternoon he woke, his throat tight and dry. He reached for the glass of water on the table by the bed and drank from it. Some water escaped from his mouth, trickled down his neck and on to his shoulders. He replaced the glass on a folded square of paper he had been using as a mat. Numbers were written on it in blue ink and in Hannah's hand. Spilled drops of water were causing the ink to run. He sat up sideways on the bed and took the telephone and dialled the blurring numbers; such an easy task, yet one he had pushed aside without knowing why. He felt a pang of guilt when his call was answered straight away.

'Oh, Kit, how wonderful. We have been so worried for you. Your father has been telephoning almost daily in case we had news.' Karoline Maierscheldt's voice was tremulous and thin, quite without its usual animation.

He told her little of his situation, just that he was perfectly all right, that he had become separated from his squadron but he expected to be back in the air in a day or two; and, yes, of course he would telephone his father to let him know he was still in the land of the living.

'Oh, dear Kit, please don't even talk of such things.' Her English was almost perfect, just a trace of French, which made her accent enchanting. He had been a little in love with her as a child, could understand his mother's powerful affection for her. She said that she and Maurice refused to contemplate the horrors broadcast on the wireless, in the newspapers and on everyone's lips. 'We will not believe what we hear. Ostriches, I'm afraid. We just apply ourselves to living day by day. For Maurice the business occupies his mind more than ever before, and I am happy that he takes such comfort from it, though numbers of our craftsmen drift away.' Then she said: 'Hannah is not here and I miss her dearly.' She was in Paris, occupying the apartment in the rue du Faubourg St-Honoré. 'She is perfectly able to continue with her design work there and, if I may speak honestly, dear Kit, it is one less anxiety to cope with. Of course, when the situation becomes clearer she will return and things will be as normal, the good God willing.'

'That day may be a long time coming,' said Kit. 'Please, you must get out while you can. Let the business look after itself. Everything is very bad now particularly—'

'For people like us,' said Karoline Maierscheldt. 'I know you are right, Kit, but it is quite impossible. You would not comprehend how hard it was for Maurice to let Hannah go. He managed it only by convincing himself that it was a scheme of his own and nothing whatsoever to do with the war, that he had been contemplating a new product line, "La Vie de Paris", composed of wonderful objects at the very edge of our technical ability. How to obtain the inspiration? He asked me this in all seriousness and told me his solution. To send our gifted young head of design to Paris, of course, and what better time than now, in spring? Each week poor Hannah is required to dispatch a sheaf of designs for "La Vie de Paris" even though our normal production begins to falter. But he does not see this, Kit. He chooses to see very little.'

'But you?' said Kit. 'Surely . . .'

'I have no choice,' said Karoline Maierscheldt. 'My place is here. And Hannah at least is safe and secure. That gives me joy.' She paused, as though turning over a phrase in her head. 'Kit,' she said, 'dear Kit, tell your mother I love her, that I will always remember. Tell her precisely that.' She cleared her throat. 'I know you have many duties, Kit, and little time. But if you could find time to talk to Hannah, even meet her, while you are in Paris . . .'

'Yes,' he said. 'I'll try.'

'Goodbye, dear Kit. I often think of our happy times.' She did not wait for him to reply. The phone went dead.

Kit made his second duty call. His father sobbed down the line. 'Oh, good heavens, what you must think of me. Terribly sorry, my boy. What an old fool. Of course, we've been worried sick but we always knew you'd come through. Wonderful to hear you. Your mother's not here. She'll be overjoyed. Know you can't hang on. Goodbye, my boy, goodbye. Make sure you come back to us safe and sound, do you hear? We know you will, just know it. So proud of you, so proud.'

Kit replaced the receiver, then picked it up again and dialled the reception desk. He asked for a bottle of 1921 Lanson and some Sevruga caviar to be brought to his room. The tray, when it arrived, bore two flutes. The waiter seemed surprised to find him alone. He eased out the cork, with a dull pop, and poured a little champagne into a glass. He waited for the froth to subside, topped it up, handed it to Kit and returned the bottle to the ice bucket. Then he set out the caviar on the ebonised console table and left.

After two glasses of Lanson Kit felt restored. It was criminal: one of the vineyard's finest vintages and he had gulped it like lemonade. The Sevruga, contained in a glass crock, had come with tiny dishes of minced onion, sieved egg white and yolk, slivers of lemon and thin triangles of toast. He began to laugh as he crammed it into his mouth, the greenish-black eggs smooth and rich, popping on his tongue. He remembered Maurice Maierscheldt offering him a teaspoon of the stuff, on a family outing to Vittel when he was no more than ten, the teaspoon wavering, Maierscheldt's face red with wine and good humour. He had favoured it ever since.

He studied his surroundings. The room's furnishings, the antiques, the silk wall covering, the heavy brocade curtains, struck him as delightful and aptly chosen. The ambience was elegant, snug and comfortable; almost sensual. He began to reflect on his good fortune, the events that had brought him here, how things might have turned out for the worse. How, even yesterday, it might all have ended in the cab of a riddled Renault truck, his fate unknown, if it hadn't been for Ossie Wolf. He heard the laconic 'I owed you one' as the American drove them away from the place of the killing. Perhaps he was wrong about Wolf. The man was a realist, ruthless, but fighting this war as it had to be fought. Suddenly he felt warm towards him, overcome by a sense of fellowship, even affection. He decided to lay off the Lanson.

Ossie Wolf had taken himself out of the Crillon and into the Tuileries. The gardens did not have the bustle of a weekend but a few children were sailing little yachts with coloured sails on the big round pond, leaning over the white stone surround that came up to their waists, their sleeves rolled up. Metal chairs and tables stood under the canopy of the nearby trees, the white umbrellas moving in the wind against the foliage. He took a double café espresso and a *croque monsieur* from the small café. At a nearby table a boy of four or five in an old-fashioned tweed outfit pointed him out to his mother. She looked across, took in the blazer and the broken nose, then said something to her son, soft and urgent, and they got up and walked away towards the boating pond. Her *café crème* was hardly begun. Ossie didn't care. The woman was plain as hell anyway.

In the Jardin du Carousel, wrapped round by the wings of the palace of the Louvre, he came to the place where, months ago, the *flic* had obliged them by taking a photograph with Kit's Kodak: Bébé and Hannah in the centre, arms round each other's shoulders, like sisters although they had only just met and, on either side, Kit and Ossie, faces set in goofy smiles. Unconsciously he touched the inside pocket of his blazer where he had slipped the cracked picture, now protected in a Hôtel Crillon envelope.

He crossed the Seine by the Pont Royal and headed along the quai Voltaire. A barge came thrusting upstream against the current, low in the water with a cargo of timber. People browsing through the books, magazines and prints clipped to the stalls on the embankment stopped to watch it go by, pushing between the stalls for a better view.

At the François 1er house on the corner of the quai des Grands Augustins the old concierge was fussing with her cats. The feline stench was strong, carrying up the winding staircase, wafting behind Ossie as he climbed towards Bébé's apartment. The concierge called after him: 'I tell you, Monsieur, she is not there.' The apartment door was not locked. The place was empty, a bland white box, balls of dust rolling across the wooden floor in the draught from the open door.

'Where has she gone, Madame?'

'I do not know. But she went at night. When they found out—'

'They?'

'*Les hommes de loi*, the men of Madame Westcott. *Ces hommes sont très fâchés.*'

'*Fâchés, Madame? Je n'comprends pas.*'

'*Furieux, Monsieur, en colère.*'

'*Ah, mais pourquoi?*'

'*Dans l'appartement il n'y a rien, absolument rien.* Gone, gone, everything.' The concierge was shaking with laughter. '*Ah, la jolie comtesse. Quel style!*'

Back at the Crillon Kit Curtis was stretched out on a sofa in the salon reading an English newspaper. He saw Ossie and folded it away. 'I thought you might have set off for Louvins on your own.'

'Why would I do that?'

'I don't know. Just an idea I had.'

'What are *hommes de loi*?' said Ossie.

'Lawyers. Why?'

'I guessed it was something like that. She's quite a girl.'

'Who?'

'Bébé's done a moonlight flit from the Westcott place. Scrammed with everything but the goddammed lightbulbs.'

'What on earth for?'

'Give me a break,' said Ossie. 'The stuff old Una had crammed into that joint must have been worth a fortune. I guess the Westcotts were aiming to ship it out before the Huns could get their hands on it. Bébé beat them to it.'

'You sound as though you approve.'

'She's sure got one hell of a nerve.' Ossie reached into his pocket. 'Remember this?'

Kit took the photograph. 'They look as though they've known each other for years.' He was struck again by how similar the women were, remembered how fast they had talked, their words falling from their lips in a jumble, so eager were they to share the rush of thought and emotion that swept over them, as though they had been waiting for this moment all their lives. But Hannah was like a sister to him, and he was anxious for her because he did not know or understand Bébé Dubretskov. She had an energy, a force, that he found disturbing, although she had barely addressed a word to him, entirely taken up with Hannah at that first chance meeting in the Tuileries towards the end of February. Three weeks or so later, on his next leave, he had treated them all to dinner at Fouquet's. He hadn't seen Ossie Wolf as a particular chum but they rubbed along all right. He couldn't deny that some sort of bond existed between them, perhaps because they were cast as the squadron's terrible twins after the Strasbourg escapade, perhaps because of what had been said that night in the church of Saint-Saulve. And for Kit, at least, the American's promotion made the situation easier. He himself had found it amusing to conform to type, young officers on the town with lovely women – it made a change from knocking about with Buster.

Then, suddenly, Bébé hadn't been available any more. For a while Ossie persisted, telephoning, calling at the apartment on the quai des Grands Augustins, looking for her at La Vosgienne, checking the faces in the crowd on the Champs-Élysées or along the rue de Rivoli. The disturbing force that Kit perceived in Bébé Dubretskov had done its work. This tough bruiser from St Louis had been hooked as surely as any adolescent experiencing his first crush.

Kit imagined it had never happened to him before, but he could not be sure because it had not happened to him either.

He was uncomfortably aware that Bébé had reached out to him as well, but in a different way. She stayed in his mind as something dark and vague like a half-remembered fragment of a dream that might have been a nightmare, elusive and never quite in focus but always about to step forward and make itself known; something you did not want to see. He could not understand these feelings. Her beauty was dazzling and she knew about art, literature and music, spoke well and wittily in God knew how many languages, was vital, full of energy and fun, and led the dance wherever the dance might be. And yet there was something distasteful, a knowingness, the merest whisper of corruption. When, as she sometimes had, she rested her hand on his arm and turned those mirror-eyes towards him she seemed to make him an accomplice in some way, ready to accept the unacceptable. Thank heavens, he thought, he wasn't sold on her too. Briefly he felt sorry for the fellow, incongruous on an elegant gilded chair, crumpled and reflective in his borrowed blazer, like one of his mother's not-quites turned down by the Midhurst golf club.

'I'm popping round to the Maierscheldts' place in the rue du Faubourg St-Honoré,' he said. 'Hannah's meant to be there but she doesn't answer the phone so I'm going to leave a note. Care to tag along?'

'Sure,' said Ossie carelessly. But he frowned a little at the mention of Hannah. She had screwed things up for him, gazing at Bébé like she was some sort of goddess. Jesus, how Bébé had loved it, like she always needed someone around to tell her how wonderful she was. And Hannah had appeared on the scene at just the right moment for Bébé, a few weeks after that rich old bundle of tweed Kitty Bannister had hauled her yellow arse back to Britain, but at the wrong moment for Ossie who had thought that maybe, finally, he was getting through.

The Maierscheldts' apartment was in a seventeenth-century mansion close to where the avenue Matignon cut north east across the rue du Faubourg St-Honoré. From the street the building was insignificant, hidden by two large wooden doors reaching to twenty feet, high enough to admit a carriage, with a smaller man-sized door on the right. Through the door a great courtyard opened up, with pathways of white gravel, laid out to a geometric pattern, running between small areas of grass hedged by box. And, set back, the central portion of the mansion itself, pale grey, tall windows ornate in the style of 1630, under a dark grey slate roof.

In his cubicle of an office close by the entrance, the concierge did not rise from his squeaking swivel-chair. 'Ah, the Maierscheldts. You mean our Jewish friends.' He knew Kit well enough but amused himself by pretending otherwise. He was full of little tricks to pass the time. Now he took pleasure in adding that Mademoiselle Maierscheldt was out and likely to be so for some considerable time. He said he would try to remember to present her with Monsieur's envelope when she returned. He pointed to his desk for Kit to leave it there and squeaked his chair as a sign for them to go.

Ossie stepped forward and caught the chair. The concierge's head snapped back. He looked up, startled.

'We'll go on up, feller,' said Ossie. 'Just to check for ourselves.'

The man reddened. 'Quite impossible,' he began. 'I have strict instructions—'

'Just the same,' said Ossie, 'we'll go on up.'

They followed the white gravel pathway to the marble steps and the central door of the mansion. Inside, the hallway was cool and rang to the sound of their feet. At the door to the apartment on the third-floor landing Kit waited for a moment, then pressed the ivory bell-button. 'I think somebody's there.' He had detected the faintest suggestion of activity within but now there was nothing, as though someone had frozen at the sound. He rang again, then pushed the envelope underneath the elaborately carved door, prodding it right through with his fingers so the concierge would not be able to withdraw it when they had gone.

Outside, as they stood on the pavement, its tar warm under the soles of their soft borrowed shoes, they saw Hannah Maierscheldt coming towards them through a shimmer of heat, carrying a big black leather portfolio. She recognised them and broke into an awkward half-run, struggling to control the portfolio that banged against her legs. She was laughing and breathless when she reached them. 'Where have you come from? Why are you here? No, tell me later. Oh, it is lovely to see you. What a surprise.' She kissed Kit lightly on the lips and allowed Ossie to peck her on the cheeks. She stroked Kit's bruised face with her long fingers, murmuring: 'My poor Kit, tell me how it happened. No, don't tell me.' Her fingertips were as gentle as the touch of a feather. She looked at Ossie's nose. 'You too? Are you sure you haven't been fighting each other?'

'I left a note for you,' said Kit. 'Pushed it under your door.'

'Oh,' said Hannah. 'The concierge had instructions . . .'

'Yeah,' said Ossie. 'He told us that.'

Kit took the portfolio from her. 'Let me carry this. What is it? Work?'

'Oh, yes, I am like a real artist, Kit, on a quest for inspiration. So many wonderful things to see. I have been everywhere. I will show you my designs. My father has great plans.'

'I heard. I spoke to your mother.'

'Ah,' said Hannah. 'She asked you to call on me.'

'Not at all.' Kit flushed. 'How could I be in Paris without seeing you? But I agreed to let her know if you're behaving yourself in the big bad city.'

'Oh, I'm in very good hands,' said Hannah, smiling. 'Come on, Mother's spy. *C'est l'heure du déjeuner.*' She had a freshness about her, a new vivacity, which made her seem immensely pretty in her dark, plain clothes, oddly chosen and quaint, and a black velvet beret.

The concierge turned in his swivel-chair as he heard them approach. He was on his feet at the sight of Hannah, assuming the demeanour of a dutiful servant. 'Please remember, Sauval,' Hannah said, 'my instructions do not apply to Monsieur Curtis. I thought you would realise that.'

'Of course, Mademoiselle. I regret I did not recognise him out of uniform. Perhaps, Monsieur, you are leaving France?' He smiled a thin smile.

'Tell me, Sauval,' said Kit, 'you appear to be of an age for the army. Why are you not in the ranks?'

'*Rhumatisme articulaire*,' said Sauval.

'They are not so particular now,' said Kit, 'with the Boches at your border. I have a meeting with General Gamelin at the defence ministry tomorrow. I will put a word in for you. I have your details.'

'It's your lucky day, Sauval,' said Ossie.

They started up the stairs to the apartment. Hannah said: 'Tell me, did you ring the apartment bell?'

'Of course.'

'And what did you hear?'

'What should I have heard?'

'Nothing.'

'That is what I heard.'

Outside the apartment Hannah rang the bell three times, one long, two short, and they heard footsteps approaching. A bolt was withdrawn and the door opened a little. A face appeared. It was Bébé Dubretskov.

She opened the door wider and stood back to let them in. She was not at all surprised to see the pilots. Kit's envelope lay on a gilt-wood console, torn apart. 'Ah,' she said to Hannah, 'now you have no need of this.' She tossed the letter down beside the envelope with no trace of embarrassment.

Hannah smiled, took Bébé's hand and kissed it. She did not pick up Kit's note and read it for herself. 'Have you eaten, *chérie*?' she asked Bébé.

'No,' said Bébé. 'I rose late. You can get me something if you like.' She sat down at a piano, selected a piece of music and began to play Schumann's *Aufschwung*. Kit looked at Ossie looking at her. She was quite a picture, hands moving over the keys, eyes closed, body swaying against the background of golden silk at the tall windows and, between, the portraits of distant worthies in elaborate gilt frames.

Hannah went into the kitchen and came back with slices of Périgord *noir foie gras* terrine on a large floral plate, half a baguette and a bottle of sweet white Monbazillac.

'I went looking for you,' said Ossie to Bébé, 'at the *quai.*'

'Was I there?'

'The cupboard was bare. Nothing but the lightbulbs. How come you left them?'

Bébé shrugged impatiently. 'What are you saying? I was required to leave. I left. That is all.' She caressed Hannah with her eyes. 'If it had not been for you *mignonne . . .*'

'They have treated Bébé quite horribly,' Hannah said.

'Who?' said Curtis.

'The Westcotts. They have behaved like brutes. Bébé, you must explain.'

Bébé took a sip of her wine, holding it in her mouth for a moment, breathing its aroma. She was sitting erect, not looking at them. Then she gave a long, reflective sigh. Kit thought it was perfectly done. She said Hannah was quite correct. The Westcotts had been quite brutish and unreasonable, brushing aside all considerations of the happy years she had spent as Una's companion. *Nom de Dieu!* she cried. It was almost as though they blamed her for the woman's death.

'Christ!' said Ossie. 'She's dead?'

'Of course she's dead,' said Bébé. '*La garce stupide* killed herself.' She glanced at Hannah. 'I'm sorry but it makes me so angry to think of her throwing her life away when she had so much to give.'

'Yeah,' said Ossie, bitterly. 'I heard she had a lot to give.' He understood very well the significance of the women's gentle touches and words of endearment: another path had opened up for Bébé, a path he could not follow. He felt anger now and wanted to provoke her, disturb her cool indifference, prove that he meant something to her even now.

Bébé was talking about the letters, it seemed like hundreds, she had received from Una, each more hysterical than the last. These American matrons, she complained, with their delicate emotions. She had given up reading them. Anyway, they were all the same, begging her to come to the States, even sending money orders to pay for Bébé's passage. No, she had not answered one of them. What was the point? She had no intention of leaving Europe and certainly not to spend time with someone who had clearly gone soft in the head. And then she had heard that the imbecile had done away with herself. *Mon Dieu*, the fuss, as though she, Bébé, had been responsible for locking the *pauvrette* in the sanatorium, as though she had arranged for her to be supplied with her favourite Sobranies but also the box of matches with which she had set herself alight. Then the stream of telegrams and letters from Philadelphia had begun, not in Una Westcott's big purple scrawl but typed, none of which she had bothered to read except for the first few, out of curiosity. It was all too boring. Forms to sign surrendering rights and claims, references to small bequests that might or might not be paid, instructions for shipping this, returning that. She had thrown them all away, of course, because everyone knew Una had wanted her to have everything.

'Have you any proof?' said Kit.

'It was her wish, I know it was her wish. She often spoke of it.'

'It's so cruel, heartless,' said Hannah, 'trying to cheat you in this way.'

Bébé said that finally a man had called round to the quai des Grands Augustins, a French man, imagine, instructing her to vacate the apartment by such-and-such a date, leaving everything as it was. 'He presented me with this,' she said, 'and was required to watch me read it.' She laughed and passed Kit a letter headed 'Pinkney Grace, attorneys at law, Philadelphia, PA'. The writer said that as all previous attempts to arrive at a reasonable conclusion to the matters in hand appeared to have failed he had instructed his associates in Paris, the legal partnership of Jabesco, Rougerie et Bouy, to evict the Comtesse Anna Lvovitch Dubretskov from the apartment on the quai des Grands Augustins and secure all contents, property of the late Una Mary Westcott. The letter was dated two weeks ago. Kit returned it and Bébé scanned it idly. 'What nonsense. She gave it all to me, everything. It was her wish, I swear to you.'

'And has she got her wish?' said Kit.

'*Qu'est-ce que vous en pensez?*'

'Jesus,' said Ossie. 'You really did it then. So where the hell is it all?'

'Oh, it is safe enough.'

'Not here?'

'Of course not here.'

'Hannah, you must be mad to get involved in this,' said Kit.

'No,' said Hannah. 'Don't you see? It is only right. There is no other way. The poor woman's wishes must be honoured. She knew her treasures would be safe with Bébé. But once they are in America it will be too late. Everything will be dispersed and sold. It is all just dollars to them. As long as the collection remains here, in France, something might be done. There is always hope.'

'These people will find you, Bébé,' said Kit seriously. 'Paris is small.'

'Oh, they have found me already,' said Bébé, 'but not exactly.' She had been moving slowly round the room as she spoke, picking up a Baccarat paperweight, an ebony chesspiece, a small jade figure of a kneeling horse, feeling their weight in her hands, inspecting them and replacing them with precision. Now she moved across to the *chaise-longue* where Hannah sat, her hands folded in her lap, and sank down beside her. They smiled at each other like mischievous children and offered their profiles to Kit and Ossie.

'Do you see?' said Hannah.

Kit shook his head. 'What exactly?'

'*Attendez*,' said Bébé. She went into the cloakroom and came back in a moment, pulling on Hannah's long, eccentric coat and velvet beret.

'*Venez*,' she said. She went to the door and Hannah held it open, beckoning to Kit and Ossie to follow. They descended the stairs and crossed the courtyard to the concierge's office.

Bébé stood framed in the doorway in plain sight. 'Sauval,' she said, 'I have lost a silk scarf.'

'I have found nothing, Mademoiselle,' said the concierge.

'Exquisite, *très cher*.'

'That's a pity,' said Sauval. 'If it turns up I will bring it to the apartment.'

'*Merci* Sauval.'

'*Bonne après-midi, Mademoiselle Maierscheldt.*'

Bébé was triumphant but Kit saw that the man seemed troubled. As they returned along the white gravel path towards the mansion he heard Sauval hastening after them.

'Hah,' said Kit. 'Is he sharper than he looks?'

Sauval took his sleeve, panting. 'Monsieur,' he said, 'Monsieur.' He wore a desperate smile. 'That business about General Gamelin . . .' He wanted to be told that the whole affair was a joke.

'Don't worry, Sauval,' said Kit. 'I won't forget.'

Bébé said it had happened as easily with the seedy little man in the black Homburg who stopped her in the rue de la Verrerie, on the way to visit the Countess Sofia. It had been so silly to forget, of course, that they would keep watch outside her mother's place. But with Hannah's clothes and identity card it had been simplicity itself to persuade him of his mistake.

Nom de Dieu, her indignation. He had become so flustered he even doffed his hat. Of course it had meant that Bébé had been compelled to hurry past her mother's door, but what of it? It was only a short-term solution. Soon the jackals would grow tired of waiting for a phantom and turn their minds to matters more serious than helping greedy Americans trace some *objets d'art*, which, after all, were with their rightful owner.

Before they left, Kit took Hannah aside. 'How is it with you? With you and this woman, I mean.'

'Oh, an *amitié amoureuse*, a loving friendship, that is all.'

'Nothing more?'

'Nothing more. I find her fascinating, amusing, like no one I have ever met.'

'You know her reputation?'

'She has been very frank with me. To be born to poverty in the midst of wealth is a terrible thing, and worse when in Russia her family were among the very richest.'

'That excuses her way of life?'

'It explains it. And anyway, Kit, she assures me that most of the tales are fables. With the American woman, for instance, she was like a daughter, although malicious tongues said otherwise.' Hannah sighed. 'Perhaps she is a little . . . audacious, but to me, so safe and dull, she's like a miracle, ready to lead a life of risks and chances.'

'You are exposed to those risks and chances.'

'Oh, Kit, don't be such a grandfather. It's been such fun, such an exciting game, like nothing I have experienced before. I am swept before it like a gull on a wave.' She took his hand. 'When must you leave Paris?'

'Tomorrow.'

'What plans have you for this evening?'

'None. I thought perhaps I might treat you to Fouquet's again.'

'Do you believe in Fate, that one can foretell the future?'

309

'What a ghastly idea.'

'What do you know of tarot?'

'Mumbo-jumbo, isn't it? Superstitious tosh.'

Hannah laughed. 'Join us tonight for tarot, you and your American. Come with an open mind and see what you make of it. Even if you remain sceptical you will find it intriguing.'

'Surely you don't believe there's something in it?'

'Come and find out. It's extraordinary. Come, to please me.'

'Where does this nonsense take place?' said Kit. 'In a tent in the Tuileries?'

'No,' said Hannah. 'At an address I will give you in the fourth *arrondissement*.'

The Countess Sofia Pulcheria Dubretskov was standing by the only window of the twin rooms she rented in the rue de la Verrerie. Beyond the dowdy house-fronts opposite she could hear the battle of motor horns in the rue de Rivoli. It sounded like a herd of startled beasts, like the cattle that, as a child, she had witnessed threatened by wolves on the summer estate at Arkhangelskoye. 'Yesterday,' she said, 'I saw a most dispiriting sight.'

'Really, Maman?' said Bébé.

'In the place de la Madeleine,' said the countess, 'I saw in the distance a cousin of mine, Prince Nicolai Boris Fedunov. This man was once highly placed in the east, a viceroy no less. Cossacks would clear the way for him. He held sway over millions. Yesterday he was running for a bus.'

'Did he catch it?' said Ossie Wolf.

The countess regarded him coldly. 'Has it been explained that divination cannot take place in an atmosphere of frivolity and childishness?' She sighed. Twenty years ago, compelled to earn a living, she had found herself celebrated by society as a guide to the occult, able to reside in some comfort in St Germain. But the fashion for *La Russe* had passed. She looked for a long moment at the photograph in the silver frame that stood on the cheap pine desk by the empty fireplace: the fancy-dress ball at the Winter Palace in 1905. Her young face was set and assured, confident that this brilliant world would last for ever. Her sumptuous pastiche of Russian national dress gave her the grandeur of an empress, a lofty triangular head-dress of jewels and pearls enhancing her height, a choker of pearls at her throat, rubies and diamonds on her bosom. Beside her sat Count Felix in the fur-trimmed dress uniform of the Imperial Hussars, hair cropped, moustache heavy and black, arrogance and impatience in his eyes, the man Bébé had never known.

Now the countess nodded to Bébé who lit an array of candles and a small incense-burner on the mantelpiece. Then the countess seated herself at the table in the centre of the room. When she spoke it was to address Hannah, as though discounting Kit and Ossie as heretics. 'The cards talk,' she said. 'They reveal the secrets of nature, the reason for things, why day is driven out by night and night by day.'

She opened a wooden box, removed a pack of antique cards, shuffled them with her left hand, then laid them out carefully, face upwards, on the table. She explained about tarot in the flat voice of one who has spoken the words many times before: the twenty-two major suits that cover all aspects of life – wisdom, justice, sacrifice, death . . . grotesque hand-painted scenes in once-brilliant Renaissance colours – and the fifty-six minor trumps, each gathered under its own element, water, fire, air and earth.

'These cards have great age,' said Kit. He wanted the woman to believe in his sincerity. He was careful not to look at Ossie.

'They came to my family from Venice many centuries ago,' said the countess, 'from the estate of Francesco Marcolino da Forli.' She did not raise her eyes from the cards. 'At court, we had a peasant woman, Katerina Semyonovna, to read these cards for us every day.'

'And did they foretell your fate?' he asked.

The countess did not look up. 'Towards the end she refused to tell us what she saw. Her fear was eloquent.'

Now she led them through the selection of the tarot suits and trumps, an intricate ritual of curious questions and rattling dice, murmuring to herself as she pencilled entries in a note-book and leafed through an array of leatherbound volumes at her elbow. Once Ossie coughed.

'No coughing, no yawning, *pas de reniflement*,' snapped the countess. 'Only restraint, honesty and an open mind. However,' she said, 'you accord with a Prince of Wands. You are hasty and violent, burdened by responsibility, cruel only to achieve the outcome you wish, essentially just. You persevere against great odds. If you achieve success it will be at a great price.' Ossie's face was expressionless in the glow from the candles. 'Your suit is the Hermit, the seeker of truth whose staff is a symbol of spiritual power but also supports him in his frailty. In certain tarot,' the countess said, 'the Hermit is Time itself, a winged man on crutches, outwardly lame, inwardly free. Fire is the element of which you are part and which is both your friend and your foe.'

She turned to Hannah and permitted herself a rare, faint smile. 'I do not need tarot to divine your character, my child,' she said. 'The Star, gentle, poetic, kind, on the brink of a transformation. But you are trusting, sometimes dreamy, and must be wary of being deceived. There is a change in your emotions, a joining together, perhaps a marriage,' she glanced at Kit, 'or a new insight into the way in which the world is perceived. You are one who understands that the approach of death gives one access to the pleasures of life. You will experience sorrow but be released from it by the Great Mother, who makes all things joyous by the subtle pressure of the waters.'

'I do not understand,' said Hannah.

The countess sighed. 'That is all that can be said.'

Bébé pushed back her chair with a snort. 'This is very boring

Maman: not amusing at all. Once it was fun but now I have grown tired of your talking cards that speak of cruelty and violence, sorrow and death. I have no wish to learn what they might say of me.'

'They say nothing of you that we do not know,' said the countess.

'Good,' said Bébé. 'So much for them. And what of our English milord?'

'Courage and strength. Calm in the presence of evil, a trust that right will prevail. Obstinate, yes, a little. Perseverance against great odds – bravery, too, in the face of certain defeat. A favourable outcome when the last words are said and the last things done.'

'That is not so remarkable,' said Bébé. 'It applies to a million men.'

'It was said of this one,' said the countess, testily.

It soon became clear that the reading was nearing its end. The countess began to gather up the cards and replace them in the wooden box. But as she moved them across the table the pattern they formed caught her attention. Her eyes remained fixed on the confusion of suits and trumps, moving from one card to the next. She did not seem to notice when Bébé turned on the electric light and began to extinguish the candles. The smoke from the wicks mingled with the pungent odours of the burning incense. The countess remained at the table, her long, thin hands together as though in prayer. She appeared to be ordering her thoughts. Then she murmured, almost to herself: '*Quelle véritable énigme*. I see a blue man falling.'

Bébé and Hannah chose to leave separately, an arrangement the countess found odd. 'Why, pray, choose to scurry down the back alleys? In this cursed blackout the rue de la Verrerie is hazardous enough.'

Bébé submitted to a brief embrace. '*Au revoir*, Maman.'

'*Un petit moment*,' said the countess. 'Mention of hazards refreshes my memory. A person called two days ago. He asked for you but chose not to explain.'

'What did you tell him?'

'Nothing, naturally. His manner was most insolent. Is there something I should know, perhaps to do with the rich Americans who threw you on to the streets?'

'Consult your cards, Maman,' said Bébé. 'Surely they will tell you.'

'Rude child,' said the countess, smiling nonetheless. 'So, where may you be found these days?'

'I will find you, Maman. *Au revoir.*'

When she had gone the countess looked thoughtful. 'I hope the time has passed pleasantly for you. How is it that you know my daughter?' She was talking only to Kit.

'Mutual friends,' said Kit.

'*Vraiment?*' said the countess, dropping into French. 'I was not aware that she had any friends, like you at least. Have you lost your heart to her?'

'No, not at all.'

'I am happy for you. Anna approaches life much as one indulges in a game of cards. Apt, you might think. The hand is dealt, this poor soul is discarded, replaced by another, a third surrendered, a fourth picked up, and so it goes on as she seeks to assemble a winning hand. A Dubretskov trait, I'm afraid, but by no means foolproof.' She glanced at the silver-framed photograph. 'Count Felix played the game for many years with great success but then, in 1917, he lost.'

They moved to the door. 'Thank you so much,' said Kit, reverting to English for Ossie's sake. 'It's been jolly interesting.'

'Countess,' said Ossie, 'how you figure those crazy cards beats me.'

'*Vous êtes bien bon,*' said the countess, 'but I believe you might have forgotten something.'

'We had no coats,' said Curtis.

'Messieurs, *plaisanterie* apart, there is the matter of one hundred and eighty francs.'

'One hundred and eighty francs?'

'*Bien sûr*,' said the Countess Sofia. 'Normally my fee for a reading is two hundred but as you are acquaintances of my daughter I am more than happy to offer a slight reduction.'

Part four

'If we're doing so bloody well why
do we keep falling back?'

Nineteen

Wednesday, 15 May 1940

When Kit ran his hand over the fuselage of Goofy Gates's
Hurricane the fabric, stretched taut across the wood and metal-
tube framework, suggested the hide of some jungle beast. For
the moment the beast was wounded: two 20mm explosive shells
had hit the rudder and port tailplane. The lower surface of the
tailplane had been almost blown away and the lack of control
in pitch had been a severe test of Gates's flying skills as he struggled to return to base. But the fitters and riggers had almost
completed the repairs, working in the open air under the hot
sun, and two fresh ammunition boxes had been installed in the
port wing by the armourers. Now they were undoing the half-
turn Dzus fasteners securing the ammunition-box covers on the
starboard side. On the leading edge of the wings the fabric
patches over the gun-ports, gone in the recent action, had already
been replaced.

Kit placed his right foot on the stirrup-step below the fuselage, pulled himself up on to the wing and moved towards the
empty cockpit. Another step, this time for the left foot, and he
was sliding into the bucket seat. He savoured the familiar smell
of fuel, oil and coolant that ran through the network of lines
like arteries to the 1,030 horsepower Merlin, providing the
hump-backed little fighter with rude life. In his mind he ran
through his old routine: his rigger Gray guiding the parachute
straps over his shoulders, deftly snapping the pin securing the

four straps of his Sutton harness, the feel of the oxygen mask over his face and the cool waft as he flicked on the supply. Now prime the engine, switches on, a good firm thumbs-up to the ground-crew and all set to press the starter button . . .

He heard someone clambering on to the wing. Flight Sergeant Jessop's face appeared beside him. 'How does it feel to be back in the old Hurribox sir?'

'Marvellous Chief. Can't wait to get back to business.'

'The boys will be pleased to see you. They've had it rough. I gather it hasn't exactly been a picnic for you.'

'When are they due?'

'Any time now. Fourth sortie of the day. They're all pretty whacked. Flying Officer Brown reckons he's had seven hours' sleep in forty-eight. You heard about poor old Windy Miller?'

'Yes, rotten luck. Sergeant Gates told me. Anybody know what happened?'

'Not a clue, sir. Went missing yesterday in a dust-up with some 109s.'

So Miller had gone. Kit remembered the A Flight weaver's hilarious mood after he had belly-landed his ruin of a machine at Revigncourt on the first day of the invasion. The little sergeant had sunk mug after mug of sugared tea and munched slabs of bread and jam, as though, having survived this time, he would survive the next. He had told the tale of his escape a dozen times. Only when it became clear that his flight commander, Ossie Wolf, was missing, probably dead, did the pilots grow preoccupied and drift away to their duties leaving him to drink his tea and eat his bread and jam alone.

'I see you're working your usual miracles, Chief.' Kit pulled himself upright in the cockpit, standing on the seat and glancing down at the ground-crew, working through their check-lists.

'Almost done, sir,' said Jessop. 'Just got to break the bad news to Sergeant Gates.'

'Bad news?'

'Manner of speaking, sir. Good to have you back.'

Kit and Ossie had arrived at Louvins shortly after one thirty. The ministry Austin, organised by Rupert Pringle, had collected them from the Crillon on the dot of midday. The car was comfortable and both men slept, waking only as the Royal Army Service Corps driver swung off the main road from Paris to Troyes and bumped across the broad expanse of grassland that served as the squadron's new base on the outskirts of the town. The scatter of concrete buildings appeared to be deserted. Nearby bomb craters revealed why.

The RASC corporal spun the steering-wheel and headed for a handful of bell tents, where airmen could be seen at work on trenches and dugouts. Apart from a few machines being tended by ground-crew, most of the squadron's Hurricanes were in the air. As Kit and Ossie got out of the Austin, Goofy Gates came out of one of the tents. He walked across to them, hands in pockets, face expressionless, a tipped Player's jerking up and down between cracked lips as he spoke. 'Back from your holidays?' he said. 'We had you down for goners.'

'How you doing Goofy?' said Ossie.

'Good question,' said Gates. 'If you believe the score-sheets we're giving a good account of ourselves, considering we're outnumbered four to one. But a bloke who ferried in a replacement Hurry this morning said he'd heard on the grapevine that Fighter Command lost fifteen pilots yesterday. One was ours. Old Windy's bought it.'

'Confirmed?' said Ossie.

'The Froggies have just found him in his burned-out kite. How long can this go on? The sky's black with the Hun bastards.'

In the CO's tent they found Brewster and Spy Turner bent over maps spread out on the rickety green baize card table, just as Kit had seen them at Revigncourt less than a week earlier. It seemed like a year. 'Ah,' said Brewster, 'so you've finished gallivanting about the countryside. Good show.' He sucked at his pipe. 'I must say, we'd written you chaps off but as you're here you might as well make yourselves useful. Find them some kit,

Spy, and get them on the roster pronto, flying tomorrow at dawn.' On Brewster's desk the single black telephone rang. 'That'll be Wing,' said Brewster. He waved them outside and took the call.

Kit and Ossie followed Turner out of the tent. The heat was oppressive and a multitude of mayflies danced in the humid air, a frenetic dog-fight on a tiny scale. Ossie thrust his hands into the cloud of insects wheeling round his head, smacked his palms together and brushed a few tiny victims away. 'For God's sake,' said Kit, 'leave them alone.'

'You'll see a few unfamiliar faces,' Spy Turner was saying. 'Three pilots plus Hurricanes straight from Operational Training. Came in a couple of days ago. Barely a moment to register their names. No time for the usual niceties, I'm afraid. The CO gave them a bit of grace to stooge around and get some more hours in but a couple have already been chucked in at the deep end. They're up now with B Flight.' He cleared his throat. 'I'm afraid Al Miller bought it yesterday.'

'We heard,' said Kit. 'Gates told us.' He ran through the tally in his mind and wondered if the others were doing the same: Dinghy Davis, Pip Fuller, Beaky Parker, Taff Evans in Fonteville and now Al Miller.

'The hell with brooding,' said Ossie Wolf, quietly, as though he had read Kit's thoughts. 'I want a slice of the action.'

'You'll find yourself with more than a slice,' said Turner. 'You can help yourself to a whole damned cake with a nice red cherry on top.'

Now, as Kit jumped down from the wing of Goofy Gates's machine, he heard the mounting thunder of Hurricanes approaching the airfield. 'B Flight's back,' shouted an LAC. A single vic of fighters dropped in over the perimeter, thumping down quickly, conscious of the threat of free-hunt Me-109s lurking near the base to pick them off at their most vulnerable. Kit hung on to the running-board of a small Morris truck as the ground-crews raced to meet the taxiing Hurricanes. He recognised Buster Brown in his open cockpit, the sliding hood pushed back, his goggles on his forehead. He gave him a wave and Buster saw him, but did not smile.

As the pilots descended from their machines the word ran round that the two replacements, Frazer and Vaughan, fresh from OTU, would not be returning from this, their first operational flight; one of them, Vaughan, in the brand-new machine, ferried in that morning. But there was more. Kenny Rains, the ebullient Claude, had also gone, throwing himself at a defensive circle of twenty Heinkel-111s. Brownings chattering, he had sailed through the killing zone that lay at the centre of the circle, hitting nothing, and the Heinkel rear-gunners had swiftly done their work. The Hurricane had dived vertically from 15,000 feet, a fireball brilliant against the deepening blue of the evening sky.

'Stupid little sod,' said Buster in the tent that served as a mess. 'He always was a press-on type. Keen to show the new boys what was what. Well, they all found out together.'

Kit's thoughts went back to when he had stood beside Rains for a pee, before their first big test against the Hun, heard again the boy's jaunty tone as they ran to their machines, about to set off on patrol over Metz. 'Got here just in time, sir.' And his reply, 'If we get some trade stick to my tail-wheel.' Little Claude had not stuck to his tail-wheel: he had thrown himself into action and picked off a Dornier Do-17 right under his nose, had secured two more victories since, a second Dornier and a Messerschmitt-110. Most people thought he was on the way to being something special and he had believed it too . . .

Buster Brown peered at Kit through a cloud of cigarette smoke. He had dark rings beneath his eyes and his cheeks were sunken like those of an old man. His right foot tapped the ground constantly. 'I must give up these bloody gaspers,' he said. 'They're giving me the shakes.' He spat out fragments of tobacco. 'I hear the Hun have been chasing you and the infernal Yank all over France. Sounds amusing.'

'Not exactly.'

'Tell me about it.'

'Do I have to?'

'No, not really. Except for one thing.'

'Yes?'

'Whatever happened to my bloody Alvis?'

Ossie Wolf walked into the tent, saw them and lowered himself on to the mashed grass close by, leaning against the central tent pole, almost joining them but not quite. He rested his arms on his drawn-up knees, hands hanging loose. His head was angled back and when he spoke he stared upwards at the expanse of green canvas. 'The guys tell me communications are fucked,' he said.

'I think that fairly sums it up, old boy,' said Buster. 'The way it works or doesn't work is this. Some Frog observer type crouching in a ditch somewhere spots the Hun at twenty thousand and thinks maybe he'll give Wing a tinkle. Wing cogitates a bit and finally gets round to giving old Brewster a buzz on that jolly little relic from the Kensington Science Museum he keeps on his desk. So we take off, in whatever direction we happen to be pointing, like a flock of split-arsed geese, and fart about looking for the sods the benighted *poilu* spotted about an hour ago and waiting for more gen. When it comes, we can't make head nor tail of it because we're almost out of R/T range and it sounds like Donald Duck calling from a tin can and it's probably a load of out-of-date bollocks anyway.' He took a drag on the Gitane. 'The only consolation is that there are so many of the Hun bastards you can't really miss them. But as for any kind of fighter control, forget it. Once we're up, boys, we're on our own. Get the picture?'

'Yeah,' said Ossie, 'and tomorrow you can show us first hand. Brewster's assigned us to your flight so we can get ourselves up to speed.' He stood up. 'Thanks for the briefing, Flight Commander, sir. I think I'm going to check me that heap of aeronautical shit I've been given to fly.'

'Which particular heap of shit are you referring to?' said Buster.

'Goofy's kite. Seems getting home on a wing and a prayer has got to the guy. Doc's prescribed a day off to get his pants cleaned.'

'If that's all it takes,' said Buster, 'I'm due a fortnight's leave. I've run out of bloody trousers.' He threw down his cigarette and ground the butt into the mud with his heel. 'I must press on. The CO needs some gen for the letters he's got to write. Your son died a valiant death defending freedom, pressing home his attack with the utmost courage, you know the form.'

'Did you have any luck today?' said Kit.

'Apart from losing half the flight, you mean? For Christ's sake, Kit, you've been spending too much time with our bloody Yank.'

'Sorry,' said Kit, reddening, 'I mean, did you get anything back?'

'I got a probable,' said Buster, 'one of the Heinkels, and Eddie Knox got a 110 confirmed. Not good enough, though, is it, one and a half for three?'

Kit found himself assigned the camp bed of Kenny Rains. Spy Turner was clearing away Rains's possessions when Kit came into the tent: a photograph of the dead pilot's parents, another of a girl wearing a sundress in a skiff, the rudder ropes resting on her bare shoulders; a Parker fountain pen next to a half-written letter; an unopened packet of Players and a box of Swan Vestas; a ragged volume of Just William stories. So this was the fate awaiting all those carefree William Browns who had passed so many merry years between the wars. Turner placed the few belongings in a cardboard box, slipped Rains's spare uniform off its hanger and said to Kit: 'What size are your feet?'

'Ten and a half.'

'Rains took elevens. You might as well try these for size. He always flew in boots.' He pushed a pair of black service shoes from under the bed with his foot. 'Sounds a bit callous but it's daft to waste them.'

Kit stretched himself out on the bed. The blankets had been changed but it still smelt of Rains's sweat, tobacco smoke and hair-cream. His eyes closed. A voice said: 'Hello. I'm Hangdog.' A pale-faced pilot officer with a tangle of dark hair flopping over his forehead was frowning down at him, keen and youthful, white teeth showing in an anxious grimace. Kit could hardly bear to look at him. Not another bloody lamb teetering on the slaughterhouse ramp.

'Hangdog?' said Kit. He pushed himself on to his elbow.

'My generally mournful expression,' said the pilot officer. 'You must be Flight Lieutenant Curtis.'

'Do you have another name,' said Kit, 'or just the one you've told me?'

'Collins, sir,' said the pilot officer. 'I've been chalked up for B Flight's first rhubarb tomorrow. We'll be flying together.' He seemed pleased and proud, regarding Kit with the ingenuous respect always seen in the faces of the unblooded when they were in the presence of those who had seen action.

'You'll be one of the OTU sprogs who breezed in,' said Kit.

'Yes, sir.' Collins chewed the inside of his cheek. 'I couldn't believe it when I heard about Frazer and Vaughan. We've been together for months.'

'Do me a favour, Collins,' said Kit. 'Just try to make sure you don't breeze out again as quickly as your chums. Now, I don't want to be rude but I'm desperate for some shut-eye.' He rolled over and went to sleep.

Ossie was quizzing Goofy Gates about the characteristics of the Hurricane he was to fly at dawn. Gates was not encouraging. 'She was bad enough before she got plastered. Christ knows what she'll be like now.'

'Bad enough how?' said Ossie.

'Well, even with full forward trim the bitch will never dive at more than 320 m.p.h. and she's always left wing low. There's also a lot of aileron snatch. And she swings to port on landing as soon as the bloody tail goes down. Apart from that, old chum, a piece of cake.'

'How about the fucking tyre pressures?' said Ossie.

'Oh, they're all right,' said Goofy. 'I checked them at the local garage this morning.'

Ossie tracked down Flight Sergeant Jessop. 'Sounds to me like the air flow over the rudder and elevator is buggered in some way, Sid. Check out the trailing edges of the fin and tailplane. Also, make sure the control cables in the aileron circuit are good and tight, no bloody backlash. And give the hinge-pins the once-over. There could be a little slackness there as well.' He placed his hand on Jessop's shoulder. 'Sorry, feller, teaching grandmother, but tomorrow I'm going to need all the advantages I can get.'

'Leave it with me, Ossie,' said Jessop. 'We'll see you right.' The American was popular with the ground-crew, partly because he showed a technical interest in his aircraft, partly because it was founded on real knowledge. As usual, he conversed with them easily, always ready to share the latest blue joke. His promotion hadn't changed that, as it sometimes did in others.

'That's swell, old buddy,' said Ossie.

'We hear you and Flight Lieutenant Curtis had quite a time of it,' said Jessop.

'Oh, hell,' said Ossie, 'we had a million laughs.' He broke off. Titch Baker, the admin clerk, was hurrying towards him. 'The CO wants to see you, sir, right away.'

'Jesus,' said Ossie, 'I can't be in the doghouse already.'

He did not like to be summoned into Brewster's presence. It usually meant trouble of one kind or another, something he'd done wrong or even something he'd done right that had given Brewster the idea he could do much more along the same lines.

As he walked at an even pace towards the CO's tent he recalled the time in February when he'd gotten a similar request. Then Brewster had made him stand for a while in front of his desk while he sorted through some papers and found what he was looking for. 'Yes, your DFM. Didn't get it, I'm afraid. Wing must have smelt a rat about your Strasbourg jaunt. They keep their ears to the ground if not their eyes to the sky.' Ossie had turned to go. 'Hold your horses, Wolf. I haven't finished yet. You should know I'm recommending you for a commission.'

'I don't want that sir.'

Brewster's face had purpled. 'I don't bloody well care whether you want it or not. *I* want it, and that's all you need to know. We're not on a peacetime footing here, Sergeant, kicking our heels in the clubhouse before we set off for a jolly old spin. We've got a full-scale battle heading our way and I want the best damned pilots around me and the best officers leading them.' He'd looked Ossie up and down, eyes shrewd. 'You saw action in Spain.'

'Yeah,' said Ossie, slowly, 'sir.'

'I seem to recall you experienced some vision of a working-class wonderland, everyone equal, share and share alike, down with the bourgeoisie, up with the proletariat.'

'Along those lines, yeah.'

'I respect your ideals,' said Brewster, 'but one reason Spain was a shambles and ended badly for your lot was that no one would concede overall responsibility and everyone wanted a say. It just doesn't work, man. In Spain you lost. Well, now you have a chance to win, and against a far greater evil than Franco and his gangsters ever were. But you're not going to do it lurking in the ranks and evading responsibility.' Brewster's colour had lightened a little as he struggled to appear reasonable. 'Look,' he said, 'I can't compel you to accept promotion but see it from my point of view. You're my best fighting pilot by far, with kills to prove it, and the men respect you, whatever their rank, because of your skill and leadership in the air. It's only on the deck that the problems begin. Let's face it, your rank is a stumbling block.

I don't hold with all this pre-war gentlemen-and-players rot but I can't have you babying beardless sprogs like Pip Fuller and his kind when they outrank you. You're unable to give orders and expect them to be obeyed. It's bloody nonsense man. That's why I want you to accept my recommendation with good grace and one proviso.'

'Can I think about it, sir?'

'You have thirty seconds. And while you're pondering I'll tell you the proviso. As an acting flight lieutenant I'll expect a damned sight more of you on the ground, so an end to your Bolshie affectations and displays of petty insubordination. It proves nothing and gets in the way of what I'm trying to achieve with precious few resources.' Brewster opened a desk drawer, dug his fingers into a canvas tobacco pouch and began to tamp down strands of pungent St Bruno's in the bowl of his briar with his thumb. 'So?' he said.

'Okay,' said Ossie.

'Okay what?'

'Okay, sir.'

'No, you clot, what are you saying okay to?'

'The promotion, sir,' said Ossie heavily. 'The way you put it, it seems I've got no option.'

'That's very magnanimous of you, Sergeant,' said Brewster. 'Is there anything else you want to say before I put in the papers?'

The innocent question hung in the air like a grenade. It would be so easy to kill this thing right here and now, thought Ossie. Should he come clean about screwing up in Spain and flying with the goddammed Fascists? How far could he trust Kit Curtis, the only guy who shared his secret? When the Englishman heard about Brewster's plan would he take the CO aside and murmur: 'I think there's something you should know about our American friend, sir, before it's too late . . . ?' Sure, it didn't sound like the guy. It wasn't his style. But folk could act in unexpected ways, particularly stuffed-shirt Limeys who'd been spooned a double dose of moral rectitude ever since they were squawking bundles in a bassinet. Then the shadow of doubt had dissipated a little. The hell with it, Ossie had decided. And the hell with anyone who wanted to finger him. He'd take his chances. The CO was right. This was an opportunity to take the fight to the enemy, do things the way he wanted. And if being a damned officer put a horseshoe in his glove, well, so goddammed what? All that mattered was beating the bastards.

That had been February, a quarter of a year ago in a world that no longer existed; a world in which events seemed likely to take a predictable turn and time had been abundant. A world in which a guy could get steamed up about stuff he couldn't change and feared might ground him for good. But now, in May, everything was streaming past like a speeded-up movie, so fast that there was only time for essentials – consider, decide, act; prepare, fight, regroup and fight again. And it was fighting, not past history, that Brewster wanted to talk about. He told Ossie to resume command of A Flight with immediate effect. Mortimer, drafted in from 11 Group to lead the Flight, wasn't up to it: on the final patrol that afternoon he had declined to engage a formation of forty Dorniers guarded by eighty 110s and had been unable to explain himself. He was to be sent back immediately, despite the desperate need for pilots. It was a question of morale. There was no place in the squadron for those who lacked resolve.

'Will Curtis be taking over B Flight, sir?' said Ossie.

'Never you mind about B Flight,' said Brewster. 'Here's a roster of your A Flight chaps. Rustle them up pronto and be as uncompromising as you like about what you expect. I want them back in the air, bristling with bloody-mindedness.'

'What about Sergeant Gates sir?' said Ossie. 'I was taking over his machine tomorrow while he had a break.'

'Bloody silly idea in the first place,' said Brewster. 'Can't imagine why I gave Doc a hearing. Tell Gates to report to me immediately.'

Goofy Gates was playing draughts with a sergeant pilot Ossie didn't know. Gates said cheerily: 'This is Plum Duff. Ponderous intellectual type. Used to be a scribbler on the *Telegraph*. All that grey matter and he still forgets to crown his kings.'

'You were right about your kite,' said Ossie. 'It's been put together like knitting. Jessop's doing his best but the thing's a goddammed death trap.'

'Stop binding, old chum,' said Goofy. 'As long as you remember left wing low you might just get away with it. Oh, and the aileron snatch. And not forgetting she swings to port when the tail goes down. Pilot of your calibre? Like I said, piece of cake. I'll give you a thought, tucked up nice and snug in my bed.'

'Oh, I'm not flying her,' said Ossie. 'You are.'

'Who says?' cried Goofy springing to his feet and knocking the draughtboard off the table. 'Who bloody says?'

'The CO,' said Ossie. 'He wants you in his office right away. I'd get a move on, feller. He's in a lousy mood. Oh yeah,' he added, 'here's a bit of good news for you. Those tyre pressures – I checked them myself and you were right, they're spot on.' He turned to Duff. 'Plum, I see you're on my roster. As of now I'm your new flight commander. I want to see the guys over by my kite in five minutes.'

'That would be Flight Lieutenant Mortimer's kite, would it, sir?'

'No,' said Ossie. 'Mine. There's nobody called Mortimer on this station any more.'

A little after 21.00 hours, the sky purple-black, the sun obscured behind the distant hills, a Merlin exploded into life and a Hurricane taxied rapidly away from Dispersal. It was dark enough for the flames from the exhausts to be startlingly bright against the long nose of the machine as it turned into wind. The Hurricane climbed rapidly to perhaps 3,000 feet and commenced a fluent display of aerobatics: loops, multiple loops, rolls off the top, flick-rolls, stall turns, vertical turns, spins, each manoeuvre flowing smoothly into the next in one continuous sequence. It was neatly done but the pilots gathered by the runway watched aghast.

'Christ,' said Buster Brown, 'who's that bloody idiot? The CO will have his guts for garters.'

'It *is* the CO,' said Spy Turner. 'He's taken himself off the sick-list. He's leading B Flight tomorrow.'

Twenty

Thursday, 16 May 1940

When he learnt that Ossie Wolf had taken over A Flight Kit experienced something uncomfortably close to a stab of envy, almost resentment. He knew very well that his reaction was infantile and did not do him credit. He resolved to keep his feelings hidden, but as the B Flight pilots gathered for Brewster's 3.00 a.m. briefing he allowed himself to express, in what he intended to be a casual aside, his mild surprise that the American had resumed command so soon.

The CO tore into him: 'Don't be so bloody wet Kit. If you want to indulge in a sulk like an Angela Brazil schoolgirl you can bugger off back to Blighty with Max Mortimer.'

Kit said nothing: there was nothing to be said. He joined Buster Brown and the rest, and Brewster told them Wing had ordered a patrol over Reims, taking off at dawn. 'Press tits at four thirty a.m.'

As the briefing broke up, Brewster took him aside. 'Don't fret boy. You'll have all the responsibility you can handle coming your way.'

'Yes sir.'

'And Kit, keep an eye out for young Collins. He's flying Blue Two.'

At 16,000 feet over Moronvilliers they picked up a dense formation of Heinkels above them, sixty strong, and higher still, more than forty 110s. By now the six Hurricanes had pulled the plug, urgently climbing on boost-override, trailing black exhaust smoke with throttles pushed through the gate, as Brewster led them round the right flank of the enemy bombers. Leading the second vic, with Eddie Knox and Goofy Gates formatted on his right and left, Kit checked his instruments, listening to the beat of his engine. Oil pressure, oil temperature, radiator temperature: all showed normal. Damn it, he'd forgotten the hood. He pulled back the canopy and locked it to stop it sliding forward if he had to get out fast. The surge of air was chilly and refreshing. He was overcome by a rush of exultation and triumph that he was back and about to rejoin the battle. He was unable to detect a trace of fear: he felt invulnerable and a pulse of pure joy ran through him. This was his purpose, his destiny. He was grinning behind his oxygen mask, on the verge of breaking into laughter. The sensation of euphoria was so strong that he checked his oxygen supply in case it was failing and making him light-headed, but it was normal.

Ahead, the machines of Brewster, Collins and Buster Brown lifted and swayed and Kit fed constant tiny corrections through the control column as his Hurricane was buffeted in their wake. He had his gun-sight switched on now and the gun-button set to fire; he made a small adjustment to his air-screw control, cool, calculated, thinking clearly. They were closing on the Heinkels fast and his thumb moved to the gun-button. He thought: at this instant I am intact, my body whole and functioning, blood circulating, brain engaged, sight perfect, reactions razor-sharp. Yet in seconds I might die. And if I die how will it be? Struck by tracer, consumed by fire or falling free through the air to be swallowed by the earth? This fragment of awareness, considered and complete, came and went like the flash of a torch in his eyes. But he was not afraid.

Brewster had taken the flight to 18,500 feet, five hundred feet above the Heinkel formation. Now he wheeled them round in a flanking attack coming in from the left. 'Echelon starboard,

334

echelon starboard. Go!' They were almost within range now. The bombers saw them and hurriedly moved closer together, covering each other as the rear-gunners opened fire. Streams of white tracer curved towards the Hurricanes as they closed in. Holes appeared in Kit's port wing and something, probably a cannon-shell, exploded beneath him. The Hurricane leapt like a startled cat, but still responded to the controls. The instruments confirmed that everything was functioning as it should.

Kit focused on one of the Heinkels that had strayed a little to starboard, the pilot probably shaking with nerves. He dived down left and, as the great bulk of the bomber swung through his sights, he thumbed the gun-button, a two-second burst allowing for deflection. Strikes appeared on the wings and fuse-lage of the Heinkel and pieces flew off near the cockpit. White smoke began to pour from its wing-roots, its wheels came down and it began a shallow diving turn to the right. Then it rolled slowly on to its back and dived vertically out of sight belching flame.

He eased the stick forward, then pulled back firmly, rocketing upwards and momentarily out of effective range to gather himself for the next attack. The Heinkel formation was in disarray now, some confused and falling behind, others damaged and losing height, turning for home, harried by the Hurricanes, pressing their assault.

Unaccountably the blue-bellied twin-engine 110s had remained aloft as though oblivious to the conflict below, but now they plunged down in screaming dives, their nose-mounted 20mm MG cannons twinkling. 'For Christ's sake Kit,' someone shouted on the R/T, 'behind you.'

A 110 flashed past him feet away, the Hurricane rocking in its slipstream. Kit rolled his machine on to its back, pulled the stick hard into his stomach and aileron-turned vertically down-wards on to its tail. He got in a long burst but the Messerschmitt banked quickly to the left, fell into a vertical spiral, as though hit, then levelled out at 15,000 feet. Kit powered down after it, dropping through a zone of crossfire from the Heinkels. A big hole opened up in his starboard wing, another cannon-shell, but failed to strike anything vital. The 110 had its throttles pushed wide open but Kit closed to within five hundred yards and tried two or three bursts at long-range. The Hun rear-gunner also opened fire but his aim was wild and wide. Another burst from the Brownings, closing fast now, and there was a spurt of orange flame from the 110's port engine, which immediately began to trail oil. Again Kit jabbed the gun-button and the 110's twin-finned tailplane was sliced from the fuselage. Connected only by control cables it whirled behind the grey-green fighter as it nosed over into a final dive to earth, exploding near the railway line close to Mourmelon.

Kit was laughing, wet with sweat, panting into his oxygen mask. 'Got you, you sods.' His body was trembling with tension. He wanted to kill again but could see no one. He was down to 8,000 feet now and seemingly alone, except for a solitary aircraft a long way off, enveloped in flames and falling in a centripetal spin from considerable height. Kit's laughter ceased and he felt sick for those who might be trapped inside the doomed machine, English or German, enduring a prolonged, hideous ordeal. When it exploded at 10,000 feet he was relieved that it was over for them. He turned the nose of the Hurricane on to a course for Louvins, the propeller a healthy golden arc in the sunrise. Several times, as the landscape passed slowly beneath him, he called into the R/T: 'Blue Leader, this is Blue Four. Blue Leader, this is Blue Four. Over.' But there was no reply. He prepared himself for the worst, but when he landed at Louvins he found he was the last to return and that all had survived. Hangdog Collins, whom Brewster had asked Kit to look out for and of whom he had seen not a sign, was Hangdog no longer, a huge grin fixed on his schoolboy features. Not a mark on his machine and a third of a share of a Heinkel probable with Brewster and Eddie Knox. The state of Kit's Hurricane prompted roars of laughter, muted only slightly when he told Spy Turner that he had accounted for a Heinkel and a 110. It was the flight's best score of the sortie, with Buster and Goofy Gates claiming a Heinkel each.

Brewster seemed content. 'Good show, Kit. Like falling off a horse, eh? Scramble back pronto and it's like you've never been out of the saddle. Now, see if you can get that kite patched up. I want us in the air again by nine a.m.'

Thirty minutes after B Flight returned A Flight was ordered up to intercept a large formation of 110s north-west of Reims. French convoys on the main highway from Laon to Reims were being strafed while squadrons of Heinkels and Dorniers bombed Laon itself.

With Beaky Parker and Windy Miller dead, Ossie Wolf found himself flying with pilots he did not know. The previous evening he had made his expectations plain: 'I got a crude philosophy. First, I don't want you guys under any illusions. You're here to kill people. It's simple arithmetic. If we kill more of the Hun, we win. If they kill more of us, we lose. Second, let's face it, fellers, the curtain's only just gone up on this show. The odds on us being around to take a curtain-call are lousy. Accept that and you'll find life a little easier.'

'Personally,' said Duff, the journalist, 'I'm banking on a long run with the original cast.'

'Prove me wrong,' said Ossie. 'Maybe we'll all end up waltzing down Broadway arm in arm.' He took a packet of Senior Service from his jacket pocket and passed it round, not lighting one himself. 'So,' he said, 'most of you boys, replacements too, have logged plenty of hours. This is good. You can handle an airplane and you understand the Hurry's little foibles. Problem: only three of you, Ferguson, Duff and Challoner, have seen any kind of action and you've still got big fat zeros against your names. I don't know why that is and I'm not here to dish the dirt. But tomorrow we're going to put things right. When we find the Hun we're going to go in quick, hit them hard and get out fast. When

I say "go in" I mean exactly that. I want to see real raw aggression, fellers. Get right up close until you see the proverbial whites and let 'em have it good, in nice short bursts, one or two seconds max. At all other times, go for height and keep a real sharp lookout. It's the guy who sees the enemy first who holds the aces. In the combat zone never fly straight and level for more than thirty seconds. And make decisions with the speed of light, even if they're wrong. Anything's better than fannying around. If you hesitate you're dead meat. And if you find yourselves under attack, turn and face the sods. The Hun like to hang together and a belligerent bloody Hurry coming straight at them with Brownings alight tends to make them thoughtful. Finally, anyone not cutting the mustard will have me to reckon with. And I'm more goddammed frightening than any sonofabitch Hun.' He gave his crooked smile. 'I guess you may have heard stuff about me, cocky colonial jerk with a big mouth and Bolshie ideas, a loner waging a private war and not fighting it like a gentleman. Well, I don't give a shit about what you may have been told. Make up your own minds as we get to know each other, and disregard what other mugs might say. But I'll tell you this much. I had to learn the value of teamwork in air-fighting and learn it the hard way. There's no way you guys can screw up I don't know about or won't find out about. Now, get over to your machines, check them out and check them out again. If anyone has to turn back with a preventable malfunction of any kind he might as well go straight to Chiefy Jessop and ask for a mop because the latrines is where he'll be working for the duration, period.'

Nobody had to turn back. The two vics of A Flight lifted swiftly away from Louvins, the blast from their propellers flattening the grass. At 18,000 feet over Craonne, just west of the Route Nationale from Laon to Reims, they caught sight of their quarry, the Messerschmitt Me-110s, dead ahead and at the same altitude, mere specks against their bullet-proof windscreens except, as they grew more distinct by the second, they were not 110s but a squadron of yellow-nosed Me-109s.

Hours before, over a bolted breakfast of bread and jam and mugs of khaki tea, Ossie had run through his plan of attack with his untried pilots. Now he directed Plum Duff, leading the second vic, to make urgent height with his wingmen Nuttall and Sailor Staples. With his top-guard in place he led Ferguson and Challoner in line astern towards the 109s, the three Hurricanes approaching head-on at 330 m.p.h. The Messerschmitts maintained their course, not deigning to acknowledge the threat or show concern. The Hurricanes were perhaps a dozen machine-lengths from the enemy formation when the first rank of the 109s opened fire, still holding position, but the British fighters had already dived and swept below them, leaving the torrent of machine-gun bullets and cannon shells to stream through thin air, striking nothing and showering to earth, spent and harmless.

Above the Hurricanes the bellies of the 109s flashed past like a shoal of monstrous fish. Then: 'Pulling up. Go!' Ossie tugged the control column firmly back, the G-force flattening him against his parachute and seat-back. He was climbing fast but throttling back a shade to make sure of his aim, wings level, the aircraft perfectly balanced, easing the stick further back still, his feet light on the rudder-bar anticipating and countering yaw. Behind him he could sense Ferguson and Challoner on the same trajectory. The pale underside of the Hun formation's tail-end Charlie passed through his gun-sight and at the same instant he loosed off his Brownings.

The 109 erupted into a nebula of fiery fragments. Ossie heard the roar of the explosion in his cockpit as he reached the top of the loop, using only gentle pressure on the controls to allow for the fading airspeed, and half rolled into a steep, descending turn to port, wings almost vertical, thumbing one, two, three bursts from his machine-guns at the 109 in the centre of the rear vic. The bullets smashed their way through the cockpit to the bellowing Daimler-Benz engine, which blew up, severing the starboard wing. The propeller, black blades projecting from a yellow spinner, hurtled free and chewed into the tailplane of the 109 immediately ahead.

Ossie did not see this, concentrating on easing back from his extreme bank to port and diving with wings lateral once again, gun-button jabbed once, twice, no time for more at the third 109, the only survivor of the formation's rear vic. This time he missed but behind him Fergie did not and the 109 spun away, trailing white smoke. A 'chute opened up at 8,000 feet. So far the attack had occupied perhaps forty seconds. And now the German squadron broke and turned to fight.

But Ossie had dived to the right, throttles wide, away from the mêlée, with Ferguson and Challoner yelling with excitement behind him. 'This is Red Leader, this is Red Leader,' said Ossie on the R/T. 'Please, gentlemen, remember you're British.' He called up Duff and told him and the others to use their height and get the hell out. 'There are some very angry Huns in your vicinity, fellers. Thanks for the insurance but this time we didn't need you.'

The six Hurricanes regrouped and headed back to Louvins pursued by seven determined 109s who only gave up the chase within sight of the airfield, when French ack-ack began to pepper the sky. The flight had sustained not a single bullet-hole.

The word went round: three kills to Ossie, including the 109 felled by the flying prop, one to Ferguson and a probable for Dicky Challoner, who had snapped off a round or two as the Messerschmitt formation scattered in front of him and reported strikes on the fuselage of a machine with a distinctive black arrow on its flank bisecting the German cross. '*Staffel* leader, you naughty lad,' said Spy Turner, at the debrief. 'That'll teach the blighter.'

Later, French observers phoned in to say they'd seen a 109 matching Challoner's description hit power cables attempting a wheels-up landing near Anizy-le-Château. It was good enough and A Flight's tally of confirmed victories rose to five.

*　　*　　*

Each flight flew three more patrols that day. On B Flight's third, taking off at 1.00 p.m, Brewster stepped down and Kit resumed command. The CO's phone had been jangling all morning. Spy Turner had fielded the calls, but now they wanted Brewster. Wing seemed rattled. There were suggestions that the squadron might be required to fall back further still, not a retreat, naturally, merely a strategic withdrawal. News of the day's successes were met with an automatic 'Jolly good. Keep it up.' The wing commander in Reims appeared to have his mind on other matters.

'How are we doing, generally?' said Brewster. He wanted a more considered response.

The wing commander roused himself. 'The chaps are performing magnificently. We're knocking them down three or four to one.'

'If we're doing so bloody well,' said Brewster, 'why do we keep falling back?'

There was a long silence. Finally the wing commander said curtly: 'You should know, Squadron Leader, that we're relocating to Troyes with immediate effect. No questions, please, and certainly no comment.' He rang off.

No one else knew of this exchange, not even Spy Turner. Brewster was reluctant to disturb the buoyant mood. The fortunes of the day had given heart to every pilot. They believed they had the measure of whatever the Luftwaffe cared to throw at them. 'How long can the bastards keep going at this rate?' demanded Buster Brown. 'As long as we get reinforcements we can give them a bloody nose every time we go up.'

When A Flight landed at eight thirty p.m, after the final patrol, the squadron had accounted for ten enemy aircraft for the loss of two. Kit's perforated Hurricane had been written off and bulldozed into a bomb crater; as flight commander he had stepped into Brewster's machine. And Goofy Gates went missing when B Flight bounced a strong force of Dornier-17s without fighter escort bombing Château-Thierry. No one saw him go down and for a while he was hardly mentioned, other than a casual 'Goofy?

Oh, he'll be all right', blandly rejecting the possibility of his death. Some types seemed to have a mark on them from the start and when they bought it, well, it was never a surprise; Windy Miller, for example, always on the edge of disaster; Frazer and Vaughan, eager and proud to be part of the show but without the hours or the nous to survive; even Kenny Rains, for all his ability, had clearly – it could now be seen – always had it coming. But Goofy? No. Stolid, unshakeable Gates would always make it back.

And, sure enough, he returned to Louvins in the back of the Renault taxi he had hailed outside the *mairie* in Montmirail, where he had landed, muddy and bloodied after his brolly-hop, shot at by French *poilus* as he descended. 'The buggers must have whanged off thirty rounds,' he said. 'With marksmanship like that the Hun will be goose-stepping up the Champs-Élysées before you can say Schickelgruber.'

Ossie Wolf had strolled up. 'Hey, Goofs, get caught out by the aileron snatch?'

'Bollocks,' said Gates. 'Glad to see the back of the bloody thing. If I'd been able to dive the bitch I wouldn't have been clobbered.'

But the habitual levity could not conceal the strain that showed in the pilots' faces, anxiety too. Each man knew that all the confirmed kills had come on their early patrols. The rest had been probables or damaged, inconclusive engagements from which they had been forced to break off, faced with over-whelming numbers. As the day took its course, the Luftwaffe Geschwader seemed to grow less complacent, putting up larger formations of bombers striking a wider range of targets and protected now by a multitude of fighters.

Intelligence from Wing was more sparse and inaccurate than ever. Orders came to intercept enemy battle fleets that did not exist or perhaps had existed hours before. Where no Hun could possibly be, they were present in hundreds. 'Once we're up, boys, we're on our own,' Buster Brown had said, and nobody could have put it better. But it was not the only thing that Buster had said. They remembered his unanswered question: 'How long can the bastards keep going at this rate?' As the day progressed, the answer was plain to see, rumbling across the skies of France even as the ground-crews prepared the squadron's battle-worn Hurricanes for whatever they might face the following day.

It was almost dark when Kit pushed back the flap of the mess tent. With the smell of grass and canvas, and the warm glow of paraffin lamps throwing shadows on the tent sides, it evoked an image he could not quite place: the beer-tent at a point-to-point, perhaps, after the horse-boxes had left, or the end of a country wedding reception in a rented marquee, the diehards clutching their drinks, reluctant to go.

Close by, Goofy Gates was draining his glass and rising unsteadily to his feet. 'Join us for a noggin, Flight Lieutenant Curtis, sir, why don't you?'

Kit moved towards the bar. Buster Brown was in the crowd, and Ossie Wolf, who introduced his pilots. Kit noticed that it was as though he had known them for years. They were very happy and rather drunk. Later, he could not recall a word that had been said. But he often thought back to that ring of faces, tension soothed by beer, anxiety all but forgotten, and hanging over everything a stink that should have been foul but wasn't: earth, spilled ale, tobacco, sweat and paraffin fumes. On the canvas of the tent moths danced, drawn to the light of the lamps, with the sillhouettes of a dozen swooping hands simulating dog-fights of the day.

Brewster joined the party briefly. He accepted a beer, then another, standing by the group with Spy Turner and Doc Gilmour, the three men tolerant and amused. Someone had cranked up the gramophone and Flanagan and Allen were doing their breathy rendition of 'Run Rabbit Run'. Buster shouted: 'I say, does anyone fancy musical chairs?' There was a scramble and clatter as the chairs were flung into a row. Ossie Wolf said: 'What the hell is musical chairs?'

Spy Turner took charge of the gramophone and the game began. The music stopped. Chairs flew and bodies tumbled as the pilots fought for a seat. Ossie Wolf found himself bundled into a corner with the beginnings of a black eye. A chair collapsed as Plum Duff and Eddie Knox threw themselves on to it at the same moment. Music again. And so it progressed. Finally Buster was victorious and Goofy Gates, lying on his back, gasped: 'Any other ideas for games you can win, you old bugger?'

Brewster accepted a final beer. He raised his glass. 'Confusion to our enemies.' The pilots roared their approval. A few minutes later, he clasped his fists over his head, boxer-style, and slipped out of the tent with Spy Turner. Doc Gilmour paused uncertainly by the tent flap. 'I don't want to spoil the party, you fellows, but tomorrow you've got a war to fight. Too much booze and—' He was shouted down and pulled back into the circle.

Someone put a George Formby song on the gramophone. Eddie Knox reeled over and seized the disc. 'For Christ's sake, this unfunny bastard's driving me mad.' He smashed it against the tent pole.

'Lighten up, old son,' cried Buster, 'I like Noël Coward's stuff.'

Things quietened down. Kit found himself next to Ossie Wolf. They chinked glasses. 'Here's to you partner.' Before Kit could reply, Eddie Knox slumped beside them. 'I want you to know,' he said, 'I want you to know . . .'

'What is it you want us to know?' said Kit impatiently. He was feeling mildly groggy but had not gone at it as hard as Knox.

'You blokes,' said Knox, 'have brought us luck. If we knock the sods down at this rate we'll wind up in the *Daily Mirror*. Let me buy you a drink.' He rose to his feet and lurched away.

'Remember this?' Buster called to Kit from the gramophone. He lowered the needle and Lucienne Delyle began to sing:

> 'Sur les quais du vieux Paris,
> Le long de la Seine,
> Le bonheur sourit,
> Sur les quais du vieux Paris . . .'

'Jesus,' said Ossie, 'I know this.' He had heard it last when he was lying in a ditch with the corpses of an English corporal and a French colonel, and an *Oberschutze* from Chicago telling him to beat it. He was startled by how vividly the sweetness of Delyle's voice summoned up the desperation of that moment. 'Jesus man,' he shouted, 'find something with a beat to it. We're meant to be whooping it up here.'

'Wrap up you soulless Yank,' said Buster.

Kit was remembering too: the suite at the Crillon back in October when Albert had found them a gramophone and he and Buster had drunk chilled Lanson and talked about the tea business, motor dealing, rowing, rugger, racing cars, families, women and shop – most of all shop: the miracle of flying, the fascination, the facets and foibles of the aeroplanes they had mastered, near-misses and hair's-breadth escapes, the Hurricane and their fondness for its bulldog character, their impatience for the action to start. It all seemed a long time ago and his head was starting to hurt.

Ossie had also gotten to thinking. He found himself running through the chain of events that had led him to Verdun and from Verdun to here. He glanced at the sonofabitch skin-and-bone Englishman sitting next to him who'd pulled off a million-to-one shot, picked him up and put him back in the air. He felt a need to say something about it but couldn't find the words. Instead he said: 'Hey, I hear you weren't too shabby up there today. So how's the glory business going?'

'Not too bad,' said Kit. 'How's the hate business?' He rose

with some dignity and made his way to the exit. Then he turned. 'Goodnight Ossie,' he said, and vanished.

'Well, I'll be damned,' said Ossie.

Much later the party broke up and a single figure remained, straddling a sagging chair, propped up against the tent pole, snoring thunderously. It was Doc Gilmour.

Twenty-one

Friday, 17 May 1940

When Maurice Maierscheldt entered the great courtyard of the
mansion in the rue du Faubourg St-Honoré and paused to collect
the key of the family apartment from the concierge, Sauval, the
man was delighted to tell him his daughter was out. 'But the
other one is there.'

'The other one?'

'*Bien sûr. La jumelle*, Monsieur. At least, that is what Madame
Sauval and I call her. It confused us at first. *Extraordinaire*. They
are as like as two peas but, of course, you know that, Monsieur.
No doubt your daughter has told you all about her very good
friend.'

'Of course,' said Maierscheldt. He took the key that dangled
from the index finger of Sauval's upturned hand and crossed the
courtyard towards the main building.

The concierge watched him for a moment or two, with the
smile of the perfect servitor, but his eyes were cold. 'Jew pig,'
he muttered, and went back into his office.

Maierscheldt let himself into the apartment and placed his business case beside the gilt-wood console. Expensive clothes were
scattered over the furniture, newspapers and magazines strewn
about the floor. Two empty Margaux bottles had been tossed
into the wastepaper basket by the desk. He heard a noise in the
bathroom and tapped on the door, concerned not to startle his

347

daughter's friend, of whose existence he had just learnt from Sauval. 'Hello?' he said.

There was a long silence and then a young woman's voice said: 'So you have found me then.'

'I suppose so, yes.'

'Which one are you? Jabesco, Rougerie or Bouy?'

'I am Hannah's father.'

There was a longer silence, then the sound of the young woman getting out of the bath. After a minute or two the door opened. She was wrapped in a white towelling bathrobe, her hair black and wet, beads of water like tiny jewels on her brow. As she held out a slim brown hand the robe parted and Maierscheldt glimpsed the curve of her breasts.

'I recognise you, of course, from your photographs,' she said easily. 'Please, sit down.'

Maierscheldt was unable to resist a smile at the stranger, who was welcoming him graciously to his own apartment.

'You seem amused,' she said.

'Surprised,' said Maierscheldt. 'Hannah has not spoken of you. Why would that be?'

'Ask her.' She pulled the front of her robe more tightly together. Maierscheldt realised he had been looking at her hard. Sauval was right. The resemblance was remarkable – so remarkable that Maierscheldt threw his mind back twenty years and ran through his minor indiscretions. He had conducted various intimate friendships with women in La Ville Lumière; Albertine the mannequin, Margot, the ripe wife of one of his best customers, little Adele who took dictation in his firm's Paris office, the energetic Gabrielle of course, Jeanne, Agnès, the troublesome Isabeau. The list was long but no longer than that of the average *homme d'affaires* in his position. Besides, at that time, before his own interest in such matters had waned, Karoline had not been warm towards him: always his advances were too clumsy or he stank of wine or particles of food had lodged in his moustache.

'Tell me,' he said to his daughter's friend, with more than a little apprehension, 'what is your name?'

'Anna,' said the girl. 'Anna Lvovitch Dubretskov.'

'And your mother?'

'Sofia Pulcheria Dubretskov. Countess.'

Maierscheldt relaxed. No exiled Russian aristocrats on his list of conquests. How could there have been when they were violent anti-Semites, convinced that the Bolshevik revolution had been plotted by Jews? All the more curious, then, this relationship with Hannah, whom this exotic creature so closely resembled. But now, as he studied her intently, he could see that she differed from his daughter in many subtle and disturbing ways. There was a challenging, unchaste quality about her, despite her youth, and she produced in him a rush of the piquant imaginings he had thought he had put behind him.

The girl was saying: 'To my friends I am known as Bébé.'

'What shall I call you?' said Maierscheldt, like a feckless adolescent.

'Oh,' said Bébé, 'I think you should call me Anna. After all, you could be my father.' She stood up and went to get dressed.

While she was gone Maierscheldt sat silently, imagining her slipping off the white towelling robe and standing naked only yards away from him in the other room; he pictured her pulling on each item of clothing, perhaps caressing herself. He was big now, the first time for months, but as the familiar impulses engulfed him he was overcome by shame, given the nature of his visit. He had allowed himself to forget, to believe for a moment that Paris was restored, full of promise and temptation. Then he heard a key in the door and it swung back. Hannah came in, holding a black leather portfolio, her face flushed from the spring sunshine, a velvet beret pushed back carelessly on her head. 'Oh, Papa, how wonderful to see you! What brings you here? No, it can wait. You must be tired. Let me get you a little something, some food, a glass of wine.' She looked around the apartment. 'You have caught us. What a mess we have made. You are angry.'

'No,' said Maierscheldt, 'I am not angry.' His bigness had subsided. 'I have introduced myself to Anna.'

'Anna, yes. Isn't she adorable?'

'Is she staying here?'

'Oh, yes, for the moment. She has nowhere to go.'

'You did not tell us about her.'

'Oh, there is nothing to tell. She came to me through Kit.'

'A friend of Kit?' Maierscheldt was taken aback and not a little impressed. Perhaps the boy he had known from a child was not such a boy, after all. He had not been granted a son, had always wished he could understand the fellow better, confounded by that air of Anglo-Saxon reserve.

'Not a friend exactly, no. Bébé was with another pilot, an American, walking in the Tuileries. We felt we knew each other from the first.'

'Like looking in a mirror, perhaps?'

Hannah laughed. 'More than that, but isn't it bizarre?' She sighed. 'Of course, she is so much more beautiful than I.'

'You have a beauty, Hannah,' said Maierscheldt loyally, 'that I suspect your friend will never possess.' However, it was true that while the resemblance was remarkable, Bébé's physical perfection somehow pointed up the deficiencies in Hannah's appearance: the angularity of her shoulders, the thinness of her legs, her meagre breasts, the faint darkness of the skin beneath her eyes, her carelessly cropped hair.

'What is it that I will never possess?' said Bébé, from the door to the bedroom. She was wearing a black dress by Schiaparelli with a short fitted jacket in hyacinth blue. Maierscheldt stood up automatically, heart pumping hard. Hannah ran over to her and kissed her on both cheeks. 'We were talking of someone else,' she said. 'For you the world will provide everything you desire.'

Maierscheldt was disturbed by the way the women were together. He had not seen Hannah like this before. She had always been an unexcitable child, impassive and self-contained. Now she sat at this Anna Dubretskov's knee, like a witless acolyte, hanging on every word and gazing up with something more than mere fondness. The look, he realised, was familiar to him: he had sometimes seen it exchanged by his wife and Diana Curtis. And when he spoke, this Anna, this Bébé, regarded him with languid eyes that held a challenge, even a threat, but of what he could not tell.

'Your designs, Hannah,' he said finally, 'they are remarkable, inspired. Everyone talks of them.'

'Is that why you are here?'

'No,' said Maierscheldt. He looked at Bébé. 'Forgive me. We have some family matters to attend to. I am sure you understand.'

Without a word Bébé uncurled herself from the Biedermeier satin-birch sofa and went into the bedroom, then returned a moment later in her street clothes. She smiled sweetly at Hannah but not at Maierscheldt, and was gone.

'Papa,' began Hannah.

'Please.' He held up his hand. 'This is not easy.' He took a beige envelope from his case and told her to open it.

Hannah peeled back the flap without tearing it. The envelope contained her passport and an exit visa. She looked at him questioningly, then understood. 'Papa, I am not leaving.'

'Hannah, I implore you. The Boches have overrun Sedan. In weeks they could be here. On every side we hear the war is lost and also . . . also what might be in store for our people.'

Hannah threw down the passport. 'No,' she said. 'I cannot go. Not now.'

Maierscheldt began to pace the room. He paused, bent over and picked up the discarded passport. 'You must understand it is not a simple matter to obtain such things,' he said. 'At present the authorities in Nancy are more than accommodating, but who knows how long that will continue?'

'I will not go,' said Hannah, firmly, 'unless we all go together.'

'That is impossible,' said Maierscheldt. 'I cannot prevail on your mother to understand. She denies everything. "Tomorrow, tomorrow, tell me tomorrow." And what is to become of the business? Am I to walk away, abandon everything the family has worked for?'

'You see?' said Hannah. 'You are compelled to take your chances. So must I.'

Suddenly Maierscheldt was in a fury. He clasped his fists in front of him, banging them together in frustration, the knuckles white. 'You must go! You must! I order you to. That is my decision.'

'Oh, Papa,' said Hannah. She was smiling, which stirred his anger still more. 'Surely France will not fall. You know we are always rescued by a miracle at the eleventh hour.' She stood in front of him, reached up and rested her hands on his shoulders.

He felt uncomfortable because of his thoughts about Anna Dubretskov and his love for his daughter. His anger subsided. 'I cannot force you, of course.' He kissed her forehead. 'But it would be one less anxiety if you did. Think of that, if nothing else.'

'I will,' she said. 'Perhaps Bébé will help me order my thoughts.' She looked at him with affection. 'You have been unlucky with your women, Papa.' Maierscheldt's eyes brimmed with tears and he held her to him.

That evening she told Bébé about her father's request, showed her the passport and exit visa. Bébé turned the passport over and over in her hand. She tapped the photograph and laughed. 'How beautiful you are. Of course you must go.'

'I cannot.'

'Because of your parents?'

'Partly.'

'Don't be a silly goose. Do not think of me. If I were in your place, *mignonne*, I would leave tonight.'

'What nonsense. Did my father ask you to tell me that?' Hannah put her arm round Bébé's neck and kissed her lips.

'Your father would not confide in me,' said Bébé. 'He views me with the greatest suspicion.'

'I could not leave without you *chérie*,' said Hannah. 'I have waited and waited, and now I have found you I could not bear to let you go.'

'It is hopeless,' said Bébé. 'No, really, you must go. Your father is right. Would you agree to leave if I promised to follow?'

'We have talked of this. You have no papers.'

'There are ways,' said Bébé. 'I know people.'

'So you say,' said Hannah. 'But people know you.'

'Ah, *oui*,' said Bébé. 'I am a fugitive. How thrilling.'

'There is a solution.' Hannah pulled back a little. 'Let the Americans have their way. Give it all back, everything, every last scrap. You cannot possibly be prosecuted. You will be forgiven. All they want is their property.'

'It is not their property,' said Bébé. 'It is mine.'

'But don't you see?' said Hannah. 'Then we could be as we were, free to be seen, with nothing to fear, free to get the papers you need. We could be together, in England, in America, anywhere.'

'No,' said Bébé. 'The price is too high.'

That night Hannah wept quietly to herself, her face turned away from Bébé so that she would not hear. When she dreamed it was of the rare, faint smile of the Countess Sofia as she talked of divination. The predictions of the tarot came to her again, like whispers in a cathedral. 'You are on the brink of a transformation . . . a joining together . . . a new insight into the way in which the world is perceived.' Then came another voice, far away and barely human, speaking of sorrow from which she would be released by the Great Mother who makes all things joyous by the subtle pressures of the water, and the words did not make sense to Hannah, as they had not made sense before. 'I do not understand,' she murmured. 'I do not understand.' But the distant voice had gone.

Twenty-two

Monday, 20 May 1940

With a squeak of ineffectual brakes, the tiny yellow Citroën Spider driven by Madame Courance, the wife of Louvins' *notaire*, stopped by Brewster's bell tent. The passenger door creaked open and the town priest, a tall, bony man, descended with some difficulty, carefully gathering the skirts of his black cassock round his knees. He had come to offer absolution, he said, to those pilots who might require it. Brewster, a negligent Anglican, supposed it would be all right and told Spy Turner to sort things out.

By now Madame Courance had also got out of the car and stood uncertainly beside it, her gloved hand resting on the steering-wheel. Brewster regarded her with something close to confusion, feet apart, hands clasped behind his back. His complexion, rose-hued at the best of times, had deepened to a cherry red. He had always responded to natural blondes and Mireille Courance, unusually in France, looked almost Scandinavian in her blondness. Some B Flight boys, Knox, Gates and Collins, were close by and Brewster heard guffaws. He recovered himself quickly and invited Madame Courance into his tent for a mug of English tea with bread and jam.

When the refreshments arrived she regarded them with some dismay, removed a cream glove and struggled to raise the steaming mug from Brewster's desk. The CO addressed her like a public meeting in fractured French, explaining in gruesome detail how many Boches the squadron had sent to their deaths. Madame Courance hid the smallest yawn, but Brewster did not notice.

The B Flight pilots had loitered. 'I saw bread and jam going in,' said Hangdog Collins.

'The CO's got a way with women,' said Goofy Gates. 'Watch and learn, son, watch and learn.'

Ossie Wolf was sitting in the cockpit of his Hurricane, helmet buckled, goggles on his forehead, humming 'Jeepers Creepers' and jiggling to the rhythm. The ground-crew had already attached the trolley accumulator and helped him to belt in firmly. Now he and the others waited, ready to switch on, hit the starter buttons and fire up. Orders for an intercept were expected at any time. A Flight had already carried out one rhubarb but without making contact, glimpsing only a handful of Fairey Battles limping back after bombing crossing-points over the Meuse near Sedan where German columns were pushing towards Rethel and Reims. Challoner, Staples, Nuttall and Duff were ranged alongside their flight commander.

Ferguson, who had not added to his 109 destroyed on Thursday, was gone: he had taken to his 'chute the day before, hit by German ack-ack as the flight strafed enemy troops east of Laon. He had been seen to land safely but close to Panzer positions and was properly in the bag. He had not been replaced and Brewster had made it known that further reinforcements for squadrons of the Advanced Air Striking Force could not be relied on. Instead fighters operating from airfields in southern England had joined the fray. But their range was limited and their sorties focused mostly on northern France, Holland and Belgium. Meanwhile the French-based units further south were expected to cope with daily losses and whatever jolly little jobs Wing cared to throw their way or they made up for themselves.

Ossie wasn't complaining. He liked it that way. He had

raised his score to eleven confirmed and was keen to see the erks paint another dinky little swastika on the nose of his machine.

The priest from Louvins was working his way along the line of Hurricanes, looking for Catholics. Ossie was surprised to see Dickie Challoner and Sailor Staples confess, the priest on the wing beside them, craning over their cockpits. When he got to Ossie he called up in English: 'Do you want absolution, *mon fils?*'

'No thanks Father,' he shouted. 'Just a 109.' He looked down the line at his pilots. They seemed chipper enough. Fergie brolly-hopping like that had been a bad deal but, hell, tomorrow it could just as easily be any one of them.

The priest was walking slowly back towards the little yellow automobile parked by the CO's tent. The sun was high and, in the rapidly rising heat, the grass runway was submerged in a shimmering mirage, an illusory silver lake.

Ossie could not remember how many sorties he had flown. It was all in his logbook, though. He was never so bushed that he didn't record his hours. Sitting on his parachute, he tried to work it out. Okay, since that memorable day when he and Kit Curtis had found themselves back in business, both flights had chalked up five rhubarbs a day. Five rhubarbs, ninety minutes each, times four. Jesus Christ, what the hell was that? Thirty hours? Sixty for the squadron. And what of the cost? After the black day when Frazer, Vaughan and Kenny Rains had bought it, the dice had fallen their way. Even Fergie might still be alive, if not actually kicking. The squadron had had the best of it so far, no question.

But they hadn't been able to mix it again as they had that first hectic day. Ossie was content for the rest of the guys, who'd been at this thing longer and needed a break, but he was also a tad disappointed. Sure, they'd knocked their fair share of Hun out of the sky but the contacts had been more sporadic. After the intense encounters of 16 May it was almost like the word had gotten round about the outfit at Louvins, almost as though the Luftwaffe had turned to another map. One Dornier crew, under Brewster's guns, had bailed out without firing a shot. An entire *Staffel*, sighting the A Flight boys above them at 20,000 feet, had just turned and high-tailed it for home. What had Buster said? 'How long can the bastards keep going at this rate?' At the time Ossie had grunted sceptically, reckoning he knew the answer. But now he allowed himself to speculate. Maybe the Hun really were feeling bruised and battered, having to explain the attrition to the fucking Führer when the whole damned show was meant to be a walkover. Maybe, just maybe, the fighter boys were making a crucial difference in what was starting to look, on the ground, like a general foul-up.

The priest had almost reached the yellow automobile when the two 109s came in from the south, straight out of the sun, at five-hundred feet and opened up with their MG-17s and 20mm cannon. Ossie could see the faces of the pilots. He watched the storm of bullets and shells rip across the grass and earth and appear to engulf him. He was not hit. To his right there was a mighty detonation, almost too loud to hear, and a fireball rolled into the sky. He was twisting in his seat to locate the ground-crew.

Incredibly they were there, looking up wildly. He primed the engine, flung them a thumbs-up and pressed the start-button. The Merlin caught immediately, and as the airmen snatched away the attachment to the accumulator and stumbled towards the next machine Ossie opened the throttle and taxied rapidly away from Dispersal, the tyres of the Hurricane bouncing high off the uneven ground with the unaccustomed speed. He was throttling up now, heading cross-wind but that was the way it had to be, powering towards the perimeter fence three hundred yards away. The Hurricane began to lift but as Ossie felt its wheels spin free he caught, in his peripheral vision, the Messerschmitts banking round to make their second pass.

Kit had been propped up on his bed writing a letter to his father.

> My dear Farve,
>
> Just a quick line between patrols. Leading the Flight again, I'm delighted to say. No contact with E/A unfortunately, but it's been quite a party of late. The chaps have been magnificent and although we have suffered some losses we have given a splendid account of ourselves. Since the balloon went up our squadron has accounted for at least thirty of the Hun. The other squadrons can tell a similar story. My personal score is six. It's wonderful to be back in the air again, even if someone is shooting at you. Far preferable to those escapades on the ground that I wrote to you about! Honestly, it's as though I've never been away. I must say we all pine for dear old Revigncourt, however, and we only hope we're not too far from the action in our new location. None of us wants to miss the party. By all accounts the Hun have swung north to try and reach the coast but they're going to have their hands full when they encounter the BEF. This might explain why our chums in the Luftwaffe seem to have been a bit distracted lately, at least in these parts.

As he paused he heard the growing roar of aircraft and put down his pen. So A Flight were up again. But now it seemed the clots were beating up the 'drome and right down on the deck as well. He pushed out of the tent expecting to see Ossie Wolf leading A Flight in a low pass just to get the CO's juices flowing. Absolutely ruddy typical. Buster had been right after all: once a line-shooter, always a line-shooter.

Then he heard a tearing, ripping sound and realised it was machine-gun fire. His eye was caught by a whirling shape a hundred yards away. A Hurricane without a tailplane was cartwheeling towards the edge of the airfield, engine screaming, propeller blades chewing deep into the ground. The cockpit hood was pushed back and Kit could see the pilot, like the hub in the centre of a wheel, powerless to do more than sit and, as Ossie Wolf had once said, enjoy the accident. Then he picked out the big white letters on either side of the roundel on the fuselage. It was Ossie Wolf's machine.

A fighter, mottled grey and green with sky-blue undersides, swept over his head so close that the wind from its propeller threw him to the ground. It pulled up into a 180-degree half-loop and rolled off the top, its mustard-coloured snout and black crosses vivid against the azure sky. A second came across, the full-throated clamour of its twelve-cylinder Daimler-Benz reaching a crescendo as it flashed overhead. The thunder of guns and cannon drowned out all thought and movement. Kit lay on his face, digging his fingers into the earth. The two Messerschmitts linked up and pulled round in screaming vertical turns. It seemed they were preparing for another attack.

He was on his feet now and sprinting towards the CO's tent. To his right, over by Dispersal, something was burning fiercely. A Hurricane waddled through the wall of flame, the black smoke parting like a curtain and curving downwards in the wake of the Merlin's prop. A second Hurricane emerged, then a third. Two hundred yards away the squadron's boxy little Morris ambulance was charging across the grass towards the source of the blaze, its rear wheels sliding and straining for grip on the long, smooth grass. Kit could see the driver and orderlies being thrown about in the cab. Behind it lumbered the heavy Crossley fire-tender, its crew struggling to pull on their protective gear.

By now, fifty feet beyond the perimeter, Ossie Wolf's machine had completed its dizzy gyrations, vaulting a low bank in a shower of grass and mud and thumping down, right way up, in a flattened circle of bushes and small trees. There was no fire, and as Kit continued to run, bent double, he made out Ossie climbing from the cockpit and strolling, nonchalant and unhurried, away from the smoking wreck.

Kit reached the CO's tent gasping for breath, the stench of fumes deep in his lungs. Brewster was scanning the sky, dancing from foot to foot with rage. He grasped a .38-calibre Webley revolver, thrusting fresh bullets into the hot chambers. 'I was issued with twenty rounds,' he roared, 'and, by Christ, I'm going to use them.' With the weapon reloaded he waved it above his head. 'Come on, you buggers, come on.' But the engine-noise of the Messerschmitts was fading now.

Behind Brewster, in the tent, Kit realised a woman was screaming, high and shrill. 'For Christ's sake,' shouted Brewster, 'put a bloody sock in it,' adding quickly: 'There's a good girl.'

Kit looked into the tent. An elegant woman, blonde and fashionably dressed, was crouched on her knees, eyes screwed shut, beating the ground with bird-like hands. She screamed until she could scream no more, breathed in deeply and began to scream again. Under her left knee, close to a tear in her silk stocking, was a crushed round of bread and jam. A priest in a black cassock pushed past him and sank down beside her, his big hands grasping her shoulders, murmuring words of comfort. To Kit the tableau made no sense. The priest helped the woman to her feet, and she fell against him, holding on to him for support.

Formed into a reassuring vic that spoke of discipline and coolness the Hurricanes of Challoner, Nuttall and Duff made rapid height, searching for the 109s, but they had done their work and were now faint specks on the horizon.

On the ground the charred remains of Sailor Staples, obscured by foam, huddled in a mess of pulverised metal tubing that, only minutes before, had been a fine-honed fighter plane; Sailor, who had chosen air over water after a life at sea in the merchant service, had never fired a shot in anger from his Brownings. But he was not the only loss. They found Len Croft, the corporal armourer, lying close by, a cannon-shell fragment in his brain, and in the bottom of a half-completed dug-out, almost severed at the waist by machine-gun bullets, Titch Baker, the admin clerk, still holding a file of daily inspection forms. One bore the hurried scrawl of Sergeant Pilot Reg Staples, pronouncing himself satisfied with the preparation of his machine. He had signed it off five minutes before he had taken absolution from the priest from Louvin.

One of the towable bowsers had also been hit and the conflagration had spread and engulfed two empty tents where the riggers and fitters took brief rests out of the sun, a small Renault van and Brewster's Humber, waiting to have a tyre changed. But B Flight's Hurricanes and a single spare machine, fresh from repairs, had escaped, gathered in the deep shadow of woodland on the eastern side of the airfield.

The little yellow Citroën was moving away now, very slowly, returning to Louvins. Madame Courance was at the wheel, trembling with shock but unwilling to be driven. 'You have more important considerations, Monsieur le Commandant,' she told Brewster. Instantly he had forgiven her screams. The priest said he would remain to provide comfort for the dying.

'There are no dying,' said Brewster, 'only dead.' But the man was insistent.

Ossie Wolf was back, chewing a blade of grass. 'Are you all right?' said Kit.

'Sure,' said Ossie. 'Who got the chop?'

'Staples.'

'I thought it had to be Sailor. Shit. Anyone else?'

'Corporal Croft and Baker.'

'Titch? You'd have thought he was too small to stop a bullet.'

Buster Brown squealed to a halt on a bicycle, skidding the back wheel. 'You chaps okay? I say, that was a pretty good show wasn't it?'

'Us?' said Kit.

361

'Them. Couple of crazy idiots coming from nowhere like that. Funny. Reminded me of two other lunatics I heard about.'

An hour after the first attack the priest from Louvins led the squadron in prayers over the bodies of Staples, Croft and Baker as they lay covered by rough grey blankets. He spoke in Latin and no one except Kit understood a word. The pilots and ground-crew stood in silence, heads uncovered.

To Kit the impromptu service rang hollow, the sing-song tones of the priest tawdry and irrelevant. Usually there were no bodies to mumble over: one moment a chap was with you, large as life, immortal, the next he'd gone. So many had vanished now, mourned briefly by the living and toasted with a mug of tea or a glass of beer, and somehow it seemed better that way. No time to find that hole in the ground where a comrade lay hidden, compressed and boneless, four foot down, or the remote hillside copse of beech and oak where he sat at the controls of a skeletal blackened machine; or beneath the Channel, dragged down by a booted foot still pinned under a damaged rudder bar and investigated by curious fish in his open cockpit.

Brewster appeared similarly discomfited. When the priest fell silent, tracing the sign of the cross in thin air, the CO led three robust choruses of 'Onward Christian Soldiers', reclaiming the initiative for the Church of England.

When the singing died away Brewster began to speak, his voice brusque and businesslike: 'These men served their country well. We will serve them well. If we had reason to hit the Hun hard before, now we will hit them still harder. Today was different but the same. Different because it happened on our own doorstep and we see in front of us the consequences of war. The same because we knew what war was before. It has taken Davis and Evans, Parker and Miller, Frazer, Rains and Vaughan, Croft and Baker. And it will take more. It may even take us all. But our job is to fight and win. Perhaps some of us won't be around to see the final victory but by sticking to our task we will help to make it come about. Of that I have no doubt. That is all. Flight commanders and Flight Sergeant Jessop, to my tent. You too, Spy.'

As Brewster turned and marched away, the remnants of A Flight landed together, with nothing to report.

Twenty-three

Tuesday, 21 May 1940

It was something special, Wing said, very hush-hush. Six Hurricanes to fly to an airfield east of Soissons, refuel and receive further orders on the ground. It sounded dicey, the way it was put, and Brewster asked for volunteers. The previous day he had reorganised the squadron, juggling with eleven serviceable aircraft, a diminishing stock of spares, seven experienced pilots, three others of proven ability but short on battle-hours, and two replacements, the last he could expect, who had just straggled in by road after hazardous journeys from reception bases to the north. He knew he would be compelled eventually to send the new boys into combat but meanwhile had set aside the spare machine for them to share and build their hours. As it was, they were little more than cannon-fodder.

The squadron now had two flights of five aircraft each: Ossie with A Flight, leading Challoner, Nuttall, Hangdog Collins and Plum Duff; Brewster and Kit sharing command of B Flight, allowing for the CO's other commitments, supported by Buster Brown, Eddie Knox and Goofy Gates. Kit had not allowed a flicker of emotion to show on his face when he learned that B Flight would only occasionally be his. Brewster had glanced at him, expecting a reaction, but had seemed satisfied when he saw nothing. But later, when Ossie Wolf was named flight leader of the half-dozen volunteers for the Soissons party, Kit had to fight to control his disappointment. Again, Brewster studied him and for a moment there was sympathy in his eyes, quickly replaced by the usual flinty resolve that brooked no challenge.

It was the first time for months that Kit had flown with Ossie, the very first with him as flight leader. He was surprised by the American's crisp commands over the R/T. No trace of flippancy, just calm, succinct and decisive.

'ETA four minutes, fellers.'

'That must be Pierrefonds to port,' said Challoner, close to Ossie's wing.

'Cut out the travelogue Red Two,' said Ossie.

At the head of the second vic Kit throttled up a touch, Knox and Gates keeping station to his right and left.

'Aircraft three o'clock, a long way off Red Leader.' That was Buster Brown.

'Okay, Red Three, I see 'em. No interest to us. Good work Buster. Keep 'em peeled fellers.'

The six Hurricanes had pierced a ribbon of haze at 6,000 feet and now they hung as though motionless in air of crystal clarity, their shadows moving almost imperceptibly on the murk below. Kit felt again the intoxication of flight. He knew that if he survived he would look back on these moments as a golden time, when his senses were heightened and fulfilled as never before and almost certainly never would be again. He was anxious that they should not pass too swiftly or go unacknowledged because one day the memories would sustain him as such memories had sustained all old warriors down the centuries.

The volunteer flight reached its rendezvous at Blérancourt without incident. Ossie led them round the airfield in a perfect curved approach. As scheduled, three fuel bowsers stood waiting by a black-painted hangar. It seemed their on-flight was going to be a long one, probably more damned bomber-escort duty, to the north around Cambrai and Arras, or even striking targets on the coast near Calais and Dunkirk, with the near-certainty of being ambushed by 109s and peppered by the Hun's viciously accurate flak. Ossie had been told to prepare for further orders on the ground and he was not alone in detecting a whiff of desperate measures about the op, not least in its demand for volunteers. The scale of the German advance was clearly immense and, whatever Wing maintained, it seemed the dam had burst.

Already, near the bowsers, small figures could be seen in air-force blue and, close to a gaggle of military vehicles, still more in British Army khaki. It was the routine assortment of light trucks and buckboards but, unusually, supplemented by two light-infantry support tanks. It was only as the flight swept in for a stream landing that Ossie became aware of puffs of smoke rising from the Vickers machine-guns in the stubby turrets of the Matildas. He hesitated, wondering what it meant. Already he had set engine mixture to rich, propeller pitch to fully fine, and on his control panel twin green lights confirmed his wheels were down. He made the decision: he was committed to the landing. He'd find out what the hell was going on when they were down. Now he was below 140 m.p.h., flaps applied, skimming over the perimeter hedge at little more than 90 m.p.h. He eased back the stick and held her off, waiting, waiting. The airspeed dropped towards 60 m.p.h. and the machine stalled gently on to the runway. As his tyres touched three huge shadows flashed across his cockpit. For a second he thought they had been bounced by 109s. But it was the Hurricanes of the second vic, still in the air and banking urgently to the right. Rumbling across the ground, his rudder swinging right, left, right and taxiing fast, Ossie headed towards the black hangar, tailed by Buster Brown and Dickie Challoner. His eyes were fixed on the two Matildas and now the sound of their gunfire was unmistakable.

He'd goofed. He cursed himself for not realising the danger, aborting the landing while he'd had a chance, however fleeting. Airmen were running towards him shouting and waving him away. One of them went down. The rattle of the Tilly machine-guns was startling now and he could hear the haphazard crack of rifles over the noise of the Hurricane engines.

Return fire, intensive and sustained, was coming from banked hedgerows beyond a narrow lane and every two or three seconds the ear-cracking boom of a sizeable gun. A Matilda rocked under the impact of a shell but for a moment seemed unscathed. Then flames erupted from its open hatch and it brewed up fiercely. One of its two-man crew pushed his head and shoulders clear of the turret, but his strength failed and he fell back into the furnace.

'Get the hell out,' Ossie Wolf shouted over the R/T, no longer clipped and cool.

'God's teeth,' yelled Buster, 'we've landed in a bloody battle-field.'

Overhead Kit had wheeled the second vic round and they came in from the south, three abreast, clipping the tree-tops. Below they could see the infantry unit of a Panzer tank division attacking Blérancourt airfield from the north-east, using the cover of hedges and patches of woodland and scrub and laying down an intense barrage of gunfire.

'Okay chaps,' said Kit. 'Let's even the odds.' The Hurricanes opened fire together and a storm of machine-gun bullets swept across the Panzergrenadiers as they lunged for cover behind brown-grey half-tracks or, caught in the open, defiantly discharged their weapons. In the armoured turret of one Hanomag a single trooper tried to track the fighters with his mounted machine-gun until the vehicle exploded around him. A five-man Panzerjager team, with a 37mm Pak anti-tank gun, was shredded by a two-second burst from Eddie Knox. By now the crew of the mobile 88mm flak gun that had destroyed the first Matilda had turned its attention to the threat from the air.

As the Hurricanes attacked for a second time, individually now, a storm of shells rose to meet them. The flak was exploding around them with a whip-like crack, the lethal splinters keening and whining like metal hornets, seeking flesh, fabric and steel. Kit had been first to go in, low and fast, skidding wildly to evade deflection shots before pinpointing the flak gun. He thumbed the gun-button and strikes sparked all over the grey steel of the artillery piece. Firing ceased as the crew dived behind the armour. Thundering across the airfield at little more than fifty feet he could see that Ossie, Buster and Dickie Challoner had scrambled back into the air. There was no obvious sign of damage to their machines.

Kit snapped his R/T: 'Out of ammo Red Leader. It's your party now.'

Knox and Goofy Gates swung into position beside him, their magazines also empty, and he led them away to a safe height.

Ossie resumed the offensive and Kit felt a stab of pity for the helpless Panzer infantrymen as the rounds from the Brownings slashed through their meagre cover. All return fire had ceased and it seemed impossible that anyone could have survived the ferocious assault. But as Ossie and the others pulled away, their ammunition expended, they saw the surviving Panzergrenadiers resuming their attack. The crew of the FlugzeugAbwehrKannone appeared intact and the 88mm flak gun returned to its original targets. Very quickly, over by the black hangar, the trio of bowsers was hit and moments later the second British Matilda, still firing its puny Vickers, was struck and blew up like the first. Clearly the flak-gun team were experts. By now the scene was largely obscured by drifting smoke but it was clear that any surviving defenders would soon be overwhelmed.

At Louvins Brewster was unfazed. 'Well, you did your best, boys. Go and grab some char.' He seemed relieved that he had got his men and machines back in one piece. It was hard to tell how much he knew about the nature of the op but it was plain he had not expected all of them to return. Wing was equally phlegmatic. 'Oh, yes, poor old Blérancourt. Overtaken by events, I'm afraid. The Hun are moving like greased lightning on that Front. By the time it was confirmed, your fellows were in the air. Still, at least they didn't get caught up in the unpleasantness. Commend them on giving a good account of themselves.

Unfortunately our chaps on the ground there weren't so lucky. Pretty well wiped out, I understand, though hopefully a few are in the bag.' A pause and a shuffling of papers. 'Check in again in thirty minutes, Squadron Leader. We may have fresh orders for you.'

The pilots had gathered round Spy Turner, clutching mugs of tea. 'I can't tell you a thing about the purpose of the op, chaps,' he was saying, pen poised over his clipboard. 'The CO didn't let on. Anyway, it's academic now, isn't it? I've got my reports to write. Tell me your tall tales and then you can shove off and wait for the next little excitement.'

'I got a half-track,' said Eddie Knox.

'Bloody sauce,' said Goofy Gates. 'That was mine. I saw bursts all over the ruddy thing.'

'You might have softened it up,' said the dour Knox, 'but I finished it off.'

'A half-share of a half-track each,' said Spy wearily. 'Anyone else?'

'And a 37mm Pak,' said Knox. 'Plus crew.' He showed with his hand how the five-man Panzerjager team had hit the ground together, dead. They all had their stories to tell, hazy recollections of desperate action. Kit gave a sketchy outline of his assault on the flak position, but that was all. He felt a little sick. He did not care to recall the sight of bodies writhing under the impact of his bullets.

Ossie ambled up. Brewster had demanded an immediate debrief one-to-one. Ossie slapped Kit on the back. 'Nice going, pardner,' he said. 'Those bastards had me flat-footed.'

'Just luck,' said Kit. 'I had a bit more time to work things out.'

Later that day Brewster learnt that the squadron was to move again, to a fresh location near Le Mans. There was no explanation other than a gruff remark about the possible need to cover further withdrawals westward. At once he began to make arrangements. This time Kit was to lead the air party with Ossie Wolf in command of the advance road party, Brewster himself following with the main road party.

When he read the order Kit was full of pride. No doubt his quick-thinking at Blérancourt had counted in his favour. The CO had been gruffly complimentary. Kit relished his approval and was curious to see how Ossie Wolf would greet the news. He was conscious of an inner need to be preferred, to dispel some of the myths of daring and invincibility that had grown up round the American. But he was to be disappointed. That evening he overheard Ossie confiding to Buster Brown over a beer: 'Me i/c a road party? I got no problem with that. No problem at all. Who the hell cares about missing out on a lousy ferry job?'

But first there was the matter of the three men killed the previous day. They lay in austere pine coffins on trestles in the church in Louvins; Staples, Croft and Baker, their names and numbers etched into hammered panels of aviation alloy and riveted to the wood. They were to have been buried with some formality in two days' time. The priest had wished it so. But the priest was to be frustrated; circumstances did not permit the novelty of a funeral service with military honours. Instead Brewster assigned Spy Turner to represent the squadron at a humbler affair. There were nearly a hundred miles to be covered on choked and perilous roads and no time was to be lost.

To the volunteer pilots the purpose of the Blérancourt op remained a mystery.

Twenty-four

Wednesday, 22 May 1940

Bébé was bored and restless. One evening, about to slip past
the concierge's office to take the air in the Tuileries, wearing
Hannah's long dark coat and beret pulled well down, she
realised he was engaged in conversation with a small man who
looked oddly familiar. She paused in the shadows and tried to
hear what they were saying. She shrank back when the conversation ended and the man came out of the office after the
usual courtesies and put on his hat. It was a black Homburg.
From where she stood he did not look quite like the seedy
salaud who had accosted her in the rue de la Verrerie but she
could not be sure and he was certainly of the type. She tried
to think of some pretext to talk to Sauval and discover the
purpose of the man's visit, but she knew it would only arouse
his suspicion.

Instead she returned to the Maierscheldt apartment and stayed
there, half expecting a knock on the door. She did not think it
would be the police: the Westcott family was only interested in
retrieving Una's collection and spiriting it away to America before
the authorities could object; as no doubt they would, unwilling
to yield up such treasures of French culture, even in the grip of
a Boche invasion. No, the Westcotts would be subtle and pragmatic, reasonable with her, even generous, but Bébé knew they
could never be generous enough. And first they had to find her.
If she could evade their agents until the crisis in Europe reached

its peak, years might pass before the world returned to normal – and who could tell what kind of world it might be?

Meanwhile she remained in the apartment and was overcome by the dullness of her existence. She felt like a prisoner, helpless and alone. And Hannah was always there, anxious and loving and always pressing, however gently, for Bébé to let the Westcotts have their way so she and Bébé could escape and be together always. She did not know that Bébé considered they had been together quite long enough. But Bébé pretended to yield a little to her entreaties, give them grave consideration, simply to make life bearable.

At Bébé's urging Hannah had told the concierge that her friend had returned to her family in Rennes. Bébé had instructed her to study the man's face carefully. He appeared only mildly curious and Bébé wondered if she had been misled by a black Homburg.

'What were his actual words?'

'Oh, the usual vulgarity, *chérie*. How like sisters we are but, with an odious wink, how unlike. You know his ways. Nothing more.'

'He senses that his time is coming,' said Bébé. 'That is why he is bold.'

She began to feel more at ease but still slept lightly at night. Often, half awake, she thought of the château of Kitty Bannister, close by the tumbling waters of the tributary of the Loire a mile or two from Azay-le-Rideau. The mountainous Englishwoman had laughed and laughed, in that booming British way, as she had followed the heavy-laden Renault *camion* in her Delage, driving like a man, big hands sweaty on the steering-wheel.

The nameless artisans with the shabby truck, paid well but not too well, had cleared the Westcott apartment on the quai des Grands Augustins with brisk, incurious efficiency: friends of friends of shady friends who honoured a certain code. They had not asked questions. They had been told nothing. But still Kitty Bannister had not trusted them enough to enlist their help in the entombment. That task had fallen to her and Bébé, dislodging the oak planks of an internal wall in a picturesque barn, cool and dry, its timbers sunk deep in raised ground well above the water-line, dry enough for grain to be stored in centuries past. But not used now, except to store the bric-à-brac of pleasure, bright umbrellas, canvas garden chairs and loungers on which Kitty Bannister's circle had sprawled through sultry, intoxicated summers, croquet sets in long pine boxes, tennis racquets, warped with broken strings, badminton nets in mouse-infested boxes, some trompe l'oeil Grecian columns on canvas frames, replicas of the Temple à l'Amitié, where Kitty and her friends had played out little scenes in homage to Sappho.

Kitty Bannister had laughed again as she and Bébé stored the Westcott treasures in the space behind the panelling, all care-fully wrapped in layers of sacking and tied with string, even bulky marble busts. They had saved the hand-made iron nails and repositioned the panels exactly as before. Then they piled the paraphernalia of summers past against the wall and stood back, inspecting their work with a critical eye, dusting off their hands. The building was perfect for their purpose. It would be impos-sible for the Americans to discover the cache. Like the anony-mous men with the *camion*, Kitty Bannister lived by a code, very English, even with her flagrant tastes and frailties. The agree-ment was a matter of trust: to store the collection for as long as it took and return one day to permit it to filter on to the market, piece by piece, at the end of an untraceable chain. For this the Englishwoman required forty per cent and Bébé did not argue. It mattered little to her. She did not intend that Kitty Bannister should enjoy a single *sou*. The only price she had to pay was to walk back through the drowsing parkland to the deli-cious Renaissance château, drink a quantity of good champagne and submit to the embrace of the woman's fleshy arms, her searching lips and fingers. It seemed little enough.

Hannah knew nothing of this. She seemed entirely happy, locked away in the rue du Faubourg St-Honoré. She no longer ventured out much, just occasional errands to fetch groceries and wine. She would sit for hours at Bébé's feet, her head resting against her knee, reminiscing about the past. She was touched by Bébé's interest in everything that had happened to her, her elegant mother Karoline, who sometimes seemed so sad and distant, and Papa, who had created a thriving business making so many wonderful things. Dear Papa, who tried to be good but sometimes drank a little too much and said silly things that people took the wrong way, impulsive, careless but lovable. She talked of their enduring friendship with the Curtis family in England, which had grown from a fabled time when Maman and Diana Curtis had spent their youth together in the severe Swiss college beside the silky waters of Lake Thun.

'Perhaps they loved like us,' said Bébé.

'Oh, no,' said Hannah. 'Do you think so? Oh, no, surely . . .'

'It is possible,' said Bébé. 'Have you never thought of it?'

'Oh, no, they are the greatest friends, never happier than when they are together. Seem to come alive, somehow. But no more than greatest friends, I'm sure.'

'But we are greatest friends, *mignonne*, and we share everything of ourselves. Why should it be different for them?'

'I don't know. You confuse me so.'

Bébé let the matter go and, to amuse herself, pretended to be jealous of Kit. 'Such a perfect English milord. The very picture. How can you resist him? Simple, honest and brave. Confess. Be honest with me. You have always been in love with him.'

'Perhaps a little, but as a wonderful brother, nothing more. You have nothing to fear, *chérie*. Of course our mothers would dearly wish it otherwise. It was always their dream . . .'

Then Hannah talked of long holidays when she and Kit, as children, played, walked and talked for hours, days, weeks, sometimes in the strange grey countryside in the far, far west of England where the Curtis family owned sizeable tracts of land.

Bébé smiled. 'He grows more irresistible by the minute.' But Hannah was telling her how Kit, so lithe and tanned deep brown, had tried to teach her the baffling game of cricket on the beach of amber sand or how to sail round the cove in his stubby wooden dinghy with the single yellow sail. 'I was such a coward. The water seemed so deep. I could swim a little but the very thought of nothing beneath my feet used to paralyse me with fear. Poor Kit. He tried to improve my swimming but I was too frightened. I used to watch him from the beach instead, lying on my towel.'

'The fool, to toy with boats when such an *enchanteresse* awaited him naked in the sun.'

'I was not naked, *chérie*. What nonsense you sometimes talk.'

'Ah, *oui*. Of course. I was forgetting. This was England.'

At the mention of England the conversation would take an inevitable turn. 'What holds you back, *chérie*? It would be perfect for us. Diana Curtis would take us in until we found a place of our own, I am sure of it.'

'Impossible. The Americans . . .'

'Oh, give them what they want. Then you will be free and we can arrange your papers. Papa has contacts . . .'

'No,' said Bébé. 'But you must go. Soon it will be too late.'

'Now I am obstinate.' A sob. 'But I know Papa is right. Things will be bad for the Jews.'

'Go, go now, and I will follow. I promise.'

'I cannot. It is too much to bear, to lose you now, even for a little while.' Crying helplessly now. 'Oh, *chérie*, don't you see? There will be danger for you as well.'

'Oh, I will make my way. I always do.' But now Bébé was not so sure.

A short while before she had talked with her mother of what might transpire if the Germans conquered France. The countess had laughed. 'Do not trouble yourself, my child. You remember Count Nicolai Boris Fedunov?'

'The man who ran for a bus?'

'Once a viceroy,' the countess had said stiffly, 'and still very much *au fait* with affairs of state. He assures me no Russian need fear the Boches. After all, the detestable Molotov signed a pact of non-aggression with the Reich less than a year ago. But that is not all. The count is convinced the pact will not endure. Hitler hates the Bolsheviks and Jews as much as we do. Inevitably he will invade and, of course, prevail and that will be our moment, the time when we will return to our homeland and things will be as they were.'

'You forget the Boches, Maman.'

'By no means. Russia is far and why should they remain if the country is once more in the hands of those of a like mind?'

Listening to the countess complacently outlining the future as she desired it to be, Bébé had been more concerned with the immediate prospect of Paris in the hands of the crude Boche soldiery. Her mother was naïve and lost in a fairy-tale. How would it help to be Russian when you were faced with a Wehrmacht trooper who had his own ideas about *la vie Parisienne*? Beauty could be a curse. *Merde*, what tedious times might lie ahead. And Count Fedunov's appraisal was perhaps too neat: if the pact was violated, as he predicted, the struggle might be prolonged and bloody. As the countess had said, Russia was far and invasions had not been notable for their success. Fine distinctions between White and Red Russians would be swept aside in the chaos and brutality. And how could the countess and her kind trust in Hitler to restore the White regime to its rightful place? If the count's assessment was correct, the man was prepared to betray his solemn promise to refrain from any act of violence or aggression.

Bébé did not talk of this to Hannah. Secretly she had begun to agree with the sad little creature. She imagined how it would be to step off the boat at one of those ugly English ports and board a train for London, a city she had seen only on travel posters or read about in books, larger than Paris, where one could lose onself but where beauty and a modicum of guile could help one make one's way among the dull, solid Anglo-Saxon potatoes. But how could it be achieved? Clearly Hannah would not get her wish – it was selfish of her to want it. Obviously they could not flee together unless Bébé surrendered Una Westcott's precious things and forfeited a fortune she now considered hers. And give it up for what? She could not imagine what Hannah was thinking. Was it sense to exchange some miserable documents worth a few francs for a future life of wealth and comfort, even if one had to be patient? And, anyway, such a sacrifice would simply prolong the deadening *ennui* of Hannah's facile chatter and pitiful emotional demands. At first the freshness of the girl had been diverting and the rich apartment a welcome haven. But now it was too frustrating.

As Hannah talked and talked, Bébé knew there had to be a solution. But for the moment she could not imagine what.

Twenty-five

Friday, 24 May 1940

'Just a lousy ferry job.' Kit had been stung by Wolf's careless aside to Buster Brown three days earlier. He did not believe that the American had meant it vindictively, intending him to hear. He had simply been expressing what he thought of the short, straightforward hop to the squadron's new base due south of Le Mans. But the following morning, when he took off at the head of the eleven surviving Hurricanes bound for Boulay-sur-Sarthe he felt that his pride and fulfilment in leading the squadron had been devalued. He did not have it in him to set up a final, low pass over Louvins in salute: it smacked of a hollow line-shoot. Even the sight of his comrades, in their neat green-brown British fighters sweeping west over the pastures and meadows of the Pays de la Loire, did not stir him as much as he knew it should. He wondered if he hated Ossie Wolf, not the man so much as his values and the way he had made his mark so swiftly, winning, with little apparent effort, the respect and recognition for which Kit had always striven.

He was also aware – and it was difficult for him to acknowledge this – that if Ossie Wolf had not risen so rapidly from the ranks his own position as the natural successor to Brewster would have been unquestioned. Yet it seemed as though he and Ossie were bound together in some way, their destinies linked, although they shared little.

He remembered when they had all played musical chairs at

Louvins. At one point during the high jinks he had tried to restore a little calm by embarking on a tale of the Great War. 'It seems,' he told the pilots, 'that during a raid over a French airfield a German pilot dropped a glove. It was expensive, fur-lined, one of a pair his mother had given him. The next day he returned to the airfield and dropped the second with a note. He had no use for a single glove and begged the finder of the first to accept this one with his compliments.' There had been a guffaw of amusement. 'That was not all,' he had continued. 'The next day the finder of the gloves flew over the German's airfield and dropped a note thanking the German airman for an act of true camaraderie.'

Wolf had broken the silence. 'If I'd been the guy who dropped the glove,' he said, 'I'd have tucked a fucking hand grenade inside.' To whoops of delight the circle of pilots had dispersed, looking for more beer, leaving Kit with only the snoring Doc Gilmour for company.

Later Ossie had come over, eyes bloodshot. 'I guess I spoiled your story.'

'Your point being that this is a different show?'

'You can't play by the rules of the game with these Nazi bastards, Kit. They'll laugh at you for your weakness.'

'So we must be as despicable as them? Trade horror for horror, atrocity for atrocity?'

'This isn't a gentleman's war for Christ's sake. How often do you need to be told?'

'Quite often I think.'

The flight to Boulay-sur-Sarthe passed without incident and Kit had been almost regretful. The Hurricanes were fully armed and the CO had made it clear that if the enemy was sighted and the situation favourable the squadron should attack. The time for strategy had passed. Now it was hit whatever you could, bombers, fighters, reconnaissance aircraft, men and machines on the ground. But the skies had been empty and Kit missed his chance to saunter up to Ossie when he arrived with the advance road party and say: 'Just a lousy ferry job, eh? How does half a dozen Heinkels and a brace of 109s sound? Pity you were stuck in a buckboard.' Not that he would ever have permitted himself to say such a thing.

From 15,000 feet, the countryside below had looked serene. But on the ground, as Ossie and Brewster, with the two road parties, had crept kilometre by kilometre towards Le Mans, the *routes nationales*, lanes, byways and railways were clogged with desperate humanity. At every town and village more fearful souls joined the shuffling multitude. Some moved south towards Bordeaux and Spain, others west to Brittany and the haven of sea-ports still untouched: Brest and St Nazaire, Cherbourg, Dinard, La Pallice, St Malo. At every step came fresh rumours: Paris was in flames, Premier Reynaud had been shot as a traitor, General Weygand had been flown to England, abandoning his command, the Boches were already in the suburbs of Dunkirk and poised at Abbeville, at the mouth of the Somme, encircling the BEF, who stood with their backs to the sea.

It had been a French sous-lieutenant of cavalry, inexplicably on leave and intent on returning to the Ministry of Defence in Paris on a borrowed British Army Harley-Davidson, who had told Brewster about Dunkirk and Abbeville. At first Brewster had been sceptical. But then he had seen that the man was serious and probably well informed. 'My God,' he had said quietly to Spy Turner, 'if it's true, then it's all over for us.' The French officer had straddled his motorcycle in front of them, saying over and over again: 'Something might have been done.' He had wrung his hands. 'It is as though France is paralysed, unable to comprehend. The government is frozen. We have been conquered, humiliated. France has lost her soul.'

In the next town there was talk of Reduit Breton, Fortress Brittany, a marshalling of Allied forces first to resist the Boches, then push them back. Apparently the mayor had heard some such report on the wireless. At first the tale had caused wild alarm among the thousands fleeing the conflict – it seemed they were to be engulfed in fresh battles – but, surrounded by the convulsions of a nation in collapse, Brewster doubted that such a stand was possible, simply empty rhetoric.

The slow-moving convoy of air-force vehicles quickly became laden with a new cargo: a pregnant woman they had found slumped beside a hand-cart with a shattered wheel; another with a crying child, stumbling under the weight of a makeshift haversack fashioned from flour-bags; more children, one with blisters the size of ten-franc pieces, barely able to walk; a frail old woman dressed in black, supporting herself with a stick, dignified and uncomplaining, who had to be persuaded by the airmen to accept their help. The young, the weary, the sick, the old – the human freight increased until every space had been filled.

When Brewster's group finally neared its destination and pulled off the road by the narrow lane leading north to Boulay-sur-Sarthe, ten kilometres further on, there were protests and pleas to continue to the coast. The airmen, disturbed and awkward, helped the women and children down, gave them food and milk, forced smiles and told them in English that they would be all right now, the ports were not so far away. But they huddled together, listless and uncertain, full of fear, as the convoy moved slowly away, down the bumpy track just wide enough for a single vehicle.

When the airmen looked back, the group had not moved. The pregnant woman had sunk to the ground, arms folded across her chest, hands clutching her shoulders, rocking back and forth. Only the old woman, resting on her stick, raised a hand in gratitude and farewell.

Soon after the ground parties had negotiated the network of sandy tracks, flanked by spiky clumps of flowering gorse, that led to the new base at Boulay-sur-Sarthe the squadron was operational. This time there were no hangars, no buildings of any kind. Boulay was just a level expanse of grassland, protected to the north and east by woods, potential cover from air attack. For a short time Brewster even established shaky communication with Wing in Troyes, then the line went dead. But the contact was long enough for him to confirm that the squadron was ready to carry out its new role, patrolling the Atlantic and Channel seaports and protecting the steady flow of merchant and Royal Navy shipping surging to and fro between Britain and France.

Both flights had completed patrols without incident. The Hun seemed occupied with developments to the north. And now, at the head of B Flight, Kit was sweeping the Channel seaboard from the Cherbourg peninsula to Le Havre. The old firm, Buster had called it, five-strong but no Brewster for the time being, just Kit, Buster, Eddie Knox and Goofy Gates with Chris Lloyd, one of the new boys, tucked away to Kit's left. The sector was reportedly quiet and it seemed a good opportunity to blood the fledgling sprog.

At 10,000 feet the green coast of England lay to port, waves breaking on the deserted beaches just as they had seven months before when Kit had imagined himself in the shadow of spectral heroes bound for war. The clarity was startling and to the north-east, beyond the bruise-like darkening of the coastline that was Dieppe, columns of black smoke curled and twisted into the air, ominous and unexplained. Immediately below them, minute against the broad expanse of the Channel, ships were crossing from coast to coast, trailing creamy wakes. The ports were thronged with vessels and the bustle almost had a holiday air, with its bouncing craft and vivid splashes of colour.

Then, against the green-blue sea where it pressed into the Seine estuary with the harbour of Honfleur ahead and the dockyard cranes at Le Havre visible, Buster Brown saw a high-wing monoplane drifting from right to left at little more than a few hundred feet. Its progress seemed impossibly slow. 'Henschel at two o'clock,' Buster shouted. 'Right on the deck.' White puffs of Allied ack-ack fire appeared round the tiny aircraft and it moved inland, banking to the east. 'Go get him, Buster,' said Kit. 'We'll stay upstairs and give you cover. Good hunting.'

Buster dropped away to the left, shedding thousands of feet in a steep, exhilarating dive, then swept round to the right to come up astern and a little below the angular big-winged reconnaissance machine. It was a Fieseler C-2 Storch, as fragile-looking as a gadfly and hanging in the air at little more than 40 m.p.h.

Brown misjudged his speed and rocketed past, almost removing its tailplane with his propeller. As the Fieseler pilot fought against the turbulence of his pass the gunner-spotter gave the Hurricane a hopeful burst from the rear-facing MG-15 machine-gun, mounted in the two-man cockpit below the notch in the gull-wing.

It was the last thing he did. Buster screwed round in a vertical turn, came in again on the nose and opened fire. The Fieseler disintegrated like a balsawood model and fluttered to the ground. One of the crew was thrown clear and somehow managed to open his 'chute, but it barely slowed his fall before he struck the earth in a cloud of dust close to a few grazing Charolais that scattered in panic. Buster Brown climbed back to rejoin the flight.

'Good show, Buster,' said Kit.

'Plain bloody murder,' said Buster.

The flight had been in the air for sixty minutes. Now they turned south for Boulay-sur-Sarthe, sighting no further Hun. The presence of the Fieseler meant that this was likely to change.

Twenty-six

Saturday, 25 May 1940

Within a few minutes' walk of the pathless tract of flat, open ground that served as the squadron's new base, stood a handsome *maison du maître*, a grey-stone building on three floors, its tall windows flanked by wooden shutters, also grey, and topped with a shallow roof of blue-grey slates pierced by a dormer on two sides. Across an extensive gravelled courtyard facing the front door were a number of outbuildings: a barn that looked older than the house, its double doors rising to more than twenty feet, and next to it a stable building, lower but of the same grey-hued stone. On the tiles of the main house doves and pigeons quarrelled and cooed and, through an archway cut into a dense yew hedge, a terraced garden fell away to the dun waters of the Sarthe.

Brewster had spotted the potential immediately. Now, with Kit as interpreter, he pushed open the heavy gate, wrought iron above, solid iron below, and stepped into the courtyard. The ungreased hinges groaned and the front door of the house opened an inch or two. At the same moment six Hurricanes bellowed overhead, little more than fifty feet above the house. A flight was on a rhubarb, bound for St Lo and Caen.

At the sight of their uniforms a woman of perhaps thirty came out of the house and watched them hurry towards her. She regarded them with a certain apprehension, occasionally shooting a glance at the receding fighters, shielding her eyes against the early-morning sun. Her hand was slender and graceful against her brow and her feet, enclosed in tiny black-laced shoes, were dainty on the rough granite steps.

Brewster was his usual gruff self in the presence of an attractive woman but Kit softened the CO's brusque enquiries with gracious French elaboration, and the purpose of their visit was quickly explained. Madame Garencières listened in polite silence to their request, sitting upright on a carved mahogany side-chair in the echoing tiled salon, icy even in the warmth of early summer. Her slim legs were crossed at the knee, her small hands folded in her lap. She made her decision quickly and asked if they wanted to inspect the barn. They followed her into the hall and a small boy clattered down the wide uncarpeted staircase, his eyes alight at the sight of the British pilots.

'*Bonjour*,' said Kit.

'*Bonjour, Monsieur*,' said the boy.

'We are to have guests, Louis,' said Madame Garencières. '*Ouvre la grange.*'

The boy raced across the courtyard and slid to a halt by the great doors. He kicked away a heavy log and the left-hand door swung outwards. He secured it by hooking a long iron stay into a ring sunk into the ground. The barn was dark with shafts of light filtering through gaps in the roof where the tiles had shifted over the decades. Two massive wine-vats stood next to each other against the far wall, surrounded by the paraphernalia of a once-active vineyard. The interior was heavy with dust and cobwebs but the tang of good wine still hung in the cool, dry air.

Madame Garencières stood by the open door, leaning on it lightly, arms folded, watching Brewster as he stumped about assessing the barn's potential. Finally, standing in the centre of the space, hands on hips, jaw jutting, he said: 'It'll do.' Which Kit translated as absolutely perfect for the squadron's purposes and a thousand thanks. And so it was agreed that Brewster's pilots would occupy new quarters with immediate effect, under a solid roof for the first time in weeks.

In the house Madame Garencières insisted on serving coffee and petits fours. Brewster crammed one whole into his mouth and slurped from his bone-china cup. The boy Louis, eight or ten, hung by Kit's chair staring at his wings.

'You have been fighting in the air?'

'*Oui.*'

'How many of the enemy have you shot down?'

'Six.'

'Six?' The boy was impressed. 'Did they die?'

'Almost all.'

'How did they die?'

'They died. That is enough.'

'What is it like to kill?' The boy was studying his face intently.

'It is not good,' said Kit, 'a bad feeling afterwards. But you do not have time to think.' He hesitated. 'It is a necessity of war.'

'I am too young for this war,' said the boy. '*Je suis très ennuyé.*'

Kit smothered a smile. It was droll, this mop-haired child confessing his annoyance. He could see Madame Garencières looking across at them but there was no amusement in her dark eyes, only sadness and concern.

'My father is fighting,' said the boy, 'my uncle too. Cavalrymen,' he added with pride, 'like the Cuirassiers of the Grande Armée. But now it is tanks they ride. My father commands a squadron of Char Bs. He made me a model of his. I will show it to you.'

Madame Garencières was beside them. 'Louis, you must not bother this young man. Besides, he has to return to his comrades.'

'*Oui, Maman.*' The boy raced away up the stairs and could be heard clattering about somewhere, high in the eaves of the cavernous old house.

'He is full of the war,' said Madame Garencières, watching

Brewster devour another petits four and brush himself off as he stood up. 'Just like his papa.' Her voice was flat, emotionless.

'Where is he stationed?' said Kit automatically.

'His division was placed between Dinant and Sedan. On the thirteenth of May our forces were overwhelmed there. All contact was lost. At first nothing was known. However, my brother is attached to the Ministry of Defence in Paris and used his influence to discover that he was burned and a prisoner of the Boches. Now we learn that he is dead. I have not had the heart to tell Louis yet. He worships his father and dreams of war as a glorious adventure.' She gestured vaguely at the park-like gardens where the shrubs and trees moved gently in a light breeze. 'They had such times together. The garden was their battlefield.' She caught her breath and swallowed. 'Even my brother, who managed to scrape a few days' leave, could not bring himself to tell the boy.'

Brewster had been struggling to follow the conversation. Now he said: 'Ask Madame Garencières if her brother was riding a Harley-Davidson motorcycle.'

Kit was puzzled but put the question. Madame Garencières nodded. '*Une moto, oui. Mais comment . . . ?*'

'Tell Madame we met him on the road,' said Brewster.

'Was he in good spirits?' asked Madame Garencières, through Kit.

'Of course,' lied Brewster. 'Eager to return to the fray.' His brow furrowed as he considered whether a nice soft billet in the hushed corridors of the French Ministry of Defence could be described as the fray.

Ten minutes into A Flight's patrol a tremulous voice said: 'Hello, Red Leader. Hello, Red Leader. Over.' It was the second new boy, Spotty Leppard.

'What's your problem, Red Two?' said Ossie. 'Feeling lonely?'

'I can't seem to turn my oxygen on, Red Leader. Over.'

'Then you're no use to me,' said Ossie. 'Head back home.'

'Roger Red Leader. Out.'

'Keep your eyes skinned Spotty,' said Challoner. 'Looks like there's plenty of trade about today.' They had all noted the criss-cross of vapour trails at high altitude, too abundant to be friendly.

Leppard's Hurricane banked to port, carefully maintaining its height, and the formation closed up, Hangdog Collins in the sweeper slot, his head constantly on the move as he scoured every inch of sky. They were passing over Ouistreham now, their progress apparently sluggish as the landscape unrolled slowly beneath them. A convoy was setting out from Le Havre, rough-and-ready merchant tramps and coasters streaked with rust, here and there a spick-and-span passenger ship. And, scurrying round them like vigilant sheepdogs, British destroyers, grey and swift, carving great wakes in the gentle green swell.

Ossie did another cockpit check: oil pressure, coolant temperature, reflector sight, range and wing-span indicators – the usual routine. It was as he switched the gun-button to fire that he felt a familiar tingling sensation sweep through his body. He had noticed it before when danger was imminent but unseen, like some primeval instinct, a warning that something, somewhere was ready to pounce. Then . . .

'Christ Almighty!' Hangdog's voice was shrill and hoarse. 'Red Leader, Red Leader, estimate forty plus bandits at two o'clock approaching from direction Calais.'

'Roger, Red Five.' Ossie could see them now: a formation of about twenty Dornier Do-17s approaching the convoy at 6,000 feet. Stacked above them at 12,000 feet, the same height as A Flight, were a dozen Messerschmitt-110s and at 14,000 feet a flight of 109s.

'Okay fellers,' said Ossie. 'Dickie and Plum take the fighters. Tim and Hangdog, we'll go for the bombers. Good luck, guys.'

'Who needs luck?' shouted Challoner. 'We're only outnumbered eight to one.'

'Line astern, line astern, go!' Ossie pressed forward on the stick and descended on the Dorniers. They were spread out below him in a striking, powerful pattern, moving over the fringes of the convoy. Rosettes of foam began to appear round the ships, opening like flowers. Beadlike strings of ack-ack rose from the destroyers but were ignored by the German crews, flying straight and level now, adhering precisely to their flight-plans. Preoccupied with their task they unloaded their bombs, veering away from their targets in graceful, descending turns. They had no thoughts of British fighters. Surely what few there were would be occupied elsewhere. Was Calais not in flames and Dunkirk on the verge of surrender, with Rommel and Guderian squeezing the Allies kilometre by kilometre, their backs to the sea? And as the land was theirs so was the air. They ruled the sky. Soon the whole of Europe would crumble before the forces of the Reich . . .

The three Hurricanes flashed through the formation of Dorniers at full throttle, one, two, three, opening fire at less than three hundred yards. Bursts appeared all over the fuselage of Ossie's chosen prey. It seemed the pilot had been hit. The bomber flopped away out of control, its engines surging, rolled on to its back and plunged vertically into the sea. The tidy formation had broken up, some of the Dorniers turning away from the convoy with bombs still in their bays. Hangdog's Brownings chewed into one and the bomb-load detonated with a searing flash, the fragments spinning and fluttering in the air like leaves and paper caught in the updraught of a bonfire. Ossie led them in for a second time. The Messerschmitts had dropped down to join the fight. A 110 made for him in a wide curve trying to get on his tail. He pulled back on his stick, screwing into a vertical turn and brought himself on to the Hun's tailplane. He could see the rear-gunner struggling to get an angle on him, the bullets from the MG-15 ripping past him, close, but nothing like close enough. He stabbed the gun-button in three two-second bursts and the *Bordschutze* fell out of sight behind the shattered canopy, the barrel of his weapon pointing skywards. The port engine stopped and began to stream white smoke that traced the aircraft's gradual descent, rising, falling, rising, before it dipped for the final time, struck the sea at an angle, bounced fifty feet like a leaping porpoise and buried its nose deep in the waves. Its tailplane stayed erect for a minute or two, bobbing with the movement of the waves, then slipped smoothly beneath the surface.

Close by, a Dornier pancaked more successfully, throwing up huge clouds of spray as its belly struck the water. A hatch flew open and the crew fell on to the starboard wing, struggling to inflate a dinghy. For a second Ossie thought of strafing them. Then he changed his mind, aware that a thousand seamen in the convoy had grandstand seats. He was down to eight hundred feet now and an ack-ack crew on the foredeck of one of the destroyers waved wildly as he levelled out and climbed away. He laughed, exhilarated and gave his cowboy yell. Then, as he clawed for height, he saw a 109 coming at him beam-on from the right. He turned to meet it, the distance closing so fast there was no time to think.

The Messerschmitt opened fire first. Ossie expected the impact of a bullet. He did not care. He was ready to die. Something slammed into the metal bulkhead just behind his head and the Hurricane shuddered but collected itself and powered on. The 109 was huge in Ossie's windscreen and still he had not fired. He was almost hypnotised by the scarlet spinner a few hundred yards away. Something was different. The flicker of machine-gun fire on the leading edges of the German's wings had ceased. Jesus, the bastard was out of ammo! Ossie did not waver in his approach and pressed his gun-button half expecting the hiss of escaping compressed air to tell him his own ammunition was gone. Again the Hurricane shuddered, this time from the recoil of its guns. No time to see if the 109 had been hit. The two fighters burst past each other, missing a head-on collision by the span of their propellers. Suddenly Ossie was clear and still in the air.

'Sonofabitch,' he said aloud. 'Sonofabitch.'

On the R/T someone said distantly: 'Hello, Red Leader, is that you?'

'Where in hell are you, Tim?' Ossie shouted.

'Buggered if I know,' said the voice, fainter still. 'I'm . . .'

A quarter of a mile away a Hurricane plummeted towards the sea, black smoke belching from its engine. Then it swooped into a steep climb, stalled and fell off the top, tipping into another desperate dive. Ossie could see the pilot, his head falling forward, then thrown back with each twist and turn of the stricken fighter. Another climb, another screaming descent and it was over, a dull explosion and a ring of fire on the dunes just east of Arromanches.

One of the merchantmen had been hit and was listing to port, its bow submerged. The bridge was missing, a tangled mass of blackened steel. A few lifeboats and rafts were pushing away from the hulk. In the sea, figures black with oil strained to reach their comrades. Near the stern of the vessel the sea was on fire. A 110 came in low and strafed the survivors. One of the life-rafts flew into pieces, spilling bodies into the mess of wreckage and oil. As Ossie dived down the Messerschmitt flew through a storm of ack-ack fire from a racing destroyer, pouring black smoke from its funnel. The 110 veered up, stalled and fell back-wards into the sea. Nearby, the stern of the merchantman was rising, rising until, with a rush, it slid vertically downwards and vanished. Two other vessels had suffered damage but were limping on, seamen hosing water on to blazing topsides, the injured stretched out on the decks. From some considerable height a single parachute of German design floated down. A tiny figure tugged frantically at its lines but could not change the course of its descent. The parachute settled neatly in the area of burning oil and the squirming figure was engulfed.

The sky was empty now. The surviving Dorniers and Messerschmitts had completed their mission and were making for home. Ossie called up the flight. Only Nuttall did not respond. The Hurricanes were widely dispersed but linked up over Falaise and headed south for Boulay-sur-Sarthe. Each machine showed signs of damage but all four put down safely, to their surprise. Dickie Challoner's was promptly declared a write-off. He protested. Flight Sergeant Jessop shook his head. 'It might not look too bad to you, sir, but we haven't got the spares. All we can do is cannibalise the poor old girl and keep some of the others in the air.'

Spy Turner drove up in the Morris pick-up and Brewster jumped out of the passenger seat. Ossie Wolf was leaning back against the fuselage of his machine. Somebody had found him a mug of tea. Brewster said: 'A close-run thing.'

'It got my attention,' Ossie said.

'What happened to Nuttall?'

'I saw him go down. No 'chute.'

'And Leppard?'

'Leppard?' Ossie tipped the dregs of his tea on to the grass. 'Isn't he here? He turned back before we hit the coast. Gremlins in his oxygen supply.'

'No sign of the chap.'

'Shit,' said Ossie. He caught himself. 'Sorry sir.'

Brewster shrugged. 'These sprogs have a habit of turning up with a silly grin on their faces and a sackful of excuses.'

'Yeah,' said Ossie. He knew that neither of them believed it. He wondered how Spotty Leppard got hit, the poor little punk. Under the twin MG-17s of a free-hunt 109 unable to believe its luck? Or maybe he'd tried to be a hero and gone in single-handed against another Hun formation? It would have been like him to try, anxious that no one should suspect him of turning chicken.

'How did the rest of you chaps get on?' said Spy Turner.

Ossie grunted. 'Hangdog and I got a Dornier each, confirmed. Plum bagged a 110 probable.' He did not mention the 109 with the red spinner. It had been a dumb engagement, pushing his luck like that. As far as he knew the Hun hadn't even been damaged and for that he had laid himself on the line.

'Two–all, then,' said Turner.

'Not good enough, is it?' said Ossie.

'It's a decent enough show,' said Brewster. 'We can't expect more. Trouble is, the Hun can afford the losses more than we can.'

Later, Brewster changed tactics. He had noticed cloud building up from the south-west. For the rest of that day B Flight carried out two-man rhubarbs, pairs of fighters hunting anything German that moved. The CO's orders were stark: 'Get in with the speed of light, hit the buggers hard and climb back into the cloud faster than a homesick angel. If in doubt don't mix it. Wait for a softer target.' He decided to fly one of the rhubarbs himself with Goofy Gates, who looked ridiculously pleased. 'They tell me you've got eyes in the back of your head,' Brewster rumbled. 'Cover my backside and I'll buy you a beer tonight.' Kit was matched with Buster Brown, the grizzled Eddie Knox with Chris Lloyd. The youngster had been shaken by the loss of Spotty Leppard. They had trained together, at Kidlington and Little Rissington, before travelling across France in high spirits to join this, their first operational squadron.

The pilots of A Flight, Ossie, Challoner, Duff and Collins, watched the rhubarbs take off at intervals, each rising quickly and vanishing into the lowering cloud-base. Only Ossie wished he was with them. Behind him, Jessop's men were working on the flight's three serviceable aircraft. For the first time it occurred to him that their task might be hopeless, that this was how it might be, meeting each day with fewer men and machines until, maybe, there weren't any more days, no more men, no more machines.

When Brewster returned his eyes were shining. 'A Heinkel confirmed, Spy, plus a probable. Gates will bear me out.' Which Goofy was quick to do. He made no claims himself, other than effectively covering his CO's ample backside as they had dropped down on six Heinkels bumbling along complacently over Nantes. 'The bastards didn't know what hit them,' Goofy chuckled. 'We were back in the cloud cover before they had a chance to say *Gott ind Himmel.*' The taciturn Knox had also added to the squadron's score, bringing down a Dornier on reconnaissance over St Nazaire. Chris Lloyd had dived with him, hitting nothing but proud of the scorched gun-patches on his wings, shot away in his first experience of combat. For Kit and Buster, patrolling the Atlantic coast from Brest to Lorient, there had been no signs of enemy activity. 'Just a jolly nice seaside outing,' said Buster.

However, a grim day ended on a more favourable note. 'Four–two after all, Spy,' said Brewster. 'That makes better reading.' But when he attempted to report to Wing in Troyes the line was dead again.

That evening, stretched out on makeshift bedding in the church-like barn facing the Garencières' house, the pilots did not talk of the two men no longer with them. The spaces set aside for Nuttall and Leppard had been absorbed. In the guttering light of two or three paraffin lamps voices were low and beer was drunk slowly. Plates of bully-beef and bread remained untouched. It was not so much the events of the day that occupied their minds, it was what was to come tomorrow.

When the small boy appeared at the door it was a welcome diversion. He stood on the threshold, rubbing one sandalled foot against the other, curious and shy.

'You're up late, Louis,' said Kit, in his perfect French.

'Ask him if he's got an older sister,' Goofy said.

'What did he say?' asked the boy.

'He says we are very comfortable here as your guests.' Kit looked at Goofy with narrowed eyes.

The boy was pleased. '*Un plaisir, Messieurs,*' he said, quaintly formal. He scanned the curious faces. 'Do you know, perhaps, of Capitaine Guynemer?'

'Of course,' said Kit. 'The French ace of aces.'

'When he disappeared in 1917 he had fifty-three victories to his name. Imagine! Do you also have an ace among you?'

Kit grinned and pointed at Ossie. '*Lui, peut-être. Il est un aviateur américain – il a descendu onze Boches.*'

'Onze!' said the boy, nodding. 'Très bien.' Then he added: 'But fifty-three . . .'

'There are certainly no bloody Guynemers this time round,' said Brown. 'You tell him that.'

'What did he say?' asked the boy, again.

Kit led him back into the courtyard. 'Show me the model tank you told me about.' Instantly the boy raced for the house, waving to him to follow, leaping up the stairs two at a time. Madame Garencières appeared at the door of the salon. She held a leather-bound book in her left hand, a cigarette in her right. Her hair was pulled straight back and gathered in a bun like a Degas dancer's. She smiled at her son's excitement but there was sadness in her eyes.

Kit climbed the stairs after the boy, two flights, and found himself in an attic, big and airy and unfurnished, except for a large plain table standing in the middle of the floor and deep wooden shelves running along one wall. The shelves were laden with a jumble of old books, battered toys and long-forgotten games in musty cardboard boxes, unfashionable china, hat-boxes and spelter figures with missing limbs, everything grey under a film of dust. The windows were barred. The boy was by the shelves, cradling a model of a French Char B tank in his arms. It was not roughly fashioned from wood, as Kit had expected, but finely crafted in metal, a perfect replica with working tracks and an opening hatch on the mono-seated turret. 'Papa made it in his workshop,' said Louis. He offered it to Kit. 'He has a workshop in the stables. I help him sometimes.'

'It's wonderful,' said Kit.

'Yes,' said Louis. 'I hope . . .' His shoulders began to shake. He smeared tears angrily from his cheeks and drew the back of his hand across his nose, sniffing loudly. Kit replaced the model tank on the shelf and moved over to the table. A miniature Grande Armée was drawn up in battle order, gloriously uniformed, regimental standards flying beside the tricolour; cuirassiers, dragoons, lancers and hussars mounted on spirited chargers, artillerymen poised for action with their light pieces and *caissons*, grenadiers of the Guard with big moustaches, bearing imperial eagles. And at the head of the colourful host the emperor, sitting on the grey-white haunches of his little Arab thoroughbred, Marengo, surrounded by his marshals, haughty under cocked hats dripping with gold braid. 'My grandfather's,' said Louis. 'Not for play. Just to look at.' Suddenly he was screwing up his face, trying not to cry again. 'That is all they are good for,' he said fiercely. 'Just to look at.'

Kit knew there was nothing to say. He put his arm round the boy's thin shoulders as Louis stifled sobs.

Downstairs he said quietly to Madame Garencières: 'I think he is ready, Madame.'

'Ready?'

'He may know already in his heart. He has strength, your son. Perhaps more than you think. Perhaps it is time to share your grief.'

'Ah, *oui*, my grief,' said Madame Garencières. 'Poor Louis. Now he will learn the price of glory.'

Twenty-seven

Monday, 27 May 1940

Hannah looked child-like, Bébé thought, as she bent over the green leather writing-desk, her head tilted, hair pushed back behind her right ear. She wrote slowly, with great care, reading through each sentence and mouthing the words before she set pen to paper. From time to time she glanced up and gave Bébé such a joyous smile, her eyes shining, that Bébé had to laugh to herself. She marvelled that she could excite such adoration and such misery in others when she felt so little herself. Once she had been curious about why this should be so but finally she had come to see it as a strength, a weapon, even.

When Hannah had finished writing she pressed the two small pages from her notepad on to the blotter and passed them to Bébé.

My dearest Papa,

I address this to you alone for obvious reasons. You see, I do heed your advice. As I explained on the telephone I am making arrangements to go to England, just as you told me to. Now you must obey me! Please, please, I beg you, do the same. Paris is ravaged with frightful rumours. No business is worth the risk, Papa. We would find protection in England, I am sure. You must make Maman understand that too. I know she finds it hard to believe ill of anyone, even the new Germany, but the horrors are real,

I assure you. I am certain that the Curtises would help us until we can find a place of our own. I talked of this to Kit when he was here and he said they would make us welcome. I have sent them a letter also, alerting them to the possibility but of course there is not the slightest hope of a reply as things are. Anyway, that is where I expect to be when, as I implore you to, you make the journey to England yourselves. Thank you in advance for transferring some money to the bank in London. The amount you mentioned is far more than I could ever need but it will help me get settled until you arrive. Papa, it will be difficult for me to write to you while I am en route but I will be in touch again as soon as I land in England. The journey is not without its difficulties as you can imagine – and grows more difficult by the day – so you must not be anxious if you do not hear from me for a while. Now please, Papa, I beg you a final time, heed my words as I heeded yours. Please follow me to England. I pray that we may all be united very soon,

Your loving daughter,
Hannah.

'Well?' said Hannah, anxiously.

'It is perfect,' said Bébé

'I ached so to tell him of you,' said Hannah.

'No, *mignonne*,' said Bébé. 'Your father sees me as a harmful influence – why worry him further when he has anxieties enough? It is better he thinks of me safely in Rennes, as you told him on the telephone. Besides, what if he had cause to talk to Sauval, who also believes me there?'

'How kind you are, how thoughtful. If only Papa knew you better . . .'

'Yes,' said Bébé, 'if only.'

Hannah folded her letter, slipped it into an envelope, moistened a stamp and adjusted its position until it was precisely square. 'How long, do you think, before it is safe to apply for your exit papers, *chérie*?'

'Tomorrow I will go to the offices of Jabesco, Rougerie et Bouy and throw myself on their mercy. I do not expect the Americans to delay in coming to terms and favourable ones at that. They are greedy for what they think is theirs.'

'They are despicable,' cried Hannah, hotly. 'It is so unjust.' She folded Bébé in her arms. 'It is too much, your sacrifice. I cannot bear it. Perhaps I should go alone, after all. How can I expect this of you?'

'No,' said Bébé, quickly. 'It must be as we arranged. My mind is made up. Tonight, when it is dark, we will take the air by the Seine and talk of our new life together. It seems I have spent an eternity in this luxurious prison.' She gave Hannah a fleeting kiss on the cheek. 'How sick I am of France and the stench of defeat.'

'What if we are seen together?' said Hannah.

Bébé smiled. 'Don't concern yourself. Sauval will be deep in his cups soon enough. And for lovers the blackout is a most discreet friend. Anyway, my pet, tomorrow everything will be as it should be.'

That morning, when Bébé had told Hannah of her change of heart, Hannah had been ecstatic. 'How wonderful! But are you sure? It is so much to ask. What swayed you? You seemed so firm.'

'There is only one course open to me,' said Bébé. 'There is bound to be a price.'

That afternoon Hannah, as excited as if she were on the threshold of a holiday, hurried to the nearby rue de Ponthieu to buy what she needed to concoct an authentic quiche Lorraine, a favourite of her family. 'Really, I am too happy for food,' she said, 'but we cannot let this evening pass without a little celebration.' When she had gone Bébé seated herself at the leather-topped desk and wrote a rather shorter letter.

Maman,

I am sorry but this seems my only escape. Life has become a great deal too complicated. I am dreadfully fatigued by it all and with things as they are I see only misery and pain ahead. You may be surprised that I have chosen this course but you will acknowledge that I was always a realist. This seems to be a logical conclusion to an existence that no longer gives me pleasure. And you know that I have always been ruled by pleasure,

Anna.

She took a small envelope from the rack, folded the note, licked the flap and stuck it down. But she did not apply a stamp. Instead she scrawled, as though in some distress, 'For the attention of Countess Sofia P. Dubretskov' and slipped the envelope into the pocket of her coat.

Bébé found the preparations for the quiche maddening. It seemed that Hannah had been making the accursed thing for hours, rolling the pastry that lay on the kitchen surface like a giant white maggot, beating the eggs. The slam of the oven door jarred her ears painfully.

Hannah insisted that the quiche should be allowed to cool a little but finally they sat down to eat. The aroma was not unpleasant and Bébé forced herself to swallow a little, sipping Gewürztraminer from a green glass. Hannah had lit candles for the occasion and the room was bathed in their flickering light. But she only toyed with the meal she had worked so hard to produce. Half of the quiche remained untouched. 'Perhaps for tomorrow,' said Hannah. 'I think I prefer it cold.'

'Yes,' said Bébé, 'tomorrow.'

The shadows deepened across the great courtyard. A yellow light showed briefly in Sauval's office before he closed his shutters. Bébé glanced at her watch. It seemed as though time refused to pass. Hannah came in from the kitchen, her face rosy from the heat. She snuggled close to Bébé, her thin fingers pressing into her arm. Bébé wanted to shake her off. She stood up quickly. 'Coffee?'

'No.'

'I think I will.' She passed into the kitchen. Everything had been cleared away. It was as though Hannah had never been there. She took her tiny coffee cup back into the salon and sat down in another chair.

'So,' said Hannah, as she often did when she could think of nothing to say. She was sprawled awkwardly on the settle and patted the cushion beside her, wanting Bébé to join her.

'So,' said Bébé, not moving.

'I have never understood . . .' Hannah faltered. 'Believe me, I am not jealous, but I have never understood about your little American.'

'He was not so little,' said Bébé. Her lips twisted coarsely, but she was quick to hide it and Hannah did not notice.

'No, taller than you, of course. But . . .'

'Oh,' said Bébé, tiredly, 'you know I have never been entirely *comme ci, comme ça*. I retain an interest, you might say. And with the Drôle de Guerre, the streets of Paris were suddenly busy with a species of man I had never met before, didn't dream existed – men with purpose and energy, almost a brutality, about them. It was intriguing. And death was at their shoulder, counting down the hours. The American was such a man, sure of himself and of what he wanted. He was crude, uncultured and persistent. For a little while I found it amusing. It suited my mood.' Then she added quickly, softly: 'Remember, *mignonne*, I was alone. Una had left me for her family.' She made it sound as though she had been abandoned. She sighed, as if reflecting sentimentally on her fleeting *amour* with Ossie Wolf. 'It was a stimulating enough experience until . . .'

'Until?'

'Until the very things that had interested me repelled me. It is often so.' Bébé caught a momentary shadow of doubt on

Hannah's face and hurried on: 'But then, of course, you and I met and everything became clear.' A diversion was called for. Bébé gave a little laugh. 'But how can we talk of my pugnacious barbarian when you have been courted by a gallant English milord since a child?'

Hannah brushed aside the tease. 'It's true Kit is part of me. To lose him would be unbearable. Perhaps he is lost already. But I believe I would know. Something would tell me. He is alive, I am sure of it. I will write to him and tell him all our news. The British Embassy will find him for me. Yes, that is what I will do.'

'Later, then,' said Bébé. 'It is growing dark. Soon it will be time for our promenade. If things work out as expected there will not be many more occasions when we can stroll together by the Seine.'

Bébé compelled herself to wait until almost midnight when she knew the boulevards, *jardins* and *quais* would be quiet, submerged in the darkness that many had come to hate. During the day the citizens could escape into the illusion of normality, familiar Paris seeming to endure as it always had done. But at night the city became another place, heavy with unseen dangers, real ones but petty by comparison with what advanced towards it over the mutilated fields of France. Indeed, it seemed to Bébé, when she reflected on this, that what she was about to do was such a little thing . . .

They prepared themselves for their promenade. Bébé pulled on Hannah's long black coat and beret. 'I love your clothes,' she said. 'You have quite changed my taste.' She gathered the coat round her, the deep collar framing her pale oval face. 'I almost feel . . .'

'Feel what, *chérie*?' said Hannah, her voice trembling a little.

'As though I am wearing your skin,' said Bébé. 'You wear mine.' She held up her favourite coat, double-breasted and severely cut, almost masculine; Una Westcott had pressed it upon her in the rue Cambon establishment of Madame Chanel.

402

Hannah wriggled into it and adopted poses like a mannequin, looking coyly over her shoulder, her eyes huge. Bébé laughed. 'Your *carte d'identité*, Mademoiselle Hollywood,' she said, and tucked the card into a small inside pocket of the coat. Her fingertips touched the envelope already there. She secured the flap of the pocket with its tiny ivory button and kissed the tip of Hannah's nose. 'Are you ready for our adventure?'

'Yes,' said Hannah. 'And just think, *chérie*, it is only just beginning.'

They left the apartment separately, slipping past the silent office of the concierge without a sound, and met at an appointed corner of the Boissy Danglas. At first the city seemed as pitch-dark as the inside of a cave but gradually their eyes became accustomed to it. A few motor-vehicles squealed round the place de la Concorde, their cast-down headlamps dim and blue, the faces of the drivers caught in the glow from their instrument panels.

The women did not encounter a soul on foot. As they expected, the gates to the Tuileries were chained and locked. They walked down the broad marble steps to the quai des Tuileries arm in arm. There was traffic here, too, but sparse and widely spaced, moving slowly, wary of the hazards of negotiating the streets by night. As far as Bébé could tell, no one took the slightest notice of the two indistinct figures moving slowly towards the river. They had passed the Pont du Carousel now. Bébé wondered what Hannah was thinking but did not care to know. It was no longer relevant. Their feet scuffed on the fine stones of the gravel pathway. The river was very close here, a black expanse, a void more sensed than seen, the water moving fast and splashing, gurgling along the edge of the sloping *quai*. At the beginning of the quai du Louvre, beyond the arches of the Pont des Art, the bulk of the Île de la Cité loomed like some huge, crouching beast. Bébé's heart beat rapidly. Her mouth went dry. To her surprise she thought her legs might fail her.

She stopped and so did Hannah. She turned, her eyebrows arched and questioning, smiling in the darkness, standing between Bébé and the river, angling her head for a kiss. Bébé touched her lips with hers, her hands light upon her shoulders. She was conscious of a rushing sound and thought it was the river but it was the pulsing of her blood because she knew it had to be now. It was the slightest of movements, as though she was simply straightening her arms. For a moment Hannah swayed, her arms rotating backwards as she struggled to stay upright. Her mouth was open in a silent scream. She stared at Bébé, horrified, unable to believe what she saw. For a moment she steadied. Bébé stepped forward quickly and this time there was no mistake. The palm of her firm, cold hand pushed hard on Hannah's forehead and then she was gone.

After a few feeble strokes Hannah felt the weight of her beautiful coat bear her down. The cold water closed over her face. Through the faint shimmer of the surface, as the last few bubbles escaped from her mouth and water filled her lungs, she saw a solitary figure standing motionless on the *quai*. She thought her chest would explode, then heard a distant voice: 'Sorrow . . . you will be released from sorrow by the Great Mother who makes all things joyous by the subtle pressures of the water.' But there was no release from sorrow. She felt her senses slipping away. She could not remember who she was or why, how she had come to this awful place. The water pressed down. All that remained of her now, beyond the agony of physical pain, was sorrow because another being had never loved her, after all . . .

Bébé watched for any sign of movement on the surface of the river. The girl had not even cried out. She would have been wise to let Kit Curtis teach her to swim as a child, Bébé reflected. But, then, even a strong swimmer could not last long in such a current. She could still taste Hannah's saliva on her lips, feel the grease on the palm of her hand where she had thrust at her forehead. She remembered her eyes. A pity that. So much better if she had gone at once, believing it was an accident, believing Bébé had loved her. She deserved that much, poor little goose . . .

Twenty-eight

Thursday, 6 June 1940

In the space of twelve days the Hurricanes at Boulay-sur-Sarthe had become a familiar sight in the skies of Brittany, sweeping along the Atlantic coast from Brest to La Rochelle and, to the north, over the Channel ports of Roscoff, Dinard, Cherbourg and Le Havre. The nine remaining aircraft had been grouped again into flights. Brewster had been compelled to switch tactics once more, waking each morning to skies without a trace of cloud cover.

When A Flight, now four-strong, was not on convoy patrol Ossie would take to the air with his increasingly unkempt trio of pilots and practise dog-fights, hurtling about the sky in pursuit of the target plane, sometimes Dickie Challoner, Plum Duff or Hangdog Collins, most often Ossie himself, seeming to read the minds of his pursuers and wriggling out of harm's way, leaving them chasing thin air. When Ossie was an attacker the others found themselves dispatched with the ruthless efficiency of a terrier snapping the neck of a rabbit.

B Flight also practised, nerve-jangling close-formation aerobatics drawn from Kit's Hendon air show routines and by-the-book attacks devised by Fighter Command that, on the page at least, still seemed solid sense.

Either way the pilots built their confidence and skill through effortless, instinctive control of their aircraft. The bold displays of airmanship were popular with the locals: eyes grew brighter, voices stronger – something, at least, was being done. And Louis Garencières, who had accepted his father's death without a word, taking himself to a secret place by the river to exorcise his grief, watched the Hurricanes at every opportunity, identifying the pilots with whom he spent his evenings, practising his English until he was packed off to bed.

No large enemy formations had been encountered, no further losses suffered since the end of May. Four unescorted Heinkels preparing to drop aerial mines on the approaches to Le Havre had been swiftly dealt with, two going down in flames, two more scuttling for home, their bomb doors still closed. A *Schwarm* of four Messerschmitt-110s had turned away from B Flight, lacking the advantage of height and the inclination for a scrap that might cost them a crew or two at this stage of the campaign. And Chris Lloyd, swiftly dubbed Tigger, had forced down a Junkers Ju-52 to the north-east of Lisieux. The tri-motor transport, unnervingly familiar as an airliner in a dozen countries, had absorbed repeated strikes on its corrugated duralumin fuselage, then waggled its wings as a sign of surrender, dropping towards an expanse of open farmland near the junction of the rivers Touques and Orbiquet. Tigger Lloyd, flustered by the helplessness of the unarmed machine, followed it down. It made two attempts to land, as though the pilot was experiencing some difficulty at the controls. On the third approach, the Junkers' undercarriage snagged the upper branches of a row of poplars and it struck the ground nose first, distributing itself over a wide area.

Back at Boulay Lloyd had been subdued and thoughtful until a French infantry battalion reported that, as well as the remains of the flight crew, they had discovered four German corpses in the wreckage dressed in the uniforms of *poilus*, each man strapped into a parachute and carrying false papers. No one was surprised.

The telephone line to Wing at Troyes repeatedly went dead. A priest had been seen near the perimeter fence watching the squadron through binoculars and had been driven away at high speed in a Citroën Avant. Several pilots reported picking up morse code signals on their R/T channel as they took off. A guard was mounted at night, the nervous airmen patrolling the perimeter, fingers twitchy on the triggers of loaded Lee-Enfields, bayonets fixed, starting at every night sound.

Brewster was summoned to Wing and, to his delight, Kit was given temporary command. But the CO was back within hours, leaping from the wing of his Hurricane and instructing him to assemble the squadron. The men gathered round as Brewster mounted a couple of empty ammunition boxes. He glowered down at them, hands on his hips, unlit pipe jutting fiercely. 'I am bound to tell you that, as of today, the British Expeditionary Force in France has virtually ceased to exist. Three hundred and forty thousand men have been successfully evacuated from Dunkirk, a quarter of a million of them our own troops, the rest French. At least thirty thousand of our own chaps have been abandoned in the rearguard, forty thousand French captured. No one knows why the Germans failed to consolidate their advantage and allowed the evacuation to take place on such a scale. That does not concern us. What matters is, they did. I understand that it has been described by our prime minister as a miracle of deliverance. But he also warned against regarding this as a victory, that wars are not won by evacuation. Hitler is now free to advance on Paris. Already, a few days ago, the city experienced its first air-raid. Apparently the French Army is organising a new front behind the Somme. No one seems to have any hope that it will succeed.' He took a deep breath. 'If intelligence is to be believed we can expect a brief respite. First Paris must be taken and the German forces are weary. So what does this mean to us? It's very simple. We are no longer hunters but defenders. Clearly we can expect significant evacuations from all the major ports remaining to the Allies in the north-west. Our job is to make sure that they take place with the minimum interference. We cannot anticipate what the Luftwaffe's next move might be.

It's likely they'll attempt to blockade the ports, aerial-mine the harbour mouths, sink shipping at harbour entrances, strafe and bomb those waiting to embark. Without our cover a lot of people, including women and children, are going to die. That's what we're here to prevent and that, in turn, means preserving ourselves and our aircraft. No mixing it, unless those under our protection are at risk. In the short-term, this objective may be more achievable than it sounds. The Hun seem a touch reluctant to lose any more machines, now they reckon they've won this thing. Also, I suppose it's just possible that the efforts of chaps like you have properly put the wind up the buggers. Long may it continue. Any questions?' There were none and the men dispersed.

Later Flight Sergeant Jessop approached him looking uncomfortable. 'What provisions should I make about my blokes, sir, if we have to pull out?'

'Don't you worry about that Chief,' barked Brewster. 'We'll sort it out when the time comes. For now your priority is to keep our ruddy kites in the air.'

Brewster had returned from Troyes with a handful of letters that had somehow arrived on a desk at Wing. One was for Kit. Posted ten days earlier it was from Maurice Maierscheldt, giving him good news about Hannah. He had spoken to his daughter on the telephone and at last she had agreed to go to England. He did not understand this change of heart. She had seemed so set against it. He had been convinced that she was being influenced in some way by her questionable acquaintance with the ridiculous name. But it seemed he was wrong for now this Bébé person had gone to Rennes. It was a great relief. As for himself and Karoline, they would make their decision in due course.

If we go away from here we know it will mean giving up everything. But at least Hannah is one anxiety less. I know she can turn to your parents for any support she might need, my dear Kit. That is a great comfort. She will, of course, be well provided for financially (I have made the necessary arrangements with a bank in London) so there need be no concern on that score. Nancy is full of rumours. It is said that our armies have been pushed into the sea at Dunkirk, that Belgium has capitulated. What times we live in. Karoline is considerably cast down by it all. There never was a better woman but she finds it hard to come to terms with the madness that confronts us on every side. She only derives contentment from reflecting on the past, on happier times. Who knows how this dreadful business will end? When you visited us in December I was guilty of many foolish remarks. I had not grasped the enormity of what was about to overwhelm us. I know you will forgive me. So, dear Kit, may this find you safe and well and may God protect you and your gallant comrades.

Kit folded the letter. He, too, felt relieved that Hannah had done the sensible thing. But there remained doubt: Bébé Dubretskov had given up so easily. In Paris he had sensed a deeper purpose in her relationship with Hannah. He recalled his distrust of her, the hint of something distasteful and corrupt. And what possible connection could she have with Rennes, that dingy granite city of the *département* Ille-et-Vilaine with its timber-yards, tanning works and textile factories? She seemed to him the essence of Paris: elegant, worldly and, quite possibly, dangerous. He could not picture her in the surroundings of a provincial backwater. He tried to stop thinking about her, and eased himself back in the rickety deck-chair he had placed in the shadow of his Hurricane wing. Somewhere, far away, he could hear the grumble of gunfire. It never paused.

Ossie Wolf came over, fresh from an uneventful patrol, still in his flying gear. His leather helmet had incised a deep crease across his forehead. His eyes were red, as though he had spent a hard night on the town, and his chin was black with two days' stubble. Kit caught the sour smell of his sweat.

'Hey, letters from home?'

'The Maierscheldts.' He squinted up at Ossie, the sun in his eyes. 'Hannah's getting out.'

'England? That's swell.' Ossie thought about it. Kit could see him framing the next inevitable question. 'Bébé too?'

'No. Apparently she's gone to Rennes.'

'Rennes? Where the hell's Rennes?'

'She never mentioned Rennes to you?'

'Never heard of the goddammed place.'

'Well,' said Kit, 'that's where she's gone. Apparently.' He looked at his watch. 'I'm on at fifteen hundred. Need to rustle up the chaps. Have any fun?'

'Zilch,' said Ossie. 'Brewster's right. The Hun don't seem to want to come out to play.'

B Flight found the same. From Cherbourg the creamy wakes of many vessels curved away north, like vapour trails in the sea, on course for Poole, Southampton, Portsmouth. The Cap de la Hague was washed with gentle breakers, green and white and all shades of blue, with spread-winged gulls moving effortlessly on infant thermals. Off the Pointe de Barfleur people were even bathing.

When Kit set off down the lane from the airfield to the house of Madame Garencières the square tower of the church of Boulay-sur-Sarthe, set on a slight rise in the ground a quarter of a mile away, was silhouetted against the darkening sky by the rays of the dying sun. In the valley grey mist was gathering over the waters of the Sarthe. The house stood square and solid, cut into the gentle slope. The lower part of its garden was partly obscured, the outlines of shrubs and trees, a summer-house and an ornate urn standing out against the rising vapour. Kit thought that one day he would like to own such a place.

He walked on slowly down the lane towards the big iron gates, savouring the characteristic heavy silence of rural France, the aroma of earth, grass and growing things, the stench of fox, horse and farmyard beasts; the sound of his feet pressing into mud and stones, flicking up water from the puddles. And yet it wasn't truly silent: still there came the far-off rumble of artillery and nearer, on a farm across the valley, a chained-up dog barked.

As he came closer to the house, he heard shouts and laughter, the bellow of a powerful engine, the revs rising and falling as someone pumped a throttle. In the courtyard a throng of pilots was gathered round a handsome boat-backed sports car, its French blue bodywork tapering back from an oval honey-combed radiator. Cycle-type mudguards, front and back, also blue, followed the line of the tall, thin wheels. There were tracks in the damp gravel, leading from one of the stable-block stalls where the doors stood open. Crouched behind the big four-spoke steering-wheel Buster Brown was staring intently at the array of instruments on the brushed aluminium fascia. 'I think we may be in business,' he yelled, to no one in particular. Louis Garencières was leaping up and down on the back seat, his hands pounding Buster's shoulders.

Buster saw Kit. 'Type 43,' he shouted, 'and jolly nice too. One of Ettore's finest. Fancy a spin? I've promised young Louis a lap of Le Mans. At least, I think that's what I promised him. Bit shaky with the old lingo. Could do with a translator along.'

'Are you off your rocker?' said Kit. 'His mother will hit the roof.'

'She's all for it. One mention of the Vingt Quatre Heures and she unlocked this beauty in a trice. Never used in anger, apparently, but her hubby's pride and joy. Thinks it's just the ticket to take the lad's mind off things.'

'That much is true,' said Kit. 'Riding with you concentrates the mind wonderfully. Is Madame aware that you're a madman behind the wheel?'

'She's about to find out old boy. She's coming with us.'

Louis sat up front with Buster, his left arm stretched along the

412

top of the door. On the corners he leant over, racing-driver style. Stones rattled against the insides of the Bugatti's mudguards as Brown drifted the corners on the loose surface. As he accelerated away hard the supercharger cut in with a banshee wail.

In the back Kit was thrown against Madame Garencières, who made no effort to pull back from his weight. She had found a linen helmet and the metal buckle was firm beneath her small rounded chin. Her dark eyes gleamed behind light chrome-and-rubber goggles. As they approached the roads that, once a year, comprised the racing circuit, Kit translated Buster's racing exploits into French and she laughed. She did not strike him as a grieving widow.

It was dark now, the big Cibié headlamps wobbling on their struts, the yellow beams stretching far ahead down the road between the twin lines of poplars. The heat from the engine wafted back, rich with the stench of oil and petrol. The noise from the exhaust was pain and joy. 'Never has this motor-car been driven in such a way,' cried Madame Garencières. 'I would not have believed it possible.'

They negotiated the darkened streets of Mulsanne with the Bugatti held to a deep-throated burble, then emerged on to the circuit at Mulsanne Corner. Immediately Buster thrust the throttle pedal to the floor, only lifting momentarily as his left foot dipped the clutch and he snicked another, higher gear. Each time the needle of the rev counter tipped the red zone, then sank back, the Bugatti surging forward, the power from the 2.3-litre straight-eight spinning its rear wheels under acceleration.

They approached the S-bend at Arnage at seemingly impossible speed, the car writhing this way and that, like a thoroughbred wanting its head, Buster feeding countless corrections through the wheel. He was hard on the brakes now, throwing them all forward, using heel-and-toe to maintain firm pressure on the brake pedal as he rolled his foot to blip the throttle and, with his left, stabbing the clutch as he went smoothly down through the gears.

Then they were clear, throttle open, the pale road streaming beneath them, lifting only slightly for the turn and the bump at Maison Blanche where, in '27, the Bentleys crashed. The fastest lorries in the world, according to the French, but still they won. Now the Bugatti was flying between the deserted grandstands and the pits, and Louis waved to an invisible crowd.

More hard braking, almost down to walking pace, squealing round the Pontlieu hairpin, then hard acceleration again, leaping over the crest of the rise before the Mulsanne straight, squashing down on to the shock absorbers as they thumped into the little dip that had caught out Perrigini in '35, then diving downhill to the straight beyond, four miles at full throttle until Mulsanne Corner and another lap. Buster took them round twice more, then eased off the road at La Rochère, just north of Mulsanne village, and quietly on to the lanes. He called over his shoulder: 'Perhaps next time we'll try it at racing speeds. You can't take chances in the dark.'

Close to midnight Brewster, still at his desk, received a telephone call. He learned that he could have saved himself a hazardous flight to Troyes. 'Wing are on the move again Spy,' he called.

'Fidgety types aren't they sir?' said Turner. 'Where to now?'

'Le Mans.'

Twenty-nine

Friday, 7 June 1940

It began with a low-level raid on targets of opportunity in Le Havre by two shark-mouthed Messerschmitt-110s. The twin-engined fighters, their under-noses decorated fancifully with large white teeth against a scarlet background, came in from the sea, strafing shipping, vehicles on the road, military positions and the complex tangle of railway lines linking the port to the rest of France. Minutes into the attack trucks and cars were blazing along the main routes into the city, stricken locomotives were expiring in the sidings in clouds of scalding steam and, near the Bassin Vauban, a gasometer erupted in an immense ball of flame that rolled upwards into the sky, like a miniature sun. It was this that caught the attention of B Flight, patrolling near Caen, fifty kilometres to the west. Instantly, Kit swung them on to a north-easterly course towards the port.

The skies above Le Havre were alive with anti-aircraft fire, from ship and shore, as the 110s continued their assault at little more than five hundred feet above the smoke-cloaked scenes of chaos and confusion.

On the point of the quai des Remorqueurs, where in peacetime the big Atlantic liners moved slowly towards their berths, the French three-man crew of a 25mm Hotchkiss *contre-aeroneufs* was struggling with the elevation and traverse of their weapon, unable to track the agile fighters skimming over their heads. They had wasted five hundred rounds already and now the loader slammed another fifteen-round box-magazine into its slot as the gunner, leaning back a little on his metal seat, waited for a fresh target to appear. He was no longer concerned with the niceties of the cannon's stereoscopic rangefinder and tachymetric projector, or even the gun-sight itself. He sat impatiently, aching with tension, ready to open fire with as little finesse or science as a gun at a pheasant shoot.

Towards the railway station, a quarter of a mile away, the artillerymen could see 110s banking round for another pass. At the same moment a third machine appeared to their right, a little higher, partly obscured by columns of black smoke. The loader screamed: '*Allons! Là, là!*' The Hotchkiss opened fire.

The high-velocity bullets ripped from the muzzle of the cannon covering the thousand-foot distance to the target in less than half a second. They flicked through the steel, light alloy and fabric of the aircraft's fuselage and pierced the reserve fuel tank between the engine and the cockpit, just ahead of the instrument panel. Instantly 240 gallons of aviation fuel exploded, the flames streaming back, fanned to white heat by the speed of the machine through the air. Engine bellowing, it pulled up into a steep climb. In the cockpit the pilot, ungloved, his goggles resting on his forehead, was submerged in fire, as though sitting in the heart of a furnace. His hands, one on the throttle lever, the other on the control column, shrivelled, blackened and cracked. The exposed skin on his face, around his eyes and upper cheeks, blistered and melted. The oxygen mask covering his nose and mouth was folding inwards, deforming, the molten rubber dripping on to his chest. The aircraft was climbing almost vertically now.

At the heart of the inferno the pilot was still a rational human being. He knew that his canopy was open; that should help. He released his R/T cable and disconnected the oxygen tube. The fire was consuming natural oxygen and without it he found himself unable to breathe. At last his senses began to fade. His hand, more like a claw, groped for the release pin securing the

Sutton harness. At the second attempt it came free. He tried to stand up, to drag himself out of the cockpit but the air pressure forced him back. He sank down, moving slowly on the glowing seat, and then the machine pivoted at the top of its steep, fast climb, stalling and rolling on to its back. He fell clear as it nosed into a spin. He was falling, the air rushing cool around his body. He tried to look down but his sight was obscured by jutting flesh round his eyes. He felt for the ripcord of his parachute, his raw fingertips touching the chromium ring tantalisingly just beyond his reach. Each time the metal touched his flesh a shock of pain ran through him. He caught it at last and screamed as he pulled at it hard. The silk canopy streamed out and opened above him with a crack. He swung lazily from side to side, rotating, then dipped into the sea close to a British navy frigate lying off the harbour mouth.

'Christ!' Goofy Gates had shouted over the R/T, as the contorted figure tumbled down from the blazing Hurricane. 'It's Buster.' He dived down on the Hotchkiss crew, his thumb trembling on his gun-button. 'You stupid bastards, you stupid, trigger-happy bastards.'

The Frenchmen did not fire. They had seen the roundels on the flanks of Buster's machine before the flames consumed them. They stood by their gun position staring upwards. One man, the gunner, extended his arms, powerless to do more than try to express remorse. The shark-mouthed 110s had vanished east unscathed, the *Oberleutnant* pilots shouting congratulations to each other over their radios.

That evening Louis Garencières came running from the house. The doors of the garage stood open. He was hoping for another spin in the Bugatti. Kit went back into the house with him. The child was puzzled by Kit's silence. The night was cold and Madame Garencières was sitting by the big open fireplace where a single hefty log was burning fitfully on a bed of white ash. At

417

first they did not understand when Kit told them that Buster would not be joining them again.

'But he is all right?' said Madame Garencières. 'I mean, alive?'

'Oh yes, he's alive,' said Kit. He knew what he wanted to add but could not bring himself to say it.

'Perhaps . . .' began Madame Garencières.

'For Christ's sake,' he shouted, in English, 'drop it, can't you? He won't be coming back. I wanted you to know.'

The boy was crying now and holding on to his mother. Horrified, Kit realised that he was crying too. He turned away. Madame Garencières was standing by him, one arm round her son's shoulders. She raised her other hand and turned Kit's face to hers. She was very small, her face tilted back, lips parted. She wiped away his tears and stroked his cheek.

'Stupid,' he murmured. 'Stupid, stupid, stupid.' He did not know what he meant. He recovered himself, conscious that the boy was watching him, sobbing. On its mound of ash the big log moved suddenly and a spurt of flame shot up. Curtis stepped away, unwilling to feel its warmth. Madame Garencières was at his side again. He felt a glass of brandy pressed into his hand. He sat down on the edge of a button-backed armchair, cradling the glass in his fingers. The alcohol burned down his throat and seemed to explode in his stomach.

Madame Garencières was sitting nearby, silent, her dark eyes full of pity. He did not want pity. Instantly he was angry. He stood up and his sleeve caught a silver-framed photograph on a walnut chess table. He bent to pick it up. It showed a sturdy French officer in pale breeches and black riding boots with spurs. A long scarf was wound round his neck, the ends coming forward over his tunic and pinned under a leather belt. A kepi was set at a rakish angle over his right eye and he held a cigarette tilted just so in a gloved hand. He was smiling the smile of the dashing cavalier. Kit thought he looked uncommonly stupid, a clown who wore spurs to drive a tank. He replaced the frame on the table. The brandy had not been a good idea.

'My husband,' said a soft voice at his elbow.

'Yes,' said Kit. He looked at the picture again. The man looked fifty at least. He did not like the thought of Madame Garencières with this posing booby. He realised, with a shock, that he was a little in love with her. He said goodnight with excessive formality.

Back in the barn, half-way down the untidy scatter of records next to the wind-up gramophone, he found what he was looking for. He did not have to listen to it to remember how it went. He did not want to hear it again, but the melody swam through his brain.

> Sur les quais du vieux Paris
> Le long de la Seine
> Le bonheur sourit
> Sur les quais du vieux Paris . . .

He took the record out into the darkness, along a path leading to the river, and smashed it against a wall. He regretted it immediately. Weakness again, loss of control. Damn it, he was cracking up. He picked up all the broken pieces of the record that he could find in the dark, took them back to the barn and slipped them into his kit-bag.

Thirty

Sunday, 9 June 1940

They sat outside Gruber's in the place de la République like reflective and detached old men. They had come to watch the crowds, to be absorbed in something close to normality, but there were no crowds and the atmosphere was far from normal. Le Mans seemed gripped by dread and people hurried past, their faces grey with anxiety.

Still, the four pilots savoured the pleasant early-evening feeling that follows a hot day. Cooking smells wafted out of the café behind them, mingling with the acrid aroma of cheap French cigarettes and a whiff of drains. They had drunk little. Their first round of ice-cold Nantaise beer stood almost untouched on the zinc table. Parked close by, so it would not obscure their view of the square, stood the Type 43. It had been hard to say no to Louis Garencières, who had wanted to come along, but it was possible they might want to go on somewhere later, although this seemed unlikely.

The boy had stood at the front door of the big house and waved them goodbye. Behind him his mother had folded her arms across his chest. Kit had very much needed her to look at him in a particular way, and when she did he experienced an odd sensation in his stomach, almost but not quite like hunger. They could have arranged to be taken the short distance to Le Mans in the buckboard but when Madame Garencières heard that Brewster had allowed a few of them a brief interlude before something big the next morning she had been insistent that they should take the Bugatti. It was mud-splashed and used-looking, just as Buster had returned it to its garage three days earlier. Kit fancied he could still make out the smudged prints of his friend's big hands on the wooden rim of the steering-wheel. He had driven them into the centre of the city himself, slowly. It was fine with the others. They knew what the car was capable of. That was enough.

Now, at the table outside Gruber's, Ossie Wolf chewed the end of a match, legs stuck out straight, hands in his pockets. Goofy Gates leaned forward, elbows on his knees, eyeing the occasional passing girl. And Peter Duff, the sardonic Plum, quietly sketched the old monastic walls of the Palais de Justice on the west side of the square, his stubby pencil running quickly over the cream pages of his notebook. These men looked harmless enough, thought Kit, but, as with the Type 43, he knew what they were capable of.

An old man came by with an armful of roses gathered into bunches, red, white and the palest yellow.

'*Bonsoir, Monsieur*,' he said to Goofy. '*Des fleurs pour votre fille?*'

'Eh?' said Goofy. Kit translated. 'Tell him I haven't got a girl,' said Goofy, 'yet.'

The old man spread out the roses on the table with pride. Kit imagined him on his small plot of land, selecting the choicest blooms, snipping the long green stems with care. The rose-grower was glancing hopefully from face to face. '*Des fleurs pour une belle fille?*'

'How much?' said Goofy.

'*Dix Gitanes*,' said the old man.

'Why not?' said Goofy, reaching into his tunic for a packet of cigarettes. 'Might soften up some crumpet.'

'The last of the romantics,' said Duff.

'There's only one guy here who can use a bunch of goddammed roses,' said Ossie. He grinned across the table at

Kit, picking up his beer. Kit felt himself flush. He pretended not to understand. He asked the old man if he had grown the roses himself. The old man said he had but coolly, seeing no chance of a further sale. His manner had changed: he no longer needed to ingratiate himself. He shuffled off, muttering, then paused, composed his features and began to lay out his blooms on another table a few yards away.

'Boy,' said Ossie, 'ain't we having a ball?'

'There's a place near Mulsanne,' said Kit, 'that sounds amusing.'

'Yeah? What kind of place?'

As they drained their beer and began to climb into the Bugatti, three British Army officers turned into the square from the rue Dumas. A small man in a pin-striped civilian suit was struggling to keep pace, breaking into a half-run from time to time.

'Well, sonofabitch,' said Ossie. 'It's Pringle.'

The ministry man saw them immediately and came over to the car. Kit turned off the engine and got out. 'Hello Pringle, what on earth are you doing here?'

One of the officers said stiffly: 'Don't you people acknowledge the presence of senior rank? Where are you stationed?'

Kit saluted crisply. 'I'm unable to tell you that, Major. Can't be too careful.'

'Don't be ridiculous,' said the Major. 'I'm military intelligence.'

In the back of the Bugatti Ossie snorted. 'Now, there's something we haven't seen too much of lately.'

Pringle said quickly: 'It's all right, gentlemen. These chaps are known to me.'

'Really?' said the major. He looked at the other officers and shook his head. 'It seems the RAF considers itself above the common courtesies of military etiquette.'

'Yeah,' said Ossie. 'We're too busy killing Germans.'

'In different circumstances,' said the major, 'I would have no hesitation in taking this matter further.'

'You mean if there wasn't a war on,' said Ossie. He was starting to get out of the car. Kit pushed him back. The army officers began to walk away. Pringle moved to follow them. 'Don't bother, Pringle,' said the major. 'We're done with you for the moment. Why don't you stay and teach your friends some manners?'

'Yeah,' said Ossie. 'Stick with us and live a little. Come and sit on my knee.'

Kit took them out of the city by the rue des Minimes and south towards Mulsanne. Pringle was pinned between Ossie and Goofy Gates, barely able to breathe. 'I can't see the point of antagonising those fellows,' he said, after a long silence. 'They can use their influence to make things jolly awkward.'

'Perhaps they can use their influence to stop the bloody Hun kicking us out of France,' said Goofy.

Half-way down the Mulsanne straight they drew to a halt outside a long, low one-storey building close to the road. 'I think this is the place,' said Kit.

'I thought you'd been here before,' said Duff.

'No, somebody told me about it.' Kit opened the door of the Café de l'Hippodrome and they went in. It seemed they were the only customers. The walls were hung with mementoes of the Vingt Quatre Heures: steering-wheels, goggles, components from shattered engines, dozens of photographs, some carefully framed, others secured anyhow with drawing-pins, and many posters bearing the names of famous marques that had battled day and night just yards from where they stood – Aries, Bentley, OM, Chenard-Walcker, Lorraine, Sunbeam, Amilcar, Delage, Aston-Martin.

'Say,' said Ossie, 'didn't Buster pedal an Aston round this raceway?'

'I'll rustle up some service,' said Kit. He found the woman

who ran the place, small and round, thrilled to hear an English accent. She was keen to make them pots of tea. Kit settled on carafes of *vin rouge* and whatever food she could find. She thought she had seen him before, racing in '37. All the English teams used the Café de l'Hippodrome.

'Surely, Monsieur, you are one of the Lagonda boys?'

'No, Madame, but one of our pilots drove an Aston-Martin in 'thirty-eight.'

'*Vraiment?*'

'Duncan Brown. But I'm sure you don't—'

'*Bien sûr*, Monsieur, Bustair. *M'accompagnez, s'il vous plaît.*'

Kit followed her into the bar. Buster grinned out of a large glossy photograph, perched on the bonnet of an Aston-Martin with a drooping headlamp, his arms round the shoulders of two other drivers. 'Bustair,' said the woman. 'He flies with you? He is well?'

Kit did not answer directly. 'No,' he said, 'he's not flying with us now. Back in England.'

'Ah,' said the woman. 'He always had the good luck, that one.' She bustled off to fetch the food and wine, pleased to be busy. No one was travelling far these days and the café was a long way from the city.

Kit did not tell the others about the photograph of Buster. Pilots who went missing were hardly mentioned and they all knew the convention, how it was. He felt now that coming here had been a bad idea. The others must have made the connection: the place was like a shrine to Buster and his kind. Everywhere Kit looked he was reminded of him. It was as though Buster was sitting at the table with them, clutching a glass with fingers burned to the bone, face unrecognisable, a symbol of the fate that might await them all. Then Kit realised he did not care. Whatever his outward form might be he was still Buster. He was alive and, knowing Buster, would very soon be kicking. And thinking this, the café became a comfort and a celebration. Yet, to the others, his expression and demeanour did not change and he waited for someone to avoid referring to Buster Brown.

'Here's fun,' Ossie was saying. 'Pringle tells us the French government is on the run.'

'Moved to Tours,' said Pringle. 'The Germans are fifty miles from Paris.'

'Christ,' said Goofy. 'What was I saying about the bastards waltzing up the Champs-Élysées before you can say Schickelgruber?'

The wine arrived with baskets of bread. Kit poured Pringle a glass from the stone carafe and he sipped it apprehensively. 'Oddly enough, that's not at all bad,' he said. He took a full mouthful. 'So,' he said, 'I gather you chaps are caught up in this Le Havre business tomorrow.'

'Who told you that?' said Kit.

'Me,' said Ossie. 'I figured the guy's on our side.'

'That bloody major makes you wonder,' said Goofy.

'Don't worry,' said Pringle. 'Your secret's safe with me. Actually, I helped to put the show together. Operation Cycle.'

'Who dreams up these crazy names?' said Ossie.

'I've got one for the whole campaign,' said Goofy. 'Operation Balls-up.'

'That's hardly fair,' protested Pringle. 'There are many factors—'

'Factors be fucked,' said Ossie. 'The Hun have just blown us away. Too fast, too efficient, too well-equipped. They got the drop on us.'

'Do you know,' said Duff, languidly, 'one of my chums on the *Telegraph* told me that Gort, our esteemed chief of the BEF, started a council of war by discussing whether the helmet, when not worn on the head, should be slung over the left shoulder or the right? Item one on the agenda.'

'That's hardly fair,' said Pringle, again. 'Lord Gort is a fine commander. Brave, stubborn, hot on detail, perhaps a little limited intellectually . . .'

'Keep going,' said Duff. 'Perhaps you'll stumble on something that might have proved useful.'

'I really cannot permit this conversation to continue,' said
Pringle. 'In certain areas the Allies have fought with great distinction against overwhelming forces.'

'So bloody what?' said Goofy. 'We're one of the areas. Still
means bugger all when you're queuing for a one-way ticket back
to Blighty.'

'Well, I think the subject's had a reasonable airing,' said Kit.
'Now, who wants more wine?'

'It's no good you fellows complaining about the circumstances
that got us to this point,' Pringle persisted. 'That's history.
Tomorrow we're faced with evacuating eleven thousand troops
from Le Havre. That's the priority. Understand, it's no small
matter getting our people out. Make no mistake, there'll be
many more embarkations, from any seaport left to us. Good
grief, we've got another ninety thousand kicking about Brittany
now, all that's left of the BEF. Sounds like an impossible task
but Dunkirk proved it can be done.' He choked slightly on his
wine and dabbed a handkerchief to his mouth. 'Of course,
without you fellows we'll never pull it off. The Germans are
devilishly close. Dieppe's already fallen.'

The food arrived on hot white plates, omelettes with cheese
and mushrooms sprinkled with chives, side-plates of cold *gratin
dauphinois* and bowls of green salad. Pringle drank a third glass
of wine. Kit ordered another carafe.

When it arrived Ossie leant over and topped up all the glasses.
Then he got to his feet. 'I want to propose a toast.' He raised
his glass. They all stood. 'To Buster, in whose world we find
ourselves.' The clink of glasses brought Madame from the
kitchen. She clasped her hands with pleasure. 'Ah, *mes garçons*,
it is just like times gone by.'

Kit looked across at Ossie as they sat down. The American
nodded. He had understood and broken a tradition that was
probably the stronger for it.

Pringle said: 'So who's this Buster fellow, then?'

'Flying Officer Brown,' said Kit. 'You met him briefly once. He can't be here tonight.' The pilots avoided looking at each other.

'Oh,' said Pringle awkwardly, 'I see. Not too bad, I hope?'

'He'll live,' said Kit.

'That's good,' said Pringle. 'They can do wonderful things these days.'

They dropped Pringle at the Hotel Moderne in the centre of Le Mans. On a wall in the courtyard was a large Bentley placard. 'I understand the Bentley boys used to stay here,' said Pringle. 'You can't get away from motor-racing can you?'

'No,' said Kit. 'You can't get away.'

Pringle turned back from the hotel door. 'Oh incidentally, didn't some of you fellows get to know a little Russian countess in Paris? Went by some ridiculous name.'

'Bébé?' said Ossie.

'Yes, that's it. I'm afraid she's done away with herself in Paris.'

'Impossible,' said Ossie. His expression was fierce, veins standing out on his temples. 'Anyway, she's in Rennes.'

'Horrible business,' continued Pringle, unable to suppress a trace of satisfaction at Ossie's reaction. In his line of work one did not forget and forgive. 'They discovered her in the river near the Pont de Conflans. Been in the water for days but her mother identified her. They also found her papers and a note. Pretty conclusive. She just seemed bored. The Left Bank was buzzing with it. Sorry to break bad news,' he added unconvincingly. 'Didn't realise you knew her that well.'

'I didn't know her at all,' said Ossie.

'Oh,' said Pringle, 'I thought perhaps you did. Strange, isn't it, what makes people do these things? By all accounts she was a lively little thing.'

*　　*　　*

Kit was unable to sleep. He wanted to, and lay on the metal bed wishing for oblivion. Around him the others snored and groaned, even shouted out, caught up in vivid dreams and nightmares. To Kit the act of drifting into sleep had become a self-conscious act. He seemed to have forgotten the knack. The luminous hands on his watch showed three and he gave up.

He pulled on his uniform and slipped out of the barn into the courtyard. His feet scuffed the gravel and he winced at the noise, walking like a man negotiating a minefield. He thought he could see light filtering through the shutters of Madame Garencière's bedroom window. Why was she still awake? He wondered fancifully if some unknown thread of communication existed between them. She often spoke words that had just come into his mind. When she looked at him sometimes he sensed that she knew his thoughts. He imagined her in bed, stretched out slim and warm under the quilt, her breasts against the thin stuff of her nightdress. He pictured the space beside her, imagined himself standing naked by the bed, turning back the covers to reveal her there, her nightdress perhaps pulled up above her waist, her arms stretched out to draw him down.

Staring hard at the closed shutters he willed her to respond to his thoughts, to get out of bed and cross to the window, ease back the shutters and watch him as he moved towards the front door. Her hair would be loose now, not gathered back. It would fall round her face as she smiled down at him from the window. But the shutters were not thrown back.

He turned away. He had probably been wrong about it all. She felt nothing but compassion for him. No more than she felt for any of the others. Here was a woman who had lost her husband, whose son had lost his father, whose country stood on the brink of defeat, humiliation and unimaginable privation, and he had fixed on her as the object of callow fantasies. He felt he had defiled her in some way, reduced her to little more than an image created to stimulate arousal.

But something inexplicable drew him to her: she provoked in him sensations he had never experienced before, powerful and disturbing, that he could not control. He moved away, through the archway to the garden, relieved to be treading on grass. He could hear the murmur of the river beyond the lawns. The garden seemed to be a living thing, the breeze whispering through the old-fashioned arbours and stirring the branches of the gnarled trees. The faint noises were like a woman's voice, a woman murmuring to him, softly yet with particular urgency; a woman lying alone, awake, behind closed shutters who perhaps even now was able to know his thoughts . . .

Near an old yew tree that had lost many branches a cigarette glowed. Kit knew there was a marble bench there. Now he could make out the dark shape of a man, arms spread along the back of the bench. The glow of the cigarette brightened as the man inhaled. Kit heard him puff out the smoke. It was Ossie Wolf.

When he saw Kit a few yards away Ossie sat up and swivelled round to make a space, stubbing out his Players on the marble, creating a shower of glowing sparks. '"Ah",' he said, in an odd, guttural voice, '"the children of the night."'

'Say again?'

'Lugosi. Dracula. "Ah, the children of the night . . . what sweet music they make." Surely you've seen the movie?'

'Afraid not. Never went in much for the cinema. Saw *Sanders of the River* once. That wasn't bad.'

'Never heard of it. What was the gist?'

'A district commissioner chap keeping peace among some African tribes.'

'An English movie huh?' Ossie lit another cigarette, the burst of flame illuminating his battered face. A few curls of black hair hung over his forehead. 'Bad dreams?'

'Couldn't get to sleep.'

'Pre-op nerves, then.'

'No. At least I don't think so. Just brooding about things.'

'Hey,' said Ossie, nudging him, 'maybe that cute little widow's getting to you huh?'

'Don't be ridiculous.'

'Oh, it's not so crazy. She don't give the rest of us the glad-eye. She's soft on you man. And who's to blame her, married to that middle-aged stiff in the fancy duds? Boy, now he's bought it you could be the answer to her prayers.'

'She doesn't pray for me,' said Kit. 'She prays for herself and her son.' Even as he said it he half hoped he was wrong, and cursed himself for a hypocrite, unable to admit his feelings for her.

Ossie was silent for a moment. This damned Englishman had a knack for changing a little gentle joshing into something serious. Suddenly he didn't feel like joking any more. He had his own concerns. 'Say,' he said in the darkness, 'do you reckon Pringle's on the level about Bébé?'

'Certainly seemed like it.'

'Sounds screwy to me. I just don't figure her doing something like that.'

'No. But you never really know anybody, do you?'

'I sure never knew anybody like her,' said Ossie. 'It was like she was something special, you know? And she was nothing, nobody, but she kinda had me hooked for a while. Jesus, who needs women in a war? Who's got time for this kind of shit?'

'I suppose there's always time for this kind of shit,' said Kit slowly, hardly aware of the obscenity. It sounded comical coming from him and they both laughed.

'Still,' said Ossie, 'kind of weird for Bébé to go out that way. I just don't figure it at all.' Dawn was lightening the sky. A few birds were beginning to sing, their calls echoing round the valley. Ossie said: 'Swell, isn't it?' He ran his hand across the grass. It came up wet with dew. 'I guess you know we haven't got a hope in hell. That in one week, maybe two, we'll be prisoners, dead or licking our wounds back home waiting for the Hun to step ashore.'

'Probably.'

'I envy you,' said Ossie. 'Whatever else happens you cling to your beliefs.'

'You make them sound like delusions.'

'Maybe so. Who cares? We all have our different reasons for getting mixed up in this thing. Who gives a damn if it comes out okay in the end?'

'Actually I think you do,' said Kit. 'There's no other reason for you to be here.' He paused. 'You once told me you were fighting to get even. I never understood. Get even with whom?'

'Pinning me down, huh? Well, at first I reckoned it was the Old Man filling my head with baloney. All some kid had to do was call me a goddammed Prooshun, a square-head, and I'd be in there hammering some respect into the sonofabitch. The Old Man loved that. Teutonic spirit, he called it, though he had a handshake like a wet catfish. And then it all went wrong. The Nazis got the country by the throat and choked it little by little. The Old Man couldn't see it. A Thousand-Year Reich? It sounded just great to him, whatever it took. And at first I couldn't see it either. Careless, because it's easier that way, and I was getting to do great stuff like learning to fly and running a Cord and dating some fancy chicks. And anyway I wasn't alone. I was soaking everything up like all the other Prooshuns in St Louis; the '36 Olympics, where the entire world seemed to reckon Hitler was a great feller, the way the country was back on its feet, the pride you saw in the faces at those goddammed rallies. Jesus, even Charlie Lindbergh was building them up good. And then I went to Spain and saw how it was, how it was going to be. And I hated the sons-of-bitches because they'd destroyed everything

I believed in. They made me ashamed of my name.' He grunted. 'That's why it's personal.'

'You can't hate a whole nation.'

'Watch me brother,' said Ossie. 'Watch me.'

Thirty-one

On the day that Brewster received fresh orders to move the squadron from Boulay-sur-Sarthe to a new location on the Atlantic coast, Paris awoke to find itself in German hands. Barely twenty-four hours earlier the French capital had been declared an open city by General Maxime Weygand as the government, already sheltering in Tours, began its final withdrawal to Bordeaux. Goofy Gates's prediction had come true. Military bands, with drums, brass and hammered dulcimers, led regiments of the German Army up the long incline of the Champs-Élysées towards the Arc de Triomphe, eyes burning, chests swollen with pride, watched by crowds struck dumb.

Three days before, eleven thousand men had been gathered from the quaysides of Le Havre and carried to safety by a fleet of oddly assorted vessels. Wing had assembled larger patrols of fighters, the various squadrons working together, and the show of strength had seemed effective. Operation Cycle had passed off largely untroubled by enemy interference from the air, although Kit had led an inconclusive attack on three Heinkels attempting to bomb a troopship as it made for the open sea. Wing had been pleased. 'Decent show all round. Now get your chaps to Nantes and do the same over St Nazaire. Operation Aerial. The navy have still got hordes to shift. But I'm sure they'll manage with a little help from us.'

'Us?'

433

The man at Wing had hesitated. 'Incidentally, Brewster, we're moving as well, to Rennes. Strategic . . .'

'Withdrawal,' Brewster had said. 'I get the picture.'

When Madame Garencières answered the clang of the bell and saw Brewster and Kit together she stood back and beckoned them quietly into the house. As they passed by her into the salon her eyes, dark under their thick lashes, met Kit's. 'I know why you have come,' she said. She bit her lip, looking uncertain and young. He wanted to hold her to him, although he had never done more than politely shake her hand.

With Kit's guidance Brewster had rehearsed his brief address in French. 'Leaving tomorrow with great regret . . . the Royal Air Force cannot thank you enough . . . such generous hospitality at a time of personal grief . . . will remember our time here with gratitude and warmth . . . gracious and beautiful hostess . . .' Kit had advised omitting 'beautiful' but Brewster had insisted '. . . may we meet again in happier times . . . Victory assured, however bleak the present situation. *Vive la France, vive l'Angleterre.*' Kit had also suggested that such patriotic fervour might be inappropriate in a domestic situation, but again Brewster had brushed aside his reservation. He liked his *vives*. They were the only French phrases he was confident about and he delivered them with passion.

Madame Garencières listened attentively, although she smiled at unexpected moments, throwing Brewster off his stride. However, he struggled on to the end, unable to see anything remotely amusing in what he said. Formalities over, he hurried off, leaving to Kit the difficult task of presenting her with a bundle of francs secured with a rubber band, which, naturally, she refused.

'Louis will miss you,' she said.

'Yes,' said Kit. 'The chaps have grown very fond of him.'

'No, I mean you. He seems to regard you with particular affection.'

'He's a grand little fellow,' said Kit quickly.

'I imagine you were a grand little fellow,' said Madame Garencières. 'Perhaps that is the bond.'

'I must say I'd like to be the one to tell him we're on the move.'

'Of course,' said Madame Garencières. 'I will find him for you.' At the door she paused. 'Kit, I feel there is something unsaid between us.' It was the first time she had addressed him by his Christian name. She pronounced it 'Keet' and he thought he had never heard anything so charming. 'Is there anything you wish to say to me,' she said, 'before I fetch Louis?'

'Well, I suppose there is.'

'You suppose?'

'Well, it's all pretty hopeless, isn't it?'

She closed the door again and moved towards him. 'Is that all?'

'Not really. I wouldn't know where to start. I'm no good at this sort of thing.'

'What sort of thing?' She leant up, her hand resting lightly on his arm, and pressed her lips to his. 'That sort of thing?'

'Yes,' he said huskily. 'Very much that sort of thing.' He placed his hands on her shoulders and kissed her again. She wrapped her arms round his waist. He kissed her forehead, her eyelids, her nose, her mouth. She felt fragile in his arms as he had known she would. A great tenderness overcame him and a strong desire, which seemed a contradiction.

'How eloquent you are,' she said. 'You express everything without speaking.'

'This is so bizarre. I don't even know your name.'

'Juliette.' She drew away from him, as though the mundane remark had shaken her from a dream. 'Of course you are right. It is all quite hopeless. Everything conspires. And yet it is such a rare thing, when it happens, that you feel you must seize it, hold it, try not to let it slip away. You would not know that yet.'

435

'You mean I am too young?'

'Never too young.' She shivered. 'But suddenly I feel old. Very old and tired.'

He held her again. Her face was warm against his cheek. 'Has it happened to you often then,' he said, 'this rare thing?'

'Only once.' She nodded at the photograph of her husband in its silver frame. 'But not with Louis. I was young and flattered, he was worldly, charming. So it goes. It is a very familiar tale, *mon chéri*.'

Kit was thrilled by the endearment. 'Your husband was also Louis?'

'The Garencières are not marked by originality. The eldest sons are always Louis. So it has been for generations. They share something else as well. At Waterloo a Louis died charging the English squares, another at Balaclava, another defending Paris from the Prussians, my husband's father at the Battle of the Marne. The thing they share is that not one lived to see his children full-grown. And now . . .'

'Now perhaps it will end,' said Kit. 'Your son has seen the cost. His father, Buster . . .'

Juliette Garencières turned away. 'Oh, what hypocrites you men are. You, more than most, have seen the cost. Tell me honestly, what difference does it make?'

'It has to be done,' said Kit. 'We cannot allow—'

'Until the time comes for another "cannot allow". Let us hope that little Louis will be lucky,' she added bitterly, 'that he will find himself in a time when things have to be done, when brave men say "We cannot allow". Otherwise I fear he will live his life unfulfilled.' Suddenly she laughed. 'Our first quarrel. In a few minutes more we shall be sick of the sight of each other.'

'No,' said Kit. 'This is a beginning, not an end. I will come back. I vow it.'

'Oh, I could love you dearly, Kit, but very much to my cost. So sincere and quite convinced you will survive. I am sure that every Louis felt the same and said the same. I know one that did. "I will come back. This is not the end. I vow it."'

'Love me dearly, Juliette, and I promise I will come back.'

'You leave me little choice,' she said, with an attempt at lightness. 'Well, I must love you dearly, then, if only to ensure your safe return.'

Later, after the buckboards had collected the pilots' kit from the barn, Kit stood with Juliette Garencières and Louis in the courtyard. 'You are quite resolved to stay?' he said.

'We will be safer here. I am sure of it.'

Kit thought of the multitudes he had seen, pressing forward from Verdun in the east, across all France and now here, where one could almost hear the breakers of the Atlantic. He hated the thought of her and the boy engulfed in the waves of fear and panic.

'You are right,' he said. 'France cannot hold out much longer. She will negotiate a separate peace. Whatever happens then must be better than this. Life will not be normal, but what should you have to fear?'

Louis shook hands solemnly. He was holding his left hand behind his back. 'Look after your mother,' said Kit. 'That's an order, soldier.'

'This is for you,' said the boy. He held out a small cardboard box. Kit opened it. Inside, wrapped in tissue paper, was the Emperor Napoleon mounted on Marengo. 'I would like him back,' said Louis, 'one day when you're passing.'

'Of course.'

'It means, you see, that you must return. Otherwise the Grande Armée will remain incomplete, without its leader.'

'It is an odd request to make of an Englishman,' said Kit, 'but, yes, I will restore him to you. I promise.'

'What a day for promises,' said Juliette Garencières. 'I will make one also. I promise I will wait.'

'Wait for what, Maman?' said Louis.

* * *

Near the airfield, where he could see the seven surviving Hurricanes being prepared for the short hop to Nantes, Kit was overcome with apprehension. It had not occurred to him before but how would the authorities of the Reich choose to regard the billeting of Allied airmen by the wife of a French officer? Surely such a thing, even if it were known, would not count against her.

He thrust his hand into his tunic pocket and touched the cool silk of the kerchief Juliette Garencières had given him as he left. 'Your lady's favour, chevalier,' she had said, sweetly ironic, indulging him.

He had presented her with his fountain pen. 'Write to me if you can at the address I gave you. Better still, go there, if you find yourselves in England, and I will come to you.'

He turned and looked back at the big house overlooking the valley of the Sarthe. He understood how it might be for a man to say goodbye to his family.

Thirty-two

Monday, 17 June 1940

In an oak tree green with lichen and missing a branch or two, brought down by a hundred years of coastal storms, a song-thrush was celebrating the dawn with a string of melodious trills. The air was rich with salt, swept in from the Atlantic by a pleasant breeze. Beyond the airfield and at the foot of the cliffs, the sea moved over the rocks and shingle, the waves pushing in and drawing back.

Kit matched his breathing to the rhythm of the ocean, taking air deep into his lungs with each breaking wave and releasing it as the backwash sucked at the strand. The song of the thrush and the pulse of the sea belonged to another world, oblivious to the turn of events on which hung the fate of millions, indifferent to the fortunes of the few damp figures stirring now under the wings of their Hurricanes. But while he breathed deeply in time to the sea, thrilling to the cascading birdsong, he felt himself part of that other world and at peace.

Overnight a heavy dew had settled on the fighters and now, above his head, moisture trickled down the wing of his machine and dripped on to his coarse grey blanket. Nearby Ossie woke and cursed. 'Somebody shoot that goddammed bird.'

Kit saw that the others were moving too, pushing up on to their elbows and peering about, eyes half closed against the light, rubbing stubbled chins, hair tangled and curling round their necks.

Most had found it hard to sleep, alert to every sound that might suggest the approach of an unseen saboteur. Reports of fifth-column infiltrators were rife. Elsewhere, aircraft had been damaged, taps on fuel bowsers opened, a shot or two fired from the cover of shrubland. A rigger corporal in another squadron, not too far away, had been discovered with a knife embedded in his chest, killed as he slept in his tent. So Kit, and Ossie and the rest had turned in beneath their fighters, pistols and Lee-Enfields at their sides, only Ossie unfazed by the prospect of a different kind of combat. Only Brewster had slept in one of the bell tents, the telephone to Wing at his side.

The Hurricanes stood armed and fuelled. From now on the pilots would have to carry out such tasks themselves. The previous evening the ground-party had left for St Nazaire twenty miles away: Flight Sergeant Jessop with his ground-crews and Spy Turner, Doc Gilmour, plus two protesting young pilots, Hangdog Collins and Tigger Lloyd. Brewster had been firm but sympathetic. 'Nine pilots, seven aeroplanes. What are you going to do? Fly tandem? It's no reflection on you fellows. You've learnt a lot in your brief time here. Now put it to good use by getting back to Blighty pronto. And make the most of your little sea voyage. We'll be back in business with a vengeance when we meet again.'

Jessop had been equally reluctant to go, fussing over his charges until Brewster pushed him away. 'Good grief, man, get your skates on. You'll miss your chance of a trip on the *Skylark*.' In the backs of the trucks the ground-crew had looked dishevelled and exhausted. They found it hard to raise the customary cheer as they moved away. They watched Brewster and the others pass out of sight behind a grove of trees. They thought about the blokes who would not be going home, their own mob, Baker, Evans, Croft, and the pilots. Bloody hell, the pilots. How many was it now? Dinghy Davis, poor old Beaky Parker, Windy Miller, young Pip Fuller, that cocky little bugger Kenny Rains.

And so it went, some of the faces seen so fleetingly they could hardly remember their names.

Finally someone said: 'Tell you what, though. I never thought they'd get old Buster.'

'*They* didn't,' said someone else. 'The fucking Froggies did.'

Behind the Bedfords, crushed into a small Austin, Collins, Lloyd, Spy Turner and Doc Gilmour had said nothing to each other as they neared the port. They pictured Brewster and his fighter boys standing by their Hurricanes on the headland overlooking the shipping striking out through the waves on a course for England. They wanted to be with them, but there was nothing more they could do. It seemed a small enough band to face those final patrols in the skies above St Nazaire.

Now, as the dawn light spread over a calm sea, the members of the ground party found themselves directed into the shuffling queues of troops, heavy with equipment and fatigue, moving towards the destroyers that would take them out to transport vessels moored in waters twelve fathoms deep beyond the harbour entrance. One made a striking picture, an old Cunarder with a single funnel, swinging placidly at anchor as though on one of her peacetime cruises in the Bahamas or the Med, before she was requisitioned. 'We might be going home in style, boys,' said Doc Gilmour. 'That's the *Lancastria*.'

At the airfield Goofy Gates was brewing tea. He had set out seven white mugs on the grass beside a little paraffin stove. Kit thought they looked like tombstones, the kind you came across on the bleak plains of the Somme, marking some brief, inglorious action, squalid and obscure. Gates stirred in heaps of sugar, the spoon clanking until Ossie shouted: 'Jesus, Goofy, give a guy a break.' Goofy sniffed and handed round the mugs.

Brewster stood a little apart, in flying kit, tracing a finger over a chart folded to show the coast. He took his tea without a word.

Goofy began to whistle 'You Must Have Been A Beautiful

441

Baby', embellishing the tune with fancy flourishes, a quavering tremolo that pierced the soul like a needle. From time to time his lips dried and he began the song again.

'Cork it, Goof,' said Ossie, 'or I'll cork it for you.'

'What's got up your nose today?' said Goofy. 'Don't you like music?'

'Yeah. And a tone-deaf sonofabitch with his lips pursed like a cat's arsehole ain't my idea of music.'

'Philistine bloody Yank.' Goofy moistened his mouth with a gulp of tea and started on 'Over The Rainbow', his eyebrows near his hairline as he strained for the high notes.

Ossie seized him and locked an arm round his neck. They staggered sideways laughing, knocking over mugs with their flailing feet. 'You little fucker,' Ossie was gasping. 'You ornery little fucker.'

Brewster slipped his chart under his arm and came over. He looked preoccupied and had forgotten his tea. 'Okay, chaps, cut out the horseplay.' He marvelled that they had the energy to fool about. At least it meant their spirits were high. He crouched down and spread out the large-scale chart on the ground. He jabbed it with the stem of his pipe. A fragment of burning tobacco fell out of the bowl and scorched a hole in La Rochelle. 'I'm going to fill you in,' he said, 'so you know just what we're up against.

'Our navy chums have got nearly sixty thousand troops to ship out.' He placed his hand, palm downwards, fingers spread, over the St Nazaire region. 'Not that it makes any difference but that number includes our own chaps. Our job is to make sure they're not interfered with, any of them. You'll find there'll be Hurrys from other outfits up there too so keep 'em peeled.' He tapped his eyes. 'No stupid mistakes. We'll fly together, working in three vics. I'll lead the first, Kit the second, Ossie the third. Everybody stay in tight. And, Gates, you're—'

'Sweeper,' said Goofy. 'Yes sir.'

'Business is likely to be brisk,' said Brewster. 'The Hun have been increasingly cocky. A couple of days ago some Stukas had a pop at *Richelieu*, the French battle-cruiser docked in Brest. No joy, but it properly put the wind up our Gallic friends. They even closed the port when a bunch of damned Dorniers came in at low-level and sprinkled magnetic mines all over the shop. We can't have that sort of thing here.' He knocked out his pipe on the side of his flying-boot. 'You chaps know what's coming as well as I do. This may be our last chance, at least for the time being, to kick the Hun in the balls. Make it count. I'm relying on you to give a good account of yourselves. Any questions? Good. Take-off in thirty minutes.' He signalled to Kit. 'Hang on boy.'

'Yes sir.'

'You knew people in Nancy.'

'Yes sir.'

'I hope they got out.'

'They didn't, sir, not all of them.'

'Just heard. The place fell four days ago. Thought you ought to know.'

Kit recalled Maurice Maierscheldt's letter. 'If we go away from here we know it will mean giving up everything.' He had known the man had no intention of going away. It would have been impossible for him. He had stayed. And he had still lost everything.

Goofy Gates was walking slowly round his Hurricane, checking the control surfaces, the cowlings, the elevator and rudder trim, just as he had done before a hundred flights, following the uncompromising routine of the professional pilot, a man who knew his stuff, had proved himself, had survived, at least this far. Kit remembered his initial distaste: a vulgar little NCO who didn't know his place. The sight of the dogged Gates busy about his machine, preparing to face whatever might come his way, made Kit ashamed of the man he had been. That man was gone. And if he should happen to come out of this business, more or less in one piece, he knew that that man would never reappear. He thought about many people – Madame Bergeret and Father Demouriez in the ruins of Fonteville; the haggard Lieutenant Dorance at the controls of the Potez, as he guided them into Menneville, accepting Ossie Wolf's silver flask of Cognac with a trembling hand; Hannah safe in England; Juliette Garencières and her son; Buster, burned and near-dead, Buster the untouchable, who had finally been touched. Faces, names, living, dead. The cost of it all and more to come. At that moment he knew he wanted to come through, to discover more about this person he had lately become, this oddly familiar stranger who seemed to have plans of a very different kind from anything that had gone before, in a very different world that lay round the corner. He did not want, after all, to be confronted by a chance for glory, for some deed of arms that might bring him crashing down to oblivion. Because now such a thing seemed possible, even probable, where before no such doubt had existed.

'I say Goofy,' Kit said suddenly. Goofy, not 'Gates' or 'Sergeant'. Goofy. It sounded odd but right. Goofy stopped whistling, startled. But he picked up on the moment. 'What's up Kit?'

'Know that Lucienne Delyle thing Buster used to like?'

'Sort of,' Goofy said. His shot at it was close enough.

Kit sensed the living and dead pressed close around him. They seemed to have great meaning, great significance, yet none at all. There was some truth contained in their shadowy faces but he could not understand it. He turned away in confusion and walked towards his Hurricane. Behind him Goofy's trills still sounded, as touching in their way as the song of the blissful song-thrush. When he reached his machine Ossie, next in line, called over: 'I'm going to strangle that little bastard.'

'He's doing requests,' said Kit.

'Yeah? Well, he didn't do mine.'

'You're a hard man Ossie.'

'Hard is my ace-in-the-hole. Hey, be careful up there today.'

'What makes you say that?'

'Hell, we've been pushing our luck for ever. Be nice to come through this thing, find out how the movie ends.'

'Well,' said Kit, 'good luck.'

'Yeah, sure,' said Ossie. 'Good luck feller.'

During the afternoon the Luftwaffe attacks intensified. Over the port great billows of smoke rolled from burning factories and refineries. Columns of troops were deluged with spray as bombs and mines plunged into the waters of the inner harbour. Dozens fell as more deadly showers sliced into their ranks. The Dorniers came in very fast and low and were equally quick to quit the scene. The air was thick with anti-aircraft fire from land and sea. French minesweepers surged back and forth, clearing channels for the destroyers, listing with the weight of scores of men clinging to their decks as they delivered them to the waiting transports in deeper water.

So far the squadron had not engaged the enemy. This was a different kind of game. The Luftwaffe was striking where it liked, often when the British fighters were chasing fresh formations that finally turned away. Now it was three thirty in the afternoon, the third patrol of the day. The seven Hurricanes taxied into position at the end of the grass runway. The bellow of their engines joined in chorus, drowning all other sound. In his open cockpit Brewster raised, then dropped his arm. They moved forward, in vics, rumbling over the ground, bumping, bumping, lifting, fat wheels spinning, folding away, fighter-sleek now, gathering together over the dappled sea, their shadows slipping across the waves, startling clouds of predatory gulls as they also went in search of prey.

On the deck of the *Lancastria*, Spy Turner watched the Hurricanes sweep across the harbour. 'Our boys,' he said to Doc Gilmour. 'Quite a sight.'

There was a roar from the able seaman by the forward hatch. 'Come on, lads, keep it moving, keep it bloody moving. There's plenty more to come.'

Turner wondered how many more the *Lancastria* could take. Already more than five thousand had filed patiently on board, pressing into a space designed for fewer than eighteen hundred. He lowered himself through the hatch on to the metal stairway leading down into the depths of the ship. He stumbled, gripping the handrail, the dim interior seeming almost dark after the brilliance of the sun outside. Ahead of him, Hangdog Collins and Tigger Lloyd skipped down the steps like gleeful children. Spy Turner, Gilmour, Jessop and the rest made their way more carefully down to the cargo hold. Behind him Turner could hear the A/B shouting: 'Move it, you lot, bloody move it. They're serving afternoon fucking tea in number-two hold.' Already the man's voice sounded a long way off.

Just short of four o'clock the Dorniers came. The crews of the Do-17s, specially trained for shipping strikes, swept towards the old liner still rolling at anchor on a gentle swell. Throughout the ship, on every deck, in every opulent saloon, down corridor after corridor of cabins, deep in the cargo holds, where thousands of exhausted men leant against their kit-bags and thought of home the sirens howled. Four bombs bracketed the hull. One missed but the blast-wave punched a hole below the port waterline. Another struck the hold containing fuel-oil. A third flew down the elegant funnel and exploded in the engine room. The fourth penetrated number-two hold where Flight Sergeant Jessop had just detailed a couple of his lads to find out where the tea and grub were being handed out. The detonations shook the sky.

'Something big's gone up,' yelled Goofy Gates, over the R/T.

'Wrap up and follow me,' snapped Brewster. The Hurricanes had been heading east, following the course of the Loire towards Nantes, anticipating enemy formations approaching St Nazaire from the direction of Tours. Instead they had come in further north, passing undetected over Le Mans and Angers and clear to select their targets at will. Nobody's fault. The sparse resource of British fighters stretched only so far. Now Brewster wheeled them as one towards the port where fresh columns of oil smoke stained the sky.

Already the *Lancastria* was down by the head and listing to port, her starboard propeller stark against the horizon like a monstrous crucifix. The sea was rising over her bow and racing down her decks, seeking any open hatch, unclosed door, gaping vent, coursing down the great main staircase with the force of a breached dam, driving before it thousands of men until the whole construction fell away and they realised dully that, for them, there was no escape. As the weight of the water stressed the hull and distorted bulkheads the list changed: she was sagging to starboard now, her elegant cruiser-stern rising foot by foot. Around her the surface of the sea was black with struggling humanity; black, too, with a glutinous film of fuel-oil. On the rolling hull more thousands bunched together, slipping and falling or jumping clear as the angle steepened and the sea advanced towards them. Some even sang 'Roll Out The Barrel', 'Rule Britannia'.

The Dorniers came in again, strafing the bobbing heads in the dark sea round the hulk, dropping incendiaries to ignite the blanket of oil. Here and there it caught, the oil bubbling as the flames took hold, the heads flaring up like candles, while in the crowded shipping lanes rescue vessels came under attack, forced to remain under way, twisting this way and that to evade the bombs and bullets, unable to heave-to and pick up survivors. Then the Dorniers turned for home.

Minutes later the Hurricanes skimmed in from Nantes. 'Six plus Dorniers at two o'clock, Red Leader, heading east, a hell of a long way off.' That was Ossie.

'I see 'em,' Brewster said. 'Curtis, Wolf, cover the port. The rest of you come with me.' He set off in pursuit, throttles wide.

As Kit and Ossie banked steeply over the harbour they looked down on a grey-black wedge lying on the surface, like a piece of burnt wood crawling with ants.

'My God,' said Kit. 'It's the *Lancastria*.'

With a final massive tremor and a scream of sheering steel the Cunarder raised her stern higher, and then she was slipping down swiftly, the point of her descent marked by immense whirlpools that gathered countless tiny figures and spiralled them down to the ocean bed. Fewer than fifteen minutes had passed since the first attack.

Ossie looked across at Kit. They were yards apart, their canopies slid back. Kit was struggling in his cockpit, unclipping his Sutton harness. He looked like a man preparing for a brolly-hop. The Hurricane was running straight and true, no hint of a problem. 'Hey, Kit,' Ossie said. 'You got a problem?'

'I think,' said Kit, gasping over the R/T like a sprinter trying to talk at the end of a race, 'they need this more than me.' Something yellow flew back from his cockpit. It struck the rudder and tumbled away. Kit fell back into his seat and fumbled with the fixings of his harness. The Mae West life-jacket landed neatly close to a few dark figures. They made their way towards it with painful slowness, and when they reached it clung on, waving.

In his cockpit Kit had dropped the securing pin of his harness. He heard it rattle on the floor. The straps were flapping loose. One, caught by the turbulence, flailed back and struck him, the metal clip biting deep into his forehead. Blood flew back from the wound, spattering the seat-back, forcing its way inside his helmet. He felt it matting his hair.

Then he heard Ossie shouting: 'Break! Break right!'

Tracer was coming past him, above and to the left. He heard the bullets zipping through the fuselage behind his head, a series of rapid explosions rather like setpiece bangers on Bonfire Night. A monstrous shadow flashed across his screen. His quarter-rolled to the right thrusting forward on the throttle, dropping the nose into a vertical spiral, the blue sea spinning, spinning, rushing towards him. He felt himself floating free of his seat no longer secured by his harness and grasped the controls more firmly to hold himself in place. He realised ack-ack bursts were rising to meet him. The Hurricane staggered under a dozen hits. He pulled out of the dive, the G-force pressing him into his seat. Momentarily he blacked out. Now he was making height rapidly, looking frantically around. The sky was clear, apart from Ossie circling a quarter of a mile away. At sea level a free-hunt Messerschmitt-110 was ditching close to where the *Lancastria* had disappeared. Flames were belching from the starboard engine. It struck the surface, bounced, disintegrated, and set the sea on fire. Ossie said: 'The bastard nearly had you.'

'He's left me with lots to think about,' said Kit. The stench of glycol was very strong. Oil was streaking back across the port wing. He looked at the gauge. No pressure. What was his height? The altimeter was smashed. He thought he should say something more to Ossie but somehow couldn't see the point. He felt dazed, his vision blurring, whether from the G-force or the blow to his head. He was passing through wispy cloud now. He could not see the ground. The engine might seize at any moment. He knew he had to jump. He waited, waited, clawing for height, striving for the bonus of an extra thousand feet. The engine noise was throbbing, wild. One moment his thoughts were lucid, the next confusion overwhelmed him. The Merlin faltered. As the speed fell off the stick and rudder control went dead. He tore off his helmet and oxygen mask severing the connections. They were snatched from his hand. Free, he raised himself into the slipstream as the Hurricane flopped over into a vertical spin. It plummeted down. Good God, she must be doing 400 m.p.h. already. The air tore at his clothes.

Suddenly he found himself floating clear, apparently supported by the air, watching his machine swallowed in the cloud beneath his dangling feet. He had lost his shoes. One foot was bare and white. Even the sock had gone. The blue veins stood out against the pallid skin. He noted the big toe, scarred and canted to the left. That frantic game of fives with Kennedy-Smith at Marlborough when he had run into the wall. He moved his arms and felt a momentary, gentle lift. He laughed. It was exhilarating. He was flying without an aeroplane.

His vision was coming and going, now sharp, now blurred like one of Farve's magic-lantern shows. Between the blue of the sky and the blue of the sea he was falling. Blue sea, blue sky. He looked at the stuff of his shirt. Same shade of blue. The trousers, too, pulling at his calves, flapping, cracking. Everything blue. Blue man falling. Who had said that? People in a room. Someone, somewhere a long time ago. It wasn't important. Only this sensation, this thrill of falling. And then he was back, as if waking from a trance and, God, the sea was close. His hand flew to the rip-cord and he pulled it hard, tearing off a finger-nail. He yelped but had to laugh at the futility of such a tiny pain, swooping down under the silken canopy to become part of a greater, more general agony. A long, grey outline swung into view. He saw he would land just aft of the destroyer's stern. Filling the deck, a crowd of people watched him come down. They were shouting, shaking fists. He wondered vaguely if the ship was German. The manner of the men who crowded the rails was redolent of hate. As he plunged through the film of oil he heard a Hurricane pass low overhead and then he was writhing, squirming to release himself from his harness, bursting to the surface in time to see Ossie circling, circling still.

'You're a very fortunate young man,' the captain was saying. 'At first I'm afraid we took you for a damned Nazi.' Kit was swaying to the movement of the destroyer, dripping oil and blood on to the floor of the bridge. Once on board he had insisted he was perfectly all right, quite able to make his report. The captain had taken him at his word. Now he thought perhaps he had been a little hasty. He gulped down the salty bile gathering in his throat. He felt the ship driving forward, rising and falling, powerful, full of purpose.

'Would that have made a difference, sir?' said Kit.

The captain didn't answer. 'Afraid you had to run the gauntlet,' he said. 'Entirely understandable, though, after what they'd been through.'

'Understandable?' He remembered surfacing near the rolling grey hull, a hundred faces staring down at him, faces black with oil, teeth startling white. 'It's a fucking German. Let the bastard drown.' He'd scraped the filth from the wings on his tunic, then pointed feebly, waving. 'Bloody hell, it's one of ours.' A small boat was near him, the water slapping against its gunwales. His head was lolling, flopping from side to side. He felt himself pulled upwards, his arms hanging down, legs numb with cold. He lay in the bottom of the boat retching, bringing up oily phlegm. Far above him, from the deck of the rolling grey ship, the voices were louder: 'Fucking RAF. Where have you bastards been? What've you been bloody doing? What the *fuck* have you been doing?'

He had very much wanted to tell them, but he hadn't known where to begin.

The captain said: 'We'll get you down below. I've got your details. We'll pass them on if we get the opportunity.'

'Thank you, sir,' said Kit. 'I suppose there's no chance of putting in somewhere, Lorient or Brest?'

'Not a hope, my dear chap. What do you think we are? Pleasurecraft for hire? Next stop Plymouth. Now, go and get some hot scran inside you.'

'You saw Kit picked up?' said Brewster.

'Sure, they got him on board all right,' said Ossie. 'The guy was on his feet.' Outside the bell tent he could hear the whump-whump of the Albion bowser refuelling the Hurricanes for the next patrol.

'At least you got your 110.'

'Yeah. He went in good.'

'A bloody business, the *Lancastria*. The pity of it is we

couldn't catch the swine who did it.' The telephone rang. 'Yes,' said Brewster. 'Yes.' He was listening intently. He put down the receiver. 'That was Wing. We're released until tomorrow.'

'Why's that, sir?'

'Search me. Who's complaining? Tell the chaps to stand down.'

Ossie ducked out of the tent. He hadn't said a word about Kit's crazy Mae West stunt. What a thing – what a hell of a thing. Thousands drowning and the dumb bastard thinks one lousy life-jacket's going to make a difference. And for that he'd lost his airplane and almost his goddammed hide. To take his eye off the ball like that, Jesus, it was unforgivable. He'd always said the guy was soft. Still, he found himself wondering if maybe, just maybe, those three guys in the water had made it.

That evening Brewster treated his pilots to a meal at the Hôtel du Parc just down the road at St Herblain. He didn't go himself. He parked himself in a deck-chair by the six remaining Hurricanes, smoking his pipe, his Webley on his lap.

At the hotel nobody felt like celebrating. The simple meal was eaten in silence. They were pleased that St Herblain wasn't on the coast. The waters of the Côte de Jade were thick with corpses. Over by the bar a dozen French *poilus* were drinking Pernod and listening to the crackling wireless half-hidden among the liqueur and *sirop* bottles.

A programme of accordion music was interrupted. An announcer began to speak, his voice slow and solemn. None of the pilots could speak French. Only Ossie knew a little. He heard the names Reynaud, Petain, the word 'armistice'. 'Jesus,' he said, 'the Frogs have chucked the towel in.' At the end of the bulletin they played the 'Marseillaise'. The French infantrymen sat frozen at the bar. Two were in tears.

At the airfield they found Brewster arguing with a French officer.

Positioned on both sides of the runway machine-gun crews had set up their weapons and trained them on the British fighters. 'I can't make head nor tail of this bloody man,' said Brewster. 'I think the sod's trying to tell us we're grounded.'

'*Pouvez-vous parler plus lentement?*' mumbled Ossie Wolf.

The French officer shrugged. He began to speak with exaggerated slowness. Reynaud was no longer prime minister. He had been replaced by General Pétain whose first step had been to negotiate an armistice.

Brewster broke in: 'Armistice be buggered! He can call it an armistice all he wants. It amounts to a ruddy surrender.'

The French officer continued impatiently.

Ossie's eyes narrowed. 'You're right, sir. He's ordering us not to take off. No more fighting on French soil.'

Brewster had the Webley stuck into the back of his belt. Now he reached behind him, gripped the butt and thrust the barrel under the Frenchman's nose. He addressed him very loudly, so that someone who did not speak English would understand. 'If you do not give your men orders to withdraw immediately I will personally blow your head off. *Comprenez?*'

The French officer took a step back.

'Furthermore my pilots will not only take off when I order them to but they will give your chaps rather more than they ruddy well bargained for once they're in the air. *Vous comprenez* strafe?' The French officer did *comprenez* strafe. He turned on his heel and returned to his men at a measured pace. They gathered up their weapons and moved down the coast road towards St Nazaire.

'Where does this leave us, sir?' said Goofy Gates.

'Wing's ordered us to leave at dawn,' said Brewster. 'Dinard, Jersey, home.'

'So, it's all over, then,' said Goofy.

'Hardly,' said Brewster. 'I'd say it's only just beginning.'

Ossie took a walk on his own, but felt that a lot of guys were walking with him. It was a pleasant June evening and on the topmost branch of the oak tree stained with lichen the same damned bird was singing its heart out, just as it had that morning, like nothing had happened, like nothing had happened at all.

Thirty-three

Tuesday, 25 June 1940

The taxi turned into the Strand from Duncannon Street and stopped. A striking young woman in a long black coat stepped out, paid the driver and entered the bank. The uniformed commissionaire, with medals on his chest, held open the door for her, saluting with a flourish as she passed, following her with rheumy eyes. Behind the counter, a cashier slipped away from his position and knocked discreetly on the manager's door. 'Excuse me sir. Miss Maierscheldt is here.'

The young woman was shown into the manager's office. He did not seem himself. His face was grave, his manner abstracted. The young woman wondered if, even now, she had made some mistake, forgotten some detail – perhaps the signature she had practised so hard, perhaps something she had overlooked in the apartment in the rue du Faubourg St-Honoré, perhaps something discovered on the cadaver they had recovered from the Seine, perhaps, perhaps, perhaps. She was perplexed and cross. She felt like stamping her foot. To have come so far. Everything had appeared perfect, her story accepted without question. At previous appointments, dealing with tedious paperwork, signing documents, at last arranging to withdraw some funds, she had been treated with the deference she expected from an institution patronised by the English king.

'My dear Miss Maierscheldt, Mademoiselle,' the manager said, with an odd, discernible sigh, 'thank you so much for coming.

So much easier to do this sort of thing face to face.'

This sort of thing? The young woman wondered if a fat English policeman was waiting outside for a signal to burst in, arrest her, take her away. She decided to say nothing. She stood motionless in front of the manager, her gloved hands clasped, her oval face pale as though already in the dock.

'Please,' the manager said, 'forgive me.' He held a chair for her and she sat down gracefully. He seated himself behind his desk. 'I greatly regret,' he began, 'I greatly regret . . .' he bit his lip '. . . I have the most terrible news.'

Still she said nothing. He seemed most sympathetic towards her. Perhaps with a little encouragement he might prove useful. She started the process immediately, reaching out and touching his hand lightly. 'Monsieur,' she said, very softly, 'say what you must.' She let her hand remain where it was.

There was a long silence. He looked down at her hand, then up at her. On the wall behind his head, next to an ebony-framed print of the Royal Family, a small clock ticked industriously. Car horns sounded over the occasional clatter and clang of a passing tram.

'I regret to inform you, my dear Miss Maierscheldt, that your parents have passed away,' said the manager.

'Passed away?'

'I'm afraid they're . . . dead.'

The young woman's hand flew to her mouth. She fell forward in her chair. The manager hurried to her side and placed his hand on her shoulder. She shrugged it off. He could not see her face. She was shaking. He stood beside her uncertainly, then crossed to the door. 'Woolger, fetch some water. Be quick about it man.' The young woman seemed to be recovering herself. 'I'm so dreadfully sorry,' he said, 'but there's no easy way to break such news.'

'Please,' said the young woman, 'I am quite myself again. You say they're dead, but how?'

It was simple enough. Residents in the place de la Carrière in Nancy had seen the Maierscheldt house visited by the German police. It was known that Jews were being identified and in some cases taken away, but there had been no suggestion that the Maierscheldts were in immediate danger. Clearly Monsieur Maierscheldt thought otherwise. At three o'clock in the morning on Sunday 22 June two shots were heard. Little was thought of it. In turbulent France such things were unremarkable and, sadly, people kept themselves to themselves. However, when Monsieur Maierscheldt, a punctual man, failed to arrive at his office on Monday an assistant was dispatched to the house. The front door stood unlocked. A note lay on the hall table. Upstairs they found the bodies. Madame had been shot once in the back of the head as she slept. Monsieur had used the same small-calibre pistol to fire a bullet into his right temple.

'Such a shocking thing,' said the manager. 'Absolutely shocking.' He admired the way the young woman had rallied herself in the face of tragedy; quite stoical, in fact. Not at all what one expected from the French. He had been dreading a scene.

'You talked of a note,' the young woman was saying. She really was wonderfully calm and collected.

'Ah yes. Your father was thoughtful to the last.'

'Not so thoughtful,' said the young woman. 'He killed my mother.'

The manager thought the remark a touch unfortunate – there was something about her tone – but she was under great strain. 'Indeed,' he said awkwardly. 'You are right, of course. But who knows what occupied the poor man's mind towards the end? I am sure he was seeking to spare your mother whatever he believed might lie ahead. And certainly he thought of you. I understand from our associates in France that his instructions are meticulous and clear. First, the funeral arrangements, of course, though naturally you can be there only in spirit.'

'The funeral arrangements, yes.' She sounded almost impatient.

'As for your father's company,' said the manager, 'well, effectively the business is yours, pending some legal niceties. I have already alerted the lawyer I recommended to you. What condition the concern will be in if – when this dreadful war concludes, we cannot know. However, your father has already taken steps to transfer substantial liquid assets to your account.'

'Substantial?'

'Very.' The manager handed her a beige folder. She read the contents carefully. Finally: 'Yes,' she murmured. 'So much.'

The manager thought this touching. 'Indeed. But what can compensate for the loss of one's parents?' He patted her hand in what he judged a fatherly manner as he took back the folder. She withdrew it rather sharply and, to his disappointment, did not display the warmth she had shown towards him earlier. She asked him a few brusque, pointed questions about the settlement and prepared to leave.

'You are settled, I hope, in your flat in Hampstead?'

'It will do for now.'

'And you are quite recovered after your escape from France?'

'Oh it was simple enough. A short sea voyage. I paid the captain more than he could earn in six months catching fish.'

'I hope we can continue to count on your business, Miss Maierscheldt.'

'Why not? I imagine one bank is much like another.'

'We like to think otherwise.'

'You must prove it to me.'

In the street the young woman hailed a taxi-cab and instructed the driver to return her to the pleasant house at the top of Holly Hill. She sat back on the slippery leather seat, entirely happy. Certainly she had anticipated that the Maierscheldts could not survive for long. That their departure was so swift and neat was wonderful, no messy legal wrangles to endure, no tedious searches in concentration-camp records to confirm their deaths in such a place on such a date. It might have taken years. Then she thought about the old barn in the Loire, hiding a secret known only to her and Kitty Bannister. She knew that for a long time she was condemned to lead a quiet, discreet life, in appalling English clothes and even a pair of wire spectacles. It was always possible that she would encounter someone who knew Hannah. But as time passed who knew how her appearance might have changed? It was simply a matter of being patient and easier to bear if she treated it as a joke. Yes, a practical joke known only to her. When the war was over how enviable life would be, for she had concluded that the Boches would be defeated. When the Americans entered the conflict, as inevitably they would, they could not permit it otherwise . . .

As the taxi passed through Trafalgar Square the news vendors were shrieking their usual incomprehensible nonsense. But today their cries had a particular urgency. She tried to read the placards but the taxi was going too fast. 'What do they say?' she asked the driver.

The man looked back at her. 'The ruddy Frogs,' he said. 'They've signed the Armistice with Adolf.'

Thirty-four

Wednesday, 3 July 1940

In the cramped cockpit of his Messerschmitt-109 Joachim Kastner set the flaps to twenty degrees and opened the throttle. He held the control column hard forward, feeling the tail come up and allowing the grey-green Emil to fly itself off the newly occupied airfield a few kilometres west of St Omer. Pull up too soon, always tempting, and the left wing was reluctant to lift. That little trait had caught out many a budding Werner Molders. The Emil was a robust machine and fast, the machine that every fighter pilot wanted to get his hands on, but even the highly skilled, those who had already flown it in battle, still had to treat it with respect and understand its ways. The Emil could bite . . .

Hauptmann Kastner was enjoying his war. In the Battle of France he had secured ten kills, six of them English Hurricanes. The Tommies had fought well and his *Jagdgeschwader* had lost good men, more than expected, more than they could spare. But, still, it had been more satisfying than Poland where air supremacy had been quickly gained and he and his comrades had found themselves assigned to ground-attack and dive-bombing duties, not what he had dreamt of when he was recruited to the clandestine German air force seven years before, although it had been enough to earn him an Iron Cross. Now he was on the threshold of promotion to *Gruppenkommandeur* and the rank of major.

There was general impatience among his pilots to finish the job. The Führer might order flags to be displayed throughout the Fatherland to celebrate the end of the war in the west, but across the Channel the English were still defiant, showing no sign of willingness to come to terms, despite their hopeless military situation. Admirable, of course, but only fools chose to fight the invincible.

He was passing above Wimereux now at 15,000 feet on a course due west that would take him over the English coast near Beachy Head. Then he would turn inland, sweeping east over Sussex and Kent before he returned to the Pas de Calais by way of Folkestone and Cap Blanc Nez. Insouciant free-hunts kept the senses alert and it was always to be hoped that a few like-minded souls would be provoked to venture up and do battle. Really, it was regrettable that the English had proved so stubborn, so unrealistic. The two nations had so much in common. But now they were alone and soon the time for free-hunts would pass. Soon the full might of the Luftwaffe would be directed at the Reich's last enemy in Europe: the ports and harbour installations that now began to fill his windscreen would be pounded to extinction, severing supply lines and stifling the Tommies' war industry. Kastner was proud of the role his wing of fighters would play in covering the mighty bomber fleets and destroying, finally, the remnants of the Royal Air Force.

He was drawing close now to the dull white cliffs of Beachy Head that fell away to the lighthouse perched on its scatter of rocks, improbable and picturesque, like a child's drawing pinned to a kindergarten wall. On a pathway leading between the clumps of gorse a figure was exercising dogs. Kastner swooped a little lower, banking inland, throttling up. He imagined that the thunder of his thousand-horsepower Daimler-Benz would tell its own story.

He climbed again, to 20,000 feet. Visibility was excellent and near Crowborough he picked up the Spitfire, about ten miles away and heading east. He increased his speed, the sun at his back. The familiar sensations overcame him: quickening pulse, drying mouth, the dangerous eagerness to engage too soon, the urge to destroy that had to be controlled, channelled into a logical, carefully planned attack. He was bearing down on the Spitfire fast now and still the pilot had not seen him. Kastner was crouching over the controls, his thumb flexing on the gun-button, squinting through the Revi reflector sight. The poor fool was as good as dead. But then, a nanosecond before he opened fire, the Spitfire rolled on to its back and dived away.

He dropped down after it, cursing his luck. What had given him away? His approach had been perfect, straight out of the sun. It should have worked. Ninety-nine times out of a hundred it would have. Perhaps the poor fool he had thought as good as dead was an old hand after all. He was certainly flying like one, flicking and feinting this way and that across the sky, always floating just out of range of Kastner's bursts of fire from his MG-17 machine-guns and 20mm cannon.

He found himself becoming disorientated as he fought to match the complex manoeuvres of the Englishman. He realised, with something close to desperation, that he was being outflown. It had never happened before. He was among the best. No one had been able to equal his ability, his touch, his instinct for the kill. He felt confused and angry, sweat soaking his overalls. Each useless chatter of his guns and thump of cannon was an affront. The Spitfire was looping above him now. Kastner looked up. He could clearly see the man staring down at him from his cockpit. He pulled back on the stick knowing that, unlike the Spitfire's Merlin, his fuel-injected engine would not hesitate, inverted at the crest of a loop. He was diving from 6,000 feet at maximum speed, well over 400 m.p.h., the machine trembling and alive. He was shouting with excitement. Yes, he had him now! He stabbed the gun-button but the streams of bullets floated wide, always yards away. The Spitfire was bottoming out of its dive.

Kastner pulled on the Messerschmitt's control column. It was heavy, almost solid, the elevators refusing to respond. So many times he had lectured his young pilots on this very trait that made the 109 so hard to drag out of a dive in anything but a gentle curve and never at this height and speed. So much for his logical, carefully planned attack. He had lost the game. He knew he was about to die without his adversary firing a shot. He had a moment left to glance up through his canopy again, see the Spitfire climbing rapidly away. It waggled its wings to tell him that its pilot had consciously flown him into the ground.

The 109 buried itself in woodland just beyond the little church of St Peter on the fringe of Southborough Common, not far from the cricket pitch. The hole was deep and filled with oil and sludge and some fragments of a man – a man who had forgotten that an Emil could bite.

Kit throttled back, the exhausts of the Spitfire cracking and popping as he floated in over the boundary hedge of his new posting. The elegant nose came up and obscured his view of the runway. He looked to the left, watching the grass rise to meet him. Gently back on the stick, holding her off, then the rumble of tyres on hard-baked ground. He taxied in, unclipping his oxygen mask, releasing himself from his harness and parachute straps.

'Well?' the engineering officer shouted.

'She'll do. No sign of rudder bias now.' He jumped down.

'And no sign of the Hun either,' said the engineering officer, nodding at the gun-patches still in place.

'Oh yes,' said Kit, 'I saw a Hun but I didn't need the Brownings.'

'Ossie Wolf was looking for you. I told him you were up. He's organised a car. I gather you're off on some jaunt or other.'

'That's right.'

'You chaps,' said the engineering officer. 'What it is to be young.'

They had given Kit a small room at the end of the long wooden hut that was home to the squadron's A Flight. Being a supernumerary instructor had its perks. And he and Ossie thought they might save a life or two before they resumed operations. They acted like irascible uncles dealing with a horde of eager nephews, trying to impart what they had learnt in the skies of France. At first the nephews, bursting with impatience, were loath to listen. They could not wait to meet the enemy in battle. Only when they had been destroyed, with chilling ease, by Kit or Ossie in mock dog-fights did they begin to grasp the brutal truth. For the moment, as in the Drôle de Guerre, the Luftwaffe was eerily inactive but everyone knew the day of reckoning would come soon enough.

In his stark little room Kit changed out of his flying gear. Nobody was about. A Flight was on readiness. In his vest and pants he pattered down the length of the hut, between the rows of iron beds and past the two coke-stoves, out to the wash-house. He showered in icy water, shaved, brushed his teeth, pushed Brylcreem through his hair.

Back in his room he selected his best uniform and set his battered service cap over his brow, its peak shadowing his eyes. He placed a piece of folded silk in his breast pocket, his thoughts in a village in the Sarthe valley.

A car pulled up outside the hut with a scrunch of gravel. Ossie Wolf sat at the wheel of a little M-type MG. 'Make it snappy feller. We're running late.' Kit lowered himself into the rudimentary seat. 'Hey,' said Ossie, 'we got reports a 109 went in chasing a Spit. About the time you were testing your kite.'

'Really?'

'The Spit didn't fire a shot, just led the guy down and let him do the job himself. We know how tough that is. Sounds to me like fancy flying.'

'Oh, probably just a lucky break.'

Ossie thrust the gear lever into first. 'Didn't see anything huh?'

'I thought you said we were running late.'

'Don't worry, brother,' said Ossie. 'I'll see we make it.'

*   *   *

464

Sixty miles away, in a side ward of the small cottage hospital, Flying Officer Brown was expecting visitors. The nurses had made him as presentable as possible. A magnum of Lanson '21 and three fluted glasses stood on his bedside table. He thought it likely that Kit and Ossie would have a tale or two to tell. They always did . . .

ACKNOWLEDGEMENTS

Some time in the mid-1980s I found myself in a small book-shop near the Cathedral Close in Salisbury. I was looking for rare titles about pre-war motor-racing. Everything they had was already on my shelves. 'Do you happen to be interested in flying?' said the owner. 'People who like cars usually are.' He pushed across a box of a dozen volumes he had just bought from the widow of a World War Two pilot; Paul Brickhill's *The Dam Busters* and *Reach For the Sky*, Ralph Barker's *Down in the Drink*, Manfred von Richthofen's *The Red Air Fighter*, Patrick Pringle's *Fighting Pilots*. Familiar stuff but well worth reading again. But at the bottom of the pile was a cheaply produced book with a stark blue cover bearing RAF wings that was new to me. It was a first edition, published by Batsford in September 1941, obviously a favourite, well used, the dust-jacket mended with Sellotape. There was no author's name on *Fighter Pilot, A Personal Record of the Battle of France*, simply a preface stating that the writer was an RAF flight lieutenant on active service at a fighter station in southern England (only later did I discover his name, Paul Richey). It chronicled the activities of Number One Squadron, flying Hurricanes close to the Franco-German border during the Phoney War from September 1939 to May 1940, and from 10 May, its gradual retreat westwards across France in the face of the German invasion. A particular image stayed with me over the years for, in the curious lull before the

Blitzkrieg, when contact with the Luftwaffe was spasmodic, the British pilots occasionally enjoyed leaves in Paris, booking suites at the Crillon and enjoying champagne cocktails before lunch. The contrast between the luxury of Paris and the deadly skies of Lorraine was bizarre.

In 2003, during a discussion about future plans with my editor at Headline I mentioned the campaign detailed in *Fighter Pilot*, that while most people were familiar with the Battle of Britain, fewer knew about the RAF's role in the Battle of France. I recalled the little nugget that had stayed with me for nearly twenty years: battle-weary pilots enjoying champagne cocktails at the Crillon. It struck a chord and *Blue Man Falling* is the result, though I should stress that Paul Richey's account was only an inspiration and his squadron is in no way related to mine.

Other invaluable sources have been *Fighter Boys*, by Patrick Bishop, *Battle of Britain*, by Len Deighton, *American Eagles*, by Tony Holmes, *Zerstorer*, by John J. Vasco and Peter D. Cornwell, *Flight to Arras*, by Antoine de Saint-Exupéry, *The French Army 1939–1945*, by Ian Sumner and François Vauvillier, *The German Army 1939–1945*, by Nigel Thomas, *The Life & Times of Pilot Officer Prune*, by Tim Hamilton, *Biggin on the Bump*, by Bob Ogley, *Spitfire*, by Alfred Price, *Homage to Catalonia*, by George Orwell, and the film *Land and Freedom*, directed by Ken Loach. I also found certain music helpful before and after but not during writing; Symphony No. 3 by Gorecki, the Pastoral Symphony by Vaughan Williams, *Les Chansons de Paris*, published by Pharaoh, and the film scores *Under Siege*, by Gary Chang, *Thin Red Line*, by Hans Zimmer, *Saving Private Ryan*, by John Williams and *Titanic*, by James Horner. Special mention must go to 'Sur Les Quais Du Vieux Paris' sung so poignantly on the eve of war by Lucienne Delyle. 'Sur Les Quais Du Vieux Paris' was written and composed by Poterat/Erwin © 1939 by Les Editions Musicales VOG, © 1951 by Les Editions Leon Angel, Les Nouvelles Editions Meridian, France, and is used by permission.

I also received great personal support from a number of generous people prepared to read the manuscript as it developed, including Squadron Leader Tom Rosser OBE, DFC, my old neighbour a/Squadron Leader Raymond Baxter OBE, new near-neighbour and fellow-writer Pamela Oldfield, and military historian Jack Livesey, who pointed out the need for such a book to satisfy the demands of 'the rivet-counters, not just readers looking for an exciting adventure story'.

Most of all I thank my wife Jan, for waiting patiently for her husband to descend from the skies of wartime France and resume normal life, the kind of life that the men depicted in this novel fought for . . .

Cover image shows pilots of 249 Squadron, the RAF's top-scoring fighter squadron in World War Two, pictured on 21 September 1940.